WHEN THE APRICOTS BLOOM

WHEN THE APRICOTS BLOOM

GINA WILKINSON

KENSINGTON
PUBLISHING CORP.
www.kensingtonbooks.com

KENSINGTON BOOKS are published by
Kensington Publishing Corp.
119 West 40th Street
New York, NY 10018

All Kensington titles, imprints, and distributed lines are available at special quantity discounts for bulk purchases for sales promotion, premiums, fund-raising, educational, or institutional use.

Special book excerpts or customized printings can also be created to fit specific needs. For details, write or phone the office of the Kensington Sales Manager: Kensington Publishing Corp., 119 West 40th Street, New York, NY 10018. Attn. Sales Department. Phone: 1-800-221-2647.

The K logo is a trademark of Kensington Publishing Corp.

ISBN-13: 978-1-4967-2936-1 (ebook)
ISBN-10: 1-4967-2936-6 (ebook)

ISBN-13: 978-1-4967-2935-4
ISBN-10: 1-4967-2935-8
First Kensington Trade Paperback Printing: February 2021

10 9 8 7 6 5 4 3 2 1

Printed in the United States of America

WHEN THE APRICOTS BLOOM

Basra Province, 1978

Huda fished the knife from the pocket of her long apricot dress. Rania eyed the *jambiya's* sharp tip and buffalo-horn handle and grinned in approval.

"That's perfect for our oath." Rania's amber eyes dilated with a jittery mix of fear and anticipation. "It's even better than the knife in the American movie."

"Last week, I saw a real American. A woman," said the younger girl proudly. "She was on the corniche, eating ice cream and watching the boats."

"I've seen plenty of foreign women in Baghdad," said her fourteen-year-old companion, not to be outdone. "Teachers and nurses, mostly. They like to picnic by the Tigris."

"Do you think they've ever sworn an oath like this?" Huda stared up at Rania. She'd grown taller and slimmer in the three months she'd been away at the prestigious Baghdad Ladies High School. Huda felt dowdy beside her, even in her favorite dress.

"What should we say?" she asked.

Rania eyed the double-bladed knife in Huda's hand. The ivory handle was stained from years of use. She took a deep breath and straightened her shoulders.

"Today we vow to be blood sisters," she intoned. "Closer than sisters from the same womb."

Impressed, Huda nodded and repeated the pledge. The two girls added a promise of loyalty and to come to one another's aid whenever called.

"Don't forget about secrets," said Huda. "We mustn't keep secrets from each other."

Rania paused, then pressed her hand to her heart. "No secrets."

"What's the punishment for breaking a blood oath?" asked Huda.

Rania consulted the cloudless sky, its blue so perfect it could break a heart.

"If the blood oath is broken," she declared theatrically, "then the penalty is sorrow."

Huda threw her a skeptical glance.

"Sorrow?" she said. "For how long? A day? A week? It's got to be more than that."

Rania raised her chin imperiously.

"Sorrow for the oath breaker," she declared, "and for the generation that follows her."

Huda nodded and echoed her words. Slowly, their eyes swiveled to the dagger. Rania swallowed nervously. Huda wondered if she would back out. Would the oath count if it wasn't sealed in blood? Without it, would Rania return to her new friends and forget all about her vow with a simple village girl?

"Do you want to skip the blood part?" Huda offered reluctantly.

"No way." Rania shook her head. "That's the most important thing."

Huda grinned in relief.

"Okay, let's prick our thumbs and press them together." She handed the dagger to Rania. "You do it, cut my thumb."

"Really?" Rania winced. "Are you sure?"

"Do it," said Huda. Rania wouldn't find many girls at Baghdad Ladies High School prepared to risk a digit for a friend.

Rania raised the knife, grit her teeth, and jabbed the point into the soft flesh of Huda's thumb.

"Ouch!" Huda hobbled about, trying not to bleed on her long dress. "I thought you'd give me a countdown."

Rania eyed the blood dripping from Huda's thumb onto the sand. Her face turned the color of summer grass.

"Hurry." She thrust the knife at Huda. "Before I lose my nerve."

Huda pressed the dagger to Rania's thumb, felt the skin resist the blade. Rania closed her eyes and turned her head. Huda pushed. The skin parted beneath the knife like a boiled egg, deeper than she expected. Rania's eyes flew open, big and wide as a calf's. They grabbed each other's hand and pressed their thumbs together.

"Sisters forever." They locked eyes. "Or sorrow for us and the generation to come."

CHAPTER 1

Baghdad, 2002

Huda paced her backyard, trying to brush off her spat with her husband. In the distance, above al-Dora refinery, columns of flames pierced the night. An easterly wind pushed the stench of the burning gas away from New Baghdad, so all Huda could smell were the orange and apricot trees by the fence. She knew the wind could turn at any time, but right then the gas flares were beautiful, like candles lined up on a giant's birthday cake.

The bell rang at the front gate. Huda paused mid-step and wondered, Had Abdul Amir forgotten his keys when he stormed off to the coffee shop? Or had her husband cooled down and decided to eat dinner with her after all? Huda hurried inside through the kitchen door. A nougat box lay spread-eagled on the counter, cellophane wrappers strewn like evidence of a hasty crime. Huda frowned and swept them into the bin. So much for her diet.

The bell sounded again. Something in its flat, insistent tone made her falter. She scurried down the hallway, heels slapping against the tile. In the foyer, she paused by a console table decorated with family portraits. The largest of the pewter frames faced the wall. Huda flipped it around. The president stared back at her, eyes dark as tar. Medals marched across his chest.

She quickly moved the president's portrait to a prominent position between a photo of her and Abdul Amir on their wedding day, and a snap of their son, Khalid, wearing a suit and tie at his thirteenth birthday party. Next, she set to work unlocking the front door: unlatching chains, turning keys, sliding dead bolts. She ran her hands over her hair and heaved open the door. Two secret police officers strode down the driveway.

Huda quivered. *Lock the bolts; hide under the bed*, she thought. But she knew that wouldn't work. These men were like dogs: show fear and they bite. Behind them, the padlock from the gate lay in chunks on the concrete. The broken metal caught the glare of the floodlights over the carport. The larger of the two men shoved a pair of bolt cutters into the pocket of his leather jacket. Huda imagined his pockets contained all sorts of instruments: for breaking, slicing, and prizing apart.

"As-salaam alaikum." Her voice wobbled. "What brings you here tonight, my countrymen?"

"Sister, my apologies for a visit at the dinner hour," called Abu Issa, the older and slighter of the two men. He too was wearing a boxy leather jacket. Men like him were never without them, night or day, even when the sun scorched the blue from the sky and the bitumen on the roads melted into sticky pools.

Without waiting for an invitation, Abu Issa and his bolt-cutting partner barreled through the front door. Their bulk filled the foyer and pushed the oxygen out. Huda retreated down the hallway, careful not to turn her back. The men followed. Sand crunched beneath their boots—no amount of sweeping could keep the desert out. The fine grains went where they wanted, just like the officers of the *mukhabarat*.

"May I offer you tea?" Huda's voice came out high and tight.

"Yes, please, dear," said Abu Issa. "Three sugars."

"Two only for me," grunted the larger man. "I'm watching my weight."

Huda waved them into the sitting room and then ducked into the kitchen. In the window above the sink, her reflection stared back at her. Her large dark eyes were even wider than normal, and her plump cheeks were whittled into tight angles. The mouth that Abdul Amir once likened to a rosebud was a bloodless line. No matter how often Huda saw it, she was always surprised by how fear transformed the most familiar face into that of a stranger.

She asked herself, why were Abu Issa and his partner here? It had been only two weeks since their last visit. *Please, Khalid*, she prayed, *forget your curfew. Stay at Bakr's and play computer games.*

Huda quickly warmed the tea in the kettle and poured it into three thimble-size *istikan* glasses. The liquid leaped over the hourglass sides and pooled in the delicate saucers. She wiped them clean, balanced the tea, sugar bowl, and spoons on a tray, and carried it into the sitting room.

"Sit, sit." Abu Issa waved her toward a corner chair—as if he were the host and she were the visitor. His bolt-cutting partner stared at her, eyes flat as night. Huda's breath bunched in her throat.

"Let us chat," said Abu Issa, "about your work at the Australian embassy."

Huda nodded. This was not the first time the mukhabarat had come asking questions about events at the embassy: correspondence and meetings, comings and goings, the latest rumors. Everyone who worked with foreigners could expect such visits. Her lacquered nails carved half-moons into her palms. *Think of your good salary*, she reminded herself. Besides, if it wasn't her job, the secret police would find some other pretense to sit on her couch, to drink her tea, to gauge her fealty.

"How can I help you, Abu Issa?" She figured a rotten tooth was best pulled fast. "Is there anything in particular that you would like to know?"

"How is your relationship with Deputy Ambassador Wilson progressing?" He sipped his tea daintily, little finger splayed in the air. "Does he trust you?"

"I do my best to be reliable and professional."

"But does he trust you? Confide in you?"

Huda returned the istikan to her lap. Once again, liquid splashed into the saucer and stared at her like a baleful amber eye.

"He hasn't told me anything unusual." She forced a smile, even as her pulse throbbed at her neck. "I do routine typing and filing, as you know. I translate his letters when he has matters to convey to our beloved government."

"And what of his wife?"

Huda blinked.

"His wife?"

"How well do you know her? Are you friends?"

"Ally seems nice enough." Huda shrugged. "Once in a while, she comes to the office to break her boredom, that's all."

Abu Issa raised the tea glass to his lips. He wore a sharp-edged ring with the president's eagle crest. If he slapped her cheek, it would draw blood.

"No doubt your boss tells his wife all manner of things," said Abu Issa. "The foreigners call it *pillow talk.*"

Huda stiffened. Her istikan rattled in its saucer.

"These Western men are reliant on their wives' advice. They call them partners." Abu Issa shook his head. "Is it a business or a marriage?"

The two men snickered, disgust audible amid their amusement. Abruptly, the Bolt Cutter sat forward and ladled sugar into his tea. The small glass looked ridiculous in his meaty hand. He would need no ring to bloody her cheek.

"These Western women, they like to talk." The humor drained from Abu Issa's laugh. "Every day they go on television and bare their shameful secrets to the cameras, for anyone to see. They confess their sins to some Negro woman called Oprah. It should not be a difficult task then, to win her confidence."

The men eyed her intently. Huda stared at the floor.

"We want you to befriend the diplomat's wife. If the West acts to destabilize our beloved nation, or God forbid, strike us again with their unholy missiles, your boss will certainly receive warning. He may let it slip to his wife. And, surely, he would make plans to send her out of the country."

"I don't think—"

"Stay close to the diplomat's wife." Abu Issa sat forward. "Watch and listen. She may give us early warning, like a dog that howls before the *sharqi* blows in from the desert."

The front door rattled. The knob thumped against the foyer wall. Khalid's sneakers squelched over the tiles in the hallway.

"Mom? Dad?"

Huda's heart constricted. She put down her tea and dashed out to the hall. Khalid loped toward her, clutching a fragment of the padlock in his fist.

"Somebody cut the—"

"I am busy with guests, my son." She blocked his path. "Go to your room and wait for me."

"But the lock . . ." He peered past her shoulder. "Who's that? Where's Dad?"

Huda grabbed both of Khalid's shoulders. She wanted to hug him tight, to crush him to her chest and never let go. Instead, she steered him toward his room.

"Do your homework. Now."

"Ouch!" Khalid twisted out of her grip. "Your nails hurt."

She fixed him with her most evil eye. It was the type of glare usually reserved for his most heinous crimes, like the time he cursed in front of his grandmother or when he and Bakr climbed the orange tree and bared their backsides at the teenage girls next door.

"Go!" she hissed.

Khalid shot a final glance past her shoulder, then slouched toward his bedroom. Huda crept back to the sitting room. The mukhabarat had finished their tea.

"We will leave you now, sister. It is late and no doubt you want to take care of your son." Abu Issa rose to his feet. "He is your most precious possession, is he not?"

* * *

It was almost midnight when Huda gave up waiting for Abdul Amir to come home and crawled into bed. Above her head, the blades of the fan pushed warm air around the bedroom. She lay on her back and cataloged the noise of the night: the buzz of the fluorescent light in the foyer, the gritty wind scraping at the windows, the click-clack of nocturnal insects. She kept her breathing shallow, listening for the dull snap of a lock or the tread of heavy boots on her driveway.

In the distance, a car rumbled. Was Abdul Amir returning from the coffee shop at last? Huda sighed like the creaking fan. These days her husband's black moods were worse than ever. Earlier that evening, when she arrived home from work, he'd been slumped in front of the television, still wearing his baggy pajama pants and singlet.

"I'm hungry," he'd grunted, eyes trained on the TV screen. "What's for dinner?"

Huda slipped out of her kitten-heeled pumps. "I picked up a roast chicken and rice on the way home."

"You're not going to cook lamb stew? You used to cook it every Thursday."

Huda ignored the whine in his voice.

"There's not enough time. Stew can't be rushed or the meat will be tough." She glanced toward the kitchen. "Is Khalid home yet?"

"He's eating dinner at Bakr's house." Abdul Amir stabbed at the buttons on the remote control. "At least my son will get a home-cooked meal."

"Come now, be fair. I didn't have time tonight."

"Tonight. Yesterday. Last week. You are always busy with your work. What sort of wife puts her family second?"

And what sort of husband sits in his pajamas all day?

Abdul Amir kept his eyes on the television. Huda remembered when she would have happily drowned in his sea-green gaze. She remembered when a kind word was never far from his lips, when he whispered little jokes in her ear. Were those days gone forever?

Was that memory, like so many, best forgotten? Huda tried once again to lure her husband from his sour mood.

"I chose a plump chicken. And I will fetch some cucumbers and tomatoes from the garden. You have a magic way with the plants, my dear."

"You should not be working for foreigners." Abdul Amir punched the remote again. "They don't respect our culture. They don't respect family. Otherwise they would realize a woman should be home in time to prepare a proper dinner."

He turned his head and glared at her. She glared back.

"Without them we would have no chicken for dinner. No meat at all."

Abdul Amir lurched from the couch and lumbered past her. She followed him down the hall and into the bedroom. He threw a checked shirt over his singlet and scowled at his master's in finance diploma hanging in a frame on the wall. After ten years of sanctions, the economy was almost dead. No one needed an analyst like him to check its pulse. Like Iraq itself, Abdul Amir's pride had taken so many hits, Huda feared it might never recover.

He swapped his pajama pants for trousers and stomped back to the living room.

"These foreigners only want to destroy our country."

"That's not true." Huda pursed her lips in irritation. Of course, she'd thought twice about working at the embassy. Anyone even remotely connected with foreigners, especially Westerners, drew the suspicion of the mukhabarat. A case of the pox was more welcome than that. But what was she supposed to do?

Abdul Amir's company wasn't the only business to close its doors. Huda's previous employer, an agricultural import-export company, had resorted to paying her with sacks of almonds or pistachios from shipments abandoned in their warehouse. Unfortunately, Huda couldn't pay her bills with rancid nuts. Then a cousin who worked as a driver at the German embassy called. He'd heard through the gossipy driver grapevine that the Australians down the road needed a secretary with good English and typing speed of eighty words per minute. When he mentioned the salary, Huda's eyes bulged. She'd swallowed her reservations about working with foreigners. Not only would this cover their debts, the salary was more than her and Abdul Amir's former paychecks combined.

"The staff at the embassy are nice people," she scolded Abdul Amir. "They're ordinary people. Like us."

"Everyone knows, Australia is nothing but America's obedient lapdog."

"You can't judge people by the actions of their—" Huda broke off as the six o'clock anthem blared from the television. The president rode across the screen in an army jeep. Abdul Amir grabbed the remote and flicked to the next channel. From a gilded balcony, the president saluted a battalion of goose-stepping troops. He growled and tossed the remote back onto the couch.

"I fear that people will question your loyalty." His words were barely audible above the television, but like most sensible people, they'd long ago grown accustomed to reading lips, filling in blanks, talking in code.

"I love my country," whispered Huda. "You know that."

"It is not what I know that matters," he muttered. "I'm going to the coffee shop."

"What about dinner?"

He had shrugged, grabbed his car keys, and stormed off, leaving her to seek comfort in a box of nougat, unaware that the mukhabarat were about to descend upon their home.

Huda rolled onto her side and checked the clock on the bedside. She wondered, Was Khalid asleep? Or was he huddled under his faded Star Wars sheets, shining his flashlight on a dog-eared copy of *Harry Potter*? The boy wanted nothing more than to enroll in the Hogwarts Academy. Pity he did not show the same enthusiasm for study in real life.

Huda's ears pricked up at the familiar rattle of Abdul Amir's

Corolla station wagon turning into their street. She swung her feet over the side of the bed and into a pair of fluffy pink slippers. A Mother's Day gift from Khalid three years ago, they were worn at the heels. In the hallway, she paused and stuck her head into his bedroom. Khalid was curled up like a snail. She continued to the front door, unlocked the dead bolts, and released the chain.

Outside, dry leaves whispered in the darkness. Abdul Amir's voice boomed from the far side of the gate.

"What the hell? Have you locked me out of my own home, woman?"

"The lock was broken." As Huda pried open the gate, she could smell the burnt molasses of *nargilah* smoke embedded in her husband's hair and clothes. "I had to replace it."

"How on earth did it break?" Abdul Amir waved his hands about like an angry prophet scolding his flock. "Do I need to punish Khalid again?"

"Please, my dear, be quiet." Huda peeked along the potholed street. Tall walls stretched in both directions, draped in flowering bougainvillea or fragrant jasmine. All were topped with metal spikes or shards of broken glass. "I'll explain everything—in the backyard."

Abdul Amir stiffened.

"The backyard?" he whispered. His hands were still raised, but now he looked less a righteous prophet and more like the victim of a stickup.

"That would be best," Huda murmured nervously.

Like his wife before him, Abdul Amir scanned the street. The wind groaned, and grains of pale desert sand scratched against their cheeks.

A razor-thin moon hovered high over Huda's backyard. The flames of al-Dora still spiked the horizon, but the wind had begun to turn. Huda's nose wrinkled at the smell of burning gas. Abdul Amir stood on his toes and peered over the neighbor's fence. No lamp glowed in their window. Their own house was dark and quiet too. Still, it was safer not to talk indoors—walls have ears, and so do teenage sons.

Abdul Amir and Huda huddled close.

"What did you tell them?" he whispered.

"There was nothing to tell," said Huda. "I barely know the woman. If she stops by the office, we chat about the weather, small talk, that's all. I mean, why would I go asking for trouble?"

Huda scanned the dim reaches of the garden: the orange and lemon trees, the vegetable patch in the corner, the wrought-iron swing seat that rocked back and forth on squeaky hinges. Abdul Amir raked his hands through his hair. In the moonlight, his fingers were pale as bone.

"What do you know about this woman?"

"Ally seems nice enough," mumbled Huda. "But it can't be long before she packs up and returns home. The heat and the sun always prove too much for the embassy wives."

And the loneliness too, thought Huda. She remembered meeting Ally a month ago, at the end of her ten-hour drive from Jordan to Baghdad. The young woman had stumbled from the embassy Land Cruiser, hand raised to ward off the sun, legs wobbling like a sailor stepping ashore after months at sea.

"All the way here, I kept looking for white sand dunes and camel trains." Ally laughed awkwardly. No one had the heart to tell her that was some other country.

Huda remembered when women like Ally had flocked to Baghdad: British nurses, French school teachers, and the plump wives of American oilmen. Tourists filled the cafés and strolled the banks of the Tigris. But nowadays, the expats were gone. So were the tour buses. The rail line to Istanbul was severed, and NATO jets shot down any planes that entered Iraqi airspace.

These days, only a handful of diplomats and United Nations workers ventured through the wide western desert to Baghdad. Very rarely did their wives join them—and like the exotic parrots at al-Ghazl pet market, the women soon went off their food, drooped, and plucked out their own feathers. Then they disappeared back into the desert, pale-skinned gypsies in four-wheel-drive caravans, leaving nothing behind but a trail of dust and perhaps a forgotten sun hat. Eventually, their husbands were posted elsewhere and life resumed happily. At least, Huda assumed it was happily. It was almost impossible to stay in touch with those outside Iraq's borders. Unwise, even, to embark on such friendships in the first place.

"What is she like, this Ally?" Abdul Amir paced back and forth. "Is she one of those arrogant foreigners who knows nothing of history and believes we're all savages?"

Huda shook her head. "I don't think so."

"Will it be difficult to befriend her?"

The moon slid behind a cloud. Huda was glad of the darkness. "I don't know," she lied. Ally wasn't standoffish at all, and Huda sensed it would be easy to draw her close.

Until this evening, Huda had thought she could handle the obligatory visits from the mukhabarat. She kept her answers brief but true and made it a rule to avoid gossip. She was only a secretary. She had nothing to hide. Besides, her Australian bosses weren't fools. They told their Iraqi staff only what they were happy for the government also to know. The rest they kept to themselves.

Huda remembered depositing her first embassy paycheck and how the bank clerk's eyes widened as he eyed her salary. His usual sneer disappeared. He called her *madam* for the first time, and asked if she'd like tea while he processed the check. She'd relished that moment far more than she cared to admit. Now, the strings attached to her job drew tight around her neck.

Abdul Amir stopped pacing back and forth across the lawn.

"Did Abu Issa offer you money?" he said.

"Money?" Huda frowned. "Of course not. No one gets rewarded for answering their questions."

"Let's be honest. They want more than that. Much more." He ripped a prickly sow thistle from the lawn. "I heard sometime they pay informants."

Huda tasted the sour gas from the refineries on her tongue.

"I am not an informant."

"You wanted the embassy job." Abdul Amir snorted. "You wanted to work with foreigners. Did you not consider there might be a price to pay?"

Huda had thought she was so smart, that she could type a few letters, take the foreigners' money, and manage the mukhabarat too. She'd ignored the voice inside her whispering, *You're playing with fire.* She searched her husband's face. His eyes were nothing but shadows.

"Have I not paid enough already?" she asked.

CHAPTER 2

Rania ducked behind one of the ornate columns lining Mutanabbi Street, but not fast enough. On the opposite sidewalk, the old poet Adnan Nawab waved to her, like a fly fisherman casting a lure. Between them ran a river of books, some stacked on low tables, but most set out on cardboard on the ground. A gust of wind whistled off the Tigris and fluttered a million pages with its brackish sigh.

"Rania, my dear!" Adnan was thin as a child, but his voice still held the power to cut through the throng at Mutanabbi book market. "Will you join me for tea?"

Rania groaned quietly. She adored Adnan, but today she had no appetite for tea and gossip. Still, he'd spotted her, so she made her way from under the shaded balcony, past the great columns, and into the heat and commotion of the walking street.

"I'm coming, Professor," she cried.

She clutched her bag tight—a backpack stuffed so full the zipper strained at the teeth—and squeezed past a stall stacked with almanacs, astronomical charts, and Korans bound in leather and engraved with jewel-toned inks. A vendor waved her toward an atlas with lands that existed only in memory: Rhodesia, Tanganyika, Transjordan. Beside him, young men squatted over college textbooks piled atop plastic sheets on the ground. Rania caught a glimpse of a dissected heart, pink arteries and blue veins laid out over two pages. She wondered, If she hunkered down beside them, might she unearth a diagram of the soul, its purple bruises and rotten patches properly dated and labeled? More important, would she find dog-eared instructions on how to remedy these maladies?

"Professor, what a blessing to see you," said Rania as she reached the steps of a whitewashed café. The clank and whistle of kettles on a gas stove drifted through the open windows. "Then again, where else would I find our nation's most esteemed poet, but at the door of Shahbandar café?"

"You are too kind," he replied. "Especially to an old man who does nothing but waste his days rewriting the same line fifty different ways."

Behind him, a group of middle-aged men passed a burbling *nargilah* pipe back and forth while noisily debating the merits of eighteenth-century novelists. Two young women in blue jeans sat quietly on a cushioned bench sipping sweet tea.

"I hear talk of a new exhibition at your gallery," said Adnan.

"The German Cultural Center is sponsoring some young artists. The theme is peace."

"Peace?" He raised a gray bristling eyebrow. "I hope the artists had good imaginations, because they could not draw from their own experience. Perhaps next time you can convince the Germans to hold a poetry exhibition. We could call it *The Gasbagging of Old Men*. What do you think of that?"

Despite herself, Rania grinned.

"It would be a fine thing, I'm sure."

Adnan limped toward the café's heavy doors, gesturing for her to join him.

"I'm afraid I can't stop, Professor."

The old man raised his ponderous brow again.

"No tea?"

Rania reddened. "I have an appointment."

Adnan snuck a glance at Rania's bulging backpack. A sigh of recognition escaped his wrinkled lips.

"I pray that your appointment goes well," he said. "After all, without you and your gallery, most of the Shahbandar's customers couldn't cobble together enough dinar for a single cup of tea."

"Well, I, uh . . ." Rania blushed again.

Sympathy clouded Adnan's rheumy eyes.

"You're not the first person who's had to sell off their books," he said gently. "There's no shame in it, my dear."

"I'm not sure my father would have agreed." Rania clutched her bag tighter. "I guess it's a mercy that he's not here to witness me trading off the last of his library for a handful of beans."

"Come now. With some shrewd bargaining, inshallah, you'll make enough to patch your roof. Or is it the hot water that needs fixing? I'm sure your father would want you comfortable."

"You think so?" Rania rubbed at an inch-long scar on her thumb, a smooth line the color of pearl. "My father always put honor higher than his daughter's wishes."

Adnan frowned, but his eyes were kind.

"Shall I come with you?"

Rania enveloped his knotted, arthritic hands in hers.

"Thank you, Professor, but I need to do this myself."

The bookseller hollered for his apprentice. His raspy call was muffled by ten thousand books. They were stuffed into bookcases that stretched fifteen feet to the wood-paneled ceiling, stacked on top of tables, and packed in crates on the floor. More were jammed into windowsills where they blocked all but the sun's most determined rays. Dust motes twirled beneath a neglected chandelier.

"That boy is never to be found when I need him." The bookseller pushed his chair away from his desk. "Please, relax while I fetch more tea to mark our deal."

Rania waited in silence as he waddled from his musty den. *He's probably gone out back to dance the* dabke, she thought morosely as she tucked her payment into her pocket. Her nose twitched at the vanilla-and-mold scent of old glue, ink, and paper slowly decomposing.

A floorboard groaned behind her, on the far side of the book-seller's front door. Silence followed. Whispers. A gentle knock. A young woman inched through the doorway. Her long dark hair could have belonged to an Iraqi, but her skin was far too pale, like Snow White's.

"Is this al-Kitab bookstore?" the young woman said in halting Arabic.

A tall man slipped in behind her. From his freckles and sun-bleached hair, Rania would have guessed he was a surfer from California. But, of course, that was impossible. Americans had been banned from Iraq for over a decade.

"Come in," Rania decided to answer in English. Like many Iraqis of her class and era, she'd attended college in Britain and spoke with a slight Oxford accent. If that didn't work, she could always switch to her passable French. "You're at the right place."

At Rania's answer, the young woman's eyes lit up. They were an unusually vivid blue—the same color as Fatima's amulet, the charm used to ward off evil designs—and they seemed to double in size as they darted over the jumbled tabletops and scaled the library ladders resting in their rails.

"This is amazing." The young woman began to spin in a slow circle. "Your bookstore is even better than I imagined."

"I'm just a customer," said Rania. "The bookseller is out back."

"Oh, I see. For weeks I've been pestering my husband to take a day off and come to the market with me." The young woman reached for her husband's arm, but he was looking at his watch like he had somewhere else to be. "Isn't that right, Tom?"

"Umm . . ." Her husband glanced about, as if he might find his answer on the shelves. A brief spark of irritation flashed in the young woman's eyes.

"I'm Ally." She extended her hand. "And this is my husband, Tom Wilson."

"Rania Mansour," she replied.

Once the introductions were done, the young woman's gaze returned to the groaning shelves.

"The market out there—so many books, so beautiful, in every language you could imagine." Ally shook her head in wonder. "And these old shops like al-Kitab, tucked away in the arcades. I feel like I've slipped down the proverbial rabbit hole. Is Mutanabbi a world heritage site? It should be. I wonder—" Ally broke off and clapped her hands over her mouth. "Sorry, I'm babbling, aren't I?"

"Not at all." Rania chuckled. The young woman was a breath of fresh air. "I remember feeling the same way when I visited the Serpentine Galleries in London for the first time. I was a student at the Royal College of Art back then. It must be close to twenty years ago."

"Twenty years? How can that be?" said Ally. "You don't look so much older than me, and I'm only twenty-seven."

"Twenty-seven? Really?" Rania peered at her from the corner of her eye. She wondered, Was it a childhood free from desert winds that kept Ally looking so young? Or was it that grief had not yet pinched her lips or reddened her eyes? Rania felt a stab of envy. In Iraq, no one neared three decades and remained so untouched.

"What brings you to Baghdad, Ally?"

Before she could answer, Tom leaned forward.

"I'm the deputy ambassador at the Australian embassy."

"The Australian embassy? Then you might know—" Rania broke off. A decade had passed since she last spoke with Huda. Why on earth was she thinking of her now?

Of course Rania's mother, the *sheikha*, kept her apprised of happenings among the tribe. Births, deaths, marriages, and successes like Huda's appointment as an embassy secretary were all relayed along the scratchy telephone line from Basra. And if she was really honest, Huda had been in and out of her thoughts ever since she began packing up her father's books for sale.

When they were young, the two of them spent hours flipping

through her father's leather-bound story collections—and substituting themselves as the heroes. The fine woven rug on the library floor was transformed into Aladdin's carpet at least a hundred times. In those moments, they were able to cast off the rigid roles they'd been born into—Rania the sheikh's obedient daughter, Huda the scrappy village girl—sharing secrets and dreams they knew others would scoff at. They thought they'd ride that magical carpet forever, closer than teeth and tongue.

But all the fabled enemies they'd fought—the sea serpents vanquished, the forty thieves outwitted—weren't enough to prepare them for what was to come. Real life in Iraq was far more perilous than a storybook monster. And their friendship was one of its many casualties. Rania eyed her empty backpack and took a deep breath. Like her father's precious book collection, Huda belonged to the past. No matter what she wished, neither could be reclaimed.

"When did you arrive in Baghdad?" she asked Tom and Ally, fixing a smile on her lips. "I hope you're enjoying our city."

"We arrived about a month ago, and I'm afraid it's been nonstop work since then." Tom threw his wife an apologetic glance. "I'd probably be at the embassy now if Ally hadn't insisted I take the afternoon off."

"I've wanted to visit Mutanabbi market ever since I first saw it on an old postcard. I would've come earlier, on my own, but I wasn't sure if I should." Ally pulled a square of black silk from her handbag. "I've been wearing this out in the market. But I see you're here without a male escort or a head scarf."

"There's no need for a scarf in Baghdad," said Rania. "But I can see how the market might be a little intimidating for a foreigner on her own."

Ally glanced up, and Rania thought she saw a touch of her own mournful nostalgia reflected in those cobalt eyes. In a blink, it was gone. If Ally had regrets, she knew how to hide them. Foreigners and Iraqis, Rania thought, they weren't so different underneath.

"You obviously appreciate fine books," said Rania. "Are you interested in other art forms? I have a gallery; it's nothing fancy, but we have an exhibition at the moment sponsored by the German Cultural Center. They are having a gathering next week, some drinks and so on in the garden. I would be honored if you came."

She slipped a business card from her pocket and handed it over. A door opened at the back of the shop. The bookseller emerged and squeezed past a column of encyclopedias. A pimply teenager trailed behind him, carrying a tray of steaming tea. The bookseller spotted the two foreigners. Within seconds, he had a tea glass in Ally's hand and another in Tom's. Rania slipped her empty bag behind her back.

"I regret I must be going," she said.

"Please stay." The bookseller's eyes did not leave the foreigners, not even for a moment. "Have some more tea."

Rania emerged from the darkness of the narrow stairwell and found Adnan Nawab waiting on the sidewalk. A young boy skipped past them with a foot-long block of ice balanced on his shoulder. Only a thin T-shirt and a scrap of cardboard separated the dripping cargo from his skin.

"The boy's errand is not so bad on a day like today." The old man wiped his forehead. "I could do with something icy myself. If you don't feel like tea, Rania, how about a juice?"

Rania nodded, and the two of them made their way to nearby Rashid Street. They waited side by side in the shade of a crumbling portico while a red double-decker bus rumbled past, then they dashed through the traffic and claimed a table outside a small juice bar. Two doors down, on the steps of a boarded-up bank, a shoe shine boy was doing brisk trade, his brushes flying back and forth. A wrinkled man shuffled by, carrying a pole slung with bagel-like rings of sesame-seed *simit*.

"I saw a couple of foreigners climb the stairs after you," remarked Adnan. "Did you meet them?"

"Let's pray the bookseller leaves a few coins in their pockets, because I invited the young woman to visit my gallery." She swirled her juice. "With luck, she'll buy a painting or two."

"Here's to that." Adnan raised his glass in a toast.

Rania clinked her glass against his.

"So, how is your daughter?" said Adnan. "I heard you'd sent her to stay with your mother. I'm sure she misses you."

Rania rolled her eyes.

"Hanan is a fourteen-year-old girl—she does not miss her mother. Her grandmother drives her from the farmhouse into Basra city every weekend for shopping and ice cream. The rest of the time she keeps her busy by taking her on the rounds out to the villages. There are many new babies, and the congratulatory visits must be made. Not that Hanan likes it. I called her last night, and believe me, she was not shy about letting me know I'd ruined her life."

Rania sighed. She'd spent forty-five minutes, dialing and re-dialing, before she got a working phone line to Basra.

"I'm dying stuck down here," Hanan had moaned to her. "The DVD player is broken. And Grandma expects me to join her while she visits every new baby in the province."

"It's not every baby. And it's only a few villages. Count yourself lucky. In my day, our tribe was bigger, and I had to do twice as many visits."

"It's not fair. I miss my friends in Baghdad."

"Come on, it's not so bad."

"All these years I had to listen to you complain about how Grandma would take off to Baghdad for weeks on end, and pack you off to stay on the farm." Static crackled down the line. "But it's fine for you to do it to me?"

Phone pressed to her ear, Rania stared at the kitchen ceiling where water stains formed a map of a derelict world.

"It's hardly the same," she replied crisply. "Your grandmother went to Baghdad to go water-skiing and wear miniskirts. I'm having no such fun. Anyway, don't fret. Basra has a very nice high school. When the school year starts, you'll make some new friends."

"I don't want new friends. I want to come home. I want to go swimming with Ghada and Ban at the Alwiyah Club."

"All in good time, my dear." Rania winced, knowing eventually she'd have to admit to Hanan that she could no longer afford the club's membership fee.

The phone line sizzled like fat in a pan.

"Hello? Hanan? Can you hear me?"

She gripped the phone tight.

"*Habibtee*, are you there?"

Static hissed.

"I love you!" Rania's words bounced off the kitchen walls and echoed in her ears.

Her chest had hurt when she hung up the phone, from love, but also from a strange premonition that time was fast running out, that events were slipping out of her control. Was it the impending sale of her father's books, the fact that Hanan was turning into a young woman, or something more? Rania didn't know, but she'd tossed and turned all night.

Out on Rashid Street, another double-decker swooshed by, nudging her back to the present.

"I'm sure your daughter misses those fancy cafés on Arasat Street." Adnan set down his glass. "Did you know there's a new restaurant with an outdoor pool and little cabanas with silk cushions? At night, you can see the blue water glowing from the footpath. I couldn't afford a thimble of tea in a place like that, but I ended up idling on the curb, a little beggar boy beside me, both of us unable to tear our eyes away."

Adnan glanced over his shoulder. The boy at the juice counter was slicing oranges. Adnan scanned the busy sidewalk, then leaned in close.

"I was outside the restaurant for just a few minutes." He lowered his voice. "Then the yellow Ferrari pulled up by the curb."

Rania's juice suddenly tasted sour. She pushed her glass away. Adnan pressed his lips together in a grimace.

"You were right to send Hanan away. If I had a teenage daughter, I would do the same."

Rania's chest constricted, just like it had at the end of her phone call with Hanan.

"Sometimes, I fear even Basra is not far enough."

"I imagine you heard that Madam al-Houri passed away last week. She stopped eating. At the end she would not even take water." Adnan hunched over the table. "She never recovered from the shock, you know. To have your daughter taken—from her very own wedding banquet—and then defiled in the most offensive way. It is incomprehensible."

"Uday Hussein is the spawn of the devil," whispered Rania. "He must shock even his own father. And who would have dreamed that was possible?"

A teenage hawker strolled the sidewalk, towing a flock of helium balloons tethered to a shepherd's hook. Rania and Adnan fell silent as he passed by. On the far side of the street, near the entrance to Mutanabbi market, a man whistled: a loud, looping note full of lechery. Heads turned. A street urchin cried, "I love you, baby!"

The balloon vendor loped across the street, toward the commotion. Rania spotted Tom Wilson, scowling, hands jammed on his hips. Behind him, Ally fumbled through her pockets. A silk scarf unfurled in her hands like a black flag. She draped it over her hair. A man next to her puckered his lips and made kissy faces.

"You see this disgrace?" said Rania. "What is wrong with the men of today?"

"I blame the cinema and the television." Adnan scowled. "Have you seen the posters outside the movie house on Sadoun Street? They make it look like Western women will lie down with anyone, anytime. Too many of our foolish young men believe that's true."

They watched the two Australians climb into a taxi and motor away.

"Ally must be a brave girl to follow her husband here." Rania fished a pack of cigarettes from her pocket. "Or foolish. Perhaps a bit of both."

Adnan eyed her quizzically.

"Would you not have followed your husband? Allah protect his soul."

"Hashim has been dead fifteen years," she mumbled, and pulled a cigarette lighter from her pocket. "Sometimes I wonder, if not for his photographs, would I be able to remember his face?"

"Don't feel guilty, my dear. Living a full life, not dwelling in sorrow, that's the best way to honor the dead."

Rania lit her cigarette absentmindedly. She'd been married less than a year when Hashim's jet was shot down during a bombing run over Tehran. She was strolling in the garden when the news arrived. Her mother-in-law's wail escaped through the open window of the kitchen and lifted the birds from the trees.

For Rania, that moment was preserved like an insect caught in amber. But most of her memories were blurry—or trivial—like her distinct recollection of the slurping noise Hashim made while eating fried eggs. Theirs had been a traditional union, matchmade by their parents, but it was far from the barbaric arrangement her fellow students at college in Britain slyly questioned her about. They imagined Iraqi girls like Rania were sold off in chains to old, ugly strangers, when in fact that was far from the truth.

Rania's and Hashim's families were old friends, and the two of them had played together as children, although that stopped once they neared puberty. The daughter of a sheikh, Rania had plenty of handsome, well-connected suitors, but she knew Hashim would treat her kindly, and, importantly, so would her future parents-in-law. When they got engaged, she didn't love him in the romantic sense favored by Hollywood. Nor did she expect to. But she was confident that given time, she would grow to love her husband, just as her mother had, and her grandmother before her.

Rania and Hashim only had a few months to adjust to their new life together. They butted heads on occasion, but once the bedroom lights dimmed, they were always eager to make up. When Hashim was called up to fight in the war with Iran, Rania was six weeks pregnant. Five months later, she mourned his death. She grieved sincerely, as a wife should, struggling to accept that Hashim would never see his daughter. And Hanan would never know her father. But as the years passed, she began secretly to wonder, what would her life have been like if she had remained married?

Like Rania's father, Hashim had been a traditional man. He would have demanded final say over all their important decisions. Would he have allowed her to move away from his family home and to open a gallery in Baghdad? That was unlikely. She'd tried many times to imagine her life if Hashim had lived, but she simply couldn't picture the details, or how it would have flowed from morning to night, from breakfast to supper, year after year. Sometimes when she talked of her marriage, it felt like someone else's story. She was just mouthing the words.

An old woman hobbled by with a roll of newspapers tucked under her arm. Rania wondered, How many widows felt the same? Were their memories as thin as hers? Charcoal sketches, a line here, a shadow there? Rania had resisted all offers to marry again and managed to build a good life for herself and her daughter. At least she had, until war and sanctions destroyed the flow of visitors to her art gallery.

She sucked on her cigarette and thought of the book merchant stroking his pudgy fingers over the last vestiges of her father's library. She glanced at her empty bag and winced. When she had handed the final book over, the calfskin binding had felt as warm as her own flesh.

CHAPTER 3

The window behind Ally's desk squealed as she pried it open, startling a trio of pigeons from the palm tree in her courtyard. In a flurry of wings, they flapped toward a traffic circle dominated by a hand-painted billboard of Saddam Hussein chatting on an old-fashioned rotary telephone. With rosy cheeks and a twinkle in his eye, he looked like a kindly uncle catching up with his favorite nephew. More likely, Ally thought, he was ordering someone's execution.

Ally hoped the squawking birds might pause, perch on the billboard, and deposit a few pasty droppings on the dictator's mustache. The birds knew better. They flew on through the bright blue sky, past tall gates and squat, sand-colored shops, in the direction of the Tigris River. As Ally eyed the billboard, a familiar *clang-clink-clang* drifted through the bars on the window. It was the neighborhood gas vendor—a skinny boy, about ten years old—beating a scrap of pipe against one of the gas canisters stacked in his sea-blue donkey cart. He followed this route every morning, banging out a melody to advertise his wares. In the past month Ally had learned his tune by heart.

When the peals faded, Ally sat down at the desk and picked up a yellowed postcard of Mutanabbi book market. On the back, a scrawl of faded ink told of parties and picnics by the river. There was a joke about a humorless boss, a pledge to write again soon, and three kisses marked *XXX*. Like the gas vendor's tune, Ally knew it by heart. It was written by her mother, Bridget, on June 12, 1970, and addressed to her father, Robert. Ally wondered, Did she already suspect her pen pal would one day become her husband?

Back then, Western nurses like her mom were paid handsomely to work in Baghdad. Inevitably some found the heat, and their homesickness, too much to bear. Not Bridget. *Who would have guessed that Baghdad possesses the world's biggest, bluest, most flawless sky? It's paradise!*

Ally liked to picture her mom as a female Marco Polo, adventuring in foreign lands. But cancer claimed Bridget early, before she could share her daring exploits with her daughter. Those untold stories had gnawed a hungry hole in Ally. She raised her eyes to the enormous expanse of forget-me-not blue outside her window and imagined her mother doing the same. For a fleeting moment, she could almost understand how someone might mistake that sky for paradise.

Now that Ally was seated, only Saddam's eyes were visible, peering over the courtyard wall topped with glittering shards of glass. She poked her tongue out at him, then flipped open her laptop. In the corner of the screen, the Internet Explorer icon sulked uselessly—its connection to the outside world severed by Saddam's censors.

She clicked on Microsoft Word. Three paragraphs stared back at her—the measly sum of all she'd produced yesterday. She re-read her description of the boy on the donkey cart, his song traveling through the streets like the jingle from some dystopian Mister Softee truck. She hated every sentence. Stuffed full of adjectives, starved of plot.

Ally straightened her shoulders and tapped at the keyboard. A few minutes later, she stopped, then hit the delete key. The cursor blinked, mocking her. She tapped out another line, frowned, and erased the sentence. The cursor moved forward, then reversed again, like a backhoe crushing her words into flat, lifeless rubble.

Ally sighed at the wreckage on-screen. Back in Australia, Tom had warned her that contrary to popular belief, the biggest danger in Baghdad was dying of boredom. Ally thought she'd keep herself busy writing a book that retraced her mother's trailblazing path. Turns out that was easier said than done. Her mother's apartment building had been torn down, her favorite riverside café went up in flames ten years ago, and the hospital where she worked seemed to have vanished into thin air.

Ally eyed a framed photo on her desk, of her mother laughing with the Tigris rippling behind her. She'd discovered the photo and the postcards only a few months ago, at her father's home, a week after his funeral. She'd been sorting through his closet, folding suits for the thrift shop, breathing in the odor of his Old Spice and fighting off tears, when she found a manila envelope tucked on a high shelf. She lifted the flap. The photo of her mother stared back.

Ally's heart had lurched like a runaway car. She hadn't seen the picture in decades, not since she was five years old. Yet somehow, she remembered every detail: the joyful wrinkles at the edge of her mother's eyes, the sun gleaming on her dark hair. The wind had pushed a long strand across her face, and she'd raised her hand to pull it away, almost like she was waving.

Last time Ally saw the photo, it had been above the fireplace in a small row house in Boston—the house where her mother died. To her lasting shame, Ally had always felt closer to the smiling young woman on the mantel than to the woman being consumed by cancer in a darkened bedroom. At some point during her mother's illness, Ally convinced herself that there'd been some mistake. How could the woman in the photo—her mother—be the same melancholy patient who smelled of cold sweat and despair?

Sometimes, Ally's mother would call for her, extend her twiggy, trembling fingers, and stroke her daughter's cheek. Ally would hold her breath, waiting for the chance to slink off to the living room, where she'd stare doggedly at the photo of the woman by the river, her real mother, smiling, with the wind in her hair. Where was she going? Ally wondered. Could she come too?

When her mother died, her father packed them up and moved them to Australia to be near his parents. Somewhere along the way, the photo vanished. When she asked about it, her father winced.

"It must have gotten lost." His voice cracked. "Now, go outside and play."

He looked so pained that eventually Ally stopped asking about the photo. Or pretty much anything to do with her mother. If she did, her father's shoulders would crumple, and soon he'd sidle to the fridge, pull out a beer, and start drinking. She'd find him at four o'clock in the morning, passed out on the couch, David Bowie turning circles on the record player, empty beer bottles on the floor.

Ally learned not to ask questions about her mother, but she didn't forget the image of her by the river, her long, shining hair loose in the breeze. More than twenty years later, Ally sank to the floor of her father's bedroom and held that photo close.

Her father's front door creaked. Footsteps clomped down the hall.

"Anyone home?" called Tom.

"In here," she called back.

"You're not going to believe what happened at work—" Tom stopped short at the sight of Ally crouched by the closet.

"Oh, babe." He squatted down and hugged her. "You shouldn't be doing this alone." He squeezed her tighter. "Do you want to go home and I'll finish this?"

Ally shook her head and passed him the photo.

"That's your mom, right? She looks so happy." He flipped the photo over and read the inscription: *Tigris River, Baghdad*, followed by looping initials Ally didn't recognize. Abruptly, Tom sat back on his heels.

"That's so weird," he said.

"What's weird?"

Tom took a deep breath.

"I got offered a deputy ambassadorship today."

"Deputy ambassador?" Ally gasped. "That's a huge promotion. Where?"

Tom handed back the photo.

"Baghdad," he said. "They want me to go to Baghdad."

In that moment, time froze. Packing up her father's belongings, Ally had never felt so unmoored, adrift without compass. Now, a spark of hope kindled in her chest. It was as if her mother's ghost had risen, tapped her daughter on the shoulder, and said, *Follow me.*

With a loud crack, the power went out. The air conditioner wheezed to a halt. Ally wondered how long the cut would last. Two hours? Three? She eyed the phone on her desk. It was a clunky rotary dial, like the one Saddam used on the billboard out front. She pressed the phone to her ear. Silence. She tapped the switch hook. Nothing.

Ally entered the number for the embassy anyway, hoping that Tom might find time in his hectic schedule to eat lunch with her. After each number, the dial click-click-clacked back to its starting point. The line crackled. A woman's voice emerged, thin as fog. A man replied, his voice even more distant, rising and falling in a sea of static.

"Hello?" said Ally. "Hello?"

The woman didn't answer. Neither did the man. Their voices grew fainter until finally they vanished altogether. A crossed line? Maybe. The head of embassy security had warned that all their phones were tapped. The embassy was sure to be bugged, he said, and their home too. If Tom and Ally wanted to talk privately, he said they should do it in their garden or outside in the street, away from televisions, radios, air conditioners, even light fixtures—anything that might provide a power source for tiny cameras and hidden microphones.

Ally put down the phone and flicked idly through a pile of news reports she'd printed up during her last visit to the embassy. Saddam had long ago barred foreign journalists from Iraq. International newspapers, foreign television, and radio were banned too. So Ally had to use the embassy's secure server to keep track of the news.

Ironically, Ally used to be a journalist herself, covering drug busts, burglaries, and the occasional homicide for the *Canberra Herald.* But then, a month before her father died, Rupert Murdoch's lieutenants retrenched her along with a third of the newsroom. She remembered she'd been futilely scouring the job adverts when Tom brought home their Iraqi visa applications.

"That's it?" Ally had eyed the flimsy document. "Just one page of questions?"

"Count yourself lucky," said Tom. "Mine was nine pages long. I'm worried they'll want a cavity search too."

"*Dependent spouse?*" Ally frowned at the form. "That's my official title?"

Tom raised his hands.

"You can always change your mind."

Ally smoothed the document with her palm and began to fill in the blanks. At the box marked "occupation," she paused and chewed the end of her pen.

"Housewife," she printed.

Tom peered over her shoulder. "Housewife? Really?"

"It asks only for my current occupation, not my whole résumé."

After that, all that remained was the citizenship box. She adjusted her grip on the pen, took a breath, and printed, "Australian." It wasn't exactly a lie. The form didn't ask if she had dual nationality, so she told herself there was no need to mention she was an American citizen too, thanks to her mother. She signed the document quickly, a rushed signature that already looked like it belonged to someone else.

Tom eyed the form like it was Eve's ruinous apple.

"I sincerely doubt they'll give you a visa."

"You underestimate the blinding power of misogyny," said Ally. "I bet those Iraqi bureaucrats won't check anything—not once they see the word *housewife*."

It turned out, Ally was right. But that was little comfort as she sat in her lonely Baghdad house, scanning some other journalist's work. She glanced through the barred window. The sky's friendly forget-me-not glow had vanished, replaced by harsh rays that bleached all the color from the garden. Nothing moved, not a single leaf or a wisp of wind. The heat silenced even the birds. Saddam's coal-black eyes leered over the stucco wall. Ally could almost feel her world shrinking. Soon, she feared, it would fit into a box on her lying visa form.

Ally eyed her reflection in the mirror by the front door and scraped her long dark hair into a bun. Embassy security had assured her that as a *guest of the state*, no one would dare lay a hand on her, that she could walk safely in the embassy district and wear her hair however she chose. Nonetheless, Ally found that left loose, her hair transformed into a pirate's flag that attracted all sorts of miscreants, curses, and lewd invitations. "*Russee, Russee,*" men cried, mistaking her for an Eastern bloc prostitute.

Screw it, Ally whispered to her reflection, *words can't hurt*. The catcalls of the street were no worse than solitary confinement inside her rented home of marble and concrete. She wrapped a thin cotton scarf around her neck, checked the bulging contents of her handbag, then fished out her keys and set to work on the front door. She turned three locks, pulled aside a bolt, and unlatched a chain, then heaved open the door.

Heat slapped Ally's face. She stumbled past a bed of thorny

rosebushes as Ghassan, their security guard, shuffled from his hut by the gate. His gray hair was shaved close to his skull. He stared at Ally's feet, revealing a shiny bald patch on top of his scalp.

"Where do you go, madam?"

Ally suppressed a frown. She hated being called *madam*. But no matter how often she asked, Ghassan couldn't bring himself to use her name.

"I'm going for a walk, Ghassan."

"Walk? To where, madam?"

"The embassy."

"You must call them first. They will send a driver."

"The phone isn't working."

"Then I will get a taxi." Ghassan headed for the gate.

"No, don't," said Ally quickly. She might be safe out on the street, where the regime was keeping watch. The backseat of a stranger's car was another matter. "No taxis."

"But, madam, you can't—"

"I need the exercise." She cut him off. They'd had this conversation many times before. "I'm going for a walk."

Ghassan positioned himself between Ally and the tall metal gate. His eyes skittered briefly across her face, then returned to the driveway. She stepped forward.

"I'm leaving now."

She took another step, wielding her strange foreign femaleness like a force field and compelling Ghassan to retreat. He grumbled under his breath and pushed open the gate. Outside, a knot of plastic bags somersaulted through the traffic circle like a tumbleweed at high noon. High above, golden dates dangled from palm trees. Others rotted in treacly heaps on the sidewalk.

Ally tugged her scarf above her collar and strode toward a set of traffic lights. They flashed amber. On and off. On and off. No one ever came to fix them, so they shone amber every day, never indicating whether to proceed or to stop, only urging caution, endless caution.

Unlike the teeming market of Mutanabbi, most of the businesses in Ally's neighborhood didn't open until the cool of the evening, so she was alone on the sidewalk, except for a woman wrapped in a black abaya selling newspapers by the traffic lights. A hoot of laughter echoed through the warm air. The newspaper vendor's three-year-old son slipped from the shadows of a cobbled alley and made a beeline straight to Ally.

"As-salaam alaikum." She squatted at eye level with the boy. "How are you, Mohammad?"

Mohammad immediately launched into their customary game of peekaboo mixed with silly faces. Ally crossed her eyes and flapped the corners of her ears. Mohammad cackled and did the same. After a few minutes, Ally pretended to steal Mohammad's nose, returned it to him, and continued on.

At the spot where the newspaper vendor stored her meager supplies, Ally paused and opened her handbag. She removed a plastic bag containing canned tuna, crayons, and a coloring book, and set it next to the newspapers. She continued past a pair of carpet shops, a tired photography studio, and a juice bar. A row of public-housing blocks loomed ahead, the same mustard hue as the desert that lapped at the city's hem. On pocket-size landings, laundry roasted on lines, socks and undershirts stiff as kindling. A black Oldsmobile cruised past the towers. The wind carried the throb of its engine toward her. The sound held no urgency: the driver had time on his hands.

Ally pulled her scarf higher. On the far side of the median strip, the Oldsmobile slowed to a crawl. Two thick-necked men with caterpillar brows and matching mustaches eyed her through its tinted glass. The passenger rolled down his window. Guttural snatches drifted across the bitumen. The words weren't listed in any of the Arabic textbooks Ally studied every morning, but she understood their intent. They were forbidden words, words wrapped in spittle, words that rattled in throats.

Muttering under her breath, Ally ignored the catcalls and plowed her gaze into the sidewalk. Eventually, the driver gave up, pressed his foot on the gas, and accelerated away. As soon as the car disappeared past the carpet shops, she pulled her scarf all the way over her hair and skittered down a side street lined with well-tended homes.

The quiet street was scented with lavender from a hidden garden, and Ally tried to flush the adrenaline from her system with a couple of deep breaths. She wondered if her mother had been dogged by sleazeballs too. Her postcards never mentioned it. And while her old photos occasionally featured women cloaked in black robes, most of her Iraqi friends wore platform boots, flared pants, and even miniskirts.

The wind pulled Ally's scarf tight around her neck, then eight cylinders growled low in her ear. The Oldsmobile motored around the corner in front of her, as if it had been lying in wait. A mix of a yelp and a groan fled Ally's lips. Behind the windshield, the men threw their heads back and laughed, baring white teeth and fleshy tongues.

Ally took a deep breath, then bolted straight toward the car. The men's mouths opened in surprise. At the last moment, she veered a sharp left into the street housing the embassy. Her sandals slapped loudly against the sidewalk, but the noise failed to drown out the obscenities spewing from the passenger's window.

The Oldsmobile drew closer. Ally could hear twigs snapping beneath its tires. She spotted the Australian flag. Moments later, an embassy guard strode out to the middle of the street.

"Madam Ally?" he called. "Are you okay?"

She shot an anxious glance over her shoulder. There was nothing but anonymous walls and high gates, and the throb of a V-8 engine lingering in the air.

Tom paced in front of his desk, clutching his blond hair like he was going to tear it out.

"I know security says it's safe to wander about, and that might be the case for me and the other blokes on staff, but certainly not for you. We need to hire you a driver. No more excuses."

Ally slumped on a cushioned bench by the door.

"Okay, you're right." She wiped sweat from her lip. "Catcalls I can handle, but not this."

Tom stopped pacing.

"So you finally agree, we'll get you a driver?"

"He's got to have an ordinary car, nothing fancy." Ally scowled at the floor. "I don't want to look like a pampered princess riding around in a limousine."

"If you want a rust bucket, I'm fine with that." Tom flicked through his desktop calendar. "But let's try to hire someone before I leave on Friday. I'll be up north for a week."

Ally sat up straight.

"Did my travel permit come through? Can I come this time?"

"I called the Ministry of Interior, and they said your application was still being processed. Sorry, babe."

"But we sent it in ages ago." Ally grabbed a cushion like she was going to throttle it. "How come your permits only take a day or two to get approved?"

"Because I am embassy staff, carrying out official business." Tom looked up from his calendar. His tone softened. "I don't blame you for feeling frustrated. Maybe you'd be better off some place where you're free to do your own thing."

"We've only been married six months. What happened to 'till death do us part'?"

"Plenty of embassy families live apart at times." Tom's freckled brow wrinkled. "Why don't you look for an apartment in Jordan? It's not so far away, and there'll be other diplomat wives to keep you company."

"Kill me now." Ally wrapped her hands around her neck and pretended to choke. "I met a bunch of those women in Amman. I thought they'd be cool and smart. Instead, they spent the whole time comparing manicures and discussing which spa gave the best massage with Dead Sea mud. And then they complained about their nannies."

Ally twisted her wedding ring around her finger. She didn't doubt that Tom loved her, but she wondered if he secretly wanted her gone. Then he wouldn't have to feel guilty about staying late at work, seven days a week, like the rest of his colleagues. At thirty-four, he was young for a deputy ambassador. He felt he had something to prove, so he worked harder, and longer hours, than everyone else.

Knuckles rapped against the door. Huda entered with a tray of coffee and water. Ally wiped her flushed, sweaty face and clambered off the bench.

"Huda, I'm glad you're here. Please, tell me the truth." She motioned to her long skirt and black T-shirt. "Am I dressed okay? Should I be more covered up?"

"You are dressed just fine." Huda gestured for her to take a sip of water.

"Honestly, do I need a head scarf?"

"Of course not." Huda patted her own hair. It was as dark and thick as Ally's but cut short in a bob and fixed with a crispy shell of hair spray. "This is Iraq, not Saudi Arabia. No woman is forced to wear the head scarf. Here at the embassy, only one of us wears the scarf. One with. Five without."

Ally scrutinized her own body for signs of wrongdoing. Her skirt skimmed her ankles, and her T-shirt was modest enough— not baggy, but not body-hugging either. She glanced at Huda. Her dark trousers sat tight on her hips, and her tailored blouse left her forearms exposed. Crimson toenails peeked from Huda's kitten-heeled pumps.

"Do you ever have any problems on the street?" asked Ally.

"Me? No, not at all." The Iraqi woman looked her up and down. "I do not see anything wrong with what you wear."

Tom blew on his coffee.

"Would you do us a favor, Huda?" he said. "Ally needs to hire a driver. Can you help?"

"I have one letter to translate, then I'd be happy to help," replied Huda. "By the way, you're due to meet the ambassador in a few minutes."

After Tom and Huda left, Ally finished her water, spread the flat cushions over the bench, and lay down. She tried to forget about the men in the Oldsmobile. As the air conditioner above her head hissed like a serpent, she tried to remember only a sky the color of forget-me-nots.

CHAPTER 4

"I told you, if you want me to read your coffee grounds, you must be calm." Huda flipped open her notepad. "Besides, Mr. Tom would like us to concentrate on finding a driver."

"I am calm." Ally set her coffee cup down on Huda's desk. "Honest."

Huda raised a brow. The girl was like a camel unable to see its own hump.

"Come on." Ally gestured at her wild hair, still damp with sweat. "Don't I look like a woman who'd benefit from a little guidance from a higher power?"

As she spoke, Ally's hands flew about like birds. Huda found her unfiltered energy hard to resist.

"Just a quick look?" said Ally. "What would it hurt?"

"Hurt?" echoed Huda.

Even though her colleagues always kept Ally at a safe distance, Huda used to believe it wouldn't hurt to entertain the girl a little, to offer her a drink and a sympathetic ear. It wasn't against the law. Not really. Now, she asked herself, how wrong could she have been? Huda turned away and searched for a pen. Bryan Adams crooned from the cassette player wedged beside the phone, but for a change, his velvet voice provided no comfort. Huda's every move, every breath, felt false. Damn the mukhabarat.

"First, let's focus on a driver," she said, "and then I will look at the grounds."

Ally grinned.

"Do not expect too much," warned Huda. "I am not a performing dolphin."

"You mean 'performing seal'?"

"Is it not a dolphin that jumps through the hoops?"

"Well, yes," laughed Ally. "I guess you're right."

Huda jotted down a few notes on the new driver and sipped her steaming coffee. The cardamom-scented brew was thick and creamy, twice boiled as required, but a touch too bitter. The cook in the cafeteria was skimping on the sugar again.

"Have you ever had one of those dreams where you think you're flying? Well, these days I dream about driving." Ally chuckled ruefully. "Since I found out I'm not allowed a license, I wake up drooling at the idea of stomping on the gas."

Huda laughed, despite herself.

"And what about the driver's salary?"

"I'm happy to pay the going rate."

"And which day of the week shall the driver have free? A Muslim may want Friday. A Christian perhaps Saturday."

"He can have two days off, whatever days he likes."

"Whatever he likes?" Huda frowned. "Be careful, people will take advantage of you."

Ally blushed. The label of diplomat's wife made her seem older than her years, but Huda knew she was still young enough to believe the best of everyone. Pity needled her side. The mukhabarat didn't give a damn about youth. Or innocence.

Ally offered her cup for inspection. "I've finished my coffee."

Huda set aside her notepad.

"First, keep hold of your own cup," she said. "Then you must still your mind. Find a quiet place inside yourself. Think of the questions you want answered."

Excitement flickered across Ally's face, followed by a ripple of apprehension. The girl was easy to read. A worm of envy wriggled in Huda's chest. She couldn't remember the last time she'd gone a day without cloaking her true feelings.

"Watch carefully," said Huda. "And do what I do."

She removed her saucer and clamped it like a lid on top of her cup. Porcelain clinked as Ally did the same. Huda raised the pieces to her chest, swirled counterclockwise, and then flipped them upside down. She set them gently on the desk, with the saucer now lying underneath the upturned cup.

"Wish me luck," said Ally, and did the same. Dark dregs drained into the pale saucer.

"Now," said Huda, "we must wait a few minutes for the grounds to dry."

Ally leaned across the table.

"I heard your grandmother was a famous fortune-teller," she whispered.

"Hush now." Huda patted the young woman's hand. "You must focus on the questions you want answered."

She couldn't disrespect the rituals her grandmother had drummed into her, even for a slapdash reading like this. Not that she expected much. The days when she could find meaning in the grounds were few and far between. Huda wondered if it was her fault, if she lacked something deep in her soul, but she knew she wasn't alone. All the ancient arts were suffering. The coppersmith and the carpet weaver were packing up shop, driven out by plastic plates and nylon prayer rugs at Cheap Ahmed's Discount Store. The great poets languished in obscurity, with barely enough dinar to buy bread. The Sufi dervishes had almost disappeared.

Huda eyed her cassette player, its tiny wheels spinning around and around. If she was a true patriot, she'd be listening to a *maqam* or *muwashshah*, but try as she might, she couldn't give up Bryan

Adams and his ballads of love. Could it be that the luxuries of modern life—of Western life—all the televisions and microwaves, were to blame? Was all this radiation and static interfering with messages from the universe?

Outside the window, a crow wailed. Huda knew whether or not she found signs in Ally's grounds, the mukhabarat would be pleased. They wanted her to draw the girl close, to ferret out her secrets. The cold ball of fear Huda had carried since the mukhabarat's visit suddenly ballooned. She had a vision of the Bolt Cutter clenching her teacup in his meaty fist. She swiveled away from Ally, breath shaky and shallow, and busied herself with paperwork.

"Is it ready?" asked the girl, a minute later.

Huda eyed Ally's upturned coffee cup warily. Perhaps she would find a kernel of truth in the grinds, not just for Ally's future, but her own as well. Huda lifted the cup from the saucer. Fine flecks of coffee adhered to the curved interior, dark islands mapped on a white sea.

"What do you see?" whispered Ally.

Huda stayed quiet. *Make them wait,* her grandmother always said. *That way they'll value your insight more.* Huda squinted into the cup. All she saw were grainy puddles of brown. She squared her shoulders and sat up straight.

"I see birds flying." She shaped her lips into a wide smile. "That means you will soon have good news. There is also a kite—that is a sign of change ahead."

She handed the cup back to Ally. While the girl peered into its depths, Huda glanced at the saucer. Patterns leaped at her: swords, towers, snakes slithering across the porcelain. Clear as day. Abruptly, the fine hairs on her arm stood to attention. She looked up. Amira Hindawi was at the door, watching her.

"Amira, I didn't see you there." Huda switched to Arabic. "How may I be of assistance?"

"Where is your esteemed boss?" Amira's lips were painted lavender, like the tongue of a snake. "I see his wife is here again."

"Mr. Tom has a meeting with the ambassador."

"What's the meeting about?"

"I'm not certain."

"Surely, it is your job to know?"

Amira sidled to Huda's desk. She glanced at Ally and bared her teeth in a facsimile of a smile.

"Reading the fortune?" she said in halting English. "What does the future say for Mr. Tom's lovely wife?"

"It was just coffee," said Huda. "We are all too busy for such nonsense."

Ally seemed to sense the tension.

"Tom asked Huda to help me. I need to hire a driver."

"A driver?" Amira pressed her fingertips together as if she were a great sage. "What about your husband, Huda? He knows Baghdad well. And he has free time, does he not?"

Huda stiffened.

"I don't think—"

"Your husband is trustworthy," continued Amira. "That is very important. Miss Ally cannot hire a stranger."

Ally perked up.

"I've got to say, I like that idea."

"That's right." Amira caught Huda's eye. "This solution will benefit everyone."

"I'll ask him," Huda mumbled. Everyone knew Amira was on the mukhabarat's payroll. She would be taking notes on this. And reporting back.

"I am going to the canteen." Amira leaned forward and swept up the cups and the saucers, obliterating the tower and the sword and the signs that screamed, *Read me.* "I'll return these dishes for you."

Huda grit her teeth. Amira offered another poor excuse for a smile and slunk away.

"I'm afraid I must get back to work." Huda made a show of shuffling her papers.

"Are you certain that squiggle was a flying bird?" Ally leaned across the desk. "Maybe it was a raven. Surely that would be a bad omen?"

Huda pushed her chair back from her desk.

"You have a good imagination," she said, "but you are no fortune-teller."

When Huda arrived home, Abdul Amir's Corolla was gone from the driveway. Huda closed the front door behind her, turned the key in the dead bolt, and slid the lock back into the catch. The scrape of metal on metal echoed along the hallway.

"Hello?" Huda kicked off her heels. "Anyone home?"

She hoped Abdul Amir hadn't gone to the tea shop. It never did him much good. Most of the men there were jobless, and hurting like him, but too proud to reach out for help. Instead, they sucked on their nargilah pipes and fanned the coals with their bitterness.

In the kitchen, Huda found a note from Khalid, saying he and Bakr were playing soccer. She opened the kitchen window. The aroma of freshly mowed grass wafted through the screen. Abdul Amir took great pains to keep the lawn lush and neat. He refused to admit that the Iraq of the fabled Fertile Crescent was gone, that the gardens of Babylon would never bloom again. Instead, when he wasn't at the tea shop, he watered, pruned, and fertilized, keeping close watch over his plants. He sought out pests and exterminated them. Weeds were consigned to the compost bin or, if they threatened to lay seed, burned in the firepit.

Huda poured a glass of water and watched the tangerine sun sink toward the horizon. Ally had said something earlier, about seeing paradise in Baghdad's sky. Now, as she watched columns of light pierce the pink and yellow clouds, it wasn't hard for Huda to imagine heaven up there. Maybe Ally was right. She had a way of finding something new and novel in things that most people had long ago stopped noticing. Huda wondered, In different circumstances, might the two of them be friends? Real friends?

In the orange tree, a pigeon hummed to its mate. Its coo was so loud it almost masked the rumble of a car turning into the street.

Huda recognized the burble of the mukhabarat's Oldsmobile, and her throat went dry. Another visit so soon—that would not escape attention. Tonight, every one of her neighbors would be in their backyards, in their quiet places, mouthing words and talking in code. The mukhabarat always brought misery. The question was, would it fall on Huda and her family alone, or would it engulf the whole neighborhood?

Huda hurried to the front door. She checked that Khalid hadn't messed with the president's framed portrait and that it remained at the front of the photos. A car door slammed. Then another. Huda scurried down the driveway.

"One moment, please. I'm coming."

She unlocked the gate and pried it open.

"I'm glad you're at home, sister, and not tardy this time in opening the gate." Abu Issa raised the corners of his mouth perfunctorily, like a bored clerk at the post office. He motioned at his bolt-cutting partner to stow his pliers. "After all, good padlocks do not fall from the sky."

Was this his idea of a joke? Huda asked herself. Was she supposed to laugh? She dithered in the gateway until Abu Issa coughed discreetly.

"Shall we have tea?"

"Yes, yes, of course." Huda's voice quivered. "I mean to say, please, enter."

Minutes later, Huda found herself in the kitchen, heart pounding like a sleepwalker woken far from her bed. The mukhabarat were in the sitting room, waiting for tea. She wondered, If she closed her eyes and prayed, would it turn out to be nothing but a bad dream? But even as she thought it, she knew life didn't work like that.

On the burner, the teapot boiled furiously. Steam spiraled toward the ceiling. Huda placed the sugar pot and teaspoons on the tray. As much as she tried, she couldn't stop the glasses from rattling in their saucers, jingle-jangling all the way back to the sitting room.

The mukhabarat had made themselves at home. The Bolt Cutter's boots were stacked on the coffee table.

"Young man, what would your—" Huda caught the reprimand just before it slipped from her lips. She stood, waiting for him to remove his boots.

"Our sister has brought us tea." Abu Issa flicked his hand at the Bolt Cutter like he was waving off a biting fly. "She needs to set it down."

The Bolt Cutter dragged his boots off the table. They thumped against the rug like cinder blocks. When Huda put down the tray, the Bolt Cutter ignored the tongs and dug his fleshy fingers into the sugar pot, rooting around among the pale cubes. Huda pressed her lips together in a thin line.

"Sit, sit." Abu Issa waved her toward the seat opposite him.

Huda perched on the edge of the cushion, spine erect, feet together, hands in lap, perfectly still except for her fingers rubbing back and forth, as if counting prayer beads.

"So please tell us," said Abu Issa, "how are your relations progressing with the foreign woman?"

"I'm doing my best. These matters take time."

"In a perfect world, we could wait until the apricots bloom. Alas, the world is not perfect."

"But there is nothing to—"

"Careful, sister." Abu Issa stared over the rim of his tea glass. "A lie takes only one moment to leave the mouth, but it can linger to the grave. Now, tell me, is your husband ready to start his new job?"

"His new job?"

"As the foreign woman's driver, of course."

Huda's fingernails dug into her palms. Damn Amira's snake tongue.

"My husband is a financial analyst, not a driver."

"I understand." Abu Issa set down his teacup. He flexed his fingers and cracked each joint. One by one, sinews and cartilage popped. "Working for a foreign woman would be distasteful for any Iraqi man, especially a loyal patriot such as Abdul Amir. But she will pay in American dollars, yes?"

"I don't think—"

"Abdul Amir will be well compensated by the diplomat's wife." Abu Issa smiled icily. "And finally, she has realized she can't parade through our streets, flaunting herself like a jezebel."

The Bolt Cutter sat forward and grunted.

"Her passport is Australian but she looks Russian." He snickered, and tea slopped into his saucer. "I saw a film once, with two Russian women. You would not believe what they—"

"Enough," interjected Abu Issa.

The Bolt Cutter snickered again.

"When the Australian woman ran across the road, her ass jiggled like—"

Abu Issa thumped his fist against his thigh.

"I said enough." He glared at the Bolt Cutter. "The foreigner may be a slut, but no decent Iraqi woman should be subjected to such talk."

Huda's cheeks burned. She rose unsteadily from her chair.

"My husband and son will be home soon. I must prepare their dinner."

Abu Issa threw another irritated glance at his partner. He got to his feet and gestured for the Bolt Cutter to do the same.

"We understand, sister." He bowed apologetically. "We'll return when you're not so busy."

Somewhere outside, a car backfired. Huda flinched. The Bolt Cutter noticed and smirked.

"Remember, you must become the foreign woman's confidante, and your husband can aid us too." Abu Issa paused by the front door. He twisted the ring on his finger. "Loyal citizens are always rewarded, are they not?"

Huda nodded dutifully. From the table in the hallway, the president watched over them.

* * *

Khalid had already gone to bed when Abdul Amir returned from the tea shop. Huda was at the kitchen table, wrapped in a pink dressing gown, smoking a counterfeit Marlboro. A deck of playing cards lay before her, divided into four columns.

"Consulting the cards?" Abdul Amir frowned. "The prophet does not approve of such superstition, even if your grandmother said otherwise."

The fluorescent light buzzed above Huda's head.

"I am playing solitaire. Besides, you know I don't read cards, and even if I did, it's bad luck to predict one's own future."

Abdul Amir opened the fridge and rifled through the shelves.

"I cooked lamb stew." Huda stubbed out her cigarette. "Shall I warm a dish for you?"

"Don't trouble yourself." Abdul Amir removed a carton of mango juice and shut the fridge door. "I'm surprised you're not in bed by now."

"I couldn't sleep."

Huda watched Abdul Amir pull a glass from the highest shelf. He was a tall man. A handsome man. People said he looked like the Egyptian singer Amr Diab, except Abdul Amir's eyes were green, not brown. She knew people were surprised when he chose to marry a plain woman like her. They thought he would pair up with Mona Karim, or one of the other beautiful village airheads. But Abdul Amir didn't want to stay in his village. He had bigger plans. So did Huda, and their shared ambition drew them together.

Not long after they married, Abdul Amir finished his university studies and Huda graduated from secretarial school. Khalid was born, and Abdul Amir made it a habit to surprise Huda with a slice of baklava or a fragrant bunch of orange blossoms. *But it's not my birthday*, she'd exclaim. He'd murmur in her ear that every day together was worth celebrating. Of course, after Abdul Amir got laid off, there was no money for surprises. Iraqi men were famously proud, and Huda knew her steady progress at work stung like salt in her husband's wounds. Eventually, even a whispered compliment cost too much.

For the first time in many years, she wondered, Would they be better off returning to the south? The village was out of the question, but what about Basra? Could they start afresh in the busy port city? Could they find their way back to the days of honeyed sweets and orange blossoms? She sighed and collected up the cards. It was foolish to dream of running away. The mukhabarat wanted something from her. There was no escape from that.

"My husband," she said, lowering her voice, "will you come to the garden?"

Abdul Amir set his glass on the counter and stared silently through the window over the sink. What did he see in his reflection? wondered Huda. Did he blame her for the lines of disappointment in his face?

Out in the garden, the palm trees swayed like dancers.

"Didn't I warn you that foreigners are nothing but trouble?" Abdul Amir dragged his fingers across his skull.

You did not complain when you saw my embassy paycheck, thought Huda.

"Well, my boss is fair, and Ally is a pleasant girl."

Abdul Amir grunted and stared at the horizon. The refineries were dark tonight. Only the stars and moon shone above their heads.

"She wants to hire a driver. . . ." Huda twisted the belt of her robe back and forth between her fingers. "Abu Issa said you must take the job."

"Me? Work for her?"

Huda nodded reluctantly.

"I am an educated man," he hissed. "I can't be expected to be at the beck and call of some foreign slut."

"Please, don't call her that."

Huda stared at her fluffy slippers. Abdul Amir stomped back and forth across the lawn. She thought of the Bolt Cutter, and how he leered as he described Ally running across the road. Had he been in the car that followed her to the embassy? Was it he who spat obscenities at the lonely young woman on the sidewalk?

She wondered, *Was it all a mukhabarat plan? Did they hope to frighten Ally into hiring a driver? Did they prime Amira to swoop in with Abdul Amir's name?* The cold ball she'd been carrying in her stomach returned. It was spiky now, as if wrapped in barbed wire.

"What should I do?" she said. "I can't simply tell them you refuse."

Abdul Amir cursed.

"I can't be this woman's driver."

"But you understand simple things like 'left,' 'right,' and 'stop here.'"

"'Left,' 'right,' 'stop here'? That's why I studied all those years?"

"Listen, I will drive Ally whenever I can. She will not bother you often. And she will pay two hundred dollars a month."

Abdul Amir paused.

"Two hundred dollars? American dollars? That is almost as much as you earn."

Huda shrugged.

"It's nothing to her. She was prepared to offer more."

"And you stopped her? Why? It's not as if you're friends."

Huda opened her mouth to argue, but prudence stilled her tongue. Abdul Amir was right. She and Ally could never be friends. No matter what she wished, it was dangerous to think otherwise.

CHAPTER 5

Abdul Amir grimaced as if Ally were about to yank out his tooth.

"Please," he hissed, "no pointing."

"Sorry, I forgot." Ally shoved her hands into her lap. "No pointing, only looking, right?"

Abdul Amir frowned. "Sometimes, better not to look at all."

On the far side of the windshield, two enormous bronze hands rose toward the sky, each clenching a 150-foot sword, the tips meeting overhead. Ally tried not to roll her eyes. She'd seen the "Arch of Victory" plenty on local television, usually accompanied by the Star Wars theme and superimposed with footage of Saddam riding a white stallion. The mighty mitts were supposedly engraved with the president's own fingerprints. Helmets looted from the bodies of enemy Iranian troops lay in jumbled heaps below, real helmets, each with its own individual wounds and stains from the battlefield.

The Arch of Victory disappeared in the rearview mirror, only to be replaced by a great copper disc slanting above the tree line like a stricken UFO. Ally felt like she was riding through a totalitarian amusement park.

"That's the Monument to the Unknown Soldier, right?" Ally remembered not to point. "Is it open to the public?"

"I do not think so," mumbled Abdul Amir.

"The National Museum is nearby. Is that open?"

On one of her postcards, Ally's mother had written of wandering the museum, resting her hand against the statue of a human-headed bull with wings, and wondering, *Is that its stone heart beating beneath my palm?*

"The museum is closed for renovations." Abdul Amir stared at the road. "Same as last time you asked."

Ally tried to quell the heartburn of frustration. She wasn't going to let it get her down. Not today. Not when she'd finally located the hospital where her mother had worked. It turned out, like so many other institutions and landmarks, it had been renamed after Saddam Hussein. As if on cue, the gargantuan dome of a new, multimillion dollar mosque came into view.

"That's the Saddam mosque, right?" said Ally.

Abdul Amir's shoulders hiked toward his ears, and he stared mutely at the road. Regret nibbled at Ally. Saddam's face might be everywhere, and his statue on every corner, but she knew darn well that no one said his name out loud. They continued in silence until they reached the Saddam Cardiac and Vascular Hospital, a six-story block of grimy concrete. As they drew closer, Abdul Amir eased his foot onto the brake.

"I will come with you."

"That's okay. You go ahead and find the parking lot." Ally gathered up her bag and pointed to a shaded seating area by the entrance. "When I'm done, I'll meet you there."

Before Abdul Amir could object, she pushed open her door and hurried up the steps into the hospital. Inside, on wooden benches, patients and their families waited for release or admission, X-rays, and blood draws. At the information desk, a man in a blue jacket greeted Ally politely.

"I'm looking for some information," said Ally, as butterflies did loop-de-doos in her stomach. She tried not to look at the two armed guards slouching by the entrance. Both were eyeing her with the same unnervingly blank gaze.

"Do you have papers, miss?" The clerk glanced at the manila envelope protruding from Ally's handbag. "Doctor's orders?"

"Actually, I'm trying to find someone." Ally pulled a yellowed photo from the envelope and slid it across the counter. "I'm looking for a nurse who worked here, back in the 1970s."

Ally knew hospital records would show her mother was American. So she'd chosen a photo of one of her Iraqi friends, dressed in a nurse's cap and pinafore. The woman had a long, thin nose and dark, dramatic eyes reminiscent of Cher. She appeared in several photos, so Ally knew she had Cher's long hair too, although in that particular shot it was pulled into a tight bun. The journalist in Ally recognized a telltale glint in the woman's eyes, the glint of someone prone to speaking the truth—even if it wasn't always in their best interest.

The clerk tapped his forefinger against his chin.

"I'll check with my supervisor," he said, then ducked into a glassed-in office.

Ally leaned against the counter and tried to act as if it were perfectly normal for her to be frequenting a hospital named after a bloodthirsty tyrant, with armed guards at the door. It was another journalistic trick: act like you belong, even if your nerves are fizzing.

As she waited, she imagined her mother in a starched nurse's uniform, striding briskly through the waiting room, stopping to comfort patients—like the elderly woman on the bench by the wall. Ally winced as the woman emitted a long thin bleat of pain. A younger woman, probably her daughter, patted her arm. For a moment, Ally wished she could trade places, wished for the chance to hold her mother's hand, to whisper in her ear that she loved her.

With a hot rush of guilt, she remembered her mother's last days and how, as her mother wasted away, five-year-old Ally convinced herself that an impostor lay in her mother's darkened bedroom, with claws for hands and fluid-filled tubes sprouting like tentacles from her arms. Ally was sure her mother was elsewhere. Perhaps she was on a daring adventure, trekking through jungle or riding camels through desert in some exotic land, or by a rippling river, with the wind catching her hair. Or maybe the explanation was simpler. Maybe she was at the grocery store, pushing a squeaky-wheeled cart laden with flour, sugar, and eggs for the cookies they made every Friday afternoon.

Maybe she'd come home soon. She'd rest her hand on top of Ally's and help her to guide the whirring mixer round and round the bowl, beating butter and sugar until they were smooth and fluffy. Her mother swiped a finger along the edge of the bowl. "Tell me, is it ready?" her mother asked, offering a snow-topped index finger. "Is it mixed enough?"

Sweet cream dissolved on her tongue. Ally nodded with delight. After cracking eggs and sifting pale clouds of flour, they put the rolled dough in the fridge. As her mother washed up, Ally hopped impatiently from foot to foot and fiddled with the cookie cutters. Ally was sure there could be no greater satisfaction than the moment she pressed the tin stars through the chilled dough. With her mother by her side, they created a sugared constellation all their own.

Maybe this Friday we'll make cookies, she'd thought, as she stared at the portrait on the mantel. She sent the young woman in the photo frame silent messages, *Please, come home soon.* But the woman stayed mum, hand raised, waving for her daughter to join her instead.

One evening, as Ally moped by the mantel in the living room, her dad came in and said that her mother wanted to talk to her. At that moment, a long moan escaped from the sickroom. To Ally's ears it sounded more animal than human. She grabbed the photo from the mantel, ran upstairs, and threw herself onto her bed. She cried and wailed and refused to come out. Later that night, her mother breathed her last.

A squawk from the hospital intercom jolted Ally back to the present. If only she could go back in time. She'd grab her five-year-old self by the shoulders and give her a good shake until she gave up the foolish suspicion that an impostor had taken her mother's place. She'd send her downstairs toot sweet. Then finally, Ally and her mother would hold hands, whisper words of comfort, like the Iraqi women on the far side of the waiting room.

For the millionth time, Ally wished she'd had more courage, more loyalty. What had her mother wanted to tell her? Was it precious advice for the daughter she'd never see grow up? Was there a secret she wanted to share? The shameful hole in Ally's chest expanded. Her mother had deserved so much better from her.

A door opened, and a middle-aged woman in a baby-blue pantsuit and head scarf emerged from the office behind the counter. Ally blinked back a tear. She straightened up, hoping her sweaty palms hadn't left an imprint of the precious package of photographs.

"My name is Mrs. al-Deeb." The woman in the pantsuit eyed Ally warily. "My clerk said you are looking for one of our nurses. Is there some problem?"

"No, no problem at all. Quite the opposite." Ally smiled in what she hoped was a reassuring manner and explained that she was writing a book about nursing history. Most Iraqis held writers and scholars in high esteem. It had been that way for over fifteen hundred years, when Baghdadi caliphs built Bayt al-Hikma, the House of Wisdom, to record the works of the world's best philosophers, scientists, and poets. Ally hoped the caliphs' love of knowledge still ran in Mrs. al-Deeb's blood.

"From what I've learned," said Ally, "the late sixties and early seventies was a wonderful period in Baghdad."

"Ah, the golden years." Mrs. al-Deeb's dark eyes glazed over with a nostalgic haze that Ally had quickly come to recognize. "You're right, those were glorious times."

"And the Iraqi health system was the best in the Middle East back then." Ally leaned a little closer. "At least that's what I've been told."

Mrs. al-Deeb beamed with pride. Ally felt a stab of remorse for manipulating her emotions, but soon Mrs. al-Deeb was regaling her with stories of a British nurse called Daphne who sang opera like Maria Callas and staged late-night limbo competitions in the hospital cafeteria.

"So, please, tell me, dear," said Mrs. al-Deeb, "who is the woman you're looking for?"

Ally's pulse quickened. She slid a few photos across the counter.

"Do you recognize any of these nurses? Perhaps someone in the background?"

Mrs. al-Deeb looked through the photos, humming a tune from one of Daphne's favorite operas. She paused at the photo of the nurse with eyes like Cher. When she looked up, her eyes had gone eerily blank, like the armed guards at the door.

"I can't help you." She pushed the photos back across the counter. "I have work to do."

"Should I come back later," said Ally, "when you've got more time?"

Mrs. al-Deeb shot a nervous glance at the guards.

"Who are you?" she whispered. "What do you really want?"

"I, um . . ." Ally trailed off nervously.

"No good will come of your questions." Mrs. al-Deeb threw another furtive glance at the guards. "Now, please, go."

Ally's fingers trembled as she shoved the photos into her handbag. She hurried away, past the mother and daughter, hands still entwined. The old woman groaned again. Her pain vibrated through the waiting room. Ally felt it like a stitch in her side long after she slipped past the guards and left the hospital behind.

Ally's doorbell buzzed. She glanced at her watch. Eight p.m. Abdul Amir was right on time. She quickly pressed the phone to her ear and dialed the number for Tom's hotel in the northern city of Mosul. Static hissed like a broken radiator.

"Damn it." Ally put the phone down. She didn't want Tom to

call later and get no answer. But she couldn't bear another night watching Saddam tributes on TV, with nothing but a bag of counterfeit "Keet Katts" for company. She grabbed her handbag and set to work on the locks and bolts of the front door.

It was dark outside, but the concrete slabs in the courtyard still radiated the heat of high noon. The perfume of the rosebushes mixed with exhaust fumes from the traffic circle, confusing Ally's senses with their benzene sweetness.

"Hello?" She eyed the quiet guard hut. "Ghassan?"

Ally tiptoed to the front gate and pushed it open. Cars trundled by, headlights skewering the ocher-tinted gloom. Ghassan was chatting through the window of the idling Corolla. Ally hurried across the sidewalk and ducked into the passenger seat.

"Hello, my dear." Huda smiled from behind the wheel. "Abdul Amir is not feeling well, so I've come in his place. I hope you don't mind."

"No, this is perfect." Ally beamed. "We can make this a girls' night out."

"Oh, my dear, I'm here as your driver, nothing more."

A concrete mixer rumbled past. Its lights swept across Huda's face, revealing eyes lined with thick black kohl and lids painted pink and purple. Diamantés sparkled at her ears.

"But you look so lovely." Ally motioned at Huda's long silky blouse and black pants. She paused and inspected her own linen maxidress and roman sandals. "I hope I'm not underdressed."

"Don't worry." Huda patted her arm.

Ally thought she saw pity in her eyes.

"You look very nice," Huda assured her.

"So you'll join me?"

Huda shrugged. "We'll see."

They motored past the billboard and through the blinking traffic lights. After a few zigzagging blocks, they turned and cruised along the Tigris. Ally eyed the deserted promenade hugging the riverbank. Her mother used to come here to unwind with her friends. On one of her postcards she called it "our weekly gossip session." Ally peered into the darkness and imagined young women strolling beside the water, music drifting from the cafés, families picnicking on the grass.

In her mother's day, Saddam was only vice president and his gargantuan palace of gray concrete had not yet sprung up on the far bank. Now his face was carved into each of the four massive turrets, granite eyes surveying every inch of the city. The palace lights reflected in the dark waters like a twisted Disneyland.

"Abdul Amir said you went to the hospital today," said Huda. "Is anything wrong?"

"I'm fine. Nothing to worry about."

"People don't go to the hospital for nothing." Huda glanced at her. "Are you sick?"

"I'm fine."

"Are you pregnant?" Huda grinned. "Please, tell me, will we have a little Tom running about soon?"

"That's not it."

"So, what is it?"

Ally hesitated. She knew she had to keep her mom's nationality secret, but surely she could share a few things about her past. Did she have to behave like a paper doll, trimmed of substance, snipped of history? Without at least a little trust, Ally suspected her friendship with Huda would wither and die, like the gardens that had once hemmed the promenade.

"Is it a secret, my friend?"

"No, it's just . . ." Ally knew Huda wasn't a gossip and that they were alone in the car. Still, it was hard not to check the back seat. "I was trying to find someone who knew my mother."

Huda's eyebrows climbed up her forehead.

"Your mother?"

"She worked as a nurse in Baghdad thirty years ago."

Huda glanced across the cabin.

"How come you never told me this before?" She frowned slightly, as if her feelings were hurt. "They had Australian nurses here? I thought they were all British."

"They were British, mostly, but there were also nurses from France, India, Australia and . . . other countries." Ally wished she could tell Huda the whole truth, but that wouldn't be safe. Not for her. And not for Huda.

"Can't your mother tell you how to find her friend?"

Ally sighed. Her secrets were like stones in her pockets, dragging her down.

"She died when I was five years old," she said quietly.

"My dear, I'm so sorry." Huda reached across and touched Ally's knee. "I didn't realize."

"Don't feel bad. It's all right."

"No, it's not." Huda stared through the windshield. "My father died when I was little. For a girl, it's not the same as losing a mother, but it hurts, even today."

Out on the promenade, a bronze statue gleamed under spotlights: Scheherazade, the fabled storyteller of *One Thousand and One Nights*. Ally's mother had written about the statue's unveiling, and every time Ally saw the graceful figure, she felt a rush of tenderness. It was not just the connection to her mom but that Scheherazade had survived—when so many other statues had been torn down and replaced by tributes to Saddam.

"I'm sorry," said Ally. "This was meant to be a fun night out."

Huda glanced at her.

"The great poet Rumi said sorrow sweeps everything out of your house violently so that joy has space to enter."

Perhaps Huda was right, thought Ally. In the darkened car, childhood losses reached out their hands and greeted each other as friends.

The car trundled by a quiet fish shack set in a patch of grass. There were no patrons at its rickety tables, only an old man roasting *masgouf* carp over a glowing firepit.

"I read that people used to water-ski right here," said Ally.

"Oh, yes," said Huda. "Young people liked to swim and water-ski. Families came to picnic, to take a nice walk, to play badminton. At night, Abu Nuwas Boulevard was the most exciting place. More exciting than Cairo. More than Beirut. There were bars and nightclubs. Fancy casinos too."

"What about you, Huda? Did you ever go water-skiing on the Tigris?"

"Me? No, never." Huda pursed her lips. "I was too busy playing blackjack at the casino."

Ally threw her head back and cackled.

"Oh, yes," Huda chuckled. "I juggled martinis in one hand, and dealt seven-card stud with the other. They called me the Queen of Diamonds."

The two women giggled, their merriment echoing through the car. Ally gazed out the window and marveled at how history always managed to repeat itself. Thirty years after her mother, she was here, sharing a laugh with a friend, while Scheherazade kept spinning her tales on the banks of the ancient Tigris.

Huda maneuvered the Corolla down a narrow street and pulled up by a sturdy gate the mottled green of old copper. Nothing could be seen beyond it, only treetops and a buttery smear of stars.

Ally unbuckled her seat belt. "Shall we go in?"

Huda eyed the gate uneasily. "I'll wait in the car."

"Please, come inside. I'm sure you'd be very welcome." Ally squeezed Huda's hand. She couldn't stomach the thought of leaving her to wait out in the car, alone. "When's the last time you had a girls' night out?"

Huda ran her hand over her hair. She reached for the interior light, flipped down her visor, and inspected her reflection in the vanity mirror.

"Will they be serving wine?" She scrubbed a fleck of lipstick from her tooth.

"I think so," replied Ally tentatively.

"Good. I need a drink."

The copper gate had been left ajar. Ally pushed it open, revealing a once grand Baghdadi home. Flakes of paint clung to the pale walls like the scales of a great fish. Light filtered through a small stained-glass window set in an iron-studded front door that looked like it had been built in medieval times. A burst of laughter came from somewhere around the side of the house.

"It sounds like the party is out back." Ally smoothed her dress. Huda dug a pack of cigarettes from her handbag.

"Go ahead. I will join you in a few minutes."

"I can wait."

"No, go ahead." Huda shooed Ally toward a stepping-stone path hemmed with lavender. It led to a large yard at the side of the house. On the lawn, a handful of people milled about a firepit. A few others congregated at picnic tables and benches. A rosy-cheeked man in a safari suit spied Ally hovering at the end of the path.

"Welcome!" He hurried past a seven-foot statue of a woman curled around a child, like a fruit around a seed. He stuck out a sweaty hand. "I'm Gunter Kops, director of the German Cultural Center. It's so nice to see a fresh face."

"Nice to meet you. I'm Ally Wilson."

"Tom Wilson's wife? I should have guessed. After all, there's not many Western women running around Baghdad. May I get you a drink?"

"A chardonnay would be great," said Ally. Gunter poured her a glass at a makeshift bar, then ushered her toward the other guests. An older Asian woman elbowed her companion, and the group swiveled toward them like a school of fish.

"Welcome to Baghdad." The Asian woman crushed Ally's fingers with her handshake. In heavily accented English, she introduced herself as the chargé d'affairs at the Chinese embassy. The other guests—all men—were either diplomats or they worked for the United Nations.

"And what do you do, Ally?" asked a silver-haired Frenchman.

"I, uh . . ."

"Ally is married to Tom Wilson at the Australian embassy," said Gunter.

"Oh, a housewife," said the Chinese woman. Her eyes went blank, like someone had pulled down a blind. She turned to the man beside her and they began conversing in what sounded like Russian.

"I thought Iraq was a nonfamily posting," said the Frenchman.

"I believe the Bangladeshi ambassador has his wife here," a Nigerian diplomat replied.

"No, she left a month ago." Gunter wiped beer froth from his lip. "Her husband sent her back home after President Bush's 'Axis of Evil' speech."

Muttering and eye-rolling broke out.

"Al-Qaeda has no stronghold here." The Frenchman sipped his wine, grimaced, and then sipped again. "This is a farce designed to distract Americans voters from their own problems."

"The regime can't keep the lights on or the phones working, let alone threaten Washington," said the Nigerian. "The Americans must know that."

"I wouldn't rule out the possibility that there's an old stockpile of nerve gas tucked away somewhere." Gunter leaned into the circle. "If things get worse, who knows what the regime might do."

"Like what?" said Ally. "Smuggle nerve gas onto the subway in New York?"

"Oh, no, they couldn't pull that off," said Gunter. "They'd use them on only the foreigners within reach—us. Or maybe they'll keep us as human shields, like they did with thousands of expats during the Gulf War." He glanced over his shoulder. "The regime can be as ruthless with foreigners as it is with its own."

The Frenchman nodded. "Remember that British journalist they accused of spying? The regime invited him here on a press tour, but when he deviated from the itinerary . . ." He paused, checked the garden, and sliced his hand across his throat.

Lukewarm chardonnay lodged in Ally's gullet.

"What journalist?" she stammered. "I never heard about this."

"That's no surprise—the world has a short memory," said the Frenchman. "It was a few years after the Gulf War. The reporter heard rumors of an explosion at a refinery, so he went to investigate. The Iraqis arrested him just outside of Baghdad, charged him with spying, and hung him at Abu Ghraib." He paused. "Of course, they tortured him for six months first."

CHAPTER 6

Rania straightened her silky blue jumpsuit, ran her hands over her long wavy hair, then stepped out of the gallery and into the backyard. She prayed that she could convince at least a few of the diplomats to buy a painting from the new exhibition. The money she'd made selling her father's books was running out fast.

"Come now, gentlemen." The stern voice of the Chinese chargé d'affaires echoed across the lawn. "No one wants to hear such wild talk."

Rania slowed her pace. Lee Ping had a fine-tuned ear for chatter that might upset the authorities. Rania considered turning around and retreating indoors. After all, the mukhabarat would have followed at least some of the diplomats here, and one of those oafish thugs could well pay her a visit later, demanding to know who said what, and to whom.

Rania turned her amber eyes to the night sky. The stars were bright, but the moon was nowhere to be seen. She wasn't surprised that it wanted nothing to do with the folly below. She took a deep breath, squared her shoulders, and continued across the lawn. Artists had always held an honored role in Iraqi society, and that afforded her some leeway from the regime's restrictions on associating with foreigners. Still, she knew she was walking a high wire.

Over the years, Rania had become skilled at fending off the mukhabarat's inquiries. She knew how to distract, flatter, and feign ignorance, how to smile even when fear bubbled in her stomach. She could always find a way to casually mention that one of the city's thoroughfares bore her ancestral name. Her family's wealth might be gone, but she was a sheikh's daughter, and that still carried some weight. In the rare case that didn't work, she'd produce her Presidential Arts Award with its dollop of bloodred wax. The sight of his signature always brought the interview to a quick close.

Tonight, however, Rania could feel a migraine coming on. She didn't want to have to stay up late, performing verbal gymnastics and dropping names for some mukhabarat brute, just because one of the diplomats drank too much wine and indulged in wild talk. Still, the bills weren't going to pay themselves.

"Rania, there you are." Gunter broke away from the gaggle of diplomats and hurried toward her. "Please allow me to introduce you to a newcomer to Baghdad."

He steered her toward a young woman—the diplomat's wife from Mutanabbi market.

"It's so wonderful to see you again," said Ally. As the conversation continued, Rania noticed her sipping nervously on her wine and glancing over her shoulder toward the gate.

"You probably find it boring here, Ally, without a job to keep you busy," said Gunter. "Did you know that Baghdad has an international school? There aren't any foreign children left, but there are some very bright Iraqi students. They always need teachers. What's your background?"

"My background?"

"What did you do before you came here?"

"She already said she's a diplomat's wife." The Nigerian ambassador sipped pomegranate juice. "My own wife tells me it's a full-time occupation—entertaining official guests, running the house, training the cook to make dishes the proper way."

"You didn't bring her to Baghdad?" said the Frenchman.

"I brought the cook instead," he replied archly. His colleagues chuckled and swigged their drinks.

Ally shifted uncomfortably.

"Would you like to see some paintings?" Rania whispered in her ear. "I can give you a tour of my little gallery."

"I'd love that." Ally smiled gratefully. She glanced over her shoulder again. "But do you mind giving me a few minutes? I just need to duck out to my car."

"Of course." Rania gestured to the side door, where light from the gallery spilled in a long rectangle across the grass. "I'll wait for you inside."

Ally appeared a few minutes later, still looking vaguely perturbed. Rania took the young woman's elbow, and they began to circle the whitewashed room, keeping in step, as if they were ladies promenading by the river.

"Are you an artist too?" said Ally. "Do you paint? Or did you create that sculpture in the garden?"

"Oh, no, I bought that sculpture many years ago," said Rania. "I just dabble, a little sketch here and there, but nothing of any great import. I try to support artists and match them with a buyer. And, as you can see, I host events in the garden from time to time."

Ally paused by a painting of three galloping horses: all slanting lines and geometric shapes in shades of orange and gray. Sharp-edged storm clouds pressed at their backs. Rania eyed the short biography pinned beneath the artist's work: Hassan Ghraib, born 1985. He wasn't much older than Hanan. Rania's heart ached. Was this what peace looked like to her daughter's generation?

"Gunter told me the theme of the exhibition was peace," said Ally, as if reading her mind.

Rania arched an eyebrow.

"Do you see peace in this work?"

The young woman blushed. "I don't know anything about art."

"Forget about your head," said Rania. "What about your heart?"

Ally eyed the stampeding animals.

"I don't see peace in this at all. Quite the opposite."

"I agree," said Rania. "Peace is a convenient theme for an exhibition, but for many Iraqis, especially our youth, it is an alien concept. It shouldn't have to be this way."

Ally glanced at her curiously. Rania was surprised too. She didn't normally share opinions like that with strangers, foreign strangers. But the young woman had an unguarded quality, an openness, that reminded her of Hanan.

The door to the garden swung open.

"Look who I found by the gate." Gunter hustled a short woman into the gallery. She raised her hand to her eyes, as if blinded by the light.

"Huda!" cried Ally. "There you are. Please, let me introduce you to Rania Mansour."

Rania froze. She'd imagined this moment so many times: what she would do and say. Now, her mind went blank. Huda lowered her hand. Her eyes were flat as a pond.

"We know each other," she said coolly.

"You do?"

Rania forced a smile onto her lips.

"Yes, we've known each other since we were children." She reminded herself to breathe, but the past had sucked all the air from the room.

"That was a long time ago." Huda turned her cheek and eyed the galloping ocher horses.

Rania's heart beat faster. She could manage the mukhabarat's questions about foreigners in her garden. Huda was different. How could Rania explain their connection? And what if the mukhabarat interviewed Huda? What secrets might she spill? Rania felt the high wire sway beneath her.

"Ally, why don't you show Gunter the painting you liked?" she said quickly. "I would love a moment to catch up with Huda. Please, excuse us."

She extended her arm and swept Huda out to the garden, so swift there was no time for her to object. She put her hand on Huda's back and steered her away from the foreigners on the grass.

"How is your family?" She directed Huda toward an overgrown citrus grove at the rear of the yard. "Your husband and son, are they well?"

"Yes, both are well. Khalid is almost fourteen now," Huda replied. "And your daughter, Hanan? How is she?"

They exchanged ritual greetings, using the time to size each other up among the orange trees. The past pressed against Rania's chest. Did Huda feel it too?

"So what brings you here?" Rania struggled to keep tremors from her voice. "Is there something I can do for you?"

"No, not at all," said Huda. "I'm here with Ally. She's my boss's wife. I work at the Australian embassy now. I'm a secretary."

"I did hear of this, from my mother. You've done very well. You should be congratulated." Rania glanced over her shoulder. The diplomats had their backs to them, blissfully unaware of the ghosts stalking the orange trees. She lowered her voice. "Forgive me for asking, but do you often socialize with foreigners outside the office?"

"I told you, she's my boss's wife." Huda frowned. "She asked me to bring her here."

"I see." Rania rubbed at the scar on her thumb. "It is quite likely that your car's number plate has been taken down. You may be followed home and interviewed."

Huda raised her chin. "Every worker at the embassy is interviewed from time to time. I can explain it to them."

"Explain? To them?"

"You associate with foreigners," said Huda. "Plenty of them. Are you never questioned?"

"But I am—" Rania stopped. "Our situation is very different."

"I'm not a poor village girl anymore." Huda stared at her. "I work at the embassy. I am simply fulfilling my work duties."

Behind them, the foreigners bayed with sudden laughter.

"You may be a secretary," whispered Rania, "but to them, that means nothing."

Huda drew herself up to her full height. She was still two heads shorter than Rania.

"I am nothing?" she hissed.

"That's not what I meant."

"Perhaps you think—"

"Here you two are." Ally materialized at the edge of the citrus grove. "I hope I'm not interrupting."

"Not at all," said Rania hurriedly. She shot a wary glance at Huda. "It's been a lovely surprise to see my friend here, after so many years. But forgive me, I better check in with my other guests."

As Rania hurried away, she wondered how long Ally had been standing there. She probably didn't know enough Arabic to have understood her conversation with Huda, but even a dead man could feel the tension in the air. And the regret, thicker than the scent of orange blossom.

CHAPTER 7

"There are too many eyes in this room." Huda hugged her arms to her chest. On the walls of Rania's whitewashed gallery, black-robed women, children picking watermelons, and warrior kings were all boxed into wooden frames. "I feel as if I am being watched."

"So how do you know Rania?" Ally tilted her head. Her gaze still held the watchfulness Huda detected in the citrus grove. "I got the impression you two aren't best buddies. . . ."

Huda ignored the question and peered at a painting titled *Three Men on a Bench*. To her, they looked like prisoners strapped into electric chairs.

"Forty dollars? So much?" She shook her head at the price tag, then surveyed the wall of oil-paint eyes: pale as moons, oversize, some crisscrossed with veins, others dead. "It's hot in here," she said. "Let's go out to the garden."

The foreigners fell quiet as Huda and Ally crossed the lawn. All those eyes again, watching their approach. Gunter darted forward and escorted them to the firepit.

"This is Huda." He puffed out his chest like a fisherman who'd netted the catch of the day. "She works at the Australian embassy with Ally's husband, isn't that so?"

She nodded and forced a smile.

"It's so wonderful to have one of our Iraqi colleagues among us," he crowed.

The foreigners erupted into a chorus of greetings. Huda told herself there was nothing to fear. Still, her heart thudded as she stammered through small talk: families, summer heat, vacation plans. Luckily, every time conversation threatened to veer into dangerous territory, a helpful Chinese woman intervened and directed talk elsewhere. All the while, she waited for Rania to reappear, but she remained inside her mansion for the rest of the night.

When Huda arrived home, Abdul Amir was in the backyard, pacing the manicured lawn. The refineries were burning gas. Huda could taste it on her tongue.

"Rania's garden was in such a state." She shook her head. "Threadbare grass, plants run to seed. Surely, she can afford a gardener?"

"How did she appear?"

"She has some gray hairs, a few lines at her eyes, but she was beautiful as always. And just as arrogant. She still believes she can tell me how to live my life."

"Old traditions die hard, especially for someone from a family like hers."

Huda scowled at the row of gas flares on the horizon.

"Rania's family is quick to abandon tradition when it suits them."

A tremor shook her, just as it had in the gallery when Rania turned to greet her, elegant as a pharaoh's queen. Huda had armed herself with the memories of all that Rania had done, and all that it had cost. But when she looked into her amber eyes, it was as if they'd traveled twenty years back in time, to when they were girls, whispering secrets in each other's ears. Despite her intentions, Huda's heart had swelled, repeating patterns it learned long ago. She hated Rania for that too.

Abdul Amir bent down and wrenched a dandelion from the lawn. It snapped off at the stem.

"It must have been difficult, seeing her again." He grunted and dug his fingers deeper into the earth until he tore out the fleshy root. "I'm sorry I couldn't spare you that."

It was too dark to be sure, but Huda sensed her husband's cheeks were flushed with shame.

"It's not your fault," she said. "Abu Issa told you to stay home."

"He was right; Ally would have left me to wait in the car. She thinks she is superior."

"That's not right, she—"

"I speak the truth, wife." Abdul Amir tossed the weed away. "So, what did you tell her? How did you explain your connection with Rania?"

Huda rubbed her aching temples. The wine and the stress of the evening had made it more difficult than usual to dodge Ally's questions, to bat her off with small talk and little jokes.

"I said that Rania and I belonged to the same tribe. That when we were young, her father was my family's sheikh."

Huda didn't mention that on the way home, she'd been tempted to pull over to the side of the road and tell Ally everything about her and Rania. But a tiny voice had whispered, *Be careful, what if the mukhabarat are listening in?* Huda didn't believe they made a habit of bugging the cars of little people, like her. But now that she was an informant, she couldn't be sure. Huda didn't know if she was being paranoid or prudent, so she'd kept quiet about her connection to Rania. The mukhabarat probably already knew all about their history, but there was no need to remind them.

Huda sighed. As much as she wanted to leave the past alone, these days it was always there, an itch at the back of her throat, a spasm that woke her just before dawn, gasping for breath. Westerners liked to proclaim that the truth would set them free. That was foolish. And dangerous. But lying to Ally was harder than Huda had foreseen.

Ally was not like the diplomat wives who had come before,

with their measured smiles and tepid handshakes. Ally told wacky jokes. She laughed too loud. She took pleasure in things that Huda had stopped noticing long ago: the iridescent shine of a crow's feathers, or a donkey cart painted the color of the Arabian Gulf. She couldn't get enough of those donkey carts, as if they were floats in a grand parade.

Huda tried to treat her dealings with Ally as a job. But her body was absorbing the repeated motions of friendship—the kisses that marked arrival and departure, the friendly pats, the playful winks—and fooling her heart into believing it was true. She was feeding the young woman sugar pills, but the side effects were surprisingly real. It was friendship by placebo.

Abdul Amir yanked another weed from the flower bed.

"So, did you learn anything of interest?"

"I don't think so." Huda rubbed her eyes, smearing the kohl she'd applied so carefully. She wanted to curl up in bed and sleep for a week. Abdul Amir wiped his hands against his trousers.

"Abu Issa and his partner stayed on after you left."

"They did?" Adrenaline drove a stake through Huda's exhaustion. "Why? What for?"

He rummaged in his pocket and pulled out a wad of bills.

"They called it a performance incentive."

Behind him, the tall flames of the refinery stabbed the night. Huda was no longer certain they were to blame for the sour taste in her mouth.

Huda checked that the doors were locked, then padded through the house, switching off lights. In their bedroom, Abdul Amir was propped up against his pillows, reading the sport section of the *Iraq Daily*. He folded the newspaper and set it down on his bedside table.

"Are you coming to bed?"

"Go ahead and turn off your lamp. I'll check on Khalid, then I'll come."

Huda tiptoed down the hall and pried open her son's door.

The odor of dirty sneakers and testosterone hung in the air. How was it possible, she wondered, that one teenage boy could be so pungent? She stepped over a damp towel left in a heap on the floor and opened the window. On the far side of the bars, cicadas chirruped and clicked.

Khalid stirred beneath his faded Star Wars sheets.

"Mom? What are you doing?" He reached for her with a long, skinny arm. Huda didn't understand how he could eat so much yet remain so thin. She had only to glance sideways at a sticky bun, and the next thing she knew, it was attached to her hips.

"What time is it?" He slipped his hand into hers.

"It's late. Go back to sleep."

"My legs ache."

"Growing pains again? Shall I get a hot-water bottle?"

The boy shook his head. His hair was very dark against his pillow.

"Maybe I'll feel better if you stroke my head?"

It had been a long time since Khalid had asked her for this, and she'd wondered if those days were done for good. She smiled and perched on the edge of his mattress.

"Roll over."

The boy pushed aside the stuffed Chewbacca doll he'd slept with since he was six. He claimed he no longer cared about the toy, yet he refused to throw it away. Even so, Huda suspected Chewie's days were numbered.

"Where did you go tonight?" he murmured.

"Hush." Huda gently scratched her son's scalp. "Go to sleep."

"Why? Did it involve one of those men we're not supposed to talk about?"

"Where do you get such nonsense?" Huda frowned into the darkness. This was not the time, or place, for such a perilous conversation. "I went to see a friend, that's all."

"Who?"

"An old friend. I haven't seen her in many years."

Huda stroked Khalid's hair. It was the exact same thickness

and color as his uncle Mustafa's. Almost every day, Huda was struck by Khalid's growing resemblance to her dead brother. Her chest ached with equal parts love and fear. It was difficult enough lying to Ally, but how much longer could she keep the truth from her son?

"Have I met your friend before?" he whispered.

"Yes, a long time ago." Huda kissed his cheek and levered herself off the bed. "Now, it's time to sleep."

Khalid grabbed her hand again. "Don't go."

Huda caught sight of their reflection in the mirror on the chest of drawers. Years ago, she'd hung an amulet at its apex to ward off the evil eye: the Hand of Fatima, with an eye of cobalt glass in the center of its palm. Her grandmother had given her the amulet and promised it would keep her safe. It had worked, so far, but even the Hand of Fatima could only do so much. She glanced at Khalid, and kicked off her slippers.

"Move over, then."

She slid onto the mattress and rested her head on the edge of Khalid's pillow.

"Who were the men that came tonight?" he whispered.

"Are your legs still cramping?"

"Who were they?"

"Khalid, be quiet and go to sleep."

"But, Mom—"

Huda put some iron in her voice.

"Your father and I have told you before, this is none of your business." She sighed, and her voice softened. "Another time, my son. Sleep now."

Khalid grumbled into his pillow, while outside, the cicadas' cry cycled up and down. Huda lay beside him and tried to forget Abu Issa and the Bolt Cutter, to banish thoughts of Ally and Rania, but her mind chattered like the insects outside. After Khalid fell asleep, Huda listened to his breath sigh in and out of his lungs. Eventually, she pried herself off the mattress. She stared at the Hand of Fatima, then shuffled from the room.

CHAPTER 8

Tom and Ally fell silent as they passed the flashing traffic lights and neared the men sipping tea and playing backgammon on the sidewalk. In the cool of evening, dice clattered. Dominoes clicked and clacked. A man tilted his head and blew out a stream of minty smoke from his nargilah pipe.

"Hello!" he cried.

Tom raised his hand in greeting and smiled. Ally tried to do the same, but her lips wouldn't cooperate. She kept her eyes down and skirted past the mismatched tables. As soon as they were out of earshot, Tom's smile vanished.

"I can't believe this," he muttered. "I get back from a week away and discover you've been playing Nancy Drew. If the woman at the hospital checked the nursing records, they'd show your mom was . . ." He trailed off, checked the sidewalk, and bent close to her ear. "They'd show your mom's nationality, for sure."

"I never mentioned my mom. Not once." Ally scowled. "There's absolutely zero chance that Mrs. al-Deeb would make that connection. All I said was that I was writing a book about nurses who worked in Iraq."

"That's enough to cause trouble," Tom grumbled. "You don't have a work permit."

"What am I supposed to do? Stay home and learn to crochet?"

A seventies Cadillac, a long, wide boat of a car, cruised toward them. The driver tapped the horn to see if they wanted a ride. Gas was far cheaper than water, and in the evening, every second motorist was a freelance taxi driver. Tom waved him off.

"I'm just saying . . ." He scanned the sidewalk again. "If anyone connects the dots, we'll probably be thrown out of the country."

"Don't be such a drama queen." Ally peered past Tom, to the corner where Mohammad's mother sold her newspapers. There was no sign of them. She wondered where they went at night. She prayed they weren't sleeping rough, in an alley somewhere.

A carpet vendor appeared in the doorway of his showroom.

"As-salaam alaikum!" he cried cheerily, as he did every time he saw them on the sidewalk. "Come have tea, my friends."

Tom nodded noncommittally and deployed his diplomat smile. Two more vendors materialized in nearby doorways, each entreating them to come, recline a while on their fine carpets, kilims, and rugs. Tom and Ally exchanged a sideways glance and crossed the road, away from the men's sharp ears.

"I know you're bored. And it doesn't help that I'm away so much." Tom paused near a shuttered souvenir store. Two letters had burned out in the fluorescent sign above the doorway, leaving dark gaps like missing teeth. "But this is why you'd be better off in Jordan."

"But what about my book?" Suddenly, Ally's eyes stung with unexpected tears. "And what about my mom? As weird as it sounds, I feel like Baghdad is finally giving me a chance to know her."

"You have an aunt in America, right? Why don't you get in touch with her?"

"Aunt Bernice is in a nursing home. Early-onset dementia."

Tom sighed, but this time, without frustration. He reached for her hand.

"Once, I heard my dad on the phone with my grandma." Ally

stared at the slabs beneath her feet. "He said it wasn't cancer that killed my mom. It was a broken heart."

"A broken heart?"

"When I asked him about it, he claimed Mom was depressed because of the cancer, and that's what he meant. But I could've sworn he was holding something back."

"Like what?"

Ally shrugged. She'd often wondered if postpartum depression had drained her mother of joy. Had Ally sucked the serotonin from her mother's body, smuggled it across the placental barrier under the cover of nutrients and oxygen, so that she thrived while with each passing year her mother withered away? Her father denied it. He told her, *Please, let it go. No good comes from dwelling in the past.*

The thing is, Ally longed to remember more of the past, something other than the burning feeling when her mother's bony fingers touched her cheek. A familiar rush of guilt swept through her. A better daughter would remember more than that. A better daughter would know how the smiling woman in the photo became the woman in the darkened bedroom. All she knew was that here, in Baghdad, she felt closer to the answer. If she left now, she'd never find out.

"I understand." Tom lowered his voice. "But don't go poking around. You could get us kicked out. Please, think about that."

"Okay," she mumbled reluctantly.

"If you plan to do more investigating, talk to me first. Don't do anything rash."

"Okay, all right, I'll talk to you first."

A light flickered in the souvenir store behind them. The door rattled, startling Ally and Tom. A middle-aged man with fat cheeks and an even fatter mustache stepped onto the sidewalk.

"As-salaam alaikum." He grinned like he'd just won the lottery. "Come inside, dear friends. Join me for a cup of tea."

"Thanks, but some other time." Tom turned away.

"Hang on," said Ally. In the window display, a fist-size statue caught her eye. She wasn't sure if it was a woman transforming into a dove, or a dove into a woman. Something in its dust-coated curves reminded her of the statue in Rania Mansour's garden. She nudged Tom's side. "Let's have a quick look."

Inside, the shop smelled of sandalwood incense. The vendor herded Tom past a display of copper teapots and toward a stand of colorful nargilah pipes.

"Have you tried apple-flavored tobacco, my friend?"

Ally hung back by the entrance and leafed through a stack of postcards. Some were almost as old as her mother's, with photos of women in bell-bottoms posing by the ruins of Babylon. Others were hand-painted with desert oases or turbaned men riding camels through ocher dunes.

She drifted to the window display and plucked the small dove from the shelf. It was surprisingly heavy in her palm, cast in bronze. She turned it upside down. The Arabic numerals for 1996 were carved into its base, alongside a pair of looping initials. Ally's breath snagged in her throat. Her eyes widened. She'd seen those initials before—on the back of her mother's photo by the Tigris.

She stared at the statue in disbelief. Could the sculptor be the link she'd been looking for? A true connection to her mother's past?

"You like this little statue?" The souvenir seller noticed her interest. He swooped to her side. "A very nice piece, indeed. You can use it as a paperweight, or maybe a bookend. Or display it on your mantel."

Ally's heart hammered in her chest.

"Where did you get this?"

"It came from a local artist." He smiled broadly. "I can give you a very good price."

Ally peeked at Tom from the corner of her eye. He was inspecting a case of watches stamped with Saddam Hussein's portrait.

"What's the artist's name?" She tried to act nonchalant. "Do you know her?"

"Oh, yes." The souvenir seller nodded vigorously, sensing a sale. "Miriam Pachachi is a very fine sculptor."

Tom closed the display case. "Found something you like?"

"Your wife is very lucky!" cried the souvenir seller. "This week I have discount sale."

Ally quickly slid the bird-woman back on the shelf. Ten minutes ago, she'd promised Tom she'd stop ferreting about in her mother's past. But even as that pledge had left her mouth, she'd suspected she wouldn't keep it. Now she knew it for sure.

"I'll come back another time," she told the vendor. She smiled apologetically, then caught Tom's eye and gestured toward the door. Her heart was still pounding when she stepped onto the sidewalk.

"What's going on?" Tom dodged a pothole. "Are you okay?"

"I'm fine, just a little tired, that's all." Ally's lie slipped out smooth as silk, even as guilt nipped at her heels. She turned toward the flashing traffic lights and told herself every marriage, and every family, had its secrets, its little white lies. Anyway, it was probably best to keep Tom out of it. That way, if she stirred up any fuss, the ambassador couldn't blame him. Or at least, he'd blame Tom only for reckless taste in wives.

Ghassan nodded to Ally and pushed open her front gate. She trudged to the curb and slid into the Corolla's passenger seat. Huda was behind the wheel.

"I wasn't expecting you," said Ally, surprised. "Where's Abdul Amir?"

"He's at the mosque," said Huda. "I hope you don't mind."

"Of course not." Ally laughed awkwardly. For a change, she would've preferred to have Abdul Amir sulking in the driver's seat. "I don't want to interrupt your weekend, that's all."

"I was happy to get out of the house," said Huda. "Where are you going?"

"I'm going to . . ." Ally tried to look nonchalant. "I'm going to the Rashid Hotel."

"The Rashid Hotel?" Huda's cheeks were striped with pink blush, but underneath, her skin turned the color of curdled milk. It was an open secret that minders, informants, and spies populated the lobby of the Rashid. It was also where the regime corralled visiting dignitaries and the few foreign journalists allowed in on brief, tightly controlled press junkets. The guest rooms were famously equipped with hidden cameras, microphones, and all manner of surveillance devices.

"I'm meeting a friend of a friend," said Ally. "He works for a business magazine in Dubai."

"He's staying at the Rashid?" Huda's eyes were wide as an owl's.

Once again, Ally wished that Abdul Amir was behind the wheel. He'd know how to handle this. He kept a Saddam watch in the glove box, and he put it on his wrist whenever he knew they'd have to pass through checkpoints. He made sure to nod and smile at the men who loitered on street corners, men who wore leather jackets despite the heat, men who Ally suspected were secret police, or at the very least, informants.

"You know what?" Ally put her hand on Huda's arm. She was stiff as a wax dummy. "I'll go another time."

Huda eyed her suspiciously.

"What do you mean, another time?"

"I'll go some other day," Ally replied vaguely.

It was a lie. The reporter wasn't just a friend of a friend. Ally had worked with him at the *Canberra Herald*, before he landed a well-paying gig in Dubai reporting on oil prices and real-estate deals. He was leaving Baghdad tomorrow, and Ally was going to see him, no matter what. He'd agreed to bring books for her—books about pioneering professional women like her mother. Ally's own books were still sitting in Iraqi customs, waiting for import stamps.

"What's this about?" said Huda.

"It's nothing." Ally grasped the door handle. "I can get a taxi."

"A taxi?" Huda shook her head vigorously. "No taxis. You can't trust those drivers."

Ally decided this wasn't the time to mention Hatim—a freelance taxi driver she'd started to use when she couldn't get hold of Abdul Amir. Hatim was friends with a security guard at the embassy, and he usually worked around the souk near her house.

"Don't worry," said Ally. "You go home and relax."

"I won't relax. Not if you're thinking about getting in some stranger's car."

Huda frowned, put the car in gear, and steered away from the curb. Reluctantly, Ally buckled her seat belt. Soon, they passed the Baghdad telephone exchange. The building was draped with a forty-foot-tall banner declaring, "Yes, Yes, Yes, Saddam!" A presidential election was looming—if it could be called an election when there was only one candidate—and the dictator hung over everything. Like a bad smell, Ally thought, or the bubonic plague.

"I'll make this a quick visit," she said. "You don't have to come inside the hotel. Unless you want to, of course."

Huda said nothing, but her eyes darted up and down, left and right. Ally attempted to lighten the mood.

"My mom used to go dancing in the Rashid's nightclub. Can you believe it? She sent a postcard, saying she'd stayed till four in the morning dancing under a disco ball."

Up ahead, a handful of people milled about on the side of the road, while a young policeman chased yet another presidential banner that had come loose from its anchors. The breeze changed direction, and Saddam's smug grin rose high above the bitumen. The policeman twirled desperately, trying to catch it. A few onlookers tried to help out, but they seemed nervous, as if they might cause offense by placing their hands on the president. Ally wondered, If those people were free, would they set that banner on fire?

Ally glanced at Huda from the corner of her eye. She wished she could tell her that she knew about the secret police haunting the Rashid Hotel, and confide that her heart was beating faster than normal too. But she'd learned that in Baghdad, truth was like a blister. If you pricked the surface, you only made the pain worse.

They motored onto the Jumhuriya Bridge. On the far bank, the palace of giant heads was hung with bunting, guard towers wrapped like Christmas gifts. Soldiers paraded about in shiny boots. Ally's peripheral vision caught the dull gleam of a mounted machine gun.

"So this fellow I'm meeting was invited here by the government." Ally tried not to stare at the machine gun. "The authorities are trying to find investors to renovate a resort at Lake Habbaniyah and they want some press coverage. Do you know the area?" Ally eyed the heat shimmering above the bitumen like a thin fog. "I think my mother picnicked there."

"It must have been wonderful in her day." Huda brightened a little. "The lake is so big it's like being by the sea. Back in your mother's time, there were swimming pools, tennis courts, restaurants, and a big beautiful hotel. But you don't need to hear about it from this journalist. Abdul Amir and I will take you there in person. We can go tomorrow and see for ourselves."

"I can't," said Ally. "I need government permission to leave Baghdad."

"Oh, of course . . ." Huda glanced across the cabin. "I stopped by your house last evening to see if you wanted to go to the market. Ghassan said you'd gone out with Mr. Tom."

"We went to look at some paintings."

"Paintings? Where?"

"Rania Mansour's gallery. She's got some great pieces, like that sculpture in her garden."

Ally longed to tell Huda that the sculpture had been created by Miriam Pachachi, the same person who took her mother's portrait. She'd never thought it would be so hard to keep secrets, but they seemed to have a will of their own. Even now she could feel them clawing at the roof of her mouth.

"I hope you are careful in your dealings with Rania." Huda frowned.

"What do you mean?"

"You can't trust anyone."

"Who?" Ally swiveled toward her. "Rania?"

"I'm just saying, you don't know who you might meet at her gallery."

"Like who?"

"Who can say?" Huda muttered in irritation, "You think they wear signs on their backs?"

Huda flicked on the radio, as if to say, *Conversation over.* She kept the music up high until they reached the boom gate at the entrance to the Rashid Hotel. A thickset guard with a Kalashnikov slung over his shoulder emerged from a guard post. He bent down and stared into the cabin. Huda opened her mouth to greet him. No sound emerged. Ally leaned past her.

"As-salaam alaikum," she called.

The guard raised an eyebrow at Huda. She gave a tiny shrug and shrunk into her seat.

"I am here to visit a guest." Ally enunciated her words carefully.

The guard frowned. "You are guest?"

"My friend is a guest. I'm meeting him here."

"Guest?" he said.

"Yes." Ally nodded animatedly. "I'm meeting him in the lobby."

Confusion muddied the guard's features. He glanced at Huda and muttered something that Ally couldn't understand. When Huda replied, her words skittered out timid as lambs.

"Excuse me." Ally leaned past Huda and held out her diplomatic ID card. It was stamped with the foreign ministry's gold seal.

"*Diplomasiya.*" Ally hooked her thumb toward her chest. "I am diplomasiya. I go to the hotel. Now."

The guard inspected the ID warily. Ally smiled again, but this time in the icy manner of a princess accustomed to having her demands met. Her confidence worked. The guard tapped his forehead in a quasi-salute, clicked his heels, and waved them on. The boom gate lowered behind them. Ally giggled nervously.

"Yes, sir, I am diplomasiya. What do you think? Am I bossy

enough to be a VIP?" Ally forced another chuckle, even as a voice inside her head said, *Calm down; act like you belong.*

The hotel rose before them—fourteen stories of gray concrete with white balconies like rows of shark teeth. A long banner rippled in the wind. "Iraqis will give their lifeblood for Saddam Hussein," it read. Ally stopped chucking and folded her flighty hands in her lap.

A doorman bustled from the marble lobby. He wore a red turban around his head, billowing white pantaloons, and curly-toed shoes, like he were Aladdin. Ally touched Huda's arm.

"Please, just drop me off in front of the lobby. The hotel will have drivers who can take me home. Don't worry about me."

A side door opened. Two men in poorly tailored suits slipped out. Their oiled mustaches, heavy boots, and barely concealed handguns screamed secret police.

"We're here now," said Huda. "It's too late."

CHAPTER 9

The doorman threw open the door to the lobby. Huda waited, but Ally didn't step inside the hotel. Like a woman on the edge of a cliff, Ally bent her head and stared at the mosaic of tiles at her feet. After a moment, she straightened her spine and trod purposefully onward. Her heel landed squarely on the pigeon chest of George H.W. Bush, cemented into a doormat.

Huda scurried in Ally's wake. Her legs were not as long, and she had to step twice on the American president before she made it into the lobby. Inside, the air was cool. The towering marble walls were smooth as glaciers. Four enormous chandeliers hung overhead.

"Is it just my imagination?" whispered Ally. "Or have we found Superman's Fortress of Solitude?"

"Not Superman," murmured Huda. "A castle in a fairy tale."

The chandeliers were draped in a thousand crystals—exactly as Rania had described to Huda almost twenty years ago. As she tiptoed into the hotel, memories unspooled in her mind. She remembered Rania returning from her first trip to Baghdad, giddy with delight after attending a cousin's wedding feast in the

Rashid's ballroom. She talked for days of women in jewel-toned Siamese silks, of dining on lamb stuffed with apricots, and dancing to disco music. Most of all, she talked about the moment she stepped under the great chandeliers.

Rania said when she looked up, it was like gazing into the sun, but when her eyes adjusted, the sparkling crystals seemed more like a constellation of stars, extending through the heavens, offering infinite possibilities. Back then Rania claimed anything was possible for a smart young Iraqi with the courage to follow her dreams. Huda had believed her.

It was summer at that time. Like most people in her village, Huda's family slept on the roof of their mud-brick home to escape the heat. Lying on a thin bedroll, while her two brothers snuffled and snored, Huda imagined the milky stars were the lights of the Rashid Hotel. She fell asleep dreaming of crystal chandeliers and silk dresses.

Even after the seasons changed and the family returned indoors to sleep, Huda continued to dream, God willing, one day she too might bathe in the glow of those miraculous lights. Now, as Huda's heels clacked across the lobby, she couldn't find the courage to lift her head. Instead, she watched the thousand crystals cast their reflection on the smooth marble floor, as if they were shimmering on the surface of a lake.

The women continued through the lobby. On a gilded couch, a white-robed sheikh with a gold Rolex flipped through a magazine. Government minders in short-sleeved business shirts nursed coffee cups and sucked on cigarettes. Plump, mustachioed mukhabarat sulked by the doors, looking like spoiled boys who'd rather be elsewhere, tormenting small animals or ripping off grasshoppers' limbs.

Every nerve in Huda's body screamed at her to turn around and sprint for the door. She wished she could've allowed Ally to visit the hotel alone, but she knew Abu Issa would require a full accounting. Or else the Bolt Cutter might be called upon to inter-

around her knuckles, one by one, until

he marble hall, someone hissed.

ied through the lobby. Men stopped what they
ned, and raised their heads like dogs sniffing the
onfident step faltered.

. . ."

grimaced. This was not the Iraqi way. And if the men
t Ally was a Russian whore, what did that make Huda?
n the corner of her eye, Huda saw Ally hesitate. Then her spine
ncurled, and once again she took on the haughty air of a princess.
Chin high, she sailed toward the reception desk. Huda followed.
Like flotsam trapped in the slipstream of a boat, she couldn't fight
the forces around her; all she could hope was to stay afloat.

A clean-shaven man in a dark blue suit darted from behind the
reception desk. He gave Huda one brief, dismissive glance, then
beamed at Ally as if she were his favorite niece.

"Welcome, madam." He opened his hands wide. "What a pleasure to greet you at the Rashid Hotel. I am Saadi, the concierge.
May I assist you to check in?" Like a well-trained sheepdog, he
looped behind the women and herded them toward the mahogany
desk. Huda trotted dutifully onward. Ally didn't budge.

"There's no need," she said. "I'm meeting a friend."

"In that case, madam, please sign our guest register."

The concierge gave a little bow and waved her toward the
desk. Ally hesitated for a moment. Once again, men shifted in
their seats, lowered their newspapers, set down their coffee cups.
Huda's breath dried up. *Stay calm*, she told herself. *Pretend you
are a sheikh's daughter attending your cousin's wedding, dressed in
a fine silk gown.*

"Ally!" A bald man with skin as pink as ham loped across the
room. Behind him, the elevator operator checked his wristwatch,
pulled a notebook from his pocket, and scribbled a note.

"Peter." Ally smiled awkwardly. "I'll just be a moment. I have to sign the visitors' log."

"They'll get your information." The bald man chuckle tipped his head toward the elevator operator. "One way o other."

The concierge's eyes narrowed into slits.

"Who is this woman?" He hissed at Huda in Arabic. "And wh are you?"

In the periphery of her vision, Huda sensed men drawing closer. Her pulse began to gallop. She offered the concierge a placating smile.

"Ally, give me your ID." She stuck out her hand. "I will sign us in."

"Good idea," said the sunburned journalist. He waved Ally in the direction of the nearest couch. "Let's have a cup of coffee while Saadi does what he must. Hotel policy, right, Saadi?"

"Yes, sir." The concierge's lips contorted. "Hotel policy."

Huda trailed Saadi to the far end of the reception desk. The wall behind it was decorated with a portrait of the president and a series of identical clocks showing the time in Baghdad, Beijing, Moscow, and Mecca. Hand trembling, Huda laid Ally's ID on the counter. Two men appeared beside her. Fat-cheeked, dead-eyed, solid as bookends.

"Madam," one of them said, "please come with us."

Huda opened her mouth, but her tongue turned to stone. The men frog-marched her through a set of doors behind the desk. Just before they swung shut, Huda caught a glimpse of Ally spooning sugar into a coffee cup, and her long dark hair shining beneath the chandelier.

The men dug their fingers into Huda's arms and propelled her down a narrow corridor. They threw open a door. Dreams of silk dresses evaporated.

"Please, don't!" cried Huda.

She glimpsed filing cabinets lined up against the wall, then one of the men grabbed the back of her neck and flung her into an office chair. Its wheels squealed as she sailed across the room. Like a small child strapped into a whirling carnival ride, Huda clutched the arms and tried not to throw up.

"Please," she cried, "I can explain."

"Shut up," barked the taller of the two mukhabarat. He had a large scar on his left cheek—a curl of purple skin, raised and swollen like a worm. His partner ripped Huda's handbag from her shoulder and emptied the contents on top of a desk.

"I'm not—"

"I said, shut up." The scarred man bent over Huda's chair and shoved his face in hers. "Are you deaf? Or just stupid?"

As the men rifled through her wallet, sweat bloomed in Huda's armpits. The sharp odor of fear permeated the air. She wished she'd let Ally take a taxi. She should have gone home and cooked lamb stew for Abdul Amir, then taken Khalid to the ice cream parlor. Two scoops of pistachio for him. Chocolate for her. Just like old times. An enormous sob rose in her chest. Why hadn't she kissed Khalid goodbye before she left, or Abdul Amir?

"Who are you?" The purple worm twisted on the mukhabarat's cheek. "And who is the foreign woman?"

Huda's words tripped over each other in their haste to escape. In a strange way, it was a relief to tell the truth. There was no risk of judgment. Not from men like these. The scarred man plucked a small blade from the desk. Huda shrunk into the chair.

"How do I know you're telling the truth?" he said.

He began to toy with the blade, tapping it against his palm, scraping dirt from his nails. It dawned on Huda that it was a letter opener, not a knife. Still, it could slice out an eye, as easy as scooping flesh from a melon.

"Abu Issa can confirm everything." Huda pointed to her handbag. "You will find his number in the side pocket."

He snatched up her bag and threw it in her face. It bounced off her cheek and tumbled into her lap.

"Hand it over," he said.

Huda unzipped the inside pocket and removed a small piece of paper. He ripped it from her fingers, dragged a telephone across the desk, and punched in the number. Huda prayed the lines were working.

"Hello?" he barked. "Who's this? General Intelligence, you say? M-5 division?"

He caught his partner's eye and shrugged.

"I'm calling for Abu Issa." Absentmindedly, he scraped the point of the letter opener across the desk, back and forth, back and forth. Huda kneaded her sweaty palms in her lap.

"Four o'clock? Okay, I'll call back." The scarred man put down the phone. He nodded to his partner, then he grabbed Huda's chair and dragged her toward him. She closed her eyes and turned her face to the side. Could he feel the terror seeping from her pores?

Boots stomped in the corridor. A fist hammered on the door. A third man poked his head into the room.

"Excuse me," he said coolly, as if he were interrupting a job interview not an interrogation. "The foreign woman is making a scene. She wants to know where her friend is. Should we detain her?"

The scarred man frowned. He grabbed Huda's throat and dragged her from the chair. Eyes bulging, she tottered on her tiptoes. He leaned in close.

"Go out there and tell the foreign bitch you have completed the guest registry." His breath was hot and sour. "Tell her there is nothing to worry about."

He released his grip. Huda stumbled backward, choking.

"I'll be talking to your so-called Abu Issa later today. If your story doesn't check out, you can expect a visit from me. Now, get out there." He shoved her toward the door. "And put a smile on your face."

CHAPTER 10

The queue outside al-Faqma ice cream parlor was six people deep when Huda hustled into line. She put her hands on Khalid's shoulders and angled him toward the patio.

"Look, over there." She pointed out a woman wiping soft serve from a toddler's chin. "They're about to leave, so see if you can get their table. And keep an eye out for your father."

Huda glanced toward the coffee shop on Hurriyah Square. Abdul Amir was still out front, chatting with the men playing backgammon. Huda prodded Khalid toward the patio.

"Your dad won't be long, inshallah."

She shuffled to the serving window. A man in a white cap and coat prepared her order, scooping chocolate ice cream into a waffle cone and ladling chunks of tropical fruit over two creamy sundaes. When he was finished, Huda carried the sweets out to the picnic tables.

"I said strawberry syrup, not orange." Khalid frowned at his sundae.

Huda raised an eyebrow.

"Don't you mean to say, 'Thank you, Mom, for this delicious ice cream'?"

"Thanks." Khalid stabbed a plastic spoon into the offending sundae. "I guess."

Huda grit her teeth and glanced at the coffee shop. Abdul Amir had taken a seat on one of the benches out front. She had a feeling he knew she was watching, but he didn't meet her eye—just like the teenager hunched over the table in front of her.

"What a beautiful evening." She waved her cone toward the setting sun. She tried to forget the terrifying encounter at the Rashid Hotel and trained her gaze on a line of seagulls flapping toward the Tigris, their bodies outlined like tiny shadow puppets against the pink-and-orange sky. On the sidewalk, Baghdadis darted in and out of cafés. Others bargained with street vendors for fabric, costume jewelry, toys, and leather shoes.

"Now tell me," she said, "how is your sundae? Do you really like it better than pistachio ice cream? You have been eating pistachio since you were a baby."

"I'm not a baby." Khalid slumped in his seat. "Don't call me that. Soon I will be a man."

"I did not say you were a baby." She lowered her cone. "But as for being a man, it is well known that a man buys his own ice cream. And, more important, he respects his mother."

"Going for ice cream was your idea, not mine."

"I thought it would be a nice family outing."

"Really?" Khalid fished a pale green grape from his sundae. "Dad must be enjoying his family outing too, seeing as how he's back there smoking nargilah with his friends."

She glanced toward the coffee shop and saw Abdul Amir throw his head back and laugh at someone else's joke. On the table beside her, his sundae was fast transforming into a lake of lukewarm cream, pockmarked by islands of tinned pineapple and a solitary cherry.

A puff of wind traveled down the street. Above the patio, lines strung with tin moons and stars tinkled. A block away, speakers crackled to life. In a minaret of blue and yellow tiles, a muezzin cleared his throat. His phlegmy preparations echoed through the sky.

Khalid tossed his plastic spoon on the table. "I'm going to the mosque."

"The mosque?" Huda eyed him with surprise. First no pistachio ice cream. Now the mosque. Had a jinni possessed her son? "Where is this sudden interest in prayer coming from?"

"Mom, you might believe in coffee grounds. But I put my trust in Allah."

Huda's jaw dropped.

"I'll meet you back here," Khalid called over his shoulder.

Bewildered, Huda watched him dart through the traffic and across the road. She sighed and dumped her cone into her husband's forgotten sundae.

"What a waste of good ice cream." Abu Issa's breath grazed her ear.

He circled out from behind her, pushed Khalid's half-eaten treat to the side, and sat down in the boy's place. Huda's throat constricted. The young couple at the next table fell silent too, as Abu Issa's mukhabarat essence spread through the patio like a cloud of cheap cologne. The speakers at the mosque hummed, and the muezzin began to wail. His prayer ebbed and flowed like a holy tide. Abu Issa leaned across the picnic table.

"I hear you visited the Rashid Hotel."

"I wanted to call you." Huda's whisper was tinny with fear. "My phone wasn't working. There was no power. The electricity is still out. I had promised my son ice cream, I—"

Abu Issa raised his hand.

"Stop babbling, woman. Do you have anything to tell me?"

Huda shot a glance past his shoulder. Abdul Amir was no longer outside the coffee shop.

"Where's my husband?" she blurted. "Did you take him?"

The words came out louder than Huda expected. The couple at the next table climbed to their feet and hurried away. A group of young men in fake Ray-Bans stubbed out their cigarettes and shuffled off, leaving behind glasses of orange juice still three-quarters full. The owner of the ice cream parlor watched mournfully as his customers retreated into the pink-and-gold haze.

"There is nothing to fear. Not if you cooperate," said Abu Issa. "I want to know everything about this visit to the Rashid Hotel."

Huda nodded rapidly.

"Ally went to visit a finance reporter for a magazine in Dubai. She was picking up a few books from him. That's all."

"Books about what?"

"Biographies about those British nurses and teachers who used to work here, back in the seventies. History, that's all."

"What else did they discuss?"

"I don't know. Two men, two of your . . ." Huda trailed off.

The remaining customers took great pains not to look in her direction. They were like members of an ancient caliph's court, milling about anxiously, while Scheherazade recited endless tales to delay the executioner's sword.

"Two of your colleagues took me to a back room for questioning." Huda kneaded her fingers in her lap. "One of them telephoned your office. Did you speak with him?"

Abu Issa said nothing. He made a show of inspecting the chunky ring on his finger.

"By the time they released me, Ally was ready to go."

"What was the name of the man she met with?" said Abu Issa.

"Peter."

"Peter who?"

"I'm not sure."

Abu Issa growled under his breath.

"What sort of answer is that?"

"I don't—"

His fist thumped the table.

"Your poor productivity is unacceptable. You must perform your duties without excuses. Do you understand?"

"Of course, I—"

"How is the girl connected to the reporter?" Abu Issa eyed her coldly.

"She said he was a friend of a friend."

"Did she go up to his room?"

"Of course not." Blood rushed to her cheeks. "Ally is a married woman."

"Married or not, these foreign women will lie down with anyone." Huda dared another glance at the coffee shop.

"Please, where is my husband?"

"He's having a chat with my partner."

Fear wrapped its icy hand around her throat. In the minaret, the muezzin fell silent. Static scratched at the gathering dusk.

"I'm to blame," said Huda, "not my husband. I'll do better, I promise."

"Fortunately, your husband is proving to be a patriotic Iraqi." Abu Issa rubbed the flat of his palm across his ring. "And what about your son, is he a patriot too? Has he trained with the Lion Cubs yet?"

Huda went cold. Every year the government took boys as young as ten and sent them to military boot camps in the desert. Often they were beaten, and it was said that to graduate, the young Lion Cubs had to tear a small animal apart with their hands and eat the flesh. Not all the boys came back. And those who did were changed inside.

"We can easily arrange entry to the Lion Cubs," said Abu Issa. "It's an honor, really. Graduates from the Lion Cubs get an express pass to the ranks of the fedayeen."

The black of Huda's eyes dilated. The fedayeen was a death squad led by Uday Hussein. They liked to make the families of their victims display their loved one's severed head on their gates. Atop the minaret, the speakers squealed, then went dead.

"There are many benefits for members of the fedayeen," murmured Abu Issa. The official title was Fedayeen Saddam—but even Abu Issa balked at saying his master's name aloud, here at the ice cream parlor, surrounded by children licking soft serve.

"Khalid's not . . ." A ribbon of pain wrapped around Huda's chest. "He's just a boy."

Abu Issa leaned back and folded his arms across his chest. The band of pain around Huda's chest grew tighter and tighter, until she could barely breathe.

"We can discuss this another time." Abu Issa glanced across the street. "I must attend to another appointment."

The wind rattled the paper-thin moon and stars strung overhead. Huda's world felt just as fragile, just as easily undone. Abu Issa needed only to hook his finger and tug, and it would all come crashing down. He rose from the table, eyed the melted sundaes, and shook his head.

"I hate to see such waste."

"Hello!" Abdul Amir waved from the far side of the road. "Over here!"

Huda dashed through the traffic to a crescent-shaped park on the fringe of Hurriyah Square. Overhead, hundreds of tiny flags stamped with the president's face fluttered like nervous doves.

"Where did you go?" She clutched Abdul Amir's arm. "I was so worried."

"Calm down, my good wife." He led her to a bench by a large fountain. Spotlights illuminated its dry mouth. "There's no need for alarm."

She glanced over her shoulder.

"Abu Issa was at the ice cream parlor. He—"

"I know." Abdul Amir rested two plastic shopping bags by his feet. "Faisal told me."

"Who?"

"Faisal. Abu Issa's partner."

"The Bolt Cutter?"

"Come now. He's not such a bad guy."

"Not a bad guy?" Huda clutched her temples. "I thought they'd taken you to Abu Ghraib."

"Quite the opposite." He hauled one of the plastic bags onto his lap and pried open the flaps. It was stuffed with slabs of dinar. "Not bad, huh?"

Three women in finely tailored abayas strolled past the water fountain. The lights reflected off tiny crystals embroidered at the cuffs and hem of their robes.

"How did you get that money?" Huda whispered.

"I told Faisal about Ally's visits to the United Nations compound."

"But why? She's only there for the evening aerobics class."

"She says aerobics, but how do we know that's true? Two weeks ago, when the UN weapons inspectors were visiting Baghdad, she made two trips there. Coincidence? Maybe. But it is information nonetheless, and that made Faisal very happy."

"I can't believe this." She shook her head.

"Believe it, wife, and be happy." Abdul Amir swapped the bag on his lap for the one by his feet and pulled out a box embossed with golden calligraphy. "You have always wanted to try the famous pastries of Abu Afif, yes?"

He pried opened the box. The aroma of warm pastry, pistachios, and rosewater escaped into the night. Huda pressed her hand to her mouth.

"You shouldn't have done that."

"Don't worry, I also got a little something for myself." He peeked inside the bag and grinned. "Six bottles of beer. Amstel, from Holland, not that cheap Turkish dishwater."

The buttery smell of the pastries made Huda's stomach turn.

"It's dirty money," she said.

"Maybe once it was, but now it's mine."

"If you must take it, then save it. For something important."

"What's so important that I can't buy a beer?"

A conga line of honking cars turned onto the square. A Chevy with cat-eyed headlights cruised at the front, carrying a bride in a frothy veil. A minibus decorated with plastic flowers followed.

Wedding guests danced in its narrow aisle, while in the back seat, musicians beat cymbals and tabla drums. Huda leaned close and murmured in Abdul Amir's ear.

"We need a passport for Khalid."

Abdul Amir reared back.

"What? Why?" He glanced left and right. "No man under forty-five years old can leave the country. It's impossible. What on earth are you thinking?"

"Perhaps if we offered an official enough money, he would bend the rules. I've heard of boys going abroad to study."

"Not ordinary boys. Not boys like Khalid. Where is this crazy idea coming from?"

The wedding bus trundled past. A young man with a trumpet hung out the door and sent a lungful of notes spiraling into the sky.

"Abu Issa said . . ." Huda's throat ached. "He said he would put Khalid in the Lion Cubs, and then into the fedayeen."

Abdul Amir growled and shoved the box of pastries back in the shopping bag.

"Did you ever consider the saying 'If you can't beat them, join them'?"

Huda recoiled. Who was this man sitting next to her?

"I can't believe you'd say that, after all that we suffered—"

"The past is dead." Abdul Amir's palm sliced the air.

"But you know—"

"What I know is that once, I had a good job. I studied hard and worked long hours. I deserved it. Then the Westerners imposed their sanctions and killed the hopes of ordinary Iraqi men, like me. I was forced to rely on my wife to feed my family." His cheeks burned. "Now you say I should sneak my son out of his own country. For what? I ask you. So he can end up a gas station attendant in the fabulous United States of America?"

"Anything is better than the fedayeen," she hissed.

"Abu Issa wants to scare you, that's all. You need to give him more information."

"But I have nothing to tell."

"Make it up then, like everyone else working for them."

Huda tried to reply but shock rendered her dumb. The wedding procession rolled past. She stole a glance at Abdul Amir. Whether a love match or arranged the traditional way, it didn't matter how well the bride knew the groom on the wedding day. Husbands could change so much; even a wife of sixteen years could suddenly find herself married to a stranger.

Abdul Amir paced up and down the garden, backlit by the flames of the refinery. He swigged on his fancy Dutch beer, stopping only to rip weeds from the garden.

"Don't overreact." He hurled a leathery rue into the compost pile. "Abu Issa has the carrot and the stick. That talk about the Lion Cubs was the stick. Give him some information, and he will be happy."

Huda pointed to his beer bottle.

"And that is the carrot?"

Abdul Amir scowled, but shame colored his cheeks. Huda noted his mixed emotions with relief. Perhaps she could still influence him. Once upon a time, he'd made a habit of confiding in her and trusting her opinion. But since losing his job, he spent more and more time brooding in the garden, or at the coffee shop with the other jobless men, all of them sucking on nargilah and bitterness.

"You can't be so foolish." Abdul Amir paced on. "Not about our son's future."

"You know what the fedayeen do. Not even women and children are spared. Do you want our son committing sins like that?"

"Of course not. But this passport idea is plain stupid. Where would Khalid go? What would he do? You want him alone in a foreign land, with no one to care for him?"

"We could send him to Damascus. My cousin is there. I'm not saying we send him tomorrow. Why don't we first try for a passport? Then we have options, in case we need them."

"What would Abu Issa do if he discovered your plan? He'd question our loyalty. Then we'd feel his stick—you, me, and Khalid." He stabbed his finger at the patio table, where he'd dumped the shopping bag full of cash, his six-pack, and the box of rosewater pastries. "Our life is not so bad. You can enjoy the finest baklava in Baghdad. I can buy a nice beer—and I did not need to pay with money from my wife's pocket."

"Beer and sweets? I should be satisfied with that? Forget about Khalid's future?"

"I warn you, do not do anything rash." He yanked a weed from the earth with unnecessary force. "Your brothers did that, and look what happened to them."

Huda flinched, as if she'd been slapped.

"If they'd succeeded, we wouldn't be worried about our son's future," she hissed. "We wouldn't have to fear he'd be drafted into the fedayeen, to kill innocent people and hang their heads from their gates."

"Your brothers were foolish and impulsive. It must run in your blood."

"Mustafa and Ali were not foolish. And they were not the only ones who wanted freedom. Tens of thousands of men like my brothers joined the uprising. Maybe more."

Abdul Amir cast a cautious glance over the neighbor's fence.

"Don't forget," he whispered. "The people who came up with that whole misguided rebellion had the power to protect themselves when it went wrong. Your brothers were just ordinary people, like us. Expendable."

"They saw a chance to be free." Blood pounded at Huda's temples. "And they would have succeeded if the Americans had lived up to their promises."

"Bah!" Abdul Amir flung his hands wide. "Your brothers should have known two things: you can't trust the Americans, and you can't beat the system. You can only adapt and work out how to use the situation to your advantage." He eyed her fiercely. "Did their deaths teach you nothing?"

* * *

As if on autopilot, Huda steered the Corolla toward the swooping expanse of concrete and steel that made up the Jumhuriya Bridge. At its feet, bulrushes stretched taller than a grown man. A checkpoint had been erected by the on-ramp. A soldier swung the muzzle of his Kalashnikov and gestured for Huda to pull over.

I haven't done anything wrong, she told herself, but her racing heart refused to believe it. Another soldier, a teenager, weaved through the line of idling vehicles. His boots were too large and his legs too skinny. He'd yet to grow into his bones—just like Khalid. Huda pictured her son bunking down in rough military barracks, while his bed with Star Wars sheets lay empty.

The soldier rapped on Huda's window.

I haven't done anything wrong.

The boy stooped over. His eyes were as blank as those of a river carp. Huda could no longer see any resemblance to her son.

"Where are you going? What is your business this morning?"

The soldier offered no greeting, no *peace be with you*, no *as-salaam alaikum*. Huda wondered, What had happened to common courtesy and respect for one's elders?

"I'm going to visit a friend in Mansour."

The soldier spat a blob of phlegm onto the crumbling verge.

"A rich friend, then?" The soldier inspected the faded vinyl of the Corolla's back seat. "You don't look like you'd have friends in Mansour. What's their name?"

"She's nobody of importance."

"A nobody, you say?" The boy wiped his ratty sleeve across his mouth. "There are so many of us nobodies these days."

He peered again at the Corolla's worn seats and faded dashboard. He stepped back and waved Huda on, toward the palace on the far bank. Huda lowered her eyes from the enormous turrets carved with the president's visage. But even after she crossed the bridge, she could feel his granite eyes boring into her back.

Her stomach gurgled. She couldn't tell if it was anxiety, the result of too many sweets, or both. After the fight with Abdul Amir, she'd curled up on the living room couch and wept until she fell asleep. About four in the morning, she got up, stiff-limbed and swollen-eyed, went out to the garden, and ate pastries, one syrupy, nutty mouthful after another, till she thought she would throw up.

Her gut twisted again. Abdul Amir would be furious if he knew what she was doing in Mansour. Some men would kill their wives for such a thing. Not him though. He never approved of beating women. That hadn't changed. She was fairly sure of that.

She passed al-Kindi souk, all the while silently rehearsing what she would say. "You owe me," she muttered under her breath. "If you ever cared, you will do this." There were many arguments she could use to achieve her goal. Some were prettier than others.

Huda took a sharp left. A block later, she turned again. She circled the block twice, checked her mirror at every corner, scanned the footpath, and peered into parked cars. Finally, she pulled alongside the curb. She adjusted her sunglasses, pulled a scarf over her hair, and then hurried along the sidewalk. She prayed no one was watching as she rang the bell at the great copper gate.

A minute later, the ancient hinges creaked.

"Huda?" Rania's hair spilled past her shoulders in frizzy waves. She eyed Huda warily. "Why are you here?"

Huda extended her palm. In it, she held a paper bag tied with string.

"I've brought lime tea from Basra. My mother sent it."

Rania stared at the offering.

"Tea from Basra?" The wind caught her words and tossed them away. Huda shifted from foot to foot. Eventually, Rania sighed and waved her through the gate.

"Take a seat in the garden. I will get us some refreshments."

"Do not trouble yourself." The words leaped forth without Huda's bidding, reflexes she thought she'd conquered long ago, suddenly resurrected. "I can prepare the tea."

"There's no reason for you to do that." Rania frowned. "Our circumstances are different now, as you reminded me last time we met."

Huda extended the bag of tea again.

"My family has always served the sheikh."

"He's been dead ten years." Rania took the bag of tea and went inside the house.

Out in the garden, a bubble-eyed gecko clung to the wall. Huda glanced at the crumbling mansion. She didn't understand why Rania hadn't moved to a house like her own, with modern wiring and plumbing. Huda thought back to the tiny, mud-brick home of her childhood. She had left that behind, and for years, she focused solely on building a better future. But the past could be ignored no longer. Abdul Amir had spoken her brothers' names last night. Now she heard them whisper among the slender leaves of the eucalypt, urging her on.

In the branches, a crow wailed. Huda glanced at the mansion. Where were Rania's servants? Surely she could afford a cook at least? But five minutes later Rania emerged from the house alone, with *istikans* of tea clinking atop a tarnished silver tray. Could she really have fallen that far?

Rania lit a cigarette and drew the smoke deep into her lungs. On the far side of the picnic table, Huda did the same, but when she exhaled, smoke emerged from her mouth not in a stream but in short, panicky puffs. She fiddled with her glass of tea. Lime-scented steam mixed with cigarette smoke and looped toward the trees.

Huda wasn't quite ready to repeat the words she'd rehearsed in the car, so she sought refuge in ritual greetings, asking after Rania's family, each one by name: her mother, Raghad; her daughter, Hanan; her aunt Muna. Rania replied with the appropriate rejoinders. Her amber stare never wavered. In the boughs of the eucalypt, the crow moaned again.

Huda shifted in her seat and waited for Rania to inquire about the purpose of her visit. Rania did nothing of the sort. She sipped her tea, puffed on her cigarette, and tapped the long gray column of ash into an ashtray. Was it possible, Huda wondered, that after all this time Rania had learned restraint?

Huda checked the path to the front gate.

"I need to ask . . ." She trailed off, nerves getting the best of her.

Rania remained still as a sphynx, head angled to the left, one knee elegantly crossed over the other.

"I need a favor." Huda cleared her throat. "Not for me, for Khalid."

Rania didn't respond. She could have been one of the statues in her garden, a goddess carved from stone, while Huda was painfully aware of her own trembling flesh, her galloping pulse, her aching chest.

"It's the mukhabarat," she whispered. "They say they'll put Khalid in the fedayeen."

"The fedayeen?"

If Huda hadn't been watching closely, she might have missed the flare of alarm that lit up Rania's eyes. Huda plowed on, words spilling forth in a breathless flurry.

"Khalid's not even fourteen years old. I can't let them take him. Please, you've got to help. I need to send him out of the country. It's the only way."

"Stop." Rania raised her hand. "You shouldn't be telling me this."

"You've got to help me. If I apply for a passport, the mukhabarat will surely find out."

"I don't see how I—"

Huda grasped Rania's hand.

"The opposition can get him out. They have ways of moving people across the border. I heard they can get passports with fake names. They can smuggle people—"

"Stop this. I don't want to hear it."

"You know people in the opposition."

"This is madness." Rania jerked her hand free. "I don't know anyone like that."

Above them, the crow gave another strangled cry. It plunged from its branch and swept low over the garden, feathers so black they shone blue in the sun. To Huda, it seemed like an eternity before the bird stopped diving and changed course, swooping up again, wings slicing the air as it flapped toward the sky. In that moment she had a vision of Khalid's future disappearing, like the black-as-night bird vanishing over the flat roofs of Baghdad.

"If you weren't connected with the opposition . . ." Huda took a deep breath and folded her arms across her chest. "Then my brothers would still be alive."

Rania said nothing, only turned her cheek and closed her eyes, as if she could wish this all away.

"You and your fancy college friends, you filled my brothers' heads with your talk of democracy and freedom." Huda eyed her steadily. "You pretended you were so brave. But in the end, you ran to your daddy and let him fix your mess. You turned your back while my brothers' bodies were bulldozed into a ditch."

Rania turned pale as milk. "I can't help you."

"Can't? Or won't?"

"There's no opposition left," she whispered angrily. "They're all in exile. Or dead."

"You must know someone."

"I don't. I swear. Why don't you send Khalid to stay with your mother? I sent my own daughter to Basra. It's safer there."

"My brothers died in Basra," said Huda. "And you know the mukhabarat are everywhere."

"I don't understand. Why are the mukhabarat so interested in Khalid? What did he do?"

"It's not his fault." Huda scowled at the patchy lawn.

Rania tapped another cigarette from her pack.

"When you came here with the diplomat's wife, I said the mukhabarat would be watching. I told you not to play with fire." She trained her amber eyes on Huda. After a long moment, she whispered, "Are you working for them? Are you trying to trap me?"

"Of course not," stammered Huda. "This is no trap."

"You must be working for them. Why else would you be gadding around with a foreigner? You're an informant, aren't you?"

"If I don't do what they want, they'll put Khalid in the fedayeen. He needs a passport."

"It's impossible," said Rania. "I can't do it."

Huda slammed her palms against the table. The tea glasses jumped.

"You have no choice."

"Who are you to say what I must do?" said Rania, her face impassive, even as her fingers betrayed her, tying and untying endless, anxious knots. With a start, Huda spotted the pearly scar on her thumb.

"I am someone who knows your secrets," said Huda. "And if you don't help, I will tell my handler that you are inciting dissent. I will tell him that I heard you insult the president."

"That's a lie."

"I will tell him that you are encouraging young men to rise up. Again."

"You wouldn't dare!" cried Rania.

"My handler will believe what I tell him." Huda's heart pounded. "Just like my brothers believed you."

"They were good men." Rania shook her head. "What would they think of you now?"

A dizzying cocktail raced through Huda's veins: anger, adrenaline, grief, guilt.

"Perhaps they would want an eye for an eye. Did you ever consider that?" She set her mouth in a stubborn line. "There's no one to save you now, Rania. Test me. See how you fare."

CHAPTER 11

The desert had claimed many acres of land since Rania's last visit to Basil's farmhouse. The wind was thick with its pearly grains. She took a step back when Basil pushed open the gate. He looked much older than she'd expected: nose drooping, philosopher's forehead more prominent than ever, earlobes like deflated balloons. The two of them stood stock-still, eyes fumbling across the other's face, trying to reconcile memories of smooth skin and plump lips. The wind whipped around them in tight circles, got tangled in Rania's hair, and tossed it about like graying ribbons.

Always a gentleman, Basil recovered first.

"My old friend!" He grasped Rania's hand, discreetly checked the road outside, and ushered her through the gate. "I am so pleased to see you. What an honor."

Pebbles crunched beneath their feet as they followed a curving driveway to a large whitewashed home. Weeping gutters had left tear tracks down its peeling facade. Rania imagined if it was lined up beside her own house, they'd be diagnosed as two geriatric patients suffering the same skin disease.

At the far end of the property, a palm grove formed a dense

green wall. Rania remembered when their serrated trunks seemed to stretch to eternity, when the Fertile Crescent still resembled its legend. But then the irrigation system fell into disrepair, and the government decided to break up big farms—at least those not owned by the president and his cronies. Basil's family was left with just a couple of acres, and the desert crept in, with its sand and thorny scrub, turning freshwater to muddy salt flats.

Basil steered Rania through the front door and into a long, windowless hallway. After the bright sun outside, it was dark as a well.

"Let's go into the drawing room. It's coolest there." Basil smiled crookedly. "I'm afraid the air conditioner performed its swan song some time ago, but we've got a fan running at least."

He deposited her in the high-ceilinged room and went to find the cook and order tea. Rania ran her fingers along a couch of threadbare Persian damask. A bookcase stretched along one wall. The naked shelves reminded Rania of her father's library, and the precious Koran she'd sold to the bookseller at Mutanabbi.

A sideboard held a collection of family photos, including a shot of Basil's mother and a friend. They looked to be in their early twenties. Dressed in knee-length frocks, they smiled broadly and strode arm in arm past the colonnades of Rashid Street. Behind them, a man in a trilby hat and another in an ankle-length dishdasha waited at a bus stop. Neither paid any mind to the young women with their bare arms and hair falling past their shoulders, marching gaily toward the future.

Rania had similar photos of her own mother dashing about Baghdad in white patent heels and frocks ordered from London, handbag blithely swinging by her side. Rania wished she could go back in time, swap places with the women on Rashid Street, and feel the breeze sweep in from the Tigris and cool her skin.

"There we go." Basil hurried into the drawing room. "Tea is on the way."

He paused beside a pair of wrought-iron garden chairs. Rania dimly remembered that two fine wingbacks used to sit in their place. They were probably gathering dust in a secondhand furniture store. Rania's gaze slid to the rug. Decades of sun streaming through the window had left the outline of the missing wingbacks imprinted in the weave.

"Tell me, how is your family? Hanan must be in high school by now." Basil gestured at the couch. "Please, sit."

Rania remained standing.

"Do you mind if we go to the garden?" She kept her gaze on the rug. "It would be wiser to talk outside."

"Outside?" The word emerged slowly, cautiously, as if stepping onto a high wire. "Is that necessary?"

Rania nodded, still unable to meet his eye.

In the garden, they clutched at straws of small talk. Basil spoke of family, old college friends, a book of poems a cousin had sent from London. Rania praised the beds of yellow rosebushes and the tidy herb garden. By a weeping willow, she spotted the wrought-iron picnic table that matched the chairs in the drawing room.

Basil directed Rania along a cobbled path. Creeping thyme grew in the cracks in the stone, and every step they took released a burst of lemony perfume.

"If I'd known you were coming, I would have asked the cook to prepare kebab."

"Just like the old days?" asked Rania softly.

She remembered how their college crowd used to pass by Basil's farm on the way to picnic at Lake Habbaniyah. On the silty shore, they'd barbecue kebab, and play Umm Kulthum or the Rolling Stones on Basil's cassette deck. Once again, Rania wished she had the power to travel back in time. She'd swim out deep into Habbaniyah's cool waters, till the shore disappeared, and all that was left was water and the wide blue sky.

Basil paused by a wooden arbor smothered in grapevines. It listed to the left like a sailboat ensnared in the tentacles of a giant squid.

"So, my dear Rania," he said. "After all these years, why are you here?"

Rania did her best to explain, forcing herself to keep going as Basil's face went rigid, first with shock, then with fury.

"This is madness." He pressed his hands to his bulbous forehead. "I can't get involved with this. Neither should you."

"I don't have a choice."

"Yes, you do. You tell this woman no."

The cook emerged from the house carrying a tray of tea. Basil motioned for her to leave it on the garden table. They waited in silence until she returned indoors.

"She threatened to tell the mukhabarat that I insulted the president," whispered Rania. "She said she'd tell them I was inciting young artists to rebel. If she does, it won't end with my head. Everyone I'm close to will be at risk—the artists at my gallery, my friends, my family."

"Surely this woman is bluffing? I thought you said she was an old friend?"

Rania sighed softly. Dry leaves eddied around her feet, and then the wind swept them toward the palm grove. Rania registered nothing of this. In her mind she saw only Huda: seven years old, squatting on the bow of a slender *mashoof*, racing along one of the tributaries veining the Basra delta.

Rania had been sheltering under a fat palm tree and wishing she were somewhere else before Huda sailed around the bend in the stream. On the riverbank, a half-dozen other skiffs were lined up in a row. Their passengers were all women who'd gathered in the long, low mud-brick house behind Rania to visit the newest mother of the al-Baidi tribe. The tribe was small, fewer than three thousand strong, but to Rania it seemed a new member was born every minute, just to spite her.

"This is the third time this week," she'd whined an hour earlier, as her mother and aunt herded her toward the curtained women's quarters.

"Try not to fidget," her mother had ordered. "And don't wake the baby."

Rania tugged at the collar of her stiff-starched dress.

"None of my friends have to do these boring visits."

"You're the granddaughter of a sheikh." Aunt Muna pinched her arm. "You have duties."

Rania slipped off her shoes, added them to the line of sandals outside the women's quarters, and crept past the curtain. The new mother reclined on a cot at the far end of the room. On the floor beside her, her baby napped in a small plastic bathtub that served as a crib. The baby's grandmother, the matriarch, quickly guided them to the plumpest cushions nearest the cot. The other guests jostled about, trading positions until all were properly seated once again.

Rania's nose itched as plumes of incense spiraled upward, collided with the thatched ceiling, and spread out in a myrrh-scented mushroom cloud. An old woman with dark skin and the scarred cheeks of a former slave brought in a coffeepot and a dish of dates. The guests watched on as Rania's mother and her aunt each accepted a small porcelain cup. Aunt Muna sipped first. She swallowed, cleared her throat.

"What a lovely home you have." She sipped a second time and smiled at the new mother. "How are you faring, dear? You look well, *alhamdulillah*."

And so began the ritual compliments, the round of questions and answers, the drinking of coffee, the snacking on dried fruit and nuts, a few jokes, and some gossip. In the plastic bathtub, the baby snored, its top lip quivering and pink. Thick kohl lined its eyes to keep evil spirits away.

Rania didn't know if the new mother had other children, but if she did, they would have been dispatched to stay with relatives. In general, children weren't welcome at these visits. They woke the baby and knocked over coffee cups. They messed about with the guests' sandals, took them outside and pretended they were swords, or set them sailing on the stream like tiny canoes. Rania was permitted only because she was an emissary of the sheikh.

As the maid refilled the coffee cups, Rania snuck toward a smaller room off the side of the sitting area. Often the hosts arranged for a woman to paint henna on guests' hands or to sell clothes or pots and pans. This time they'd hired a perfume vendor. The middle-aged merchant was plump as a fig, nestled amid her stock of jewel-colored vials. Pale twigs of arak lay in neat rows beside cones of incense. She eyed Rania's frilly dress.

"You must be from the sheikh's family?"

Rania nodded.

"Come here, dear." The woman hooked her finger. "Come smell my perfumes."

"I don't care much about the smell," said Rania. "All I want is a red bottle and a blue one too."

The woman cocked a brow.

"You want frankincense? And jasmine too?"

"As long as one bottle is red, and the other blue."

"I'm at your command." The woman showed her long teeth. "Now tell me, how much money did your mother give you?"

A few minutes later, perfume in hand, Rania crept out the back door. She wandered past rows of okra, cucumber, and eggplant. Hens clucked in a coop. Drawn by the burble of the swift-flowing stream, Rania slipped out the back gate. She strolled toward the bank, rolling the vials back and forth: red in one hand, blue in the other. Rays of light hit the curve of colored glass and emerged from the other side bright as cloth dying in a vat. She raised her hands and cast red and blue stripes across the fine sand.

Rania propped one hand on top of the other. The two beams merged into one thick band of purple. She wiggled the red vial and kept the blue still, creating a pulsing purple stripe with a rippling ruby frill. It reminded Rania of an exotic sea snake or an eel, like the one she'd spied on her ninth birthday poking from the rocks of the Basra corniche.

That was a big day, her ninth birthday. Her father had taken her and her mother to eat ice cream at the Sheraton Hotel. Then he'd hired a man at the pier to take them to the playground on Sinbad Island in the middle of the Shatt al-Arab river. Her father spent the fifteen-minute journey reciting Sinbad's adventures battling serpents and devil birdmen. Meanwhile, Rania had hung over the side of the boat and searched for more neon-striped eels.

A bead of sweat ran down her back, and she crept under the shelter of the fat palm tree. Below her, the stream frothed and hissed. She raised the red vial to one eye and the blue to the other and made bicolor binoculars. Then Huda swept into view, mid-river, crouched on the pointy-beaked bow of the mashoof.

Huda's grandmother sat in the middle of the skiff, a squat figure enrobed in black. Huda's ten-year-old brother, Mustafa, stood at the stern, steering the vessel with a punting reed thicker than Rania's arm. Whittled to a point, it doubled as a spear for hunting ducks or dark-scaled bunni fish.

The stream was running high and the current twisted like a startled snake through sand. Mustafa leaned his weight on the punt. The canoe's nose turned, and the vessel cut a foaming line to the bank. Huda leaped from the bow, her long apricot dress fluttering behind her like a goldfish tail. She landed with a thud, and her bare feet sunk into the sand. Mustafa followed and the two children hauled the mashoof onto the bank beside the other skiffs.

Huda's grandmother passed the girl a brightly woven saddlebag. Mustafa held the boat steady as she climbed from the vessel, one short, plump limb after the other. She reminded Rania of a black-robed teddy bear. The old woman straightened the purple dress she wore under her abaya and adjusted her scarf over her hair. She stepped into slippers that Huda had removed from the saddle bag, then waddled toward the women's quarters.

Once his grandmother left, Mustafa raised the sharp end of his punt.

"I spotted a pheasant's nest back up river." He looked in his sister's direction, but Rania had the feeling he wanted her to hear too. "I'm going to get us a bird for dinner."

"Can I come?" said Huda.

"Girls don't hunt." Mustafa puffed out his chest. "It's a man's job."

Huda scowled at his back as he waded north along the narrow bank. She peeked at Rania from the corner of her eye.

"You're the sheikh's granddaughter, right?"

Rania smoothed her starched dress.

"And who are you?"

"The fortune-teller's granddaughter. Of course." Huda wedged her hands on her hips. "Didn't you recognize my *jaddah*? She visits the sheikh's home twice a month, sometimes more."

"You're lying."

"I am not." Huda picked a pebble from the bank and hurled it into the water. "Haven't you ever noticed the henna on your jaddah's temples?"

"The spirals?"

"The sheikha suffers terrible headaches, right? Well, my jaddah cures them with henna and special prayers. She knows how to ward off the evil eye and how to make potions for stomachaches and broken hearts. She can read coffee grounds too."

"My father says fortune-tellers trade in ignorance."

Huda snorted.

"Well, he is a man. They don't know everything."

"If your father hears you talk like that, he'll beat you for sure."

Huda eyed her evenly.

"My father is dead."

"Oh," mumbled Rania. "I'm sorry."

Huda shrugged.

"He died when I was a baby. I have two brothers though. Of course, they would have to catch me to beat me, and I am too fast for them." She tossed another pebble in the stream. "I'll show you. Come on, let's race."

"I better not . . ."

"Afraid I'll beat you?"

"Of course not," lied Rania. Huda was a village girl. They were always fast.

"Then to the chicken coop and back. Let's go!"

The two girls sprinted to the coop and back, then twice ran a looping circle around the house. Huda outran Rania, but not by much. The girls collapsed on the riverbank, panting, skinny legs splayed out before them. Huda's bare soles were painted red. Rania eyed them curiously.

"Did your grandmother cast a spell to make you so fast?"

"No, silly. The henna cures any cuts on my feet. Don't you know anything?"

Rania tossed her hair.

"I know how to add and subtract. I can do my times table. I can count to one hundred in English and French. I can read and paint and draw. Can you?"

"Well, I can draw. . . ." Huda picked up a stick and dragged it through the sand. "See?"

"What is that? A crow?"

"It's my water buffalo! Can't you see his horns?"

"They look like wings to me." Rania stuck her hand in her pocket and removed the tiny perfume bottles. "Here. Hold these to the sun."

The two girls took turns shining red and blue light on the sand, then Rania uncorked the vials, and the girls daubed themselves with jasmine and frankincense.

"These are my magic potions," boasted Rania. "Strong enough to defeat even the smell of that stinky chicken coop. They cost me five dinar."

"Five dinar? You paid five dinar for perfume?"

"It's not so much."

Huda's eyes widened. She rifled through the pockets of her dress.

"I have magic too. I can tell the future. Want to see?"

She opened her fist, revealing a jumble of tiny bones, a seashell, and a few glass beads.

"These are my tools." She inflated her chest. Rania saw the resemblance to her brother in her round face. "My jaddah is teaching me all sorts of things, like how to read bones and coffee grounds. If I see a peacock in the grounds it's good news for the future.

Rats are bad. I would be inside now, helping her, but you know kids like me aren't welcome at the birth visits. Not that I mind. It's so boring."

"My whole life is taken up by these visits," grumbled Rania. "I feel like I'll never be free."

"Hah!" Huda sat up straight. "Let's see." She cupped her tiny talismans in her hands and tossed them onto the sand. "Wait, that's what my jaddah says. Give me time to look. When I am ready, I will tell you what I see."

The two girls were on their hands and knees, charting the future in wishbones and shards of shiny oyster shell when Rania's mother emerged from the house.

"My mother is going to Baghdad for a month," whispered Rania. Overhead, a white-tailed hawk turned circles in the sky. "I will stay at my grandmother's house. Come find me when your jaddah visits next."

High above Basil's garden, a hungry hawk prowled the sky, as if it had flown out of Rania's memory and taken root in the present.

"So who is this woman?" demanded Basil. Rania knew he wouldn't be satisfied with tales of birds and boats and village girls with oyster shells.

"Her brothers were killed in the uprising," she said. "She knows I used to be involved with the opposition. She thinks I influenced her brothers to rise up."

"Do I know these men?"

She shook her head. "Mustafa and Ali were village boys."

He eyed her curiously. "Village boys?"

Rania dragged her hands down her face. Of all the memories that had come back to her, the one that hurt the most was of the last time she saw Mustafa. He was in the hallway of her apartment in Basra, his face lit by yellow lamplight. A photo of her dead husband hung in a frame on the wall. To Rania, it seemed he was watching them: his widow and the village man, alone, at night. Out in the street, gunfire had crackled and spat. A helicopter thudded overhead. More than ten years later, Rania could still recall how her heart kept time with the *thwack, thwack, thwack* of its blades.

"Ten thousand men died during the uprising," said Basil. "Why does this woman blame you? What are you not telling me?"

"Nothing." Rania stared at her feet, barely daring to breathe. "Clearly fear has driven Huda mad. She's so desperate to save her son, she'll turn me in if she doesn't get what she wants."

"And what exactly is that?"

"A passport for her son and an exit visa. She thinks the opposition can get it for her."

"What opposition?" spluttered Basil.

"You can't have lost all of your contacts. There must be someone."

"Who? Tell me, who?" Basil threw his hands toward the sky. "Rami was killed. Raed was executed. Sami and Kareem fled and never came back. Naseem disappeared in Abu Ghraib."

He drooped like a marionette with severed strings.

"If your friend thinks the opposition can save her, she's living in a fantasy."

"If we don't give her what she asks, both of us will suffer."

Basil's eyes snapped toward her.

"What do you mean, both of us?"

"You know the mukhabarat and the lengths they go to." Rania dug her fingers into her scalp but that wasn't enough to banish the visions of power tools, branding irons, and fizzing electrical cables.

"Forgive me," she whispered. "I lack the strength of a martyr; I don't have the courage of Imam Husayn. I wish it weren't so, but I know in the end the mukhabarat would find a way to break me. And then I'd have to give them names."

The wind dragged a tear across her cheek.

"I'm sorry, Basil, but if you don't help me, one of those names will be yours."

*   *   *

On the way back from Basil's farm, on the highway between Ramadi and Fallujah, a road train appeared in Rania's rearview mirror. She watched it grow: an oil-stained truck dragging two grimy trailers. She steered her shuddering Volvo toward the edge of the blacktop. Burnt-out cars sprawled on the shoulder of the desert, their twisted chassis like dinosaur skeletons protruding from an archaeological dig.

The road-train soon caught the old Volvo and pulled out to overtake. As Rania battled the pull of its slipstream, her muscles knotted all the way up her spine. Yet even when the tanker sped on ahead, Rania remained hunched over the wheel, shoulders aching, while shrapnel from her past exploded all around. She wondered, Was Basil still out by the grape arbor, cursing her name? Or was he already seeking out his long lost contacts in the opposition?

Rania rolled her aching neck from side to side but her muscles stayed tight as a bow. Dead men's faces flashed before her eyes. She tried to empty her mind, told herself that mourning the past was a luxury she couldn't afford. A poisonous treat. When another road train appeared in her rearview mirror, she was glad for the distraction.

As she sped on, Rania caught an occasional glimpse of the Euphrates River, wending like a green ribbon through the Mesopotamian floodplains. Mostly it was scrubby desert, but every now and then she passed fields of rolling wheat, just like in the old days of picnics and swimming parties. The Volvo clattered past a sign pointing the way to the ancient ziggurat of Aqar Quf. The mudbrick pyramid was built three millennia ago to honor the ancient gods. Many times, invading forces had hacked at its crumbling sides, but it remained over 150 feet tall, weathered into the head of a great stallion overlooking the wide desert.

If she was a loyal Iraqi, Rania would have kept Aqar Quf and the glories of Mesopotamia in mind, but on the inky highway, returning from Basil's farm, she allowed herself to revisit Iraq's other history. The history absent from school textbooks. The unspeakable, unprintable, unthinkable past. The damage done by their own. She sucked it up. Swallowed it down. Over and over, a bulimic on a sorrowful binge.

Rania's eyes were veined and swollen by the time she reached the first of the sandbagged machine-gun nests on the outskirts of Baghdad. She removed her ID card from the glove box and rested it on her lap. It took two hours to negotiate the multiple checkpoints. The process required everything she had: her languid smile and cooing voice, her family name, her charm. At the third checkpoint, a young man with oil-black eyes took the last of the money she'd earned selling her father's books.

By the time she turned off the smooth highway and onto the potholed backstreets, Rania was hollow as a drum. The Volvo puttered past concrete apartment blocks, moldering mansions, and graceful mosques, until, finally, Rania pulled up outside her gate. As she slid her key in the gate, insects turned frantic circles under the streetlight. Once inside, she secured the latches and bolts behind her. Only then did she notice the front door was ajar.

"Hello?" Rania's voice wobbled in the gloom.

She pushed the door wider. At the far end of the hallway, yellow light leaked from the kitchen.

"There's nothing worth stealing," she cried. "Unless you want a painting for your wall."

The kitchen door creaked. A shadow flickered, then morphed into flesh.

"Hello, Mother." Hanan extended her arms. "Are you going to welcome me home?"

CHAPTER 12

Huda's eyes watered as she waited on the bench in Abu Nasser's photography studio. Khalid pressed his nose into her shoulder.

"The smell from the darkroom is worse than rotten eggs," he muttered. "Almost as bad as Bakr's farts after a lunch of lentil stew."

"Hush!" Huda pinched his arm. "Abu Nasser may have lost all sense of smell, but he's not deaf." She leaned close to Khalid's ear. "And remind me never to serve Bakr lentils."

She gazed at the photos that filled Abu Nasser's walls. Among the obligatory portraits of the president, there were families with baby girls in frilly frocks and boys in tiny bow ties. A soccer team held aloft a gleaming trophy. A folk band hugged lutes and goat-skin drums. But mostly there were wedding shots: grooms and young brides with henna-painted hands and trepidation twinkling in their eyes.

A mirror hung on the wall for Abu Nasser's clients to check their hair and makeup. The spotty glass caught the reflection of Khalid lounging against Huda's side, like a young pasha resting on a plump cushion. Another wave of vinegary gas seeped from the darkroom. Khalid wrinkled his nose and scrunched his eyes, and for a moment Huda imagined she saw Mustafa in the cloudy mirror, chasing her along the riverbank with the rotting carcass of a freshwater crab.

"Perhaps Abu Nasser has a side business in pickled onions," she whispered.

"Or maybe he keeps camels back there." Khalid grinned. "Camels that eat lentil stew."

Huda went to pinch his arm. Instead, she tickled his ribs.

"How long will this take?" He wriggled away. "I'm supposed to play soccer with Bakr."

Before Huda could answer, Abu Nasser hurried from the darkroom.

"Sorry for the wait." The old photographer herded Khalid to a carpeted stage at the far end of the studio. "Can I interest you in adding one of my deluxe settings?"

He dragged a floor-to-ceiling backdrop of alpine mountains behind the stage.

"Oh, no," said Huda. "That won't do."

"If you don't like Mother Nature, I have plenty more." The old photographer unveiled a vista of the Eiffel Tower. Next came Piccadilly Circus, and then the Roman Colosseum.

"For an extra two thousand dinar, your son can journey around the world." Abu Nasser flung his skinny arms wide. In his baggy black shirt, he looked like a cormorant sunning itself by the Tigris. "What mother would not want that for her son?"

"If only it were that simple," mumbled Huda. Worried that Abu Nasser would catch the ugly fight between love and fear going on behind her eyes, she busied herself fixing Khalid's collar and combing his hair.

"I'd like a white background." She licked her thumb. Khalid grimaced and pulled away before she could smooth his eyebrows. "Nothing fancy, thank you, Abu Nasser."

"Are you interested in a portrait to hang on your wall? I stock a lovely variety of frames."

"Passport size is what I need."

"Passport size?" Abu Nasser stopped and tilted his head. Once again Huda thought of a cormorant eyeing a fish in the reeds. "You have travel plans abroad?"

"That would be wonderful, but no." She tittered nervously, and wondered, Could Abu Nasser be a mukhabarat informant, like her? "This is for a locket. A gift for my mother. Passport size will fit perfectly."

Abu Nasser pulled a bare screen behind his stage.

"Passport size comes in a set of four. You can't buy one only."

"Four is fine. Thank you."

Abu Nasser sighed and straightened Khalid's shoulders. He switched on a tungsten lamp and retreated behind his camera.

"Okay, young man, give me a smile."

"No!" Huda lurched from the bench. "No smile. Just a straight face, looking right at the camera."

Abu Nasser glanced up from his viewfinder.

"First no lovely backdrop. Now you say, no smile?" He jammed his hands on his bony hips. "It'll look like a mug shot. Shall I fingerprint him too?"

"His grandmother is very old-fashioned." Huda smiled like the petrified brides on the wall. "Back in my mother's day, a photograph was a once-in-a-lifetime event. She still thinks it's serious business, not to be made light of."

"Well, it's your money," the old man muttered. "If you say no smile, then that's what you'll get."

A few minutes later, Abu Nasser retreated to his darkroom to develop Khalid's photos. The boy slouched on the bench beside Huda.

"The stink of those chemicals is going to kill me." He buried his head in his hands. "Unless I die of boredom first."

Huda glanced through the window fronting onto the sidewalk. The wind pushed a plastic bag down the street, picked it up, and lifted it high into the sky like a balloon that had escaped a child's hand. Over by the traffic lights, a beggar woman hawked newspapers to passing motorists. The wind clutched at her tatty abaya. The fabric, like the woman, had faded with age and countless hours spent outside, under the scrutiny of the sun, and every man and dog that passed by.

"How much longer?" groaned Khalid. Huda patted his arm. When she glanced outside again, Ally was on the far side of the street, walking briskly in the direction of the embassy. Tom must have gone into work, even though it was Saturday. Huda felt a stab of pity. Ally's days must be long and lonely. No wonder she was the only diplomat's wife left in Baghdad.

Huda wondered if Ally had tried to call Abdul Amir before setting out. She rarely contacted him on weekends anymore, not since Huda showed up in his place to ferry her to the Rashid Hotel. Huda remembered the glow of the Rashid's chandeliers, and the *clack-clack-clack* of her heels against the marble floor. Suddenly, she was short of breath, as if the mukhabarat with the purple scar still had his hand wrapped around her throat.

She took a deep breath and watched Ally duck into a small delicatessen. A few minutes later, she emerged with two bulging plastic bags. A moment later, a small boy toddled out from an alley. Ally smiled as he ran toward her, waving a stick in the air like a make-believe sword. From her corner, the newspaper vendor watched, unsmiling, as Ally ruffled the boy's hair.

Ally played with the child for a minute, then she deposited one of the plastic bags by the wall, alongside the woman's stock of newspapers. She bent down, pretended to steal the child's nose, and then strode on in the direction of the embassy, without looking to the woman for thanks. Huda admired her generosity. If she'd been the one handing out groceries, she would expect to hear, "Allah, bless you, sister," or even better, "May you live a long and happy life."

The newspaper vendor scanned the street warily. Was she on the lookout for mukhabarat? Weeks ago, Abdul Amir noticed Ally's interest in the boy and his mother, and reported it to Abu Issa. He sent one of his men to interview the woman about Ally:

how often she stopped by, where she went, what she said. Huda examined the woman's stiff spine, her razor-sharp cheekbones, and hooded eyes. Like anyone else, the newspaper vendor knew it was dangerous to get close to foreigners. Still, she needed the food Ally provided. And the girl always made her son smile—perhaps that made it worth the risk.

Huda watched Ally disappear down the road. She wished she could fling open the door of the photography studio and call after her. She wished they could stroll to the riverside, like people did before, in the golden years, the years of plenty. Most likely Ally would crack some jokes, or point out how the sun's rays split into rainbows as they bounced off the blue dome of a mosque. She wished they could simply be friends, free to speak their minds.

But Huda knew that after being warmed by Ally's unfiltered cheer, she'd be required to provide a full accounting of every word. Abu Issa would chastise her for failing to unearth an ugly secret or some snippet of information to pass on to his superiors. The Bolt Cutter would crack his thick, hairy knuckles, one gristle-laden pop after another. Huda knew she had no choice, but the closer she got to Ally, the greater her shame grew, like a microscopic toxin multiplying beneath her skin.

"Your photos are ready." Abu Nasser returned from his darkroom, bringing with him yet another wave of malodorous gas. Huda took a final glance at Ally disappearing down the road. Her eyes stung, but this time Abu Nasser's chemicals weren't to blame.

Huda pulled over by the soccer field behind the Palestine Hotel. A pigeon keeper had loosed his flock from their cage atop a nearby apartment block. The birds looped through the cloudless sky then flapped in tight formation across the field.

"Are you sure about this?" Huda peered through the windshield. "Where's Bakr?"

"He'll be here." Khalid unbuckled his seat belt. "We're a little early, that's all."

"How early? I don't want you wandering about and getting into mischief."

He rolled his eyes and threw open the car door.

"Kiss your mother goodbye first," said Huda.

He offered his cheek, mouth twisting, like he'd sucked on a Basra lime.

"You're sure Bakr's mom will drive you home?" She tried to wipe a smudge of lipstick from his cheek, but Khalid evaded her and clambered out of the car.

"Mom, stop worrying."

"Be good. Stay safe!" she cried. "I love you, my darling."

As Khalid jogged toward the dusty field, Huda slumped into her seat. Those last five words felt like the only honest things she'd said all day. Huda rested her forehead against the steering wheel. How long could she keep lying to her husband, to Ally, to her friends and neighbors? How long could she fool Abu Issa and the Bolt Cutter? And what about Khalid? When the truth finally came out, she feared he'd curse her name.

Huda dragged herself upright. Khalid was idling on the fringe of the soccer field, hands shading his eyes, as if he were watching her car. She turned the key in the ignition and waved goodbye. He didn't respond. Perhaps he wasn't looking at her. Maybe he was tracking the pigeons wheeling above their coop.

Huda didn't understand the birds. Did they not harbor the urge to fly toward the sun, to eat wild rice, and drink from a babbling stream? Born in a cage. Raised in its stinking confines. Was a handful of seed and a saucer of dirty water really enough to keep them in place? Was that all it took to change the nature of a bird, to extinguish its need to be free?

Huda waved at Khalid one last time. Her stomach churned as she tucked the passport photos deep in her handbag, alongside Khalid's identity papers and a thick chunk of cash. She motored in the direction of the river, crossed the swooping bridge, and turned toward Mansour, all the while keeping constant lookout for roadside checkpoints. Finally, Huda arrived at the great copper gate. Rania pried it open before she had a chance to ring the bell and led her straight to the garden.

"We're to go to Shorja market." Rania's words were barely audible amid the rustling of the eucalypts. "They said to pass by the spice stalls and wait near the old hammam."

"The bathhouse?"

Rania shrugged.

"None of this was my idea."

Huda clamped her handbag under her arm. Ten thousand people visited Shorja market every day, and common wisdom said a third of them were pickpockets. Some carried blades to slice open bags just like hers.

"May I use your bathroom first?"

Rania glanced at the house. Her mouth twitched. For a moment Huda wondered if she was going to refuse.

"Go through the gallery to the hall. It's the first door on your left." She pulled a pack of cigarettes from her pocket. "We need to leave soon to make it on time."

In the bathroom, Huda removed the scarf from her neck and used it to lash Khalid's documents to her waist. She wound the fabric tight as a girdle, hopped up and down and jiggled her hips. Satisfied no pickpocket could pry the papers loose, she buttoned her shirt, unlocked the bathroom door, and collided with a ghost from her past.

"Oops, sorry." A fourteen-year-old version of Rania rested her slender hand against the wall. Huda's eyes bulged like a character in one of Khalid's science fiction comics, suddenly transported back in time and space.

"Do you need this, madam?" The girl held out a hand towel. "Mom told me to replace it this morning, but I forgot."

Huda blinked.

"Your mom? Of course." Huda laughed out loud—a high-pitched peal that wobbled toward hysteria. "Silly me. I should have realized."

The girl's long curly hair and aquiline nose were identical to her mother's. But it was the proud tilt of her chin and her level amber gaze—even when confronted with a babbling lunatic in her bathroom—that made her seem like she'd walked straight out of Huda's memory.

"You're so tall. So pretty." Huda pressed her hands together. "But then again, I always knew you would be beautiful, Hanan."

Confusion crept into the girl's eyes.

"Forgive me, but have we met before?"

"Your mother and I are old . . ." Huda paused. "I grew up in a village near your grandfather's farm. We're from the same tribe."

"Oh, the tribe." The girl's lips twisted, and Huda was reminded of Khalid's reluctant goodbye kiss. "My mom says ours is a small tribe, but they sure seem to have a lot of babies."

"Well, I only had one. His name is Khalid. You two used to play together."

"Khalid?" A spark flared in Hanan's eyes. Suddenly, she grasped Huda's hand and led her to a collection of photographs displayed on a wall. Hanan pointed at a picture of a baby swaddled in muslin, watched over by a curly-haired toddler.

"Is that your Khalid?"

Huda leaned in close.

"Oh my goodness." She chuckled softly. "I remember when this was taken. You two were so cute together."

"So, you're the Huda Mom told me about."

The smile melted from Huda's lips. What had Rania said? Had she taken her daughter into the garden, beneath the swaying eucalypts, and whispered about blackmail, informants, and the mukhabarat?

"Yes." Huda couldn't bring herself to say her own name aloud. "I am Khalid's mother."

"My mom told me all about you."

The girl stared at her, eyes wide, unblinking.

Shame bloodied Huda's cheeks.

"Oh, yes," said Hanan. "If she sees a boatman on a river, my mom always says, 'Huda could sail better than that.' If I scrape my toe, she says, 'Huda could mix up a magic salve,' like the one you made for the scar on her thumb." The girl giggled. The sound cut Huda to the core.

It had been twenty years or more, but Huda still remembered the salve Hanan referred to, and the scar. Huda had been at the sheikh's farm. Her grandmother was busy giving readings and dispensing advice in the women's quarters, when Huda snuck out to the farmhouse kitchen. Rania was already there, virtually vibrating with excitement. She'd seen an American film where two friends pledged undying loyalty by slicing their hands and mixing their blood. She'd proposed Huda and her do the same, with a few twists of their own.

"I've got the honey," said Rania, in a stage whisper. "What about you?"

Huda rifled through the pockets of her long apricot dress. She produced a small bottle of brown glass, borrowed from her grandmother's saddlebag. Huda uncorked the bottle and carefully measured out a teaspoon of foul-smelling liquid. Rania's nose wrinkled.

"Tincture of myrrh," whispered Huda, before mixing it with a generous glug of honey harvested from the sheikh's hives.

Next she retrieved a dented tin from the depths of her pocket and scooped out an oily paste made of Palestinian thyme. Its herbaceous aroma of mint and lemon neutralized the stink of the myrrh. Rania peered over Huda's shoulder.

"Is that it?" she whispered, disappointed. "What about some henna?"

"I knew you'd say that," said Huda. She untwisted a small scrap of paper and poured a generous pinch of red henna powder into the concoction. It was a waste, really. Thyme, honey, and myrrh were more than enough to do the job, but Rania put great store in henna, ever since the day she met Huda, with her bag of runes and henna-painted feet. Rania grinned with satisfaction as Huda mixed the dye into her salve.

"We should hurry." Rania glanced over her shoulder. "The cook could come back any moment."

Quickly, Huda scraped the mixture onto a square of banana leaf, then folded it into a neat package.

"Let's go somewhere they won't think to look."

"Not the stables, then," said Rania.

"What about the riverbank, over by that stork's nest we found last year? Do you remember?"

"Of course I remember," said Rania.

Huda hurried outside, trying to hide her relief. Rania had been away in Baghdad for almost three months—a lifetime for twelve-year-old Huda. She feared Rania would forget all about her, now that she was a student at the prestigious Baghdad Ladies High School. Huda imagined Rania and the other highborn girls trading tips on where to vacation in Britain, or which Paris bakery had the best croissants. Huda had no doubt they ordered them in flawless French.

The two girls hurried past the sheikha's fragrant rose garden, then the cavernous garage with the family's collection of shiny motorcars.

"So what did you do for fun in Baghdad?" asked Huda.

"You know," Rania shrugged. "The usual stuff."

What was this stuff? wondered Huda. She had no idea what was "usual" for a student at Baghdad Ladies High School, and Rania was more mysterious than ever. As they crept past the stable, a sleek gray mare poked her nose from the window of her stall and whinnied. Huda pulled a floppy carrot from her pocket.

"What else have you got hidden in there?" giggled Rania. "A mother goat? A top hat? A fishing rod?"

"I've got what we need for our ceremony," she said, determined to show Rania that she could be mysterious too.

The mare snuffled the treat from Huda's palm, and the girls continued on, past the vegetable garden and the sheikh's beehives. They paused when they reached a wall of tall grass.

"You're not scared, are you?" said Rania.

"Of course not." Huda raised her chin. She might not know how to order breakfast in French, but the wetlands were her domain. "Let's go."

Hemmed in by hissing curtains of grass, the two girls followed a narrow goat track to the river. Rania eyed the silty shore nervously.

"What now?"

"Come on," said Huda, slipping off her sandals and feeling the sand between her toes. "I'll show you."

She had to admit, she was enjoying the situation. Rania usually seemed so confident, so adult. In Baghdad, she had celebrated her fourteenth birthday, shed the last traces of baby fat, and returned to the farm taller and more beautiful than ever. Huda felt dowdy beside her, even in her best apricot dress. But at least here, surrounded by rattling cattails and fleets of clucking waterfowl, she was in her element.

"I have one more special item in my pocket," she announced.

Rania leaned closer. "What is it?"

Huda paused, milking the drama, just like her grandmother did before revealing the signs in the coffee grounds. With a flourish, she extracted a knife from her pocket. The double-bladed jambiya was no machete, less than six inches long from the tip to the base of the buffalo-horn handle. But when Huda held it aloft, the curved blade caught the sun and split it into rainbows.

"This is for our blood oath," she proclaimed.

Rania's eyes grew round.

"Where did you get it?"

"It's Mustafa's. He won't notice it's gone until he and Ali return from hunting ducks. I've learned how to do that too, you know. I can balance a spear in my palm, just like my brothers. Soon I'll make it fly where I wish . . ." Huda trailed off, suddenly unsure if her hunting credentials would impress a student at Baghdad Ladies High School. "I've been studying English too, every day."

"Shall we do this?" Rania glanced over her shoulder. "They might miss me at the farmhouse."

Huda cut down a thick cattail with the dagger, then used it to mark a large circle in the sand.

"We have to stand inside the circle," she said. "Or else it'll just be an ordinary promise, not a blood oath."

They stepped into the circle, grinning, and ran through their plan.

"Today we vow to be blood sisters," Rania intoned. "Closer than sisters from the same womb."

"Don't forget about secrets," said Huda. "We mustn't keep secrets from each other."

Rania paused, then pressed her hand to her heart.

"No secrets."

"If the blood oath is broken, then the penalty is sorrow."

"Sorrow?" Huda was unimpressed. "For how long? A day? A week? It's got to be more than that."

Rania raised her chin.

"Sorrow for the oath breaker," she declared. "And for the generation that follows her."

Huda remembered pressing the dagger to Rania's thumb, and how the blade cut deeper than she expected. The girls grabbed each other and locked eyes.

"Sisters forever." They held their bleeding thumbs together. "Or sorrow for us and the generation to come."

Immune to the gravity of the moment, a trio of ducks landed with a splash at the edge of the river, waddled up the bank, and quacked bossily, as if to say, *Are you finished?* The girls had giggled, as Huda pulled the banana leaf package from her pocket and dabbed the rust-colored salve across Rania's wound.

"What's going on here?"

Rania strode down the hallway, fists clenched at her sides. Huda's memories of magic salves gave way to the present—where blood oath had become blackmail. She shrank against the plaster wall, feeling very small.

"Look at this, Mom." Hanan pointed to the photo of her and Khalid. "I was just showing—"

"Huda, we must go." Rania's gaze could have cut glass. "We can't be late."

"You're going out?" said Hanan. "Can I come?"

"Another time, my darling." Rania hustled the girl toward the staircase. "Go to your bedroom and do your homework. While I'm gone, don't open the gate. Not for anyone, you hear me? I'll be back in a couple of hours, once I've finished my . . . business with Huda."

Hanan sighed. She glanced over her shoulder at Huda. "I hope you come again."

Huda nodded and smiled, then turned away before her guilt spilled out her eyes.

"Shall I drive?" she asked Rania.

"I'll take my own car. That way, once we're done, we can go our own ways. We'll meet at the southern entrance to the spice bazaar. You know it?"

Huda nodded, relieved she wouldn't have to sit side by side with Rania in the close confines of the Corolla. That would be too intimate. She needed time alone to banish her girlish nostalgia, and forget about childhood friendships, magic salves, and blood oaths. She needed time alone to think of her dead brothers, time to rebuild the vengeful fire in her chest.

Beneath Shorja's web of faded tarpaulins, the air was hazy with cinnamon, myrrh, and dust kicked up by a thousand feet. Blinking in the aromatic fog, the two women plunged into the narrow alleyways of the spice bazaar.

"Try to keep up." Rania glared at Huda, then she forged ahead, skirting past a vat of bright green capers bobbing in vinegar. Huda shot daggers at her back, and struggled through the shoppers seeking out purple sumac, yellow turmeric, and powdery chunks of indigo. Someone dropped a bag. It exploded like a cardamom cluster bomb.

Vendors urged Rania to stop and taste a briny olive or sniff a sprig of sage. She sailed on, the crowd seeming to part before her, while Huda scurried in her wake, murmuring, "Excuse me, haji, perhaps next time."

Huda squeezed past bowls of henna powder in shades of red, brown, and green, and remembered her grandmother delivering the same potions and powders to the sheikh's farm. She was thinking of those lost golden days when she walked into Rania's back. Rania was holding a jar of twigs, like a little girl who'd just unwrapped a music box with a ballerina twirling inside.

"Do you remember . . . ?" Rania trailed off.

Without another word, she pushed the jar into the vendor's hands and hurried on. Pain stabbed Huda's side. Of course she remembered the twigs. One rainy day, she'd taught Rania how to shred a stick of arak and use it to brush her teeth. Afterward, Rania said it was better than Colgate. Had she told Hanan about that too?

She followed Rania around a sharp corner. The dun-colored dome of an old hammam rose above the stalls. Tongues of steam twisted from its star-shaped vents.

"Women's hours are over for today." The bath keeper perched on a stool by the entrance. "You'll have to come back tomorrow."

The two women sidled into the shade of the hammam's brick walls. A barefoot urchin with matted hair emerged from the crowd and tugged on Rania's sleeve.

"Madam, can you spare a coin for me?"

As Rania fumbled with her handbag, Huda pulled a couple of dinar from her pocket.

"Buy some flatbread or a pot of yogurt." She pressed the purple bills into the boy's palm. "Don't waste it on sweets. They'll rot your teeth."

The child raised his enormous eyes, and for a moment, Huda felt as if she were peering into a deep green well.

"Listen to me," he whispered. "Those you seek are waiting in the Khan Murjan."

"The old inn? It's been boarded up for decades."

Rania leaned in. "What's going on?"

"You've got five minutes." The boy kept his eyes on Huda's. "Otherwise the door will be closed. They said there's no second chance."

"But the Khan Murjan is on the other side of the souk."

"I know a shortcut." The boy pulled her toward the farthest alleyway. "Trust me."

Huda held back, swamped by a sudden sense of déjà vu. She'd asked the same thing of Ally. *Trust me*, she said time and time again, to keep the girl close and the mukhabarat satisfied. The skin at the back of Huda's neck prickled. Was the emerald-eyed boy a liar, just like her?

"Let's go." Rania pushed Huda toward the thronging alley. "I want this over and done with."

The boy wove through the crowd. Huda and Rania struggled after him, dodging a man with a trolley full of clucking chickens. Two women blocked the path. As wide as they were tall, they haggled noisily over a consignment of nightshirts like they were negotiating the sale of their firstborn. Huda elbowed past them as the boy zigged and zagged through the houseware stalls. A boy sprawled motionless atop a huge mound of cheap dish towels, and Huda wondered, Could he really be sleeping amid this din, or was he dead?

A small hand shot out from a gap in the wall. The boy pulled Huda into the shadows and thrust his finger to his lips. Rania was already there, back flattened against the rough bricks. Huda froze. Two beefy men in leather jackets bulldozed through the crowd. They were mukhabarat dispatched to monitor the souk, and to sniff out malcontents.

Huda waited until they passed, counted slowly to ten, then poked her head into the alley. The urchin leaped past her. The two women staggered after him. In the grain bazaar, a donkey blocked the way, its cargo of bulging burlap sacks too wide for the narrow space. The crowd erupted into curses.

"Get your mule out of here, you fool." A shopper waved his fist in the air.

The grain merchant dragged at his donkey's reins. Huda

hopped from foot to foot as the snarl of impatient marketgoers slowly cleared. She craned her neck and tried desperately to spot the boy's matted hair. She guessed her heart must have done a thousand beats already. Surely that meant five minutes had passed.

Rania pushed past and stood on her tiptoes.

"There he is!" She grabbed Huda's hand, and yelled, "Make way, please!"

As it had earlier, the crowd parted on Rania's command. Huda shook her head incredulously as the tall woman pulled her on. This time, instead of finding their passage jammed, the two of them were swept forward, like leaves floating on a stream. They sailed through the clothing market, past mountains of second-hand jeans, suit jackets, and baby bibs, until they were deposited at the entrance to Khan Murjan.

The ancient inn was boarded up. Thick cobwebs coated the gate, and centuries of rust had fused the locks. Huda's heart sank to the cobblestones.

"No one's been here for years. What a waste of time." Rania turned on her heel and stalked off without a word of goodbye.

Huda slumped against the caravan's ocher wall. Defeat mixed with the sweat running down her spine. She patted her pocket and prayed the urchin hadn't stolen her purse.

"Huda!" Rania reappeared at the far corner of the inn. She crooked her finger, then disappeared again.

Huda scurried after her and found a side door to the inn slightly ajar. Bullets had left one corner of the iron door cratered as the moon, but never managed to fully penetrate the ancient metal. Huda climbed the steps and peeked inside. The musty smell of mold scratched at her nose. She glanced back at the busy stalls. A vendor had dressed six mannequins in rainbow-colored house-coats. They were lined up against a wall like they were waiting for a firing squad.

CHAPTER 13

Inside the Khan Murjan, Rania stood with her back to the old metal door and waited for her eyes to adjust to the muted light. Somewhere, water dripped against stone. The sound echoed like a heartbeat through the great arches that formed the ribs of the old inn. She crept toward the cathedral-like central chamber, where columns of dust swirled below ancient skylights. The lights seemed to form a pattern, like the star charts used by travelers who once stopped here on their way to Mecca.

"You're late." A man stepped from the gloom. Rania wondered how long he'd been there, watching her. "You were supposed to be here ten minutes ago."

"We didn't have much time." Rania did her best to appear unruffled, but she could hear the tremor in her voice. "And the crowds are thick today."

"She's right," said Huda. Rania startled as the woman slipped in behind her. A memory flashed through her mind, of a small girl stalking a grebe at the edge of a fast-slowing stream. Even when the bird was in Huda's hand, it barely registered what had happened. It seemed she'd lost none of her stealth.

"Even if your messenger delivered us on Aladdin's carpet," said Huda, "we would have struggled to make it on time."

Rania bit back a smile. Huda had kept her quick tongue too.

The man drew closer. He was short in stature, with thick, bristly hair. Despite being magnified by black-rimmed spectacles, his eyes were small and squinty, reminding Rania of a mole emerging from its burrow.

"Well, you're here now." He waved them toward a tall staircase. "So let's carry on."

Rania felt a twist of self-loathing. No timid mole would have the courage to be here, in defiance of the regime. He led them to a balcony ringing the second floor, then paused near a low door set in a brick alcove. Scores of identical alcoves ran along the perimeter of the Khan Murjan, leading to dormitories that once sheltered travelers and students at the nearby mosque.

"You look familiar," said Rania. "Have we met before?"

"For obvious reasons, I try to avoid giving out personal details. I usually ask people to call me Kareem." He paused, his eyes probing hers. "But I believe you once knew my brother."

"You don't mean . . ." Rania peered at him. Those eyes. That hair. "You're not Ahmed's brother, are you?"

He nodded soberly. Rania bent her head.

"I pray that Allah keeps him close."

He nodded and yanked on a thick bolt. The door opened a crack. The faint yellow light and oily stench of a kerosene lamp leaked into the hall.

"Wait here," said Kareem, before slipping inside and pulling the door shut behind him.

Huda crossed her arms.

"I'm sorry for the loss of his brother." Her eyes were cold as the ancient stones. "But at least his mother has the comfort of one son left alive."

"That's not fair. I—"

The door groaned behind them. Kareem beckoned for them to enter.

"We are ready for you."

We? thought Rania. *How many people are waiting inside?* She was struck by visions of an inquisition, with murderous judges seated in a row. Why had she allowed Huda to bully her into this? If she refused to continue, would Huda really make good on her threats? The young girl she'd first met on the riverbank wasn't that cruel. She had honor, more than her share. But Rania knew honor was a two-bladed sword. Loyalty on one side. Revenge on the other.

"Come on." Huda nudged her forward. "They're waiting for us."

There was no panel of judges inside in the claustrophobic room, just one man with the chubby cheeks and white beard of Santa Claus. Still, Rania couldn't shake the feeling it was an inquisition. She wasn't worried by the black turban that marked the man as a Shi'a cleric, or the fat turquoise prayer beads looped around his wrist. It was the judgmental look in his eye, as if he had already decided she was a sinner.

"Sit, sit." Kareem waved the women toward two plastic stools, while he joined the cleric behind what appeared to be an old school desk. Gray smoke twisted from the kerosene lantern in the corner. "We don't have much time, so please tell us what you need."

Huda coughed and cleared her throat.

"I need a passport for my son," she said. "Or the mukhabarat will put him in the fedayeen."

"Why have the mukhabarat taken such an interest in your son?" Kareem eyed her curiously, but the cleric kept his eyes focused on the wall just a few inches above the women's heads. "What's so special about him?"

Huda blushed a painful red that spread from her cheeks down her neck and to her chest. She stared at the floor and mumbled that she was an informant spying on her boss's wife, and the mukhabarat were using her son as leverage. A stitch of pity needled Rania's ribs.

"Why didn't you simply tell them you couldn't do it?" said Kareem.

"Sir, you are a very educated man. From your accent, I can tell you come from a fine family. Probably like Rania, there is a boulevard with your surname." Huda shifted on the stool. "I've no doubt you have suffered. Many great families have been pushed aside, and ignorant peasants from Tikrit have taken their place. Nonetheless, you are still someone. Someone who can say no and possibly live another day."

She sighed, a spluttering sound like a lantern being snuffed out.

"I was not schooled abroad. My family never owned a library of books. If you don't believe me, ask Rania. She'll tell you, I'm a nobody."

Rania twisted about.

"That's not what I—"

The cleric raised his hand for silence. It was the first time he'd moved, and the prayer beads clacked loudly at his wrist. He leaned toward Kareem and whispered in his ear. Kareem nodded.

"Let's move on," he said. "First, practicalities. We need two passport photos of your son."

"Yes." Huda nodded eagerly. "I have them."

"Also, his birth certificate."

"Yes."

"We will need a copy of your housing card with current address."

"I have a copy with me."

"A letter of authorization from his father."

Silence.

"What about a letter from me, his mother?"

"The government changed the law a few years ago," said Kareem. "The father's signature is now required. If he has passed on, an uncle or grandfather may sign."

The cleric's lips twitched with approval. Rania tasted the kerosene fumes at the back of her throat.

"Finally, for a passport, we will need seven hundred dollars from you. An exit visa is an extra two hundred dollars."

"Nine hundred dollars?" exclaimed Rania. "She's just a secretary. It'll take her years to find that sort of money."

"I'm sorry," said Kareem. "The price is out of our control."

"But she can't—"

"It's all right." Huda cut her off.

Disbelief dragged at Rania's jaw.

"I will need some time," said Huda. "But I will get your money. I have the papers and photos with me, and I have one hundred dollars too. I can bring the rest when I get the passport."

"It doesn't work that way." Kareem rapped his knuckles against the desk. "First, we are not the ones who will handle your documents. We will let you know the procedures for that later. Second, you need to supply the money in advance."

Huda sat up tall. She kept her eyes level with the men.

"How do I know I can trust you?"

Rania bit her lip. Huda had courage, that's for sure. But then again, she always had.

"Likewise, we also need to know you can be trusted," said Kareem. "You say you are an unwilling informant for the mukhabarat, but how can we be sure?"

The cleric shifted his eyes from the wall and trained them on Huda. When she blushed and looked away, his lips twitched with pleasure. The cleric whispered in Kareem's ear, then sat back in his chair and rested his hands on his belly, like a man at the end of a feast.

"You will need to keep us updated of your instructions from the mukhabarat," said Kareem. "And we will let you know what you should tell them in return. For a start, tell them that the Australian woman you're monitoring has been behaving suspiciously. Tell them that you think she's hiding something."

"I don't understand," said Huda.

"You don't need to understand," he said. "But if you want a passport for your son, you'll do what we say. For the moment, that's all we have to offer you."

Kareem ushered them toward the hall. Before they filed out,

the cleric rose from the desk. He was taller than Rania expected, and his turban almost brushed against the damp ceiling.

"If we meet again," the cleric's voice creaked like the old door, "make sure you cover your hair like respectable women."

Blinking in the sunlight, the two women stumbled down the steps of Khan Murjan and into the crowd of shoppers.

"I've done what you asked." Rania tucked her bag under her arm. "There's no need for us to meet again."

For weeks, she'd been dreaming of the moment she could bid Huda goodbye. She was surprised when regret flicked in her chest like a fish swishing its tail.

"I suppose you're right." Huda's big eyes were flat with exhaustion. She looked like her grandmother after she'd read too many coffee cups. The crowd pushed them deeper into the alley, toward a busy corner where the path divided into two. Huda veered left, Rania right.

"Do one last thing for me." Huda's voice rose above the din of hagglers and hawkers' bells. "Tell Hanan that I will pray for God to grant her happiness."

A lump formed in Rania's throat. She tried to reply, but like swimmers caught in a riptide, the two women were swept away. Rania drifted past stalls selling dried dates, walnuts, and pistachios. Vendors called for her to stop and taste a fig or a lick of wildflower honey. The thought of food made Rania sick, but the smoke of the kerosene lantern had left her throat raw. She ducked into a teashop and ordered a glass of lime tea.

"*Numi basra?*" The old man behind the counter rinsed a glass and set it on a saucer. "How many sugars?"

Rania held up three fingers. It would need to be very sweet to wash the bitterness from her mouth. She perched on a stool at the entrance to the shack. When the old man delivered her istikan, she didn't wait for the steaming tea to cool. Rania's scalded tongue gave her an excuse for the tears in her eyes.

A barefoot boy squeezed through the crowd. His hair was matted, but unlike the child who led them to Khan Murjan, he had brown eyes, not green. Rania wished their little guide would pass by again. Perhaps she'd take him to buy a leg of roast chicken, then he'd have meat to go with the bread and yogurt he'd promised Huda he'd buy instead of sweets. She sipped the tea and searched the crowd for those emerald eyes. Kareem strolled by.

Rania slapped down a few dinar and hurried from the tea stall. She caught up with Kareem out on the street, not far from where she'd parked her car. He glanced up and down the sidewalk.

"We shouldn't be seen together."

"Why not?" said Rania. "We have plenty in common. Like Huda said, my ancestors have a boulevard named after them, and yours have a statue on a square."

"Had a statue." Kareem frowned. "It's been replaced."

"Come." Rania ushered him around the next corner. "One of my relatives keeps a pharmacy here, although I don't think he's had a customer since 1995."

The power was out when they arrived at the pharmacy. Ropy cobwebs hung in the windows. Rania wondered if her cousin had finally given up on his business, but the front door was unlocked, so she slipped inside. She found him out back in his office, snoring in a rocking chair. He could rest easy, knowing if thieves visited his pharmacy they'd find nothing of value. His shelves were bare.

Rania left him sleeping, returned to the front room, and locked the door.

"Where is your little friend, Huda?" Kareem brushed a cobweb from his sleeve. "Or should I call her your blackmailer? It's quite the Greek tragedy you two have going on."

"I don't think I'll see her again. Unless her son doesn't get a passport." Rania ran a finger along the counter, leaving a line in the dust. "Tell me, what game are you playing with her?"

"Game?" Kareem blinked. "What do you mean?"

"I'm surprised you agreed to meet with us. What's in it for you?"

"I had a visit from our mutual friend Basil. The way he told it, this was a chain of dominoes ready to topple. Huda was going to betray you, then you'd give up Basil. He'd do the same to me, and so on. Obviously, I couldn't let that happen."

"Please explain to me, why is the cleric involved?" Rania drew herself up tall. "And how dare he tell me to cover my hair? This is Iraq, not Saudi Arabia."

"I agree with you. The head scarf should be a woman's choice."

"The president may be the devil," whispered Rania, "but at least he recognized that women deserved equal recognition under the law. Once, we were the envy of all our Arab sisters. Now men like the cleric have convinced him to cut back women's rights."

"I hear what you're saying." Kareem sighed like a teacher badgered by a know-it-all student. "I understand your concern."

"You understand?" Rania growled and dug her cigarettes from her bag. "Then why have you teamed up with the cleric?"

"Right now, we can't afford to pick and choose our allies. The cleric has a strong network."

"But he doesn't want democracy—he wants a regime of a different kind. One where men have all the power. He wants Iraq to be the sort of country where a woman can be stoned to death because she had the misfortune to be raped." Rania jammed a cigarette between her lips. "It's madness."

"We must be practical. Most of the opposition fled to Britain and the United States long ago. Nowadays, men like the cleric have the numbers and the resources. We need to join forces."

"To replace one system of repression with another?"

"As I said, they have numbers. But don't forget, we have the brains. The politicians in Washington and London listen to us. Do you think they want to deal with the clerics? No, of course not. When the regime falls, they will help us end up on top."

"Come on, now." Rania lit her cigarette and dragged the smoke deep into her lungs. "The Americans don't care about us."

"Perhaps. But they do care about oil. Once the sanctions are lifted, we can sell it to them at a much better price than the Saudis. They get cheap oil. We get freedom. To achieve our goals we need to use both the cleric and the Americans."

"You know what they say, lie down with dogs, rise with fleas."

"Calm down," said Kareem. "You've done what was needed to keep your friend happy. You don't need to be involved any further."

"That brings me back to my original question." Rania blew out a long stream of smoke. "What game are you playing with Huda? And why are you interested in the diplomat's wife?"

"The foreign woman means nothing to us. She is just a means to test your friend's loyalty." He chuckled dryly. "If the foreign woman was an American, or even a Briton, it'd be a different story. Especially if we need to prod Washington into action."

"What do you mean?"

Kareem checked his watch.

"We're wasting time with hypotheticals. Forget it." He peered through the dirty window. "Look, it's useful to have someone like your friend on the inside, a double agent."

"Huda is no James Bond."

"She has a stiff spine. She is resourceful. Obviously, she is prepared to lie when needed. And blackmail too. She seems very well qualified."

"Huda is a good person at heart." Rania's fingers rubbed against her scarred thumb. "She lost her two brothers to the cause, and she can't bear the thought of losing her son."

"God willing, she'll get his passport and everything will work out fine."

"Don't play games with her."

"Stay out of this, Rania."

A floorboard creaked in the back office. Her cousin was awake. Kareem swiftly unlatched the door and slipped outside.

Her cousin staggered from the back of the shop, groggy with sleep.

"Rania?" He wiped his glasses. "Is that you?"

"Yes, it's me." Rania pressed her hand to her temple. "I've got a terrible headache."

"Let me take a look on my shelves, dear." The chemist shuffled behind his counter. "I might have a sachet of aspirin. Let me check. I have a feeling I sold it last year."

Hanan grabbed Rania's sketchpad from the kitchen table and used it to fan a cloud of cigarette smoke out the window.

"Mom, you're producing more pollution than al-Dora refinery." Her nose wrinkled. "We need a big chimney stack. You can sit under that whenever you feel the need to smoke. It's not good for the health, you know."

"I should be glad my daughter has such good sense—at least in some areas." Rania ground her cigarette into a chunky ashtray. "Happy now?"

"Of course I'm happy. I'm back home in Baghdad." Hanan rummaged through the refrigerator and pulled out an egg. "Can I cook this? It's the last one."

"Please, eat it. I just sold a painting for Leith, so he's bringing me another three dozen eggs."

"You're taking commission in eggs?" Hanan rolled her eyes. "You can't pay in omelets at the Alwiyah Club."

Rania clambered from her chair and set a pot of water on the stove.

"A few of my friends still have membership. I'm sure one of them would be happy to host us at the club before you leave for—"

"Before I leave?" Hanan's eyes doubled in size. "What do you mean?"

"Well, darling, school starts soon. Your grandmother will come to take you back to the farm."

"No way. I told you I'm not going back."

"This is not negotiable." The buzzer sounded at the gate. "That's probably Leith now."

"Or maybe it's that sculptor who owes you money," muttered Hanan, "with a bowl of last week's tabbouleh or a chunk of moldy cheese."

"Very funny, my dear. Now put your egg in the pot. The water is almost at a boil."

Rania hurried outside and peered through the crack in the gate. Two men waited on the sidewalk. New buyers? she wondered. From the fine cut of their business suits, they could be sanction busters who smuggled in cigars and Johnnie Walker for the regime. Plenty of black marketers had moved into the neighborhood. They paid cash for historic mansions, demolished their roman columns and latticed balconies, and put up brick boxes with central air-conditioning in their place. Most of the time, they couldn't tell Chagall from Charlie Brown. But they didn't pay with eggs either.

"As-salaam alaikum." Rania heaved open the gate. "Welcome to my gallery."

The men turned. One of them stepped close, as if to embrace her. Rania dodged backward.

"My dear Rania." The man chuckled throatily. "Still as lovely as always."

"Malik?"

Another well-fed chuckle escaped his lips.

"I would have called, but your telephone isn't working. If you like, I can send someone around to check the wiring. We've got some fellows lounging around at the Ministry with not enough work to do."

"What a lovely surprise." Rania lied smoothly. "I haven't had anyone from the Ministry of Culture stop by in quite a while."

Once upon a time, the Ministry had been a valued patron: commissioning new artworks, building museums, even ensuring old poets got a decent pension. Like everything else, it had withered from war and sanctions—except for the Division of Presidential Works, which continued to pump out gilded statues and gold-leaf portraits that would make even the vainest caliph blush.

Malik cocked a finely groomed brow.

"Are you going to invite us in?"

"Of course." Rania's laugh tinkled like broken glass. She waved them toward the garden. "Please, make yourself comfortable while I fix some tea."

She hurried to the kitchen. Hanan glanced up, spoonful of egg halfway to her mouth.

"What's wrong? No moldy cheese?"

"Go to your room."

"Mom, it's a joke!"

"My darling, it's not you," said Rania hurriedly. She didn't want Malik catching sight of Hanan. Along with keeping the conveyor belt of presidential art humming, he'd also ingratiated himself into Uday's clique, and they were always on the lookout for innocent young women. "This is important. I want you to go to your room."

"But I haven't finished my—"

"You cannot be seen or heard. Understand?" She snatched up a canister of tea. "Please, do what I say, and afterward we'll go shopping for a new dress you can wear to the Alwiyah Club."

Hanan lay down her spoon. Steel clinked against porcelain.

"I don't need a new dress," she said quietly.

"Good girl. Hurry now."

As Hanan tiptoed out the door, Rania noted the counterfeit smile on her daughter's face. It looked very much like the one she saw on her own face sometimes. Sorrow stabbed her side. What was she teaching her daughter? How to appease the cruel? How to keep the corrupt happy? She waited until she heard the creak of Hanan's footsteps overhead, arranged the tray of tea, then put her hip and shoulder against the kitchen door and pushed it open. Malik blocked her way.

"What on earth?" Rania startled. Glasses rattled on her tray. "I asked you to wait in the garden."

"I wanted to take a look inside the gallery, in case something caught my eye." Malik rested his hand against the cracked plaster of the hallway and made a show of admiring the family photos on the wall. "What's this? No photo of our nation's beloved president?"

"It's being . . . reframed. The roof sprung a leak and the backing got wet." Rania tipped her head toward the hall rug with its faded roses and turtle doves. "See, the water left a stain."

"I can't stay long," said Malik, "so forget about the tea."

Rania bit her lip. Refusing to take tea was a blatant insult, but she was happy to bear the slight if it meant Malik would leave sooner. Through the square of stained glass in the front door, she could see his colleague pacing back and forth.

"The good news, my dear Rania, is that I've come to commission a painting." Malik straightened his tie. "I need a portrait of the president and his sons—for Father's Day."

"What a lovely idea." Rania's lie trotted out like an obedient dog. "Would you like me to prepare a list of artists who may be suitable?"

"I already have someone in mind," he replied absently, still peering at Rania's family snaps. "Did you know that we recently invited a German journalist to Baghdad? He visited your gallery, yes?"

The teacups rattled again.

"That's true."

"Well, that ignorant barbarian toured our Museum of Presidential Art and wrote a most unflattering review. Ostentatious, he said. Can you believe such a thing?"

"He must be a fool. Blind too. There's no other explanation."

"As you know, our leader is a sensitive soul. So he wants something even more refined than usual this time. He wants an artist with a delicate touch."

"We have plenty of talented artists who would be honored."

Malik ran his eyes up and down her slender form.

"He wants you, Rania."

Silence sucked all the air from the hall.

"I don't do that anymore," she stuttered.

"What do you mean?"

"I put my paints away long ago."

a bottle of wine to an Arasat restaurant, they'll pour it into a coffeepot and bring it back to your table."

"Really?" said Ally.

Hatim grinned conspiratorially.

"You want to stop at a liquor shop?"

Ally laughed.

"Whereabouts should I drop you?" he asked.

"At al-Reef Restaurant," she said. "I'm going to eat and then do a little shopping."

Ally stared out the window so she didn't have to look Hatim in the eye. She had no intention of lunching at Baghdad's finest Italian restaurant or wasting time in fancy boutiques. She had an appointment with the sculptor, Miriam Pachachi. Gunter had managed to track her down at her brother's home, three short blocks from Arasat Street.

Hatim's Passat rolled to a stop outside the restaurant's red-and-white awning.

"Can I meet you at the opposite end of the street?" Ally held tight to her handbag, as if her falsehoods might escape its leather mouth. "In front of the big fountain?"

"Sure, take your time." Hatim gave her a thumbs-up.

As he motored away, Ally's shoulders softened with relief. She'd figured she could get to Miriam's house and back again without Hatim noticing—unlike Abdul Amir, who rarely let her out of his sight. Tom maintained Abdul Amir was simply being protective, but regardless, she felt stifled.

With her eyes hidden by dark glasses, Ally discreetly scanned the street. A shoeshine boy dozed in the narrow strip of shade by the restaurant. Across the road, a waiter swept the sidewalk outside an ice cream parlor. Ally pulled her scarf over her hair and hurried away from Arasat, into well-kept backstreets lined with sturdy gates.

Ally stuck close to the walls and did her best to keep her pace steady, not too fast or too slow, trying to look like she belonged. She pretended to remove a pebble from her sandal, so she could check if she was being followed. The only person she spotted was

Malik laughed curtly.

"In these hard times, few can afford to retire. Besides, the opportunity to paint our dear leader should renew your inspiration."

He returned his gaze to the photos on the wall. Rania flinched as he ran his fingers over a picture of Hanan in her school uniform.

"Your daughter is the very image of you, Rania." Malik stroked the thin wooden frame. "Our president enjoys meeting with Iraq's new generation. You should bring her to the palace. His sons would like to meet her too."

"I can't." Rania clutched the tray tight. "She stays with her grandmother now."

"In Basra?" Malik perked up. "Did you know Uday is building a new palace there? It's going to cover all of Sinbad Island. I'm sure he would love to have your daughter at his housewarming party."

Rania stood very still, tea and sugar pot perfectly balanced, and calculated the paces needed to reach the gun in the hall closet. It was her husband's old service revolver, hidden on the top shelf under a stack of scarves. Malik gave her an oily smile and slid a bulging envelope from his jacket pocket.

"This deposit should help to prevent any more water leaks." He laid the envelope on her tray. "I'll stop by soon with the next payment, and you can show me your progress."

Malik let himself out the front door. Rania remained in the hall, eyes locked on the envelope as if it was a venomous snake or a severed head—even though it was well known the president preferred to send heads home in boxes, not on trays.

CHAPTER 14

Ally found Hatim at his usual location outside the Karadah souk, leaning against the hood of his timeworn Volkswagen Passat, chatting with the other drivers waiting for customers to emerge from the market.

"My Australian friend!" He straightened up and waved his lanky arm. "You need a ride?"

Ally skirted toward him, past stalls laden with bunches of fragrant parsley and peppery arugula. Hatim loped to the far side of his car and opened the passenger door for her.

"Did you remember to bring me that recipe for kangaroo stew?" He slid into the driver's seat. "My wife promised to make a big vat this weekend."

"Darn, I forgot." Ally played along. "How about I give you the recipe for emu pie instead?"

"Emu is too spicy," Hatim dead-panned. "It gives me indigestion."

Ally giggled and fastened her seat belt.

"How's your wife?" she asked. "Is she back teaching?"

"Yes, the new term started, so she's busy in the science l[ab] Hatim carefully steered the Passat away from the curb. "She a few rowdy students this year. She says it will be a miracle if t don't set the classroom alight with their Bunsen burners."

"And your little girls?"

"Ruby and Hela have just started grade one." Hatim flip down his sun visor and passed her one of the photographs he pinned underneath. "What do you think?"

Ally examined the shot of Hatim's six-year-old twins in t school uniforms: blue pinafores over white shirts, jaunty scarves tied at their necks.

"They get cuter every time," she said.

"The other day, Ruby drew a design for the world's big castle. She said she will build it herself one day." Hatim bear "She takes after her father, you see."

Before the economy went into freefall, Hatim made a g living as an architect. Ally could easily picture him at a dra[fting] board, pencil tucked behind his ear, measuring angles and ting dimensions. Now, his family scraped by on his wife's teac salary of five dollars a month, government rations, and what Hatim could make ferrying passengers to and from the mark[et].

"Where are we going?" he said.

"Arasat Street," Ally mumbled sheepishly. It was Bagh[dad's] ritziest strip of boutiques and restaurants. She and Tom had there for dinner once or twice, but it was hard to have an app when she knew her meal would cost more than her taxi d made in a month.

Hatim nodded and smiled. Ally wondered, Did he ever his wife to Arasat Street, back when he was an architect? H never betrayed any bitterness. If their situations were reversed hoped she'd have such a generous heart.

"You should have come to Baghdad twenty years ago, my tralian friend. Every street was as lively as Arasat." Hatim p out to overtake a boy on a donkey cart. "Even now, if you l

a gardener pruning back a stand of pink flowering spurge, the same thorny plant used to make Jesus' crown of thorns.

It took less than ten minutes to reach the address Gunter had supplied. Ally had imagined a house like Rania's: grand but crumbling, with peeling paint and sagging gutters. Instead, a silky-smooth driveway led to an eighties-era villa of brick and tile. A row of faux-Roman columns sat out front.

Staring through the bars on the gate, Ally's heart galloped. Would Miriam remember her mother? Would she help to fill the aching hole she'd carried inside since she was five years old? Or would she recall only that her mother was American and throw her out on the street? Ally took a deep breath and pressed her finger to a button on the wall. An electronic bell blared from a hidden speaker, startling a sleepy pigeon from its tree.

The bell tolled on and on, like Big Ben at midday, until Miriam's older brother, Farouk, pried open the gate. He'd been expecting Ally, and politely waved her past two concrete lions guarding the front door.

"How did you learn of my sister's artwork?"

"I came across one of her pieces in a souvenir shop," said Ally. As far as Farouk knew, she was just a diplomat's wife with a fondness for art. She was careful not to mention seeing the statue in Rania's garden. If her mother's citizenship caused any strife, Ally wanted to make sure trouble rained down on her alone.

"Well, my sister's work is not everyone's taste," sniffed Farouk. "That's for certain."

Farouk's plump wife was waiting inside the foyer, all brassy-blond highlights, crimson nails, and leopard print. Amal purred like a fifty-year-old kitten and kissed the air beside Ally's ears. Her heels click-clacked as she led the way to a sitting room. At the threshold, Ally faltered. A larger-than-life Saddam Hussein stared at her from a painting above the mantel.

The president was decked out in a white suit with wide lapels, like John Travolta in *Saturday Night Fever*. Instead of a disco ball, white doves circled above his head. Ally choked down her surprise. She didn't know where to look. At the ostentatious fountain splashing in the corner? At the mural of the Swiss Alps that covered an entire wall? Or at a second presidential portrait— a toga-clad Saddam in a Roman chariot, elbow bent like an archer's, shooting rainbows at the sky?

Amal emitted a screech, and a maid scurried into the room. She set a tray of tea on a low table with four naked brass nymphs for legs.

"Is Miriam here?" said Ally. "I haven't come at the wrong time, have I?"

She'd arrived at the gate full of contrary emotions: excitement, fear, longing for the mother she never knew. Now she felt absurd, sipping tea while Saturday Night Saddam boogied over the mantel. A voice inside her whispered, *Is this really happening?*

"My sister doesn't get many visitors these days." Farouk frowned. "You should know, she's a little eccentric."

"Eccentric?" Amal raised one ruthlessly plucked eyebrow. "Be honest, she's crazy. It runs in the family."

Farouk's features darkened.

"Not you, *habibee*." Amal patted his cheek. She turned to Ally and whispered conspiratorially. "It's only the women in his line who are crazy. Lucky he only has one sister, or we'd need a bigger house to keep them all."

"There's plenty of space," grumbled Farouk. "My sister has a room on the upper floor and a small studio on the roof terrace."

Amal rolled her eyes. "That scrap heap? I'd like to—"

"You'd like to what?" A skinny woman with close-cropped silver hair strode into the room. "Grind up Michelangelo's *David* to make a marble counter for your kitchen?"

While Amal reminded Ally of a pampered house cat, her sister-in-law looked more like a scrappy feral, the hairless type, without an ounce of fat to smooth her wrinkles. Miriam bared her teeth in a caustic smile.

"Or perhaps you want to melt down Rodin's *Thinker* for bracelets and earrings?"

"Farouk!" cried Amal. "Tell your sister she can't talk to me like this."

"Ladies, please." Farouk raised his hands. "We have a guest."

"Actually, she is *my* guest." Miriam crooked her finger at Ally. "Please, follow me."

Ally followed her up the marble stairs, nose twitching at the peculiar perfume that lingered in Miriam's wake. It was only once they crossed the roof terrace and entered the studio that she realized it wasn't perfume but the scent of linseed oil, charcoal, and loamy oil paints embedded in Miriam's hair and caftan.

At the far end of the room, sunlight streamed through the windows and made a million dust motes dance. The walls were papered with paintings, sketches, old photos, and pictures torn from magazines. Paintbrush bouquets protruded from tin cans. Shelves held jars of nails, screws and bolts, coiled lengths of copper wire, bottles of ink, a hammer, saw, and pliers. Stacks of old newspapers rotted in the corner.

A dozen flimsy watercolors had been strung up on a line to dry, all with the same snorting horse galloping through sand dunes, watched on by a dark-eyed woman in a translucent veil. Miriam eyed them disdainfully.

"A first-grade art student could produce this rubbish, but it's the only thing that sells nowadays." She stopped short. "That's not what you're here for, is it?"

Clumsy with nerves, Ally rifled through her handbag and removed the figurine of a woman transforming into a dove.

"I bought this recently." She held it forth, like a peace offering.

Miriam plucked a pair of spectacles from a pocket in her caftan. She turned the figurine upside down and squinted at the markings on its base. A small snort of recognition escaped her lips.

"I don't work much with brass anymore. Too expensive." She glanced at Ally. "Is that what you want? Another figure like this?"

"Uh, not exactly. I have something else you created." Ally pulled the photo of her mother from her bag. Her fingers trembled. "Do you remember taking this picture?"

Miriam inspected the photo quietly. She flipped it over and read the inscription, then eyed the faded image again. Ally's blood rushed in her ears. The twirling dust motes reminded her of musty light in her mother's bedroom. The turpentine and moldering newspapers smelled like disinfectant and despair. She remembered her mother reaching out to stroke her face and almost cried out at the memory of how she turned away.

Miriam glanced up at her.

"I should have seen it earlier." Her eyes glowed like tiny torches. "You're Bridget's daughter, aren't you?"

"You remember my mother?"

Miriam took another long look at the photo, then returned it to Ally's hand.

"I didn't know her well. Not really."

"But you took the photo, right?" Ally refused to let this turn into another dead end. "Do you remember anything about that day?"

Miriam began to pace back and forth, caftan swishing at her feet.

"If I recall, I took that photo the first time I met your mother. A group of us had gathered at the promenade along Abu Nawas. We were celebrating the launch of a new literary magazine. I still remember the slogan: 'Radical art and radical politics.'" She glanced at the door, then lowered her voice. "It was published by the youth wing of the Communist Party."

Ally blinked in surprise.

"A communist magazine? In Iraq?"

"It was communist for a while, then socialist, then democratic socialist, then back to communist again." Miriam redoubled her pacing. Watercolor horses fluttered in her wake. "The British colonialists were gone. We'd overthrown their puppet king. For a brief moment, we believed we could create a new world." Her chin jutted forward at an angry angle. "We were young. We didn't realize that moment of daylight was just the eye of the storm."

Ally struggled to digest the news.

"I had no idea my mother was involved in politics."

"I don't know either. It's possible she was just there because of Yusra."

"Yusra?"

Miriam stopped pacing.

"Your mother never mentioned her?"

"She didn't get a chance. She passed away when I was very young."

"Did she?" Miriam cocked her head to the side. She gave Ally a strange, probing look. "You really do look just like her."

A worm of anxiety wriggled in Ally's chest. Had Miriam remembered her mother was American? Enemy number one. Miriam pulled a key from her pocket and unlocked a tall cupboard. The shelves were a jumble of string, glue pots, and fabric scraps, like the brightly colored lining of a bower bird's nest. Muttering to herself, Miriam rifled through a shoebox.

"Here." Miriam thrust a bony hand toward Ally. A photo quivered between her fingers. "This is Yusra Hussain."

Ally's heart leaped. It was the nurse from her mother's photos. She was out of uniform, leaning back in a swing, long hair streaming behind her, wearing that same tell-it-as-it-is smile. A two-story house with gray and white trim sat in the background. Beyond that, purple-flowering tamarisk trees framed a line of silvery water.

"I took that photo in Yusra's garden on Eighty-Second Avenue, by the river," said Miriam. "Her mother served the most delicious baklava I'd ever eaten."

"So this is Yusra, my mother's friend." Ally held the photo tight. If Miriam hadn't been watching, she would've pressed it to her heart. "Do you know where I can find her?"

"Yusra can't help you," she said slowly. "You should leave it alone."

"What do you mean?" said Ally.

"Some things are best left in the past."

Ally frowned. "That's what my father always said."

Miriam held out her hand for the photo. Reluctantly, Ally passed it back. The older woman put the photo back in the shoebox and locked the cupboard.

"I'm sorry," she said, wiping her hands against the folds of her caftan, "I have another appointment. You better go now."

"You want me to go?" Dismay dragged at the corners of Ally's mouth. "Did I do something to offend you?"

"I'm tired, that's all."

It was obvious that wasn't true. Miriam opened the door to the roof terrace. A rectangle of light slanted through the opening, illuminating a shelf of plaster heads, hands, and rounded hips. Behind the body parts, a portrait of the president, plump-lipped and smiling. Turpentine fumes caught in Ally's throat.

"Would you at least give me Yusra's address or a phone number?" Ally pressed her palms together. "I don't need to mention your name. We can keep this between you and me."

Miriam laughed sourly.

"Didn't anyone ever teach you? Two can keep a secret only when one of them is dead."

The wind had picked up by the time Hatim turned onto Eighty-Second Avenue. Grains of sand bounced off the windshield and scratched at the Passat's rusty flank.

"This doesn't make sense." Ally peered at a grimy oil depot ringed by razor wire. "We should be near the river."

"This is Eighty-Second Avenue." Hatim frowned slightly. "But there's no river out here."

Ally scanned a smattering of houses surrounded by gray sand. None looked like Yusra's home. A guard post appeared on the side of the road. It was a little larger than a phone booth, with a thatched roof being slowly shredded by the wind. The young soldier on duty shielded his eyes as they approached, and Ally pulled her scarf higher over her hair. Hatim threw her a skeptical glance.

"You really know someone out here?"

"Not exactly," mumbled Ally. "I'm looking for a woman who lives on Eighty-Second Avenue. At least, she used to."

"Does she have a name?"

"Yusra." Ally paused. "Yusra Hussain."

"Hussain?" Hatim shook his head. "There's got to be half a million of them in Baghdad."

Ally searched for a flash of purple tamarisk or a glimmer of silver water.

"This is not the most scenic route." Hatim glanced in the rearview mirror. "Maybe we should go back to Arasat Street."

"But she said Eighty-Second Avenue. . . ." Ally squinted at what appeared to be a scrapyard. No one moved about in the wreckage-strewn compound. She wondered if it had been bombed by the United States or Iran, or if its owners went out of business after the sanctions hit and abandoned their plant to the sun and the wind. In Baghdad, it was hard to tell what had been destroyed and what had simply been forgotten.

"If we keep going," said Hatim, "we'll end up near the Rasheed Airport."

"The airport?" Ally's heart accelerated, abruptly, like a runner at the bang of the starter's gun. Rasheed Airport housed the regime's grounded air force jets. It was the sort of location that embassy security had warned her to avoid. The authorities wouldn't take kindly to foreigners who ventured there, diplomatic status or not. "We should turn around."

Hatim nodded with relief and made a U-turn at a small gas station.

There were no jokes about kangaroo stew or emu pie on the journey back to Karadah market. After Ally paid and unbuckled her seat belt, Hatim motioned for her to wait.

"Miss Ally, I am always happy to drive you." He lowered his gaze to his lap. "But I like to stay near the market. Much better for you too, if you stay close to this neighborhood. This is a nice area, but other places, other people . . ."

Slowly, he raised his eyes. They were like mine shafts, with truth glimmering at the very bottom. He didn't say anything. Didn't mouth any words. Instead, he allowed her a glimpse, rare and dangerous, of things they both knew, but couldn't speak aloud. It was intimate, in a way that made Ally ache.

"I understand." A lump formed in her throat.

Hatim turned away and stared through the windshield.

"I don't want you to get in trouble," he said. "That's all."

He kept his eyes on some undefined point in the distance, until long after Ally closed her door and disappeared down the street.

The wind slammed the front door shut behind Ally. She hurried to her desk and flipped open her laptop, determined to write everything down while it was still fresh in her mind. As the laptop powered up, she struggled to make sense of what she'd learned from Miriam. Her mother? A communist?

Ally's hands hovered above the keyboard. Finally, with a clack, her fingers hit the keys.

Radical art and radical politics.

She eyed the words on the screen dubiously. It was true, the 1970s was a freewheeling time in Baghdad. But were young women really banding together to agitate for political change? Ally reached for the small collection of memoirs and textbooks that Peter had brought from Dubai and selected a history of Iraqi politics. It fell open to an image from 1958, when the Iraqi army rebelled against a puppet king installed by the British. In the grainy photo, the mutilated body of the crown prince dangled from an ornate balcony.

Ally grimaced and turned the page to a timeline of coups, crises, and countercoups, stretching through the sixties and seventies. She ran her finger down a long list of political groups: pan-Arab Nasserites, social democrats, Baathists, Kurdish nationalists—and communists. It said the communists had enjoyed great popular support, but by the end of the seventies their leaders had largely been exiled, executed, or locked up.

Ally put down the book and stared at her laptop.

Radical art and radical politics.

Again, her fingers tapped the keys.

Yusra Hussain, 82nd Avenue. By the river?

She thought back to the stretch of lonely roadway, the thatched guard post, the wind whipping up gray sand like spray from a dirty wave. She opened the textbook again, and her breath stopped dead in her throat. The final chapter of the book had been ripped out. All that remained was a row of fragile white teeth pressed against the spine.

Ally was certain the chapter had been there before. She remembered one photo in particular—a still from a video taken just days after Saddam assumed power. It showed a parliamentarian being marched from a grand hall, the whites of his eyes wide and rolling, like a terrified calf's. In the background, Saddam puffed on a cigar. A list of sixty-eight names dangled from his hand. Those sixty-eight men were marched off, one by one, and shot. A few were spared, but only after they were made to gun down their fellow parliamentarians.

Ally leafed forward and backward, pulse accelerating with each page. But the photo and the chapter on Saddam were gone. The wind rattled the front door, startling her. She imagined the mukhabarat testing her locks, slipping inside, sifting through her photos, tearing pages from her books, copying the files on her laptop.

Yusra Hussain, 82nd Avenue.

A shiver inched down Ally's spine. She'd intended to record every detail of her visit to Miriam's house, the talk of communism, the unsettling ride through the wasteland of Eighty-Second Avenue. She wanted to document that painful flare of honesty in Hatim's cinnamon eyes. She wanted to honor it the only way she knew how, to put it down in words, make it permanent, refuse to allow it to drift away like dust.

She sighed and dug her fingers into her forehead. She couldn't write it down. None of it. She couldn't risk the mukhabarat seeing Hatim's name. Or Yusra's. Or words like *Communist Party, radical politics*, and notes on mutilated kings. Wind whistled through the narrow gap beneath the front door, bringing with it sharp grains of desert sand. Ally wondered if the mukhabarat were parked outside, right now, biding their time, while the same wind gently rocked their car.

She rifled through her mother's photos, removed the shots of Yusra, and then stuffed them deep into the pocket of her handbag. She couldn't risk leaving them unattended. Next, she changed the login and password to her laptop. She eyed the screen.

Yusra Hussain, 82nd Avenue.

Gloomily, Ally pressed the backspace key. Letter by letter, the young nurse's name disappeared. The skin on the back of Ally's neck tingled. She glanced over her shoulder and the boxy, wood-paneled television caught her eye. Embassy security had warned about hidden surveillance. Was it possible the television contained a tiny camera, feeding like a parasite off the TV's electrical supply?

She padded across the marble floor and pulled the power cord from its socket. Next, she clambered onto the sofa and tried, unsuccessfully, to peer past the furred slats of the air-conditioning vent. She took the lamp from her desk, unscrewed the bulb, then turned it upside down and inspected the cord snaking from its base. Gingerly, she picked up the phone. Static whispered in her ear.

Ally wondered if the mukhabarat were watching right now or listening in. Did they note down all of her and Tom's conversations? Or had they grown bored of Ally's complaints? Did they go and refill their coffee, let the tape roll on and on, while she moaned about her empty days? She tiptoed down the hall to the bedroom and flicked the light switch. Disgust tickled the back of her throat. Did agents of the mukhabarat watch her and Tom in bed?

Ally crept back to her desk, shoulders hunched. *Yusra Hussain,* she repeated silently to herself, *Eighty-Second Avenue.*

CHAPTER 15

Through the square of stained glass in Rania's front door, her visitor resembled a Picasso: green cheek, purple eye socket, swoop of dark hair.

"Ally?" Rania called. "Is that you?"

"I've come for my painting," the girl called back. "You were going to frame it, remember?"

"One moment." Rania took a deep breath, stitched a smile onto her lips, and unlatched the door.

Ally took a step back.

"Rania, are you okay?" Concern surfaced in her cornflower eyes. "You don't look so good."

Rania hurried past her to the gate and wedged the bolts shut.

"How did you get through the gate?"

"Your friend, Malik, left it ajar." Ally held up Malik al-Bashad's gold-lettered business card. "I met him outside, on the sidewalk. He invited me to visit him at the Ministry of Culture."

"Did he now?" Rania struggled to hide her loathing. A few scant minutes ago, Malik had been in her hallway, running his plump fingers over Hanan's photo once again—erasing all doubt that her daughter was just a passing fancy. He said once Rania's portrait of the president was complete, she should bring both the canvas, and her daughter, to the palace. Uday wanted to inspect his father's gift before it was presented. *To test its quality*, he'd said.

"Did you come alone?"

"My driver brought me." Ally eyed her curiously. "Do you know Abdul Amir? He's Huda's husband."

Rania shrugged noncommittally. She couldn't bear to talk about Huda now. First she had to stop her heart from hammering and scrub the rage and fear from her eyes. She waved Ally toward the stepping-stone path.

"Please go on ahead to the garden while I fetch your painting."

Ally stretched out her hand.

"Are you sure you're okay?"

Rania replied with a tight nod and slipped out of reach. She had a habit of revealing more to Ally than she'd intended. She feared if she let her inside now, poured her tea, and sat across the kitchen table, she'd break down and confess about Malik, Hanan, and the half-finished portrait waiting inside her studio. Maybe she'd let slip about Huda and the mukhabarat. That sort of honesty always felt so good in the moment, but it was a dangerous drug.

"I'm a little busy right now, that's all. Make yourself comfortable in the garden." Rania backed inside and shut the heavy door behind her. Hanan was sitting on the stairs, snacking on a handful of pistachios.

"What are you doing?" Rania hurried over the creaking floorboards. "I asked you to stay in your bedroom."

"I heard your visitors leave," said Hanan. "And I was hungry."

"Well, I've got another visitor now."

A scowl twisted Hanan's features.

"What did I do to make you so ashamed?"

"I'm not ashamed of you, not at all." Rania's chest ached with a mix of guilt, love, and fear. "But right now I've got a client out there waiting to buy a painting."

"Will it be enough to pay our membership at the Alwiyah

Club?" Hanan brightened and sat up straight. "They're showing movies by the pool next week."

"Maybe . . ." Rania kissed the top of Hanan's head and hurried into the kitchen before Hanan could spot the tears in her eyes. Soon she'd have to tell Hanan that her grandmother was coming this weekend to take her back to the farm. She prayed she'd be safe there. At least for a year or two. Then what? she asked herself.

Rania put the kettle on the burner and grabbed a paper bag of tea. Hanan had found it tucked at the back of the pantry this morning—Huda's carefully tied package of numi basra. Rania didn't want to sit in the bittersweet steam of Huda's tea, so after scooping in the leaves she left the water to boil, retrieved Ally's painting from the whitewashed gallery, and carried it out to the garden. Ally was staring at the statue of the mother curled around her child.

"You seem to be drawn to this piece." The wind pulled at Rania's hair. "Would you like me to find out if the sculptor has any smaller works available?"

"Oh, no, don't do that," said Ally quickly. "But tell me, do you work much with this artist? Am I likely to bump into her in your garden?"

"Miriam Pachachi is her name. To be honest, these days I only see her at weddings or funerals." Force of habit made Rania glance over her shoulder to check if anyone was listening. In the 1970s, Miriam had been active in political circles—too active for the authorities, even in that relatively liberal time. It was only her family connections that saved her from prison, or worse.

"Miriam has often been called a black sheep." Rania patted the statue's sun-warmed flank fondly. "Like many artists, she is driven by the desire to communicate. But sometimes you can't put your message into words, so you paint a storm cloud, or you cast it in metal."

"These things that can't be put into words . . ." A shadow passed briefly across Ally's face. Before Rania could ask what troubled her, the young woman removed a chunk of dinar from her handbag. "Please, let me pay you for this painting."

She began to count out her dinar, flipping the blue notes over her finger, one by one.

"Malik al-Bashad was very chatty when I met him outside," Ally remarked. "He said you have a lot of admirers at the Ministry, including him, I suspect."

Rania wondered what else that bastard had said. Had he told Ally that she was painting the president's portrait, that she'd taken money to make the tyrant's eyes sparkle and his lips ruby red?

"Malik and I attended the Baghdad College of Fine Arts at the same time," she mumbled. "It was before I went abroad to study in London."

Ally glanced up from her counting.

"Have you ever thought about moving back to the UK?"

Rania gave a small shrug. She knew it was hard for outsiders to understand, but the idea of leaving Iraq seemed contrary to the laws of physics, as if asking metal to defy the pull of a magnet, or the tide to turn its back on the moon. Iraqis had given their lives for this land, men like Huda's brothers, Mustafa and Ali. Didn't she owe it to them to stay?

From the corner of her eye, Rania saw the curtain in Hanan's bedroom window shift. She remembered the tiny studio she'd rented all those years ago in London's Earl's Court. She'd sit by the window, watch the parade of passersby, and try to imagine all the millions of different places they might end up. Perhaps, back then, she could have stayed in London happily. But now, it was too late. Like gravity, loss kept her pinned in place.

When she first learned of Mustafa's death, grief had run through her body with electrical force. She felt it drill deep into the earth beneath her feet, so deep she thought she'd never move from that spot again. But Hanan was different. If she left now, perhaps she could have a chance at true happiness.

"Forgive me," said Ally, interrupting Rania's reverie. "Baghdad is your home, not London. That was a stupid question."

"No, it wasn't," blurted Rania. She imagined Hanan exploring

London's cobbled lanes, far from Uday, far from Saddam. Free from fear.

"I'm too old to start again." Rania words rushed out like it was their one last chance. "But for a young woman, perhaps it would be different. If she's smart and hardworking, a young woman could make a good life in London. What do you think, Ally? Am I wrong?"

"It's true," she said. "London is one of the world's great cities."

Rania's mind lurched into overdrive. In a year or so, Hanan would turn sixteen. Rania had a cousin in London, as well as friends from her college days. Surely, they'd take Hanan under their wing. And it didn't have to be forever. One day, God willing, it would be safe for Hanan to return.

A gust of wind raced through the garden. It plucked leaves from the eucalypt and sent them spiraling toward the grass. Rania saw nothing of this. Instead, she did math in her head—it would take at least a year to pay the bribes for a passport. Rania eyed the dinar in Ally's hand. For a moment, she felt like a starving woman hovering over a warm loaf of bread.

When her mother arrived this weekend, Rania decided to ask if she had any jewels hidden away, sequestered for an emergency like this. But she suspected they were already in the hands of Basra's moneylenders. Her mother had expensive tastes, and the moneylenders never said no to the sheikha. She eyed the wad of bills in Ally's hand again.

"Did I tell you, my dear, I'm staging a new exhibition? But I must warn you, the works are more expensive than usual. The inspiration is Scheherazade. You know her?"

"Of course," said Ally. "She's the narrator of *One Thousand and One Nights*: 'Aladdin's Magic Carpet,' 'Sinbad's Adventures,' 'Ali Baba and the Forty Thieves,' all those great tales."

Rania shot her a sideways glance.

"Many people know Scheherazade's fables, but they haven't heard the tale of the storyteller herself." She let her words out smoothly, slowly, softly, making Ally lean closer, drawing her in. "Scheherazade told all those stories, one after the other, because if she stopped, her husband, King Shahryar, would have killed her." Rania paused to milk the drama. "He'd already murdered one thousand women—virgins he deflowered in the royal bed, and then strangled the next morning, because he didn't trust they'd stay loyal."

Rania took the bundle of dinar from Ally's hand and handed over her painting.

"Scheherazade had no choice," she said. "She told her king those stories to stay alive."

"I never knew that." Ally glanced at Miriam Pachachi's statue again, like she was seeing it for the first time. "I assumed she created those stories of her own accord."

Rania felt an overwhelming urge to confide in her about the portrait waiting in her own studio. The young woman had a generous heart. She might lend her the money to get Hanan to safety. Even as Rania thought it, a voice inside her whispered, *Don't act rashly. Don't lose your head.*

Ally was the last person she should confide in. The mukhabarat were monitoring her. The cleric and Kareem seemed to have an interest in her too. And there was Huda. It was hard to keep secrets from her. Even if Ally swore secrecy, Rania knew from experience that Huda might worm the truth out. No, for now, it was safest to send Hanan to the farmhouse under the sheikha's protection. A tinny buzz swept through the garden. Rania cast an anxious glance at Hanan's bedroom.

"Ally, can you excuse me a moment," she said, then hurried to the front of the house.

"Rania?" Her cousin Hala's voice floated over the top of the gate. "I've been trying to call but your phone is down."

"I know." She pried the gate open. "It's been playing up for two—" She broke off.

Hala's face was ashen.

"What is it?"

"Your mother suffered a stroke last night. They're transferring her to a hospital in Baghdad. It doesn't look good."

It was not the slap of the orderly's mop against the concrete floor that woke Rania. It was silence. She lurched from her chair and scrambled toward her mother's hospital bed. The heart monitor was dead: no beep, no hiccupping red line.

"Don't be alarmed," said a nurse at Raghad's bedside. She brushed a strand of long gray hair away from the old woman's face. "The power cord was caught around her arm. I'll switch it back on after I turn her. We don't want her getting bed sores."

"What time is it?" Rania's mouth was dry as bark.

"Five in the morning."

The nurse peeled back Raghad's top sheet. Rania averted her eyes. Her mother would hate the ugly feeding tube taped to her nose and the way her skinny limbs poked inelegantly from her dressing gown. She'd once joked that when her time was up, she wanted to go dressed in her furs and gold. As the nurse rolled Raghad onto her side, Rania bumbled about the periphery, fluffing her mother's pillow and feeling thoroughly useless. The nurse pressed a switch on the heart monitor. Raghad's pulse flicked across the screen. Rania eyed her mother closely, hoping for a sign of consciousness.

"The doctor said there's been bleeding in the upper part of the brain," she whispered. "But still, it's not impossible that she'll wake up, is it?"

"I'm not a doctor, but if she is no longer responding to light, sound, or pain, the outlook can't be good." She eyed Rania solemnly. "If the feeding tube was removed, we could keep her comfortable throughout."

"Let her starve to death?" Rania shook her head. "She wouldn't want it."

"I doubt your mother would want you to feel guilty, either."

"There's no avoiding that."

Rania's laugh was fifty percent sob. She'd already betrayed her mother. Even as she sat at Raghad's bedside and stroked her limp hand, her mother wasn't foremost in her prayers. Instead of reciting the Koran as a proper daughter should, all she could think of was Hanan. She'd planned to send her back to Basra, far from Malik's lecherous reach. But now, with Raghad nearing death, her last safe harbor was gone.

Rania pressed her hands to her eyes, desperately trying to think of a way to find money for a passport for Hanan. The regime had long ago taken most of her family's land, just like it did to Basil's clan. Then they drained the marshes and diverted the waters her tribe needed to prosper. But Raghad had sailed on regardless, flying her extravagant flag. She'd barely been admitted to hospital when the moneylenders began to call in their debts. Rania imagined they were stripping the farmhouse right now, taking the rugs and chandeliers, tearing the copper plumbing right out of the walls.

She thought of the envelope of cash that Malik left as a down payment for the president's portrait. Would the finished work earn her enough to secure Hanan's passage out of Iraq? As Rania did math in her head, she cursed the president, his sons, and his enablers. They'd taken so much. Now they denied her the chance to mourn her mother with her whole, undivided heart.

Kareem removed his glasses and tucked them in his shirt pocket. Without the thick lenses, his dark eyes seemed even smaller than Rania remembered from their encounter at the Khan Murjan. He nodded at the old bookkeeper waiting by the door.

"Thank you, haji," he said. "We won't be long."

"Take your time." The old man pulled the door shut behind him, leaving them alone in the cramped back room, surrounded by battered filing cabinets, boxes of computer paper, and messy stacks of manila folders. Rania's throat itched from dust and the faint acid stench of decaying documents. Kareem brushed down a stool and indicated for Rania to sit.

"I was surprised to hear from you," he said. "I thought our business was complete."

"Unfortunately, there have been some problems since we last spoke."

"With your friend Huda?"

"She's not my friend," said Rania, even as an unexpected pang of wistfulness twisted beneath her ribs.

"I'm reminded of that old saying, 'A friend knows better than an enemy how to do you harm.'" Kareem smiled coldly. "I don't want to impose on my bookkeeper's hospitality any longer than necessary. So please tell me, what can I do for you?"

"I need a passport for my daughter, and an exit visa."

"You know that women can't travel without male permission."

Rania's eyes narrowed.

"Your friend the cleric must have rejoiced when that law came into effect."

"Why are we rehashing this? Later we will have the luxury to pick and choose our allies. At the moment, we must take support wherever we can find it."

Rania swallowed down a retort.

"When the time comes, I will find a way to deal with that ridiculous regulation. First, I need a passport for my daughter."

"Why now? The Americans are pledging to rid us of this regime, and suddenly you want to leave?"

"It's—" Rania broke off. Even hidden in the claustrophobic backroom, with its dented cabinets and moldering papers, the words still didn't want to leave her mouth. "It's . . ."

"Yes?"

"It's Uday."

Alarm flashed in Kareem's eyes.

"One of his clique came to my gallery to order a painting. He's come back since. Both times, he said the president's son wants to meet my daughter . . ." Fear squeezed Rania's throat. "I thought I could keep Hanan safe by sending her to my mother in Basra, but now that's impossible."

A small brown moth fluttered from an overstuffed bookcase.

"I understand your concern. I have two daughters myself."

Kareem crossed his arms. "First, we will need four photos of Hanan, plus her birth records and citizenship papers."

"Yes, I can do that." Rania nodded gratefully.

"The fee for your daughter's passport will be two thousand five hundred dollars, plus five hundred dollars for an exit permit."

"Three thousand dollars? How can that be? You told Huda her son's passport would cost nine hundred dollars, visa stamp included."

"Well, Huda is useful to us. She is a mukhabarat informant and that has value in itself."

"That's not fair."

"Surely the most important thing is to get your daughter to safety as soon as possible. So please understand, if you want, how should I say, express service, it costs more."

"Huda pays nine hundred dollars, but I have to hand over three thousand? I was a loyal member of the opposition. Does that not count for anything?"

"From what you told me, Huda's family made plenty of sacrifices for the cause."

"But three thousand—"

"Look here," Kareem cut her off. "Huda may be paying nine hundred for her son's passport, but she won't be getting it any time soon. Once she is no longer of use to us, we may supply her son with a passport, and even that is not certain. In fact, from what I hear, the boy may want to stay and join our fight. But if you want a passport for your daughter quickly, my dear Rania, you will have to pay."

CHAPTER 16

From a picnic bench on a covered pontoon, Ally watched an egret flap along the edge of the Tigris, its long, skinny legs trailing behind. The bird landed with a splash and began to stalk the rushes, beak slicing the water like a scythe. Above it, the sky stretched in every direction, huge and impossibly blue. No wonder her mom called it paradise.

Huda wiped a scrap of flatbread through the remains of a bowl of hummus. A platter of fish bones lay beside it, stripped clean during their lunch of roasted *masgouf.* She pushed a dish of plump olives toward Ally.

"Would you like something more to eat?"

"That was delicious." Ally leaned back from the table and groaned. "But I'll explode if I eat any more."

Halfway up the pebbled bank, a waiter emerged from a mud-brick kitchen. He trudged past a crackling firepit, descended a zigzagging set of steps, and bounced across a gangplank connecting the pontoon to shore.

"Tom's going to regret missing this masgouf," said Ally, as the waiter collected their plates. "You know, I should move up north to Mosul. I'd probably see him more often."

"We can come again when he returns," said Huda. "He'll be back soon."

"Not for another four days." Ally felt a twinge of jealousy. "After the election."

Quickly, Huda pointed to a trio of jade-headed ducks paddling past the pontoon.

"Do you see the birds?"

Ally noted the change of topic. She was tempted to ask if Huda had attended any of the election rallies she'd spotted, with musicians and dancers onstage, and secret police skulking about the fringes. But a voice inside her said, *Why ruin a lovely afternoon?* She told herself to keep quiet, to enjoy this riverside picnic, like her mother had done so often thirty years ago. Ally stared at the limitless sky and wondered, Was her mother up there, with her father, in a paradise colored perfect blue? Guilt prodded her chest. Her father wouldn't want her here, in Baghdad, trying to dig up the past.

"The past is dead, that's what your mother used to say," he answered, every time Ally asked about her or the portrait that supposedly went missing during their voyage from the United States to Australia. "She'd want us to get on with our lives. It doesn't help to dwell."

If she persisted with her questions, he'd go silent. Before too long, Ally knew she'd find him drowning his sorrows in a long-necked bottle of beer, and David Bowie would reappear on the record player in the lounge room.

Young Ally couldn't understand it. Her dad loved her mother, with her adventurous, globe-trotting past. He sought solace in Ziggy Stardust, jetting off in his starship toward an unknown universe. But perhaps, as he listened to Bowie wail that *nothing will keep us together*, he was reminding himself that it was best to stay rooted in the present, feet firmly planted in the safety of his own backyard. It was cold and lonely up among the stars.

Ally tried to stay out of sight. She tiptoed silently up and down the hallway between her bedroom and the lounge room, guilty and fearful of what her questions had unleashed. Her father's pain emanated from the lounge room, growing larger and more palpable with every song, with every trip to the fridge to collect another beer. What would happen if she insisted on answers? she wondered. Her father's grief was almost a creature unto itself. It had a pulse. She was too scared to test it, but she suspected it had teeth too. Teeth that could bite.

Eventually, the neighbors complained about the loud music that went on until dawn, and her grandparents noticed the pyramid of beer bottles collecting by the back door. One day, when Ally was at a friend's house, they staged some sort of intervention. Her father promised to pull himself together. And when Ally got home, her grandma made her promise she'd stop asking about things that made her dad sad.

Her grandma said it was better that way. It did no one any good, she said, rehashing what was gone. It became an unofficial family motto, that refusal to dwell on the past. During the years to come, her mother's memory grew distant and hazy. But the hole in Ally's chest only deepened. Despite this relentless march forward, she knew in her heart something vital had been left behind.

Huda sighed, leaned back in her chair, and pulled her sunglasses over her eyes.

"I could fall asleep right now," she murmured.

The river gently slapped the pontoon's side. Ally searched for fishermen, but there were none out on the water. There were no other diners either. When Huda invited her to lunch, she said the restaurant was a popular spot. But like most Iraqis, she often spoke of decades-old history in the present, as if ordinary people could still sail the river without threat of punishment and had money to spare for fine masgouf.

Like her father's dogged refusal to talk about his lost wife, there was a gap in Iraqi history too. It was as if time, and collective memory itself, stopped when Saddam seized power, when war, sanctions, and tyranny brought the cosmopolitan "golden years" to a bloody end. Nowadays, there was only the glorious past or the future. The pain that came in between, no one spoke of aloud. At least, not to Ally. She wondered if Huda had known all along that the riverside restaurant would be deserted. Perhaps she chose it because there'd be fewer people to witness her consorting with a foreigner. Ally couldn't blame her for that.

"You know what . . ." She pushed her chair away from the table. "I might go for a little stroll and walk off some of that food."

Huda removed her sunglasses.

"A stroll?"

"I won't go far." Ally gestured for her to stay put. "Don't worry."

"Who says I'm worried?" Huda climbed out of her chair and linked arms with her. "It's a perfect day to stroll by the river."

The two women paused at the top of the zigzagging steps. The Tigris burbled below them, sunlight reflecting off the ancient river. From the masgouf firepit, a graceful thread of smoke twisted into the bluest of skies. Ally wished that more people could see what she did: beautiful waters, and a generous friend. Huda and her countrymen didn't deserve the suffering inflicted on them. Huda might pray in a different manner than Ally, bake her bread flat instead of leavened, but underneath that, they weren't so dissimilar. They just wanted the chance to break bread in peace. Ally knew it sounded cliché, but weren't clichés born from a greater truth?

Huda squeezed her elbow.

"I wish more foreigners had a chance to taste our masgouf. They might see Iraq differently if we got to share a meal on the river."

Ally laughed in surprise.

"What's so funny?" Huda looked a little miffed.

"You've got to add mind reader to your list of talents." She draped her arm around Huda's shoulder. "I was thinking the exact same thing."

Huda gestured north toward a line of tamarisk trees with tightly curled purple buds.

"Why don't we head toward Eighty-Second Street?"

Ally stiffened.

"Did you say, Eighty-Second Street?"

She eyed the purple tamarisk and the silver stretch of water. Did Miriam Pachachi misspeak when she said Yusra lived on Eighty-Second Avenue? Did she mean Eighty-Second Street? Ally's pulse jumped at her wrist.

"My mom had a friend who lived on Eighty-Second Street."

"Is that so?" Huda stared at her, but all Ally could see was her own reflection in the dark sunglasses. She glanced over her shoulder. There was no one else on the river road. Only her and Huda, and the breeze hissing through the trees.

"They worked together." Ally dug the yellowed photo of Yusra in her nurse's cap from her handbag. "I don't know which house she lived in, only that it was on Eighty-Second Street, close to the river."

As Huda inspected the photo, the ache Ally carried inside expanded.

"Let's check it out," she said, and set off toward Eighty-Second Street. Huda hurried after her.

"How will you find her?"

"I'll knock on doors." Ally tried to sound confident. "Someone might recognize her."

"Knock on doors?" Huda gaped. "That will never work."

Huda was right, of course. On Eighty-Second Street, doors stayed locked. Windows barred. Occasionally someone cracked open a gate, glanced at the photo, then quickly said goodbye.

"I'm sorry, my dear. It looks like we're in the wrong place." Huda glanced at her watch. "We should go if you want to make it to your aerobics class on time."

Ally spotted a cheerful row of potted geraniums at the very end of the road, abutting the river.

"One last try," she said, and hurried forth.

Huda followed her through the gates of a plant nursery stocked with rosebushes, bougainvillea, and palms of every size and shape. The nurseryman—a skinny fellow in a grass-stained dishdasha— was napping under the fat-leafed canopy of a fig tree. Ally grabbed a lemon sapling in a plastic pot.

"Maybe if I buy something it'll loosen his tongue."

"It's better if I do the talking," said Huda. "Otherwise you'll end up paying a pharaoh's ransom for that little plant."

Huda coughed loudly to wake the old man. He opened one eye, then clambered quickly to his feet. Ally offered an *as-salaam alaikum*, then Huda launched into a stream of fast-flowing Arabic. Ally waited by her side, smiling awkwardly, trying to follow along as the two bartered over the lemon tree.

"He wants fifteen thousand dinar." Huda rolled her eyes. "It must grow golden fruit."

"Tell him he can have it, but first ask him if he knows Yusra." She passed the photo to the old man. Ally thought she glimpsed a flash of recognition in his rheumy eyes. His brow wrinkled, and he muttered a few quick words.

"What'd he say?"

"He says she doesn't live here."

"But he recognizes her, right?"

The old man gazed at the photo, shook his head, and handed it back.

"Keep trying," said Ally. "Ask if he knows of any nurses living nearby. Or maybe he knows where she moved to? The woman we're looking for would be in her fifties by now."

The nurseryman shot an uneasy glance at the gate.

"My dear, this man is not accustomed to foreigners. He'll probably talk more freely if it's just me and him." Huda pressed her arm. "Trust me."

Reluctantly, Ally drifted deeper into the nursery. Overhead, black shade cloth diced the sunlight and patterned her skin with tiny squares. At the river's edge, she stopped and glanced back at the nurseryman and Huda. Hope inflated her lungs as she pictured her mother in this same spot, with the same breeze cooling her cheek.

A little farther down the bank, a kingfisher perched in a weeping willow, motionless, eyes fixed on small fish and freshwater crabs scuttling among the bulrushes. In a flash of blue, the bird speared the water. When it emerged, a fish wriggled desperately in its beak.

"I've got your plant." Huda materialized suddenly at her side and passed her the sapling.

"The old man drove a hard bargain, but I bartered him down for you."

Ally's heart thudded like a mallet against her ribs.

"Did he say anything about Yusra? Does he know where she lives?"

Regret carved an arrow in Huda's brow.

"I'm sorry. He knows nothing."

The ache in Ally's chest expanded again.

"I was sure he recognized her."

"He was confused," said Huda. "He was thinking of someone else."

"Someone else? Who?"

"No one who knew your mom. I double-checked."

"Let's ask him again." Ally started toward the fig tree.

Huda grabbed her arm.

"He doesn't know anything, and I have to get home. Khalid has a soccer game. I can't be late."

Frustration vibrated through Ally's body. Was this truly another dead end? Did Huda really do everything she could to get answers? Or did she just want Ally to stop asking questions? In the empty lot next to the nursery something rustled. The two women fell silent. Huda squinted through the wire fence.

"It's just a lizard. There must be plenty of them hiding in the scrub."

A slab of weathered granite caught Ally's eye. It was engraved with curling script.

"What's that?"

Huda slipped her arm through Ally's.

"Please, we should go. You'll be late for your aerobics class." She steered her toward the gate. "Besides, we've been poking around for too long. People get nervous, you know. Someone might call the police."

CHAPTER 17

Huda pulled the seat belt over her shoulder, and hoped Ally couldn't hear her heart thumping in her chest.

"When that old man looked at the nurse's photo, it seemed like he recognized her." Ally slid into the passenger's seat. "Didn't you think so?"

"Not really . . ." Huda jammed her keys into the ignition and pulled out onto the road. She tuned the radio to Youth FM. The crooning of Spandau Ballet filled the cabin.

"I always liked this band," said Huda, as fish and flatbread did anxious somersaults in her stomach. "The singer has such a beautiful voice. Not as good as Bryan Adams, of course, but still very nice."

A car turned onto the road behind them. Huda glanced in the rearview mirror. Were Abu Issa and the Bolt Cutter checking up on her? She'd seen them before, tailing her.

"Is it possible there's another Eighty-Second Street?" asked Ally.

Huda shook her head. The old gardener hadn't said much about this nurse called Yusra, just a couple of words, but it had been enough to make Huda bite the inside of her cheek.

"Her family used to live here, long ago," the old man had muttered. "But their house was bulldozed. . . ."

He'd lapsed into wheezy silence, but Huda knew the words left unsaid—traitors had their houses bulldozed. That's why, when Ally knocked, people closed their doors and slammed their gates. What was she doing with a traitor's photo in her handbag? Did she have any idea how dangerous that was?

"I felt like the old man recognized Yusra." Ally twisted toward her. "Maybe we can come back another day and try again."

"I put your lemon tree in the trunk of my car." She tried to change the topic. "That old man sure knew how to drive a hard bargain."

"Oh, thank you." Ally fumbled for her handbag. "How much do I owe you?"

"Nothing. It is a gift."

"That's very kind. But, please, I want to pay."

"Keep your money," said Huda. Abu Issa had told her to keep Ally in her debt. He said it would make her easier to control. "Remember, Abdul Amir and I are always happy to help when you want to buy something. Otherwise, those merchants will take the skin off your back."

"You mean, the shirt off my back?"

"The skin is more painful, no?"

Huda navigated toward an elevated freeway. The car behind them peeled away. In the shade of the looping on-ramp, a young boy watched over a flock of yellow-eyed goats.

"Did you know that Rania Mansour's mother suffered a stroke?" said Ally. "She's in hospital in Baghdad."

"My cousin mentioned it." Huda pressed her foot on the accelerator. "I hope the sheikha recovers."

"I was there when Rania got the news."

Huda felt an unexpected twinge of jealousy. She knew it was ridiculous, but when she pictured Ally comforting Rania, a tiny part of her wished she could have been the one to stroke her hair while she cried.

After the call from her cousin, Huda had drifted outside to the carport and searched for her old set of runes. She had a vague idea that they might reveal Rania's mother's fate. After ten minutes of rummaging through the cobwebbed corners of the garage, she found a small cedar box coated in a fine layer of dust. Butterflies fluttered in her stomach. She pried open the lid. Inside lay a small leather pouch, and within that, half a dozen pearlescent seashells, a few tarnished brass coins, pebbles the color of storm clouds, and the fragile bones of a small bird.

It had been twenty years or more since Huda last held the talismans, and when she picked them up, the bird bones crumbled to dust in her fingers. Tears welled in her eyes. She remembered Rania crouched beside her, urging her to empty the bag, to chart their futures in the scattered patterns of bones and coins. They would have been young teenagers then, hiding behind the tall grass near the river at the back of the sheikh's farm.

"What do you see?" Rania had quivered with excitement. "Will I travel to London this year?"

Huda frowned. Rania had only just returned from another year at school in Baghdad, and already she was dreaming of flying away.

"Don't rush me," said Huda.

The tall grass hissed and swayed.

"If Mama leaves me behind on the farm again, I swear, I'll die."

"Must you always be so dramatic?" mumbled Huda. "Surely, some time at home won't kill you."

In years past, Huda would have scoffed even louder, but she'd become wary of tempting fate. Just a month ago Mustafa had sliced his foot on an old knife head buried in a riverbed. Days later, he was struck with a violent fever that set his teeth chattering. Lying on a bedroll in their back room, Mustafa called for *Baba* to bring him a drop of water. Huda shivered at his call. Their father had been dead more than ten years.

Huda's grandmother had tried all the usual remedies—black cumin seed potions, turmeric poultices, and honeyed herb tea. The flame within Mustafa only grew stronger. Grandmother rested her ear again his chest, then dug through her cavernous medicine bag.

"Huda, fetch a candle," she ordered.

When Huda returned, the old healer held a buffalo horn inscribed with powerful *hadith*. Like a ribbon of fine lace, the holy script looped around the curves of the blackened ivory.

"Roll your brother onto his stomach," muttered Grandmother.

She circled the base of the buffalo horn over the candle flame, then, when the bone was warm, she pressed it between Mustafa's shoulder blades. His skin was already so hot, Huda was surprised it didn't sizzle. She stroked Mustafa's sweat-sodden hair, while her grandmother rocked back and forth, whispering prayers. Every time Mustafa moaned, pain twisted in Huda's side. He'd always seemed so invincible. But when she pressed her fingers to his wrist, she felt only a thin quivering thread, easily unspooled, or sliced in two.

She closed her eyes and promised God she wouldn't complain when Mustafa teased her. She wouldn't sulk when he forbade her from joining him and Ali on their hunting trips. *I'll be good*, she pleaded silently, *just let Mustafa live*.

Grandmother pried the bone from the base of Mustafa's neck, revealing a dome of pink flesh. Suddenly, a slender knife glittered in her wrinkled hand.

"Don't hurt him," blurted Huda.

"Shush, girl," growled Grandmother. She pressed the point of the blade into the pink dome at Mustafa's neck. A dozen times she pierced his burning skin. Huda tightened her grip on her brother's hand, as the network of tiny incisions wept clear fluid, not blood. Grandmother repeated the process ten times, covering Mustafa's back with weeping pink domes. When she was done, she shuffled outside to comfort Mama, who was anxiously grinding a mountain of turmeric and cumin seed.

Huda remained, crouched by her brother, their shadows shimmying beneath the yellow candle flame. She whispered the same prayers Grandmother had set in motion, holy words and curlicues of smoke rising to the ceiling. Within an hour, the mounds on Mustafa's back subsided. An hour later, his fever broke too. Only then did Huda allow a tear to crawl down her cheek.

A month later, as she cast her bag of talismans across the silty riverbank, Huda found herself once again holding back tears. Ever since Mustafa's illness, she'd felt the need to keep those precious to her close: her two brothers, Mama, Grandmother, and Rania too. As she searched the scattered bones and shells for signs of faraway places and distant journeys, she wondered, How long would it be before Rania left for good? How far could their bond stretch? Did their blood oath still bind them? Or was it more like that skipping thread at Mustafa's wrist, capable of snapping with a sharp tug?

Rania raised her amber eyes from the runes.

"I heard that Mustafa has been ill." She rested her hand on Huda's shoulder. "I heard you stayed by his side for a week."

Huda blinked in surprise. And relief. Rania had been keeping track of her too.

"Cast your talismans one more time," urged Rania. "Let's see how long it will take Mustafa to recover fully. How long before he's back teasing us? Perhaps this will be the summer when us girls finally take charge."

"The chance would be a fine thing," said Huda.

"I heard your mama makes Mustafa sit three times a day with a warm poultice strapped to his foot. So, while he's laid up, you can show me how to throw his spear. By summer's end, I might even be as good as you."

"As good a shot as me? I don't fancy your luck."

Huda giggled and cast the runes across the sand again. She scolded herself for putting so little faith in their friendship. After all, blood oaths were stronger than distance and time, weren't they?

*   *   *

"Huda, are you okay?" Ally peered at her from the passenger's seat. "I'm sorry, I should have realized you'd be worried about Rania's mom too."

"I'm fine." Huda stared doggedly at the freeway unfurling before them. That wasn't enough to banish the tears from her eyes. "It was the weeping willow back at the nursery. I'm allergic, you see."

Ally eyed her doubtfully.

"I dropped off some food at the hospital for Rania's mom," she said. "I'm not sure what else I can do. . . ."

"Pray for her." Huda worked hard to keep her voice level. Why is it, she thought, that we Iraqis are the least pious Muslims in the Middle East, yet we have the most cause to pray for Allah's mercy?

They sped on, across the southern fringe of Baghdad. Below the freeway, mud-brick huts were scattered about like dice: one-room, crumbling cubes baking in the sun. Dust coated everything. Even the leaves on the poplar trees.

"So this aerobics class I'm taking you to, is it popular?" asked Huda, desperate to change the subject. "Have you met anyone interesting at this class?"

"There's Barbara, she's from Germany. Inez is from Colombia. They're both working for the UN's oil-for-food program."

In her head, Huda repeated the names, Barbara, Inez. Abu Issa usually paid a bonus for details like that, money she stashed away to pay for Khalid's passport. She prayed that the names would keep him satisfied and that he wouldn't ask about traitors or homes razed to the ground.

"You must enjoy this aerobics if you're coming back for the third time this month."

"Fourth time, actually."

"Fourth time?"

The wind thrummed against the windshield.

"Well . . ." Ally looked sheepish. "It was a last-minute thing. The phone was dead, and I couldn't call Abdul Amir. So I hired a driver near the Karadah market."

Huda's jaw unhinged.

"You went in a stranger's car?"

"Don't worry. Hatim is a lovely guy. His wife is a teacher. They've got two little girls."

"That's what he told you? How do you know he can be trusted? He could be anyone."

A robber. A rapist. Or mukhabarat. This "Hatim" could be an older version of the Bolt Cutter, monitoring goings on in the market zone. Huda could picture him: doing the rounds of the meat and vegetable stalls, comparing notes with his informants, checking the coffee shops for malcontents. In the heat of the afternoon, he'd nap in the front seat of his car, dreaming of new punishments to inflict on the disloyal.

"You must call for Abdul Amir. Always. Promise me."

"But I've seen plenty of women take taxis."

But they are not you. Huda grit her teeth. If the mukhabarat knew someone else was driving Ally about, unmonitored, surely she and Abdul Amir would be punished.

"If anything happened to you, Abdul Amir would feel terribly guilty. Mr. Tom would not want you getting in some strange man's car, either."

Ally fixed her mouth in a stubborn line and stared out the window at al-Sha'ab Stadium. The sports arena appeared to be deserted, but everyone knew that in specially built chambers beneath the stands, Uday Hussein tortured athletes who didn't live up to his expectations. Huda couldn't remember exactly when she first learned of the dungeons in the stadium, or who told her about the iron-maiden coffin lined with a thousand spikes to pierce those shut inside. It was one of those facts, universally known but never spoken of publicly: a few whispers, the tilt of a head, the sighting of a footballer with a bloody hole where his ear should have been.

Ally leaned forward. "What's that?"

In a dry gully, a long trailer glinted beneath a web of sand-colored netting. A twenty-foot missile sat in its bed, snub nose angled toward the horizon.

"Oh my God." Ally craned her neck. "That's a missile."

Huda stared doggedly through the windshield. Ally swiveled about.

"You saw it, right?"

"Not really . . ."

"It was right there. A big missile."

"I was watching the road."

Ally stared at her in disbelief.

"So about the lemon tree," said Huda, desperate to change the conversation. "If you really want to pay for it, you can."

"The lemon tree?" Ally's eyes widened. Frustration flickered in their blue depths. She massaged her temples, as if she had a headache coming on.

"It was ten thousand dinar." Huda's lie slipped out smooth as butter on bread. "That's how much I paid."

A gritty wind sliced the muezzin's call into ribbons. Huda probably wouldn't have noticed the call to prayer, but a man in a brown dishdasha had pulled his bicycle over to the shoulder of the road and was rolling out a mat of palm leaves. This was Iraq, and only the most pious stopped on the side of the road to pray.

Huda watched the man and his bicycle dwindle in her rearview mirror, then her gaze fell to her handbag, open on the passenger's seat. Ally's money spilled from its mouth. Ten thousand dinar. Twice what she'd actually paid the old gardener.

Guilt crept through her chest. She eyed the purple notes, with the president's face inked on every one, and wondered, How long before Ally worked out Huda was making money off her—promising vendors she'd get them a good price as long as she kept a cut? Perhaps Ally already suspected her. She'd been in Baghdad for some time now; maybe like everyone else, she'd learned it was best to turn a blind eye.

It was after that, that events became confused for Huda, as if someone had taken a film strip and cut out two of every three frames. She was left with disjointed images—pulling to the curb, removing her key from the ignition, searching for a patch of grass. She didn't have water to cleanse herself before prayer, but later she found grains of sand in her hair, so she must have struck her palm against the soil, blown the dust from her fingers, then run her hands over her face and hair. She had only the vaguest recollection of turning to Mecca and mouthing the *takbir.*

What she recalled most clearly was the scratch of the mustard grass as she pressed her forehead to the ground. The sun burned the back of her neck as she recited prayers for protection over and over, until the words lost all meaning. The wind tossed her words into the sky. *God is great* mixed with fine desert sand and disappeared into the blue.

Later, she turned into her driveway and parked the Corolla in the carport. Huda remained behind the wheel for some time, trying to make sense of her roadside prayer. She told herself she should feel more at peace, but in truth she was more rattled than soothed. When would these lies end?

"Mom, are you hiding in here again?" Khalid appeared at the rear of the carport. "What's wrong?"

Huda shoved the cash in her handbag and clambered from the car.

"Are you hungry, my dear?" she asked. "Did you eat a proper lunch? Let me make you a snack."

From the corner of her eye, she spotted her battered box of childhood keepsakes. She wished with all her heart that the runes had held on to their powers, that the tiny bird bones hadn't crumbled to dust, that she had more than seashells to help her find a way forward.

CHAPTER 18

In Rania's studio, an empty canvas waited by the window, taunting her. Reluctantly, she inspected the photo in her hands. There was the president—in jodhpurs, riding boots, and a tan jacket. He carried a hunting rifle under his elbow. The gun's walnut stock gleamed in the sunlight. He was gazing across Lake Habbaniyah, where fat cattails fringed a sweep of muddy shore. In fields all around, yarrow bloomed among thorny manna trees. The president's face was tilted to the sky, tracking a neat arrowhead of ducks. Uday lurked behind him, smirking.

Rania tried to swallow her revulsion and homed in on the flat-topped blooms of yarrow. Somewhere in her paint box lay half a tube of cadmium lemon. That shade would match. The doorbell buzzed. Rania put down the photo and hurried out to the hall.

"Mom?" Hanan wedged open the kitchen door. "Are you expecting visitors?"

"I'll see who it is," said Rania. "Now, be a good girl, and go up to your bedroom."

Hanan opened her mouth, as if she was going to argue. Rania

planted herself in the middle of the hallway and pointed to the stairs. Hanan sighed and slunk away, but Rania knew she couldn't keep her hidden away forever.

She hurried down the hall, worried that she'd find Malik at the gate. Had he come to inspect progress on the presidential portrait? Or to once again put his hands on Hanan's picture, as if she was a gift he couldn't wait to unwrap? Rania pried open the hall closet and checked that her husband's old pistol was still concealed under the scarves. The bell sounded again.

Outside, Rania peered through the gap in the gate. It wasn't Malik on the sidewalk.

"What are you doing here, Huda?" she hissed. "I thought our business was done."

"I heard the news about your mother," said Huda, clutching a sack of tea to her chest like a pitiful bouquet.

Rania was suddenly struck by a memory of Huda's grandmother pouring glasses of fragrant numi basra as she dispensed advice in the women's quarters of the farmhouse. Rania wanted nothing more than to go back to that time, to when she and Huda would sneak away, lie in the long grass, and dream of the future.

"I'm sorry." Huda turned away. "I shouldn't have come. I'll leave you in peace."

Rania hesitated, then unlatched the gate.

"Come in," she said.

The two women followed the stepping-stones to the garden and settled at a picnic bench in the shade. A crow kept watch, marching back and forth in the pale-limbed eucalypt. Silence gathered about them.

"I wanted to stop by earlier, but I was very busy at work, then of course there was the election. . . ." Huda trailed off and slid her pack of Marlboro Lights across the table. "I hope you managed to find enough time to vote."

Rania felt nauseous as she remembered how she'd ticked *yes* and exited the plywood voting booth with a plastic smile so wide her cheeks ached. The poll monitor was watching her, so she swallowed down her revulsion and joined the woman next to her cheering, *Yes, yes, yes, Saddam.*

"Of course I voted," she muttered. "I don't need more trouble with the regime."

"More trouble? What do you mean?" Alarm flashed in Huda's eyes. "Did they find out about Kareem and the cleric?"

"It's not that."

"What is it, then?"

Rania eyed Huda carefully. Could she trust her with the truth? Despite all the hurt they'd caused each other, they both wanted the same thing—to keep their children safe.

"One of Uday's men has been here." Rania lit her cigarette and drew hard, like she was running a race to see who would burn out first, her or the roll of tobacco. "He wants to take Hanan to his palace."

Huda flinched.

"You can't let that happen."

"You think I don't know that?" Rania exhaled a shaky stream of smoke. "I went to see Kareem. I asked him if he could get Hanan a passport and an exit visa."

"And?"

"He wants three thousand dollars."

"Three thousand?" Huda's mouth fell open. "No one has that sort of money."

"Ally does." Rania sighed. "I thought about asking her for a loan, but it's too risky."

"You're right." Huda frowned. "The mukhabarat are monitoring her. She might let something slip. What about your mother? She must have—"

"Debts. She has huge debts. The farm has been mortgaged twice. Her creditors are already pressuring me."

"I don't understand—Khalid's passport is not costing half that." Huda reached across the table. "We must fix this, for Hanan's sake."

The leaves in the trees hissed. Rania and Huda locked eyes. In that moment, past and future, loyalty and betrayal, all seemed to collide. Rania remembered the moment they sliced their thumbs, mingled their blood, and swore not to keep secrets.

"Kareem and the cleric are lying to you." Truth escaped before Rania had time to change her mind. "They've got no intention of giving Khalid a passport. They're using you."

"How do you know?"

"Kareem admitted it."

High overhead a flock of pigeons turned in a loop, like a necklace of gray beads, and then flapped toward the Tigris.

"That means I need a new plan to keep my child safe." Huda took a deep breath and squeezed Rania's hand. "And so do you."

Huda nudged her cigarette pack closer to Rania.

"Then it's agreed? If Kareem won't help, we'll pay people smugglers to take Hanan and Khalid across the border together. They'll have to watch each other's backs. I don't see another way, do you?"

"If only my mother . . ." Rania petered out. *What sort of daughter secretly prays for death to claim her mother?* she thought. *Surely, I'll burn in hell.*

"I'd take them myself," said Huda, "but the mukhabarat are watching me too closely. At least if I stay, I can tell Abdul Amir that Khalid is having a sleepover at Bakr's house. It will buy some time, enough for the kids to get across the border, at least."

"You're sure Abdul Amir won't help?"

Huda shook her head.

Rania wasn't surprised. No one wanted to give up, flee, abandon their homeland. No matter how much they suffered, Iraqis couldn't let go of the glorious past. They refused to admit that Mesopotamia was dust, that Babylon was desert. Was it inner strength that kept them hoping? Or was it shame that kept them from admitting the truth? Maybe both.

"How much do you think this will cost?" said Rania. "And

how do we know the people smugglers won't take our money, then dump the kids in the desert and leave them to die of thirst?"

"My mother may know someone who can help, but I can't call her up and ask. The lines aren't secure at the embassy, and I'm sure they're monitoring my home phone. I'd have to go to Basra in person."

"There's no time for that." Rania glanced toward Hanan's bedroom window. "All Malik need do is whisper in Uday's ear."

"You're right. We can't delay." Huda dug her fingers into her scalp. "I admit, I'm not surprised that Kareem and the cleric are trying to use me. I'm scared they'll get their hooks into Khalid too."

"What do you mean?"

"Khalid is the sort of impressionable boy that Kareem and the cleric would love to manipulate for their own ends. Not so long ago all he cared about was *Harry Potter* and *Star Wars*. But recently he's started going to a new mosque, and then coming home full of talk about martyrs and holy wars and how he wants to avenge his family's suffering."

Huda stabbed the butt of her cigarette into the ashtray. When she looked up, a cold fire burned in her eyes.

"I remember when his uncle Mustafa said the same thing. Three days later they bulldozed his body into a ditch."

Deep inside Rania, guilt flared like an old wound that should have been stitched.

"I warn you," Huda hissed, "if this goes wrong, you better not leave Khalid to twist in the wind. On my grandmother's grave, if you betray my family again I'll—"

"I'm sorry." Rania's voice cracked like a tea glass dropped on a marble floor. "Truly I am. I tried to save Mustafa and Ali. I went to my father and begged him for help. I cried at his feet."

"Ever since you were a little girl, you had your father wrapped around your finger. He gave you everything you asked for. After your husband died, the sheikh even bought you an apartment in

Basra and let you live there alone. No other widow enjoyed such freedoms. And you want me to believe he refused your pleas to save my brothers?"

"But it's true," whispered Rania.

"Your father had influence." Huda's eyes narrowed till they were thin and sharp as blades. "He could have gone to the authorities and convinced them to spare my brothers. But he never even tried. You were too busy helping your fancy friends, your friends with college degrees and honorable names, too busy to plead for mere village boys."

"I begged my father." Rania pressed her hand to her stinging eyes. "He wouldn't listen."

"The sheikh helped so many in our tribe. Why not my brothers? Why didn't he save them?"

"Because . . ." Rania trailed off. Many years ago, she promised Huda there'd be no secrets between them. She'd sworn a blood oath. Did she really think she could cast that aside without consequence?

"My father refused because . . ." Rania choked up. "He wanted to protect my honor."

"Your honor?" Huda glared. "What are you talking about?"

"Do you remember the first night of the rebellion?" Rania's vision turned inward and traveled back in time to her apartment in Basra, from where she watched tracer fire carve arcs in the night sky. "It was as if the entire city was suddenly alive. We'd been squashed under the regime's boot for so long, barely daring to breathe, let alone whisper what was truly in our hearts. But that night was different. We were frightened, yes. But that night, the first night, we had never felt so free."

In the eucalypt, the crow moaned and shuffled about.

"When the fighting started, my father came to my apartment to make sure I was safe." Rania stared at a crack running through the table, laid silent by a familiar rush of guilt. *No secrets*, she told herself.

"He found me with Mustafa," she said quietly.

"I don't understand." Huda shook her head. "What was Mustafa doing at your apartment?"

"My husband was dead, Huda. That night I was not with his brother, who was meant to take his place. I was not with one of those men with an honorable name." Shame scorched Rania's cheeks, her neck, and the thin skin at her chest. "I was with Mustafa. A village boy."

Shock rose like a moon in Huda's eyes.

"You mean . . . ?"

"For some time, he'd been stopping by to see if I needed help. I had that little car, remember?" Rania's smile was nine parts misery. "Mustafa would check the air in the tires, that sort of thing. Sometimes he would stay and drink a glass of juice. We would talk about the village, about you and your new job. He would play with Hanan. I was lonely. He was too, away from the village."

"You and Mustafa?" Huda stared at her, openmouthed. "How long did this go on?"

"It was only one night." Rania forced herself to keep going. "But you know the type of man my father was—honor, reputation, the family name—nothing was more important to him. When I came begging and pleading for him to save Mustafa, it only made it worse."

She stopped and dragged her hands across her face like she was wiping at a stain.

"If the regime had not done it," she said, "my father would have killed Mustafa himself. And poor Ali, he was innocent of everything."

"This can't be." Huda pressed her hands to her temples. "Why didn't you tell me before?"

"You blamed me for Mustafa's death—and you were right." Rania sighed like it was her final breath. "If I had not been so weak, if I had more self-control, perhaps Mustafa and Ali would be alive today."

"And you encouraged them to fight, to join the rebellion."

"Mustafa had no idea I was involved with that. We never talked about politics, not till that night anyway. I remember the helicopters whirring overhead. From my balcony, we could see tracer fire over the Shatt al-Arab river like a thousand shooting stars."

A gust of wind swept through the garden and made the trees dance.

"I let my emotions take over. But I didn't tell Mustafa to go and fight. That was his doing."

Huda shook her head.

"We were closer than sisters. Why didn't you tell me the truth?"

"My father threatened to kill me if anyone found out." Rania raised her burning eyes. "Be honest. You would have blamed me too. So I packed up my things and moved to Baghdad. I thought it was best for everyone."

Huda opened her mouth as if she was about to argue, but then she stopped and looked away: at the mansion's patchy roof, the insects darting about the citrus grove, the statue of the woman curled around her child. She looked everywhere but at Rania, whose face had crumpled like an old paper bag. Above them, the crow rocked back and forth on his branch, moaning like he could feel their pain.

CHAPTER 19

The telephone on Huda's desk chirruped. She startled, still buffeted by the spinning top of emotions that had engulfed her since leaving Rania's garden—regret for time lost, fear of what was to come, grief, a fragile spark of hope, and a lingering trace of distrust. Could they do this? Could they keep the vows of loyalty they pledged so many years ago, defy the regime, and keep their children safe? The phone chirruped again. Huda took a deep breath and raised the handset to her ear. Even before the caller spoke, she sensed the miles between them, static rushing down the line like wind whipping across the desert.

"Good morning, this is John Wales. I'm calling from Dubai." After five years working at the embassy, Huda could recognize an Australian accent. This man sounded different. British perhaps. "May I speak with Ally Wilson?"

"Sorry, Ally is not here." Huda knew the mukhabarat monitored the lines at every foreign embassy, and she listened for a telltale click or hum beneath the static.

"Ally doesn't know me," the caller continued. "I work at *Business Middle East* magazine with her former colleague, Peter Francis."

The hair stood up on Huda's arms. Peter Francis was the re-porter from the Rashid Hotel, the one who drank tea with Ally while the mukhabarat interrogated her out back.

"Peter is away on leave," the journalist continued. "But the Iraqi government is keen to get more investment, so they've offered us another press visa." He laughed. "Usually, they're as rare as hen's teeth. Would you tell Ally I'm coming? I'd love to meet her."

Huda couldn't hang up soon enough, wishing she could wipe the conversation from existence. Ally had said Peter Francis was a friend of a friend, delivering books for her—not a *former col-league*. Had she been lying all this time?

Huda opened the filing cabinet beneath her desk. A green folder contained a copy of Tom's visa application, with Ally's form paper-clipped at the rear. It listed her occupation as "housewife."

The phone chirruped again. Huda reached for it warily, like it might bite.

"Is this Mrs. Huda al-Basri?" a woman demanded gruffly. "I'm calling from New Baghdad High School."

"Is this about Khalid?" Huda checked her watch. School was over, and Khalid should have been at the amusement park by now. For weeks, he'd been saving his pocket money so he could ride the bumper cars. "Is something wrong?"

"Principal al-Quds wants to speak with you," said the woman. "That's all I know."

Principal al-Quds folded her hands atop her tatty desk. The wood was scratched all over and pockmarked by deep gouges, as if it had been in a knife fight. The concrete wall behind her was bare except for a portrait of the president. The lone window was cracked. The glass had been plastered with masking tape, but the wind slipped through anyway and made a high-pitched keening sound.

"Please, believe me, Khalid is a loyal Iraqi." Huda fumbled with her bag, as if she might find an excuse in its pockets. "He wanted to march with his classmates in the president's victory parade. But he was sick with fever. I made him stay in bed. His absence was my fault, not his."

Huda glanced at Principal al-Quds. The woman was as blank as the wall. She pried open her wallet.

"Our family would like to make a donation to support the school's celebrations of our president's glorious victory." Huda slid all the dinar she had across the battered expanse of desk. "You can decide how to use it, Principal al-Quds, for whatever purpose you think is best."

Principal al-Quds didn't move. She eyed the money like it was a viper slithering among her manila folders and collection of cheap pens. Huda cringed and tucked her hands in her lap.

"I know you have a well-paying job, Mrs. al-Basri," said Principal al-Quds. "No doubt this allows you privileges others cannot afford. But that does not mean your son can flaunt the rules. Not when it comes to demonstrating his love for his country and his president."

"Of course, you're right. It won't happen again."

"Khalid's teachers report other missed classes as well. How do you explain this?"

"I can't . . ." Huda shook her head in bewilderment. "His father and I will make sure he misses no more school, or any other parades. Please believe me, Khalid is a good boy. Please, give him a chance to prove himself trustworthy."

Principal al-Quds stared across the scarred expanse of wood. *What does she see in my eyes?* Huda wondered. *Liar? Sinner? Traitor?* Shame painted her cheeks red. She used to consider herself a moral woman. Now she lied every day, accepted payoffs from the mukhabarat, and negotiated kickbacks from merchants eager to separate Ally from her cash. She blackmailed Rania, a woman who used to be her closest friend. Now, she'd added bribery to her sins.

"I am a mother, like you." Principle al-Quds rapped her fingers on the desk. "So I will not report Khalid's absence from the parade. For the moment . . ."

"Thank you, Principal al-Quds. Blessings upon you, and blessings upon your family."

Bowing and mumbling apologies, Huda backed toward the door.

"Wait." Principal al-Quds flicked her index finger toward the wad of dinar. "Take that with you, Mrs. al-Basri. I'll keep my morals instead."

Huda waited in the parking lot of the Baghdad Fun Park, face still burning with shame, and stared across an artificial lake at the turquoise dome of Martyr's Monument. The fountains in the lake had been switched on to celebrate the president's victory in the referendum, and a veil of spray drifted across the water, through the parking lot, and toward the gates of the amusement park.

Huda counted four guards standing watch at Martyr's Monument, then she glanced at the man in the booth by the entrance to the parking lot. Two more guards slouched by the turnstiles to the amusement park. As if on cue, Khalid appeared behind them. Huda slid out of the Corolla and raised her hand. Khalid waved back and loped through the rows of parked cars.

"I'm starving." Khalid jogged toward her. "What's for dinner?"

"Is that how you greet your mother?" Huda steered him toward a bench overlooking the lake. From there, no one could approach them unnoticed. "Sit down. I want to speak with you."

"I'm hungry," said Khalid. "Can't we talk on the way home?"

"No, we cannot," she snapped. "Sit down."

Khalid scowled and slumped onto the bench.

"I have just come from your school," she said.

Khalid shot her a startled glance, then quickly looked away, across the lake toward the glittering dome rising a hundred twenty feet into the sky.

"I was summoned for a meeting with your principal."

Khalid grew very still. Huda glanced over her shoulder. The old man was still in his booth. The guards at the amusement park paid them no attention.

"Principal al-Quds told me every student marched in the victory parade yesterday—except you. How can that be? Surely, you are not so foolish as to skip a parade honoring the president?"

"I, uh . . ." Khalid swallowed. Out in the lake, the fountains shot jubilant jets of water high into the sky. The sun transformed every drop into its own perfect rainbow.

"Don't you know what happens to boys who do not attend rallies? Don't you know their entire families can be punished?"

Huda flicked an anxious glance at the guards across the lake.

"Do you remember Professor Hafez who used to live on the corner of our street?"

"Sort of . . ."

"Professor Hafez did not march in a rally at his college. So the police came and took him away. They kept him for three days." She turned to Khalid. "What do you think they did all that time? Do you think they drank tea and talked about soccer?"

Khalid studied his boots.

"When Professor Hafez eventually came home, he'd lost his job. A week later, his whole family disappeared in the middle of the night. Maybe they moved somewhere else. No one knows." Huda glanced at the monument. "But it all happened after Professor Hafez skipped that rally."

"I didn't think anyone would notice," mumbled Khalid.

"You must understand your actions have repercussions. For you. For me. For your father."

"What's going to happen?" Khalid's lip trembled. "Am I to be punished? Are we all going to be punished?" His words spiraled into the sky, squeaky with fear.

"I did my best to convince Principal al-Quds to overlook your absence. We have to hope my efforts were enough." Huda knitted her fingers in her lap. "Where did you go on the day of the march?"

"Nowhere, really," Khalid mumbled. "I was hanging around the soccer field, that's all."

"That's all?" Huda glared.

"Dad gave me some money for helping to weed the garden, so I bought a kebab and had a cola on Sadoun Street."

"That parade was for the president. Participation is nonnegotiable."

"But why, Mom?" Khalid clenched his fists. "Why must we parade through the streets, acting all overjoyed, when really we have no choice? Everyone must vote yes or else they disappear, like Professor Hafez."

Huda's heart pounded. Defying her was one thing, the regime another.

"The authorities take note when people fail to show their loyalty." She clutched his arm. "Keep your head down and follow the rules."

"Like you and Dad?"

"Yes." Huda sighed. "Like me and Dad."

"So I should take money from the mukhabarat too?"

Huda flinched as if Khalid had cursed the prophet. She wanted to take him home and scrub his mouth out with soap. The boy snatched a piece of gravel from the ground and hurled it at the lake.

"Do you think I haven't noticed all the suspicious chats in the sitting room with Abu Issa and his friend?"

"Abu Issa? Who told you his name?"

"He came over one time when you were at work. He asked me if I'd thought about joining the Lion Cubs. He said loyal young men get rewarded by the government."

Huda paled.

"Don't worry." Khalid kicked his foot against the ground. "I didn't tell him that I would sooner die than fight for this government. I didn't tell him the regime murdered my two uncles and ten thousand other good Shi'a."

"Shut your mouth, Khalid." Huda's voice leaped from her throat, wild as a dog. "Have you gone mad?"

"Me, mad? What about you? You drink tea with the mukhabarat in the morning, then in the afternoon you sneak off to cry over that photo of Uncle Mustafa and Uncle Ali. You know the one—you hide it in your bedside drawer instead of keeping it by the front door where it should be." He scooped another pebble from the dirt and threw it at the gushing fountains. "What would your brothers think of you and the mukhabarat? May God keep their martyred souls close."

His words hit Huda like a punch to the jaw.

"Khalid, you can't talk like this. Especially not now."

"Not now? Then when?"

"Have patience, my son." Huda squeezed his hand. "But for now, I beg you, be quiet, follow the rules, show respect for the government."

He scowled. "It's all lies."

"Please do what I say—don't skip class. Go to school, and profess your love for the president even when you want to bite your tongue so hard it bleeds. Our situation is going to change. I promise you."

Khalid laughed sourly.

"I hope you don't think the Americans are going to rescue us. We Iraqis must take control of our own destinies."

Control our own destiny? Huda remembered her brother Mustafa saying those same words. Fear snaked through her body and left her rooted to the spot. Khalid glanced past her shoulder. Suddenly, he looked much younger, like he was still a little boy.

"Mom?" His eyes widened. "What's going on?"

Huda swung about. A police car sped into the parking lot. The old man had left his booth and was standing in the middle of the road with his hands above his head, like he was appealing to God. Another man ran toward him, clutching a rifle. The two guards by the amusement park rushed toward the police car. Over by Martyr's Monument, four guards became eight.

Huda hauled Khalid to his feet and hustled him into the Corolla. More cars lurched into the parking lot. Civilians this time, slamming on their brakes, paying no heed to the white bays painted on the tarmac. Their drivers jumped out and sprinted inside the amusement park. Moments later, a woman hurried though the turnstiles, herding four children before her.

"Mom, what's going on?" cried Khalid.

"Quiet, my son." Huda stamped her foot on the accelerator. "Put your seat belt on."

As they sped toward the exit, she cranked her window down. The old man was still out in the street, wandering in dumbfounded circles.

"What is it, haji?" she cried. "What's happened?"

"It's insane!" he yelled. "Why would he do this to us?"

A gunshot echoed in the distance. Huda thought she saw a cloud of dust advancing from the west, but maybe it was fear drifting across the city, smelling of cold sweat, honking horns, making grown men bellow for their children and women pray for God's mercy.

"Go home. Lock your doors." The old man clutched his bald scalp. "It's a presidential amnesty—every thief and murderer in Iraq is out on the streets."

Huda marched Khalid through the front door. The house was quiet. The television was off in the sitting room.

"Go to your room," she said curtly. "I will call for you after I have had a chance to talk with your father about a suitable punishment."

"But, Mom—"

"No argument, Khalid. Understand?"

He slunk to his room and pulled his door shut. Huda checked the locks on the front door and the windows, then hurried through the kitchen. Abdul Amir was outside at the patio table, nursing a can of beer. The jut of his chin said he was spoiling for a fight.

"You won't believe the news." She sidled out the back door. "The authorities have emptied the jails. All the inmates are out on the streets."

"That's madness." Abdul Amir bumped his knee as he lurched from the bench. Three empty beer cans wobbled atop the picnic table.

"The ticket seller at the amusement park said the president wanted to thank the people for his election victory. Murderers, rapists, thieves—they're all walking free," she said. "How could he think this would make us happy?"

"As if we don't have enough to worry about." Abdul Amir downed the rest of his beer in one large gulp and stomped toward the kitchen. "I'll check the locks."

"I took care of it. I fastened all the windows too."

Abdul Amir paused. He made a noise halfway between a sigh and a growl and continued into the kitchen. He returned a minute later with a fresh beer and that furious set to his jaw.

"You've taken care of everything already? Then I guess there's no point in me doing anything." His laugh was as rough as a burr. "Everyone knows, Huda always does it better. First you were the star pupil at secretarial school and then the model employee. And when your pathetic husband loses his job, you get an even better position working at an embassy." He flung his arms wide. Beer leaped from his can and splashed on the pavers. "How come everything always goes your way?"

Huda took a step back.

"Come now, Abdul Amir. What sort of talk is this?"

"I used to think you were blessed, all these gifts falling into your lap one after the other. Now I realize it's all because you know how to work the system."

"Me?"

"How else could a barefoot village girl like you end up with air-conditioning, a refrigerator, a television, and still have enough money left over to buy baklava and paint her toenails a different color every week?"

"That's not fair." Huda jammed her hands on her hips. "This is the beer talking."

"The beer?" Abdul Amir croaked out a laugh. "Did you notice I am once again back to drinking Turkish dishwater? No expensive Amstel for me."

Huda glanced at Khalid's window. The curtains were drawn.

"What has got into you?" she whispered.

"I met with Abu Issa today. I had information I figured was worth at least six cold Dutch beers and a box of sweets for you." Abdul Amir wiped the back of his hand across his mouth. "Abu Issa said you'd already given them much better information about that stuck-up bitch Ally Wilson. He laughed and told me to ask my wife for an allowance."

Abdul Amir hurled his can at the gathering dusk. It cartwheeled past Huda, spraying ribbons of beer, and clattered against the back fence.

"Abdul Amir, calm down."

The phone rang inside the house.

"Where's the money Abu Issa paid you?" said Abdul Amir. "What have you done with it?"

"I don't have any money." Huda prayed he hadn't found the stash of bills in the tea canister at the back of the pantry.

"You're saying Abu Issa is lying?"

"He is mukhabarat. He wants us to lose trust in each other. It makes his job easier. And if he can humiliate a decent man, more fun for him. I don't—"

"Mom?"

Khalid materialized at the kitchen door.

"Mrs. Wilson is on the phone."

Huda pressed her hand to her forehead. Amid the chaos, she'd almost forgotten about the journalist who called Ally a former colleague. Surely the mukhabarat would want to know more.

"Tell Mrs. Wilson I'll call her back later."

"Are you sure?" Khalid's gaze flicked nervously between her and Abdul Amir, who'd stalked off and was glaring at the columns of burning gas. "She sounded sort of upset."

Huda closed her eyes wearily.

"Go tell Mrs. Wilson I'll be with her in a minute."

Huda hovered for a moment at the edge of the lawn, hoping the old Abdul Amir might miraculously return, take her hand, and point out a new flower in the garden bed. As she turned to go inside, she noticed weeds had sprouted in the grass at her feet.

The Corolla jerked to a halt outside Ally's gate. Huda scrambled onto the sidewalk. Cars raced around the traffic circle, honking furiously, their headlights carving tunnels in the swirling dust. Ghassan cracked open the gate.

"What's going on, Ghassan? Ally said you have some sort of family emergency." Huda glanced past his shoulder. Ghassan's wife was in the doorway of his hut, wiping her eyes with her abaya. "You must have heard the news. They've opened all the jails."

"I know, believe me. My wife has been at Abu Ghraib. Her younger brother was sent there two months ago for stealing a car. She had the sense to come home when she couldn't find him, but my mother-in-law is still out there. She's vowed to check every jail in Baghdad."

"Doesn't she realize it's not safe?"

"The boy is her youngest. Her baby. I need to go find her."

"But if you leave, who's going to stand guard here?"

Ghassan shrugged. "I'm sorry."

The front door rattled, and Ally pried open the door. Huda glanced at Ghassan.

"Please wait a couple of minutes while I talk with Ally."

She made her way inside reluctantly. In addition to the telephone lines, Ally's house was sure to be bugged. She prayed the girl wouldn't say anything stupid.

"Is Ghassan's wife okay?" Ally locked the door behind her. "I couldn't understand everything he said, but I think her brother has gone missing."

Huda wasn't sure if it was the light of the low-hanging chandelier, but Ally seemed a little feverish. Her eyes glowed too brightly.

"I told Ghassan if he needed to go, I'd be okay, but honestly, I'm a little nervous."

Ally paused. She glanced at the chandelier and then eyed the television. Huda realized that she too must suspect someone was listening in. She wasn't as naive as she appeared. Not by half. Ally lowered her voice.

"Is something going on?"

"Ahh, well . . ." Huda tried not to be obvious, but habit took over, and she too scanned the lights, lamps, and air-conditioning vents. "The government has decided to make a prisoner amnesty. It's a reward for the president's victory in the election."

"What do you mean?"

"All the inmates have been freed."

Ally's jaw unhinged.

"All the prisoners are out? Now? Roaming the streets?"

"Where's Mr. Tom? Isn't he back from his trip up north?"

"A meeting got pushed back till tomorrow morning. He decided to stay an extra night." The girl kneaded her hands together. "When he hears about this, he'll freak out."

"As any husband—" Huda stopped herself. She didn't want to be heard criticizing the president's gift to the people. "In that case, Ghassan must definitely stay here tonight. He can't leave."

"I don't think I can make him stay, not if . . ." Ally trailed off. She turned to the window and gestured at its thick bars. "This place is like Fort Knox. I'll be safe in here, right?" She hugged her arms around her chest. "Right?"

Huda stared at the floor and wondered, Were the mukhabarat copying down their conversation, recording the knock of the wind against the windows and the frantic honk of the traffic outside? Did they analyze the silence too, that rose now and ran its chilly fingers along the women's spines?

Abdul Amir emitted a rumbling snore. Huda squinted at the clock on her bedside table. The neon dial read 1:15. She sighed, slipped out of bed, and padded down the hall to Khalid's bedroom. He lay motionless on his narrow bed, Chewie tucked tight under his arm. Huda watched his chest rise and fall beneath his pajama top. Tears welled in her eyes, so sudden it frightened her.

Huda crossed to Khalid's window and peeked through the curtain. Ally was in the garden, rocking back and forth in the swing seat, watching the flames of al-Dora. She'd been right—Ghassan could not be convinced to stay. Huda couldn't leave her alone, not with thousands of criminals newly freed from their cells, so she'd phoned Abdul Amir to warn she was bringing the young woman home with her. He'd retreated to his bed, and stayed there, reading the sports section, until his six Turkish beers lulled him to sleep. He'd been snoring ever since.

Huda crept from Khalid's room, tiptoed through the kitchen, and slipped out the back door. A hoot of laughter drifted over the fence, followed by the salty-slick aroma of lamb roasting on a spit. Three doors down, the Rani family was celebrating.

Ally clambered to her feet.

"I couldn't sleep."

"Me too." Huda waved her back into the swing seat. "Sit, sit. We can keep each other company."

"How's Abdul Amir's migraine?"

"He's all right, my dear." Huda ferreted through the pocket of her dressing gown for a pack of cigarettes and made much ado of flicking the flint on her lighter, nursing the tiny flame, all so she could avoid eye contact while she lied. "It usually takes him a day to recover, so he may be a little blurry-headed tomorrow."

Huda sat on a bench by the orange trees. The moon fell through the quivering leaves and dappled her skin with shadows.

"I'm sorry I've put you out," said Ally. "Tom is sorry too."

"Well, he must attend to his duties."

"His embassy duties?" Ally smirked. "What about his manly duties?"

Huda smothered a laugh.

"You tell me. You're the one bringing it up."

"What's that?" Ally cupped her hand to her ear. "Did you say, getting it up?"

Huda laughed out loud. "Who knew diplomats' wives were such brazen hussies."

"How dare you." Ally stuck her hands on her hips and feigned offense. "I'm not a sleazy diplomat's wife. I'm a high-class *Russee* hooker. Just ask any man driving by. He'll tell you."

The women tittered like sparrows.

"In all seriousness . . ." Huda blew out a stream of smoke. "How is the pay for a high-class hooker? I need some extra cash."

Ally cackled and collapsed sideways onto the swing set. Huda doubled over, shaking with laughter. *You're hysterical,* a voice inside her snapped. *Don't forget—Abu Issa will want answers.* Huda's laugh petered out. If she had to pry into Ally's past, best to do it here, in the garden, with their words camouflaged by the rustling leaves and the music from the al-Ranis' party.

"Someone called the embassy today, wanting to speak to you."

"Me?" Ally sat up straight. "Who was it?"

"A journalist."

"Really?" The word sidled slowly from Ally's lips.

"He works with your friend, Peter Francis." She peered at the young woman on the swing, but it was too dark to read her eyes.

"Did he say what he wanted?"

"He said you used to work with Peter Francis." The sour taste of betrayal rose in Huda's mouth—even though she had done worse to Ally, ten times over. "A *former colleague,* that's what he called you."

"Thanks for letting me know." Ally feigned nonchalance. "Did I mention that Tom asked me to thank you? I'm glad I called him. He'd just heard about the amnesty himself."

Huda frowned. Did Ally really think she could dismiss her questions so easily?

"What did the journalist mean by *former colleague?* Are you a journalist?"

"No, of course not," said Ally quickly. "I was a secretary."

"A secretary?" Huda almost laughed out loud.

"That's right." Ally folded her arms across her chest. "But in Australia we call it an executive assistant."

"Then why did you put 'housewife' on your visa form?"

"You checked my visa form?"

"Of course not." Huda withdrew deeper into the moon shade of the orange tree. "I handle the paperwork for all the embassy visas. I remember yours said 'housewife,' that's all."

"My, what a good memory you have." Ally sighed, long and loud. "The truth is, I got laid off almost six months before I filled out that form. Budget cuts, my boss said." She stopped rocking in the swing seat and kicked her heel against the lawn. "I tried to find another job, but there wasn't anything out there. After months of looking for work, I didn't feel I had the right to call myself anything but a housewife."

Huda couldn't picture Ally as a secretary, but part of her story had a vague ring of truth. She prayed the explanation would satisfy Abu Issa. At the al-Ranis', someone turned up the stereo.

"Sounds like they're going to be partying till dawn." Ally paused for a moment. When she spoke again, her voice was softer than the breeze. "What did your neighbor do, anyway? Did he say the wrong thing? Did he make a joke he shouldn't have?"

Huda took a deep breath.

"He killed his wife."

Ally's head snapped back like she'd been clipped on the chin.

"And his family throws him a party?"

"Tonight he has a party. Maybe tomorrow his dead wife's brothers come to settle the score."

Ally stiffened.

"What do you mean?"

"When people cannot get justice, they take matters into their own hands." Huda knew that among the crowd outside Baghdad's jails, some were eager to greet loved ones. Others were waiting to take revenge. She remembered that white-hot hunger well.

moment, Huda pictured herself leaping on the Bolt Cutter's back, tackling him to the ground, and gouging his eyes out. She'd do it if she had to—like one of those legendary mothers who fought off wildcats, lifted crashed cars, or performed superhuman acts of strength to save her child.

"Please, follow me." She shepherded the men toward a tall wooden gate at the side of the house, then down a path of concrete slabs to the backyard. "Take a seat at the picnic table. I'll fetch tea."

"I'll take a slice of *khobuz*, if you have it." Abu Issa smiled superciliously. "Jam too."

Huda headed to the kitchen, bristling. She wasn't running a cafeteria. She put the coffee on the burner, then ducked down the hallway to Khalid's room. As she opened the door he jerked away from the window, eyes bulging.

"Is it about the parade?" he cried.

"Not at all." Huda hugged him to her chest, but not as tightly as she wanted, fearing if she did that she might never let him go. For Khalid's sake, she needed to stay calm. She looked him in the eye, unblinking. "This is not about you."

Khalid pulled away from her and peeked through the curtains once again.

"How do you know?"

"Because I do," she said firmly. "Now get away from the window."

She peered past his shoulder. The Bolt Cutter looked like a gorilla lounging on her swing seat. She pointed to a comic lying on Khalid's bed.

"Stay in your room and read quietly. I don't want to hear a sound from you. Understand?"

"But, Mom—"

"You're already in serious trouble, young man. Don't make it worse."

She left him sulking and sniffing, and returned to the kitchen. She put together a tray of coffee, khobuz flatbread, and ramekins

"When it comes to family," she muttered, "people do what they have to."

When she looked up, Ally was curled up, knees tucked to her chest.

"My cousin Sara, she . . ." The young woman paused and stared up at the sky. "Her boyfriend beat her to death. She was twenty-eight years old."

"Oh, my dear, I didn't realize," said Huda. "I'm so sorry."

She'd always imagined life outside Iraq to be one bright, shiny day after another, where girls like Ally zipped about in cute convertibles, joined their friends for cupcakes as big as a child's head, then went for a romantic dinner with a handsome man like Tom. At times, she envied Ally's easy life, her freedom, the luck that saw her born in a country free from strife. But of course, fate didn't pause for borders, or wealth, or age.

"Nights like tonight," said Ally, "I can feel all the miles between me and my family."

She stared up at the moon as if she were searching its craters and dark seas for a different ending. Guilt ballooned beneath Huda's ribs. She wished, for what seemed like the thousandth time, that the two of them could be free to speak their minds. She wondered if Ally would ever consider helping Khalid and Hanan, hiding them in an embassy Land Cruiser and spiriting them out of the country. Even as she thought it, she knew she'd be a fool to ask. A reckless fool.

Just like she'd told Rania, the mukhabarat were watching her. No doubt her phone and home were bugged. Ally didn't have decades of practice in biting her tongue. One slip, one whisper, and it would all be over. Huda rose from the bench and squeezed in on the swing. Another peal of laughter hurdled the fence. Ally flinched at the sound. Huda felt grief pulse through the young woman's body, like it did through her own.

Bleary-eyed, Huda and Ally shuffled out the front door and into the morning sunlight.

"Careful," called Abdul Amir. He put down the long-handled pruners he'd been using to trim a tree in the front yard. "The wasps are agitated this morning."

No wonder, thought Huda, eyeing the papery hive dangling from a branch just beyond their wall. The insects would have been disturbed by the al-Ranis' all-night party, like the rest of the neighborhood. Not that anyone could sleep soundly, thanks to the president's amnesty.

"How are you feeling this morning, Abdul Amir?" said Ally. "Is your headache gone?"

"It's okay." Abdul Amir avoided her eyes and peeled off his garden gloves. "You want me to take you home?"

Huda touched Ally's elbow.

"Promise me, you'll come straight back if Ghassan is not there."

"I will, thank you. Tom should be home in a few hours too." Ally smiled, but Huda detected a glimmer of unease in her eyes.

"If he is late, you must call me," she said. "I'll be here all day, listening for the phone."

In addition to the amnesty, the president had declared a national holiday. *Hip, hip, hooray,* she thought sarcastically. At least it would give honest people time to reinforce their locks and the bars on their windows. Abdul Amir wiped his hands on a towel and headed to the carport. Once he was gone, Ally swiveled toward Huda.

"I owe you," she said quietly. Huda went to wave her off, but Ally reached out and trapped her hands. "I learned an Arabic proverb recently: 'a true friend walks in when the rest of the world walks out.'"

Huda's throat began to ache. "It was nothing."

"Not everyone is brave enough to open their home to a . . ." The young woman blushed and trailed off. "I've been enough trouble. I should go now."

Huda tried to muster an appropriate reply: *No problem at all. You're welcome. Come any time.* But the words refused to obey.

Instead, Huda stepped forward, wrapped her arms around Ally, and hugged her. In the carport, the Corolla rattled to life.

"I'll open the gate," muttered Huda, blinking back tears.

As Abdul Amir reversed into the street, Huda collected his garden gloves and rested the long pole topped with pruning blades against the house. An agitated wasp flew in from the sidewalk and buzzed her like a kamikaze. Huda retreated to the front door, but as she reached for the knob a low burble stopped her hand. Faint at first, the familiar growl of the Oldsmobile's V-8 engine grew louder. Huda wrenched open the door and stuck her head into the foyer.

"Khalid!" she hollered, heart loud in her chest. "I have visitors. Stay in your room."

The Oldsmobile pulled up on the far side of the gate. Huda had been expecting this visit. That didn't stop goose bumps from prickling her spine. She knew there was no hiding the journalist's phone call. In fact, she'd called and left a message for Abu Issa, knowing he might already have seen a transcript of the call or listened to a tape recording. On the far side of the garden wall, a car door slammed. Then another.

Huda closed her eyes. She told herself to focus, to expel all distractions, to turn to her center, like her grandmother did when she was seeking insight. Huda took a deep breath, straightened her shoulders, and returned to the gate.

"As-salaam alaikum." She slid the bolt loose.

"Wa alaikum as-salaam." Abu Issa strolled in from the sidewalk. The Bolt Cutter lumbered after him.

"Did you get the message I left last night?" Huda bobbed her head at Abu Issa. "A foreign journalist contacted the embassy."

"Let's talk about this inside," he said.

"Inside?" Huda planted herself between the men and the front door. She was almost certain this visit had nothing to do with Khalid skipping the president's victory parade. But what if she was wrong? What if Principal al-Quds had turned them in? For

of butter, date molasses, and buffalo cream, then carried it all out to the garden. Abu Issa had made himself at home, legs stretched out, basking in the sun at her picnic table.

"Please, take some food and drink," she said, hoping he would choke on it.

Abu Issa tore off a strip of bread and dipped it into the molasses.

"So, a journalist called the embassy." He dunked the jammy morsel in the cream. "What did he say?"

"His name is John Wales. He said he worked with Peter Francis, the journalist Ally visited at the Rashid Hotel."

Abu Issa stared at her with the same dead eyes she'd seen during their encounter at the ice cream parlor, when he first threatened to put Khalid in Uday Hussein's death squad. Huda eyed the butter knife resting on the tray, imagined it a dagger.

She began to recount the phone call. All the while, she had a numb, out-of-body sensation, as if she were an invisible spectator watching from above: the two men in their leather jackets, and her, arms folded over her chest, making herself as small as she could possibly be.

"So the foreign woman is a journalist. And a liar." Abu Issa and the Bolt Cutter grinned at each other. "This is very useful."

Huda glanced at Khalid's curtained window. She remembered their argument by Martyr's Monument, and the disgust in his voice as he asked, *What would your brothers think of you . . . ?*

"I think you're mistaken about Ally." The words slipped out before she could stop them. "It's true she worked with Peter Francis at some business magazine in Australia. But she wasn't a journalist. Ally was a secretary, like me."

Abu Issa stared at her.

"A secretary?"

"In Australia they give it a fancy name, *executive assistant.*"

Abu Issa pushed his coffee aside.

"And you believe her?"

"Yes," she said firmly. "I believe her. I've done what you asked, and fooled her into trusting me. She tells me all sorts of things you wouldn't expect. Just last night she told me about a beloved cousin who died young. She even told me about, well . . ." Huda paused for dramatic effect. She glanced at the Bolt Cutter, then bent close to Abu Issa and whispered, "She confided about her *relationships* with her husband. It's not entirely satisfying, apparently."

"Unsatisfying?" Abu Issa smirked. "That's no surprise. He has no mustache. He wears short pants in public. Only a hairless boy would do such a thing."

"I'm sure she was telling the truth." Huda giggled slyly. "About her husband, her work at the magazine, all of it."

For the next fifteen minutes, as Abu Issa sipped coffee and took his fill of bread and cream, Huda told tales, made up gossip, complained about Ally, and poked fun at Mr. Tom. She felt like a courtier from ancient times desperate to keep a fickle caliph happy. When the coffee and khobuz were finished, she escorted the men to the front gate.

"*Ma'al-salāmah.*" She fashioned her lips into a smile. "Go with peace."

She closed the padlock and waited for the Oldsmobile to growl to life. Instead, Abu Issa and the Bolt Cutter dallied on the sidewalk, puffing on cigarettes and trading spiteful jokes.

"That hairless girly-boy can't get it up."

"I should give the slut a taste of a real Iraqi man."

Rage rose in Huda's chest, a hot rage that blinded her and roared in her ears. She darted silently across the lawn, retrieved Abu Issa's long-handled pruners, and crept back to the front wall. She flexed her fingers and weighed the tool in her hand. She thought back to her brothers, and how they'd speared fish and fowl with nothing more than a sharpened reed.

The two men on the sidewalk crowed again. Huda thrust the blade high. The pruners punctured the wasps' papery nest. She twisted it sharply, left to right. Wasps streamed forth like black and yellow lava, buzzing furiously. Huda scampered through the side gate just as the Bolt Cutter bellowed. A second later, Abu Issa let out a high-pitched curse.

Huda fled down the path of concrete slabs, feet barely making a sound, pruning pole balanced at her shoulder, just like her brothers sprinting through wetland meadows. In the backyard, she paused to listen to the Bolt Cutter shriek and Abu Issa squeal.

Just like hairless boys in short pants, she thought triumphantly, and carried the tray of tea and jam back inside the house.

CHAPTER 20

A breeze swept through the bars on Ally's bedroom window. It was uncommonly cool, and in the darkness outside, eucalypts and palm trees shimmied at its touch. Tom snored softly, bedsheet wrapped loosely around his hips. Ally eyed his moonlit silhouette and guilt ran its nails down her back. She still hadn't told him that a journalist called the embassy asking for her, a former colleague. The prisoner amnesty had gotten him worked up enough.

Ally rolled onto her back and stared blindly at the fan whirring overhead. She felt like a cartoon character with a tiny devil at one ear and an angel at the other. One whispered not to worry, she was no longer a reporter. She was a diplomat's wife, with diplomatic immunity. Then the other creature leaned in close, hissed that the bloodthirsty lunatics of the regime would do whatever they wanted. Diplomatic niceties be damned.

A gust of wind made the trees creak. Sand splattered against the window, insistent pinpricks, tap-tapping away. Ally gave up on sleep and crept to the kitchen. She pulled the curtain aside, just an inch, and peeked into the night. On the far side of the wall, Saddam peeked back. With a shiver, Ally thought back to the night of his prisoner amnesty, and Huda's questions in the garden.

She couldn't put her finger on it, but something felt off about Huda's claim that she remembered seeing "housewife" on Ally's visa form. Thank God she'd already come up with an answer for tricky situations like that, mixing the lie about being a secretary with the truth about how much it hurt to be unemployed. After all, the best lies had some honesty at heart. Ally grimaced at the billboard. Honesty? What did that mean? In Baghdad, few could afford the luxury.

Don't get paranoid, she told herself. Still, she couldn't shake Huda's prying from her head. The secret police had most likely heard the journalist's call to the embassy. Did they visit Huda and order her to find out more? Ally's head began to ache. She let the curtain fall and returned to bed. Suspicion slipped between the sheets with her, nuzzled close.

She buried her head in her pillow and prayed it was all a figment of her imagination. But she knew she had no choice but to put distance between her and Huda. Whatever lay behind her curiosity, Huda wasn't a diplomat's wife. She couldn't risk getting caught up in Ally's lies.

Ally sat at a table on the edge of the al-Faqma's patio and raised her ice cream cone in a toast.

"*Fe sehtak,*" she said. "Cheers."

On the sidewalk, a shoeshine boy grinned and raised his cone in reply. A man in a white smock emerged from al-Faqma's kitchen.

"Is he bothering you?" He gave the boy a stern look. "Shall I get rid of him?"

"Not at all," said Ally. "Ice cream tastes better with company."

The man looked at her like she was slightly mad, then he shrugged and smiled. The shoeshine boy had done the same when she first offered him ice cream.

"I wondered who the second cone was for." The man straightened his smock. "I hope young Faisal remembered to thank you. He's not a bad boy. He never tries to pick my customers' pockets, but sometime he forgets his manners."

"He's been a perfect gentleman." Ally raised her cone in another toast.

Faisal chuckled and licked his fast-melting scoop of pistachio.

"Ally?" a voice called. "Is that you?"

Huda hurried across the sidewalk. She was shiny with sweat, and clearly agitated.

"What are you doing here?"

"Getting ice cream," said Ally slowly. "What about you?"

"Where's Abdul Amir?" Huda squinted at a coffee shop nearby. A few taxi drivers idled at its sidewalk tables, waiting for customers. "He's not smoking nargilah, is he?"

"I'm not sure," mumbled Ally. "I couldn't reach him."

"He didn't drive you?"

"It's not a big deal." She licked her ice cream half-heartedly. "I did a bit of sightseeing, that's all."

"*Sightseeing?*"

"I went to the Sayed Idris mosque."

Huda's mouth turned down at the corners. Ally pretended not to notice. The mosque was featured on one of her mother's postcards, with its aquamarine minaret gleaming in the sun. Ally had wanted to see it herself, feel the same ancient carpet beneath her bare feet, and run her fingers along jeweled grid work protecting the casket of the long dead saint.

"You shouldn't have gone there alone." Huda folded her arms across her chest.

"I didn't." Ally tried to act unruffled. Above her head, a line strung with tin stars tinkled gaily. "Hatim drove me."

"Hatim?"

"I've mentioned him before. He's the driver I use if I can't contact Abdul Amir."

Anger flashed in Huda's eyes.

"You promised you wouldn't ride with strange men."

Ally grit her teeth. What was she supposed to do? Spend her days braiding her hair? Perhaps she could crochet her very own padded cell?

"Hatim is a good person. And he helped me find the mosque a lot faster than if I'd gone there and wandered about on my own."

"Does Mr. Tom know this? And have you forgotten that thousands of criminals are now free to roam about?"

"I don't need Tom's permission to leave the house." Ally tried not to roll her eyes. "And the amnesty came with a condition, didn't you hear? Anyone breaking the law from now on gets, you know . . ." She glanced over her shoulder, then sliced her hand like a knife across her neck. "Embassy security says crime has actually fallen."

"So you decide to drive around with a stranger? Don't you realize you can't trust anyone? After all I've—" She broke off, red lips like a wound.

The tin stars tinkled again.

"Let's not argue about this." Ally tried to hide her frustration. "As it turns out, I couldn't go into the shrine. Not even wearing a head scarf. No foreigners allowed. Not anymore."

"If you had asked me first, I could have told you."

Ally stared woefully at her ice cream. All she could taste was the sour tang of suspicion. *What the hell is Huda doing here, anyway?*

"Shouldn't you be at work, Huda?"

Huda sighed in exasperation.

"The school called and said Khalid didn't show up for class after lunch. His friend Bakr thought he might have gone for ice cream."

"Oh." Ally felt relieved and foolish at the same time. "Believe it or not, I saw a boy who looked a lot like Khalid outside the mosque."

"Are you sure?"

"I only got a quick glimpse of them."

"Them?"

"Khalid and the imam," said Ally. "At least, I think it was the imam. He sort of reminded me of Santa Claus. He had chubby cheeks and a curly white beard. All he needed was a red furry turban."

Huda pressed her hand to her mouth.

"This Santa Claus, was he tall or short?"

"Uh, tall. He was very tall, in fact. Do you know him?"

"Did you see anyone else?"

"Well, there was a man in a suit."

"Did he have thick glasses?" demanded Huda.

"He did, yes." She eyed Huda curiously. "Who is he?"

"No one. Forget it."

Huda stared at her with eyes wide as a lake, but Ally had the feeling she wasn't seeing her at all, that she was picturing some other time and place. Ally felt a pang of sympathy. She'd thought she was the one with secrets, but she'd begun to realize everyone had secrets here, enough to drown in.

"Can I help?" she offered. "We can look for Khalid together."

"No, better I go alone."

"Don't feel too bad." Ally gave Huda's hand a brief squeeze. "When I was a teenager, kids cut school to go shoplifting or smoke cigarettes. At least Khalid's going to the mosque."

CHAPTER 21

Rania sat at the bar in the Alwiyah Club's restaurant. The high-pitched laughter of children splashing about in the pool drifted through the open windows, along with the thwack of balls on the tennis courts. Rania checked her watch anxiously. She'd promised to bring Hanan to the club, but soon she'd have to return to the hospital and relieve her cousin, sitting watch at her mother's bedside.

A plump woman strolled past the bar, licking an enormous ice cream cone.

"How is your diet progressing, Amal?" chimed the woman's whip-thin companion. "Is this another of your miracle regimes, where you can have all the ice cream and sugar you want, as long as you eat nothing but grapefruit on Wednesdays?"

"You should try a little more sugar, sister-in-law," she replied. "Perhaps it will help with your bitterness."

The skinny woman snorted and turned to leave.

"Rania?" she exclaimed. "Is it you?"

"Miriam Pachachi?" Rania's eyes widened. "It's been a long time. Too long."

"So long, you probably thought I'd died," she chuckled.

"No such luck," snapped the plump woman, and sashayed away. Miriam rolled her eyes.

"Please, join me for a few minutes." Rania gestured to the barstool beside her. "Tell me, are you still sculpting?"

The two women talked art and traded gossip, while nearby a plump waiter attempted to impress a table of young women snacking on french fries and falafels.

"Your drinks, mademoiselles," he declared, dispensing frosty glasses of mango and pineapple juice with a theatrical bow so low it split the rear of his tuxedo pants, like a polyester sea parting before Moses.

Rania and Miriam battled to hide their mirth.

"It's times like these," said Rania, "when I wish the club still served alcohol. A sight like that deserves to be toasted with a champagne cocktail."

"That was Madam Raghad's favorite drink," remarked the silver-haired bartender. In his dapper bow tie, he was as much a fixture of the Alwiyah Club as the massive mahogany bar. "She always liked an extra sugar cube in her glass."

"My father loved Bloody Marys," said Rania. "He claimed the tomato juice canceled out the alcohol."

"That reminds me of that poor boy who had that crush on you," said Miriam. "Do you remember, he drank all those Bloody Marys to try and work up courage to ask you to dance? He ended up falling in the swimming pool."

"That wasn't me," laughed Rania, waving her hands back and forth in protest. "Time is playing tricks on you."

The bartender topped up their juices, then left to help erect a large screen on the Alwiyah's lawn. Later, once the swimmers tired of the pool and the tennis players downed their racquets, the French movie *Carmen* would play under the stars.

"Do you remember that wonderful bronze you sculpted, of the mother curled around her child?" said Rania. "It must be ten years now that she's been watching over my garden."

"Praise God you came just in time to save her." Miriam ran her fingers through her cropped silver hair. "I was going to have to sell her for scrap."

"I couldn't bear the thought of her melted down and turned into plumber's pipes and bathroom fixtures," said Rania. "Believe it or not, I recently thought I had a buyer for her."

"A buyer?" Miriam raised an anorexic eyebrow. "Who has money nowadays for a bronze this size?"

"A diplomat's wife," said Rania. "I think you'd like her. She's a young Australian."

Miriam blinked in surprise. She paused and scanned the dining room. The young waiter was off changing his trousers. The young women had left for the garden.

"This woman . . ." Miriam lowered her voice. "Is her name Ally Wilson?"

"You know Ally?"

"Don't get involved with that girl," whispered Miriam. "She's dangerous."

"Dangerous?" Rania exclaimed. "Why on earth would you say that?"

"She says she's Australian." Miriam leaned closer, so close that Rania could feel her breath against her ear. "Really, she's an American."

Rania recoiled.

"That can't be."

"On my mother's grave, I tell you, I knew her mother. I'm not wrong."

"I'm confused." Rania pressed her hand to her forehead. "How did you know her mother?"

"There's no point digging up the past." Miriam eyed her mournfully. "Besides, sometimes it's safer not to know everything. The fact is the girl shouldn't even be in the country, let alone admiring art in your backyard."

"Miriam, are you ready?" Her sister-in-law appeared at the entrance to the dining room. "I'm leaving. Will you make your own way home?"

"Tether your camel, I'm coming." Miriam squeezed Rania's hands between hers. "Be careful. Americans promise the earth, but we Iraqis are always the ones who pay for it."

Rania remained at the bar, too shocked to move. How could Ally have betrayed her like this? Didn't she realize what the regime did to Iraqis who consorted with Americans? Couldn't she feel the sword hanging over all of their heads?

She tried desperately to recall every conversation they'd ever had, all the confidences they'd shared. Rania had a horrible suspicion she'd let too much slip. Paranoia unfurled its dirty tentacles inside her. What was an American doing in Iraq when everyone knew they were forbidden?

Over the years, Rania had plenty of people pass through her gallery claiming to be interested in art but clearly seeking information—ambassadors, attachés, so-called businessmen from the Gulf. It wasn't hard to imagine the CIA sending an operative undercover as a diplomat's wife. She'd always thought Ally was a good listener, but thinking back, it was almost as if she'd been taking mental notes so she could go home afterward and write it all down.

Calm down, a voice inside her cautioned. *Don't overreact.* She couldn't afford to make any mistakes, especially not now that her and Huda's plan was beginning to take shape. Rania took a deep breath and tried to loosen fear's icy embrace. Maybe Ally wasn't a spy. Perhaps there was another explanation.

Rania glanced through the window. The bartender was busy setting up the outdoor cinema on the wide lawn. Behind him, Hanan and her friends were batting a helium balloon back and forth, playing a game of volleyball in slow motion. But for Rania, time seemed to be speeding up. She felt each second tick away, and with it, the need to get Hanan to safety grew ever more urgent.

CHAPTER 22

Huda hurried down the stairs of a decrepit apartment block with Rania two steps in front of her, both of them anxious to leave behind the people smuggler in his cramped fourth-floor flat. The close confines of the stairwell magnified the clatter of their heels. Rania cursed as she stumbled on the hem of her abaya.

"Careful, don't break your neck." Huda's heart slapped against her ribs. She wondered, Had anyone noticed them? Was an informant phoning the mukhabarat, right now? Beside her ear, an inch-wide crack zigzagged through the concrete.

"Let's keep moving." Rania wrenched her abaya away from her ankles. "I need to get back to Hanan."

The women skittered through the foyer and out to the unpaved street. After the gloom of the apartment building, the sunlight stung their eyes.

"I hate these damn robes." Rania picked her way past a chain of potholes.

"Most of the women here wear them." Huda lifted the hem of her abaya and leaped across the gutter. "It's better for us if we blend in."

Huda threw another glance at the squat apartment block. Its dun-colored walls were the same shade as the dirt road, the rubble-strewn lot next door, and almost every other building in the slum of Saddam City. There were no trees to provide relief, no flowering vines. Thick dust coated every surface. The only hint of color came from the jade dress of a little girl standing on the corner, bouncing a baby on her hip.

Rania glanced at the boarded-up windows of the smuggler's flat, then slid into her car. She slammed the door shut, catching her robe. She growled and tore the fabric free.

"Calm down," said Huda. "Now you'll have to sew a new hem."

"I can't believe it." Rania jammed her key in the ignition. "That creep wants almost as much money as Kareem does, and the kids don't even get a passport out of it."

"And we can't be sure he won't dump them in the desert."

"My friend Bashir said two of his cousins used this man's services." Rania steered the Volvo past a goat nosing for scraps in the trash. "The difference is, his cousins were full-grown men, not two kids barely in their teens."

"I agree." Huda glanced in the rearview mirror. "I don't trust him."

Inside the stifling apartment, the smuggler had stood with his back to the boarded-up window. Huda could see the outline of his body, his skinny neck, and the prickly stubble of hair on his head, but his face was all shadow. Huda couldn't read his eyes, but she heard the slobbery lick of his lips as he named the price for smuggling their children out of Iraq.

"What do we do now?" Rania navigated past a market cobbled together from plywood, plastic sheets, and pieces of corrugated metal. Men sat out front with baskets of tomatoes and burlap sacks of grapes. A little boy hawked cheap cigarettes. "My car would never make the journey, but perhaps I could rent a vehicle and drive the kids up north to the Turkish border. They could cross on foot."

"It won't work," said Huda. "Last time Ally's husband returned from a trip up north, he said the number of checkpoints had doubled. It's because of that warmonger George W. Bush, and his axis-of-evil talk. The same is happening near the borders with Iran and Syria."

"What about Jordan, then?"

"You heard the smuggler—the only way to get there is through the desert. You'll get bogged in the sand unless you have a new SUV or a Land Cruiser like they have at the embassy."

"The kids need passports and exit visas," said Rania. "I don't seen any alternative. We have to convince Kareem and the cleric to help us."

"How? We've got nothing to bargain with."

A muscle twitched in Rania's cheek.

"Listen to me," she said, "Kareem says the US is just waiting for an excuse to attack, and then he believes Washington will hand power to him and his supporters."

"So?"

"Kareem and his group want to prod America into action. They want a crisis, a crisis that will give the Americans a reason to invade. The sooner the better."

"What's your point?"

"We offer Kareem a deal." Rania stared grimly through the windshield. "He gives us the passports and visas. In return, we give him Ally."

Huda blinked.

"Ally?"

"The girl has been lying to us this whole time. She's an American."

"American? No, she's Australian. I've seen her passport."

"In that case, Ally must have dual citizenship. She's been hiding it."

Huda's mind whirled. *Ally, an American?*

"Even if this was true, how would it help us?"

"I told you," sighed Rania, "the opposition wants to trigger a crisis. Nothing would anger the US more than Baghdad taking an American hostage."

"A hostage?" Huda's fingernails dug into the faded leather seat. "You can't be serious."

Rania kept her eyes on the dusty road, the scabrous sidewalk, the plastic bags and rusty cans heaped in the gutter.

"The American CIA has used diplomats' wives as spies before. How do we know Ally's not one too? She lied to get into Iraq, and she's been lying ever since."

"Come on, that's crazy."

"She's always asking questions and nosing around."

"That's because she's a journalist, not a spy."

"A journalist?"

"She admitted to me she worked at a newspaper, but then she tried to convince me she was a secretary. Can you believe that?"

"An American and a journalist." Rania's eyes glittered with tears of betrayal. "I hate to say it, but that will suit the opposition even better."

Huda felt sick to her core.

"We can't do this."

"Look, we tell Kareem we have the information he needs to trigger the Americans. But we won't give him the details until our children have their passports and are on their way to the border."

"What about Ally? If she's an American . . ." A shiver took its time crawling down Huda's spine. She'd betrayed Ally time and time again. She'd lied and blackmailed and taken kickbacks. But handing her over to the regime was a depth Huda wasn't ready to plumb. "We don't know what the regime might do. They could send her to Abu Ghraib. Or worse."

"That's why we need to time this carefully." Rania turned the wheel. "We encourage Ally to take a trip to Jordan, a little holiday. Once her exit documents are ready, we reveal what we know to Kareem. Hopefully, Ally makes it out before the opposition feeds our information to the regime."

"Hopefully?"

"In the worst-case scenario, we make an anonymous call to the embassy and tip them off. Ally can take refuge there. The regime is not going to drag her out."

"How do you know that?"

"We don't have time to debate this." Rania slammed her palm against the steering wheel. "Any moment, Uday could decide he wants Hanan. He's a rapist. A torturer. A murderer. And by this time next year, Khalid could be in the fedayeen, learning to slice innocent women's heads from their bodies. Is that what you want?"

"Of c-course not," stammered Huda.

"Ally will be all right. She has diplomatic status. She has money and options in life that our children will never have. My daughter is my priority. Khalid should be yours." Rania guided the Volvo away from the slum and accelerated toward the freeway. "Besides, Ally is not as naive as she pretends. If she's a journalist, she'll probably end up writing a book and making a fortune out of this."

Huda waited at her desk, trying to appear relaxed even though sweat was beading on her palms. She'd already set two cups of coffee on her desktop, hoping steamy tendrils of cardamom would convince Ally to join her after she finished up in Tom's office. The girl's smile had grown stiff after their row over her *sightseeing*, and over the past couple of days, she seemed even more distant and gloomy. Guilt poked Huda in the ribs. She took a deep breath and reminded herself, the girl was a liar, just like her.

Huda checked her watch again. As if on cue, the door to Tom's office opened.

"Ally, my dear friend, how are you?" Huda motioned at the two cups on her desk. "Please, join me. I've got coffee for us."

"Maybe next time." Ally kept walking. "I'm afraid I've got a few chores to knock out."

Huda hurried out from behind her desk.

"Please, stop for a while."

"I'd love to, but I need to stop at the market on my way home."

Something in her voice made Huda wonder if Ally was lying again.

"How about I do a reading for you." She gestured for her to take a seat. "I can take a look at the grounds. Perhaps they will have some secrets to share."

The young woman eyed the two coffee cups.

"A reading?"

"It would be fun, don't you think?"

Huda waited as Ally eyed the cups of coffee. Not long ago, she'd believed the young woman was so easy to read, but nothing was clear anymore, not even Ally. Finally, the young woman pulled out a chair and sat down.

"Remember, my dear, you must think of a question while you drink." Huda offered another counterfeit smile. "You can ask yourself, will I take a journey soon? Are there any adventures coming up in my life?"

"Adventure?" Ally frowned. "Not likely."

"It sounds like you need a holiday. You should take a trip to Jordan."

"I've got to admit, I've been thinking about taking a little break from Baghdad." Ally paused and lowered her voice. "The problem is, with all this tension with Washington, some of the other embassies are starting to withdraw nonessential staff. If I go, the bureaucrats in Canberra could decide to keep me out too. After all, I'm the poster child for nonessential."

"Don't say that," said Huda quickly. "You deserve a little holiday. You like scuba diving, yes? You should go to the Red Sea. You can see a whale shark there."

"I don't know."

"They have some lovely spas too. You could really relax."

"I'm worried if I go, I won't be able to come back. Maybe in a few months, when things calm down . . ." She raised her coffee, gulped the last few mouthfuls, then slid her cup across the desk.

"Okay, my dear," said Huda. "First, you must take your cup

and saucer back in your hand. Do you remember? Follow what I do."

Ally copied Huda's motions, slipping the saucer on top of the cup and swirling the pieces at her chest.

"Careful now," said Huda.

She flipped the china upside down. Ally held her breath and did the same. Her cup slipped sideways, squealed like a tiny mouse. Ally caught it with her fingertips and slid it back into place.

"Now," said Huda, "close your eyes. Forget about everything but the question you want answered. Put that at the center of your mind."

After waiting a few minutes, Huda broke the seal between Ally's cup and saucer, and turned the cup upright. In places, the congealed grounds rippled like tides. In others they were pockmarked with craters. Huda's pupils widened: three signs stood out, clear as day.

"What's that?" Ally sat forward and pointed at a grainy squiggle. "Is that a snake?"

Huda ransacked her mind for the most convincing lie.

"You won't believe this." She faked a chuckle. "But there is clearly a sea or an ocean in your future." She pointed at two grainy puddles. "See, it is parted down the middle, like the Red Sea before the Prophet Moses."

Huda flicked her finger toward a blob of grinds.

"Look here," she said. "This is a sign for your home, your family life." She made a show of scanning the grounds, taking her sweet time, like her grandmother taught her. She clucked a couple of times, then shook her head. "I don't think you need worry about anyone keeping you apart from Mr. Tom. I see no sign of that here. You can see for yourself: the grounds have formed a small mound; they are rounded. That means contentment."

From under her lashes, she watched Ally lean a little closer. Huda pointed at the saucer.

"And look here—this line is a road. It's the sign of a journey. I'm not kidding, my dear, this is what your cup says." She leaned back in her chair, like she was reclining on a sandy beach. "Even the coffee grounds say you deserve a nice holiday at the Red Sea. After that, you will come home refreshed to your husband."

Ally smiled half-heartedly.

"You said while I drank my coffee, I should focus on the questions I wanted answered. But I wasn't thinking about a vacation." She pushed the cup away and stood up to leave. "I was thinking about my mother."

As soon as Ally said goodbye and disappeared down the hall, Huda snatched up the cup. The three signs were still there. At the base, a tower. On the side, a snake. By the handle, the sword. Huda looked away, took a deep breath, and then eyed the cup again. Tower. Snake. Sword. Loud as a scream at midnight.

Huda left the old nurseryman at the top of the riverbank on Eighty-Second Street, staring morosely at the currents braiding midstream. She ducked under the shade cloth and hurried past a row of potted fruit trees, back toward her car. Huda's chest felt tight, and when she put her hand to her heart, she saw that the shade cloth had patterned her skin like a henna talisman painted by her grandmother's hand.

Huda wished she could hide herself in the soft folds of her grandmother's robe and listen to the old woman divine a way forward, chart a path through the dangers ahead. Her grandmother would have understood straightaway the signs in Ally's coffee cup. The tower: a secret leaked to an enemy. The snake: betrayal by a friend. The sword: death, of course.

At first Huda thought the message in the grounds was sickeningly clear—if she and Rania betrayed Ally and traded her secrets for their children's safety, the girl would end up dead. But Ally had said she was thinking of her mother while she sipped her coffee, and Huda suddenly remembered the faded photo of Yusra, the nurse whose home had been bulldozed. The young woman's face kept coming back, and Huda had wondered, Was this the message of the tower, the snake, and the sword?

Huda's grandmother would have been wise enough to understand the symbols. In any case, she wouldn't have done what Huda just did: force the truth from the nurseryman's wrinkled lips with a combination of threats and bribery. Stick and carrot. It had worked for Abu Issa, why not for her? Huda trudged from under the shade cloth, trading the humid shadows for sunlight, clear and sharp as diamonds.

She glanced over her shoulder. The nurseryman still hadn't moved from the riverbank. Huda wondered, was he eyeing the money she'd given him the same way she did when Abu Issa slipped cash into her palm, like it was a scorpion that might turn and bite? The venom was still in her veins, because a moment later she found herself wondering, how much would the mukhabarat pay for news of a traitorous nurse and her connection to Ally? Enough to afford Khalid freedom?

The nurseryman told her that Ally had been back here too, just yesterday. When he spotted her pulling up in a taxi—no doubt driven by Hatim—the old man hid inside a lean-to of corrugated tin where he stored his tools, fertilizer, and pesticide. He stayed there until she gave up and slouched away, clutching that faded photograph in her hand.

"Why does she want to stir up trouble?" he'd asked Huda. "And why the hell do you?"

Huda pulled her head scarf over her hair and hurried away from the nursery. She didn't want anyone on Eighty-Second Street noting down her number plate, so she'd parked on the rise overlooking the masgouf restaurant and its bobbing pontoon. She'd even stopped by the kitchen and told the cook she was thinking of bringing a friend for lunch of roasted fish, building the lie she'd use if the mukhabarat came calling, demanding explanations.

She hurried to the Corolla and slid into the driver's seat. A long, low sedan sailed past. Huda's heart stopped mid-beat. The driver had the Bolt Cutter's blocky profile. He turned toward her. Huda saw blue eyes, not brown. His lips were thin, unlike the Bolt Cutter's fleshy red mouth. But he had the same carp-eyed stare. Huda trembled as she pulled the belt over her shoulder and turned the key in the ignition.

Huda's heels clacked rapidly across the sidewalk outside Rania's house. She rang the bell at the copper gate, then huddled by the wall, folding in on herself like a card player closing a bad hand. When Rania finally opened the locks, Huda squeezed past her without waiting for an invitation and hurried toward the garden.

"What's going on?" Rania scurried after her.

"I think I was followed."

"Here? Now?"

"I saw a brown Cadillac behind me an hour ago over near the river. I spotted it again on the expressway." Huda's pulse throbbed at her wrist. "I think I saw the same car just a few minutes ago on al-Kindi Boulevard, so I parked and went into the souk. I snuck out the alley behind the market and came here on foot."

"What if they saw you?" Rania's gaze flicked toward Hanan's bedroom on the second floor. "What if they come here? What do we tell them?"

"We say we're old friends." A blush crept across Huda's cheeks. "Friends from childhood."

"Why have you come, anyway?" said Rania. "Did you convince Ally to leave? Has she applied for an exit visa?"

Huda shook her head.

"She's not interested. So I lodged an application for her."

"You what?"

"I filled out the form for an exit visa and forged her husband's signature. Apparently you're not the only artist here."

Huda checked the path to the gate. Her ears strained for the rumble of an approaching car or the flat buzz of the bell.

"I'm supposed to meet with Kareem tomorrow," said Rania.

"I don't like this plan." Huda's nerves fizzed like a length of burning fuse. "If Ally hasn't left by the time the regime finds out she's American, they might—"

"I told you already." Rania cut her off. "In that case, we call the embassy with an anonymous tip. She'll have enough time to make a run for the border, or she can take refuge inside the embassy. She'll be safe enough."

"I can't have her blood on my hands."

"Don't be dramatic. That's not going to happen," said Rania. "If you want to back out, that's your choice. But I'll do whatever I need to do to keep Hanan safe."

Huda straightened her shoulders.

"I've got a new plan," she said. "And if it works, we won't have to sell our souls to the mukhabarat or to Kareem and the cleric."

Rania eyed her skeptically.

"So what is it?"

"It came to me at the river, after I talked with a nurseryman." In her mind's eye, Huda saw dregs of coffee stretching out like the dark side of the moon. "It turns out, Ally has more secrets than she even dreamed."

CHAPTER 23

While Huda locked her car, Ally waited at the top of the riverbank and inhaled the aroma of roasting fish drifting from the kitchen of the masgouf restaurant. Below, the Tigris rippled south, the crests of its milky-tea waters waving at the sun. Ally shaded her eyes and watched the shadow of a cloud sail across the river, climb the opposite bank, and vanish from view.

"We're not the only ones at the restaurant this time." Ally turned to Huda and pointed out the silhouette of a lone diner seated on the bobbing pontoon.

Huda smiled tightly and started down the zigzagging steps.

"Tom told me you took a day off," Ally called after her. "But I didn't realize you had organized another masgouf lunch. How long have you been planning this?"

"It was a last-minute idea, my dear."

Ally scanned the quiet riverside, then followed Huda down the pebbled bank. Nimble even in heels, Huda made it to the water's edge first and disappeared under the awning. Ally hurried across the ramp.

"Wait up. I'm not as fast—" She paused as the pontoon swayed, feeling the river rush beneath her feet. The diner she'd glimpsed earlier swiveled toward her.

"Welcome, dear." Rania adjusted a pale scarf over her hair. "Please, sit and join us. I ordered a round of Pepsi."

"Rania, this is a surprise. . . ." Ally's eyes flicked from Rania to Huda and back again. The two women were blank as freshly painted walls. "What are you doing here?"

"Don't worry," said Rania.

"Join us," said Huda.

Ally hesitated. She felt like an addict who'd just walked into an intervention.

"Please, sit." Rania patted the bench beside her. "We have a favor to ask you."

"A favor?" said Ally.

Huda and Rania traded glances. Ally slid warily onto the picnic bench.

"I guess this favor involves more than a cup of sugar?"

Rania and Huda laughed sharply. The sound reminded Ally of breaking glass.

"It's about Khalid," said Huda.

"Is he skipping school again?" Ally shook her head ruefully. "I'm sorry, I opened a can of worms with that one."

"I'm glad you told me, but that is not it. I mean, it's not . . ." Huda trailed off.

"This involves Hanan too," said Rania.

"A favor for your kids?" The tension in Ally's shoulders eased a little. "Sure, I'd be happy to help. What would you like me to do?"

Huda leaned across the table.

"Khalid and Hanan need to leave Iraq. And we need you to get them out."

Ally sat very still as shock flooded her system.

"You're kidding, right?"

Huda stared at her. Her pupils were so wide Ally feared she might fall in.

"The secret police are going to put Khalid in the fedayeen."

"The fedayeen?" Ally gasped. "Uday's militia?"

"They'll turn Khalid into a monster, a murderer. I can't let that happen."

Rania inched toward Ally.

"And Uday's friends want to take Hanan to his palace." She leaned closer and put her mouth near Ally's ear. "Did you know, Uday keeps a pack of wild dogs in a cage? And when he's done with a girl, sometimes he lets the dogs tear her to pieces."

A pebble rolled down the slope. The waiter trudged down the steps toward the pontoon. The women's huddle dissolved. Huda and Rania pasted on smiles. Ally busied herself with her handbag, needlessly rifling through pockets and unzipping zips, while the blood drained from her face.

The waiter clattered across the ramp, balancing a tray with three small bottles of Pepsi and a bucket of ice. He set three glasses on the picnic table and ladled out ice cubes with a small set of tongs. The river surged for a moment. The waiter paused, cube halfway to glass, and softened his knees like he was surfing. Ally faked a smile.

After the waiter left, Huda and Rania explained their plan and what would happen if she didn't save their children. Each new horror crashed on Ally like a wave, one on top of the other, so fast she didn't have time to catch her breath. The women swayed on their benches, while the Tigris pulsed below, moving relentlessly south, immune to the desperation of those struggling on its surface.

"I'd like to help, I really would," stuttered Ally. "But it's too dangerous. Tom will never agree. I can't do it."

"Yes, you can." Rania gripped her hand. "You tell Tom you are going to Jordan for a holiday. Huda already has the exit permit for you. She will use the embassy Land Cruiser to drive you out of the city. I will meet you at Lake Habbaniyah with the children. They will get in the vehicle with you, and then you drive straight to the border."

"What about the embassy? They'll notice a missing vehicle."

"I will change some travel orders," said Huda. "And I know

where the keys for the vehicles are kept. You don't need to worry about that."

"Please, listen," said Rania. "After Lake Habbaniyah, you simply keep going until you near the Jordanian border. Then you turn off the road and drive due north. Five miles later turn east and keep on going until you cross the border. "

Ally glanced up the riverbank, at the waiter sitting near the firepit, puffing on a cigarette like it was just another ordinary day. How was that possible? she asked herself. Couldn't he feel the earth shifting beneath them?

"Let me get this straight," she said. "You want the kids to go with me, while you and Huda return to Baghdad?"

"I can't leave until Allah decides to gather my mother to his side." Rania took a shaky breath. "And if anyone asks about Hanan, I'll say I've sent her to Basra. Uday is summering at his northern palace, so with luck, it'll be a month or more before he bothers trying to hunt her down. By then, God willing, I'll have the money to join her in Jordan."

Huda cleared her throat. "I would take the children myself, but my absence would be noticed immediately by the mukhabarat."

"I don't understand why the mukhabarat are targeting you, Huda."

"I work for the embassy." She sighed. "Also, I am friends with you, a foreigner."

Bile rose in Ally's throat. She'd always suspected their friendship put Huda at risk, but Khalid and Hanan were only children, innocent in all of this. A voice inside her whispered, *What would the regime do to an American journalist who lied her way into the country and tried to smuggle Iraqis out?* She thought back to the reporter arrested in Baghdad and branded a spy. She could see his battered body, like it was right in front of her, dangling from a rope.

"If you can't deliver the children to Amman," said Rania, "then take the detour near the border and let the kids cross on foot by themselves. They will have some money, water, and food.

Then you can return to the highway and exit at the official border checkpoint. You will cross the border legally. And the side trip will cost you an hour or two at most."

"An hour or two," said Huda. "That's all it will take to save our children. Surely that's not too much to ask?"

Ally fumbled for a reply. She felt strangely numb, as if she were outside her own body, watching herself at the picnic table, pale as sand, fingernails digging into her palms.

"I'm sorry," she whispered. "I'm so sorry."

Huda and Rania traded glances. Huda trained her eyes on Ally, like she was reading the fine print on her soul.

"I have something to show you," she said.

Ally trailed Huda past a row of potted geraniums into the mottled shade of the nursery on Eighty-Second Street.

"What are we doing here?" Ally glanced over her shoulder. The nurseryman was back by the gate, nervously plucking at his dishdasha, head swiveling left and right. "Did you pay him to keep lookout? Is that what the money was for? Don't tell me he knows about this too?"

Huda shook her head, then beckoned Ally on.

"It's not far away."

Ally hesitated.

"I don't like this."

"You want to know about your mother, right? And her friend?"

Before Ally could ask more, Huda pried apart two lengths of rusty wire separating the nursery from the vacant lot next door.

"Slide through," she said.

Ally eyed the prickly purple thistle, flowering chamomile, and scraps of rusty tin poking from the earth. Dust and dirt coated a mound of broken concrete. Bright yellow dandelions had sprouted in its patchwork of crevices.

"Hurry up," said Huda. "Before someone sees us."

Ally slid reluctantly between the wires. Huda picked her way toward a pile of dry branches.

"The nurseryman man must have covered it up." Huda dragged a large palm frond to the side.

Ally bent down to help.

"Covered what up?" She grabbed another frond.

"Careful!"

Too late, its serrated edge sliced Ally's palm.

Huda tutted and pulled the last of the brush away.

A weathered slab poked from the earth. Ally remembered it from her first visit to the nursery. She leaned closer. The slab was made of sandstone, with two lines of Arabic script carved across its face.

"Is this a headstone?" she said slowly.

"Can you read it?"

"The second line says 1952 to 1972, right?"

"What about the line above that?"

Ally brushed dirt from the words carved into its face. Huda laid her hand on Ally's shoulder.

"It says 'Yusra,'" said Huda. "'Yusra Hussain.'"

Ally moaned, so quietly it could have been the wind.

"Yusra's dead? She's been dead since 1972?" Ally touched the scarred marker. "How did this happen? She was so young."

Huda squinted at the humid shadows of the nursery. The old man had disappeared. No insects buzzed. No lizards scrambled through the thorny grass. Even the river was quiet, its deadly currents hidden beneath a surface so smooth it could have been glass.

"Yusra was executed," whispered Huda. "For treason."

"Executed?" The word rang in Ally's ears, so shocking she almost believed it had come from someone else's mouth.

"From what I was told, Yusra joined the youth wing of the Iraqi Communist Party. Her cousin was already a member, and he convinced her to come to their meetings. She was not a high-ranking member. She was not important at all. But the party fell out of favor. It was banned, and that was enough for the regime."

Ally's throat constricted.

"You were right, Yusra did live on Eighty-Second Street," continued Huda. "But the regime demolished her family home. That's part of the punishment for traitors." She glanced at the mound of broken concrete. "Rubble is all that's left. That, and her gravestone."

Ally asked herself, *Could it be any lonelier, this small, sad slab buried under palm fronds and dust?*

"The regime doesn't care who it harms," said Huda. "An innocent young nurse means nothing to them. It will do the same to Khalid and Hanan, unless you help us."

"Tom won't agree to this." Ally wrung her hands. "I'm sorry."

"Did you know traitors are forbidden proper burials?" said Huda. "Yusra was lucky to have her name on that stone. Most people don't get that. " She paused and eyed the burial slab. "I know this, because my brothers were called traitors. They were executed too."

"Your brothers? Executed?" Once again, Ally's voice sounded like a stranger's in her ears.

"No one wrapped my brothers in burial shrouds. No one got to say prayers as they were laid to rest." Pain eddied in Huda's eyes. "For months afterward, my mother couldn't leave our house, because if she cried in public the regime would have had her whipped."

Ally felt like a traveler gone astray, who'd crossed too many time zones, too fast and too often, who could no longer tell day from night, who didn't know the right words to say, or how to comfort the woman beside her, rigid with grief.

"I'm so sorry." She reached for Huda's hand. "Why didn't you tell me before?"

"Because secrets aren't for telling." Huda looked suddenly much older, her wrinkles deeper, her eyes weary as the hour before dawn. She brushed a patch of dirt from the gravestone. "Your mother didn't understand about secrets either, Ally. That's how Yusra ended up dead."

CHAPTER 24

Many years ago, Huda saw a young woman from her village swept away in a flood. Now as she looked at Ally, struggling to comprehend all she'd been told, she remembered the moment the sandbar collapsed beneath the young woman's feet, how her mouth opened as the water seized her, but no sound escaped, not even a scream. She waited for Ally to say something, anything, but eventually Huda had to continue on alone.

"Your mother knew about Yusra's political activities, and one day she let it slip to a mutual friend. That friend was . . ." Huda battled to keep her voice level. "That friend was an informant for the mukhabarat."

"The mukhabarat?" Ally spat out the word with such disgust, it made Huda cringe. "You're saying my mother told the secret police about Yusra? Why would she do that, for God's sake?"

"Not the secret police," muttered Huda. "An informant. They're not the same."

Ally clutched her temples.

"I can't believe this."

"I imagine your mother trusted the person she confided in. Maybe they really were friends."

"Friends?" Ally's mouth twisted. "Her and the informant?"

Huda stared at the pitiful headstone.

"Not all informants are willing. Most of them want a peaceful life, but then the mukhabarat come calling, demanding otherwise. This friend of your mother's, this informant, maybe she had to do it to save her family." She prayed Ally wouldn't see the blood rising in her cheeks. "It's complicated."

"My mother and the informant," said Ally slowly, "they're to blame for Yusra's death?"

"In Iraq, every friendship is a risk." A tremor surfaced in Huda's voice. She forced it back down, but it remained just under the surface, threatening to give way at any moment, like a sandbar dissolving beneath her feet. "You never know who might turn you in for something as small as a joke, or an offhand comment. Perhaps it will be your best friend who gets your tongue cut out. Perhaps it will be a colleague at work. Perhaps they don't want to betray you, but the mukhabarat will harm their children otherwise."

"I thought my mom was some sort of brave explorer. Now I find out she was a fool." Ally crushed her hands to her eyes. "A dangerous fool."

"Don't condemn her," said Huda gently. "We're all in danger here. Even you."

"Me?" The girl looked up. "What are you talking about?"

Huda glanced over her shoulder.

"I know you're a journalist. And someone told Rania that you're American."

Horror mushroomed in Ally's eyes.

"Who said that?"

"It doesn't matter," said Huda. "But it's enough to land you in Abu Ghraib, or even on the executioner's block. And if the mukhabarat find out, they'll want to know why Rania and I didn't tell them first. They'll say we're not patriots." She glanced at the lonely headstone. "Maybe they'll call us traitors."

Ally turned a seasick green.

"I never wanted to cause trouble," she said. "I'm such a fool, just like my mom."

Tears began to slip from the corners of Ally's eyes, reminding Huda of that river breaking its banks. Mustafa had been there too, when the sandbar gave way, and instantly he leaped in the water to save the young woman. But she panicked and clawed her way up his back, locked her arms around his neck, until the river dragged both of them down. The tips of the waves looked like teeth, swallowing them up. Eventually, Mustafa thrashed to the surface. Alone. He'd had to wrench the girl from his shoulders and release her to the river's arms.

Guilt pushed the oxygen from Huda's lungs. She wished that the Tigris would rise up and swallow her, take her down to its silent, silty depths, where there was no right or wrong, no lies or betrayal, no manipulation. She winced as Ally bent over the sandstone marker and tried to wipe the dirt from Yusra's name.

"It's my fault." The words leaped from Huda's mouth before there was time to think, like Mustafa plunging into that stream.

Ally straightened up. There was a peculiar look on her face, like she already knew what Huda was going to say.

"What do you mean?"

Huda eyed Yusra's lonely grave, a traitor's grave like her brothers'. She took a breath and forged on, praying it would wash the stain from her heart.

"You're not to blame. And neither was your mom." She took Ally's hand in hers. "The informant would have drawn her close. Just like I did to you."

CHAPTER 25

Ally stomped along the river road, back toward Huda's car, gravel crunching beneath her heels. Below her, the pontoon tugged at its moorings. Rania had left, and their table had been cleared. Ally lurched to a halt. Like tiny spiders, suspicions hatched in her mind.

"Is Rania working for them too?" She whirled toward Huda. "Is Rania an informant as well?"

"Please, keep your voice down." Huda glanced over her shoulder. "And, no, she's not. She's a victim in this, like her daughter. And Khalid."

Ally hurried on, muttering curses, and trying desperately not to panic.

"Ally, please, calm down."

Huda reached for her arm, but Ally shied away. She needed space and time to think. The last thing she wanted was Huda's false sympathy clouding her judgment.

"Tell me," she said. "Exactly what have you been reporting to the mukhabarat?"

"Nothing."

"Oh, come on. You're an informant. By the very definition, that means you're giving them information."

Huda's big eyes shone with tears. Ally wondered, Was that a trick she practiced in the mirror? Did the mukhabarat give her lessons on how to fake a smile, how to make a hug feel warm even if her heart was unmoved?

"I only told them little things," Huda stammered, "here and there."

"Exactly what were these 'little things'?"

"Really, it was nothing."

"Stop it," she hissed. "If you want me to help you, you better start telling the truth."

Fear flickered across Huda's face, barely visible, like a fish among the reeds.

"One time, I mentioned Barbara and Inez."

"Barbara and Inez? What do they have to do with this?"

"Nothing, like I told you," said Huda. "I simply reported that you did aerobics at the UN with two oil-for-food inspectors called Barbara and Inez."

"We do jumping jacks." Ally slapped her hand against her forehead. "We're not trading state secrets."

"Like I said, mostly I have nothing to report. I just provide a few details about your daily activities. It's not like you were doing anything suspicious, until, well . . ." Huda paused. She glanced at the Tigris, like she might find an answer in its tides. "I didn't tell them about either of your visits to Eighty-Second Street."

"You know that I went back?" Ally felt sick. "Have you been following me?"

"No, I never, I swear. The nurseryman told me. He said he hid in the tool shed when you came." Huda eyed her. "No Iraqi likes to talk about the dead. They're not coming back, no matter how much we pray. It's the living we need to think of. We need to think of Khalid and Hanan."

Ally squinted at the perfect blue sky with its perfect fluffy clouds, and prayed this wasn't really happening. But even as the wish formed, she knew there'd be no miracle. God wasn't going to save her, just like he never saved Yusra. Or Huda's brothers. What about Khalid and Hanan? Would he turn a blind eye to them too?

"Let's be honest." Huda leveled her gaze. "You've done plenty of lying too."

"I haven't lived in the US since I was five years old, not since my mother died. And I haven't done a scrap of reporting in Iraq." Ally tugged on the passenger door.

"Wait," said Huda. "If there's anything more you want to ask me, do it now."

Ally scowled.

"You don't get to set a timetable for this."

"You don't understand." Huda glanced over her shoulder. "There might be a microphone in my car."

"A microphone?" Ally felt as if she was still on the swaying pontoon, with the Tigris pulsing beneath her feet. "In your car?"

"I can't say for sure. But the mukhabarat know I don't want to be an informant. They may be listening in on me . . . and you." She stared at her kitten-heeled pumps. "So if you want to ask me anything, do it before we get inside."

Ally searched the sky again, but it was too big and too bright.

"Are you telling the truth about Yusra and my mom?"

Huda nodded. "It's the truth. I'm sorry."

Ally couldn't be sure if she saw concern or calculation in Huda's eyes. The Iraqi woman unlocked the car. Ally raised her hand.

"Wait."

Back at the nursery, she'd drilled Huda about her lies: exactly when she started informing on her, Abdul Amir's role, the names of the men she reported to and what they looked like. But all the while, she avoided the most important question, kept her back to it, even though they could both sense it circling like a shark, its fin slicing the surface every now and then, a small, dark hint of the animal below.

"Were we ever really friends?" Ally didn't want to ask this

question, not because Huda might lie, but because she might not want to hear the truth. "Or was it all part of the act?"

"I'm your friend, of course." Huda bent her head. "I couldn't sleep last night trying to think of how I could prove this to you. But honestly, what can I do or say? You need to look into your heart. Do you really believe our friendship was a trick?"

"Why would I trust my heart?" Ally's eyes stung. "I obviously can't tell friend from enemy, just like my mom. And she got Yusra killed."

"We can't fix your mother's mistakes, or mine." Huda eyed the muddy river. "But perhaps we can beat the mukhabarat. If we stay loyal to each other, if we trust each other, then maybe we can change the patterns of the past."

CHAPTER 26

The aroma of roasting chicken filled Huda's kitchen. The phone jingled. She laid her knife next to a mound of sliced eggplant, wiped her hands on the kitchen towel, and grabbed the handset from its cradle.

"Hello?" Ally's voice reverberated down the line. "Huda?"

Huda gripped the phone tight. It had only been a few hours since she dropped Ally at home.

"My dear, I can't talk right now." She prayed the girl wouldn't say anything dangerous on the line, and that the mukhabarat weren't taking notes. "I will stop by your house tonight when I go to the market. We'll talk then. Now is not good."

"Listen, I—"

"Really, it's better if we talk later. I am frying eggplant. It's—"

"Please, listen." The girl's words surfed in and out of a buzzy fog of static. "I'm going to Jordan for a short holiday. I want to leave tomorrow."

"Tomorrow?" Huda pressed her hand to her chest. "That's too soon. It's impossible."

"The day after, then. No later."

"But I need to organize a car."

"I can't put this off." Ally's pitch began to climb. "Really, I can't delay."

"Okay, be calm. I will get everything ready for you to travel. Thank you, Ally. Thank you."

As Huda hung up, tears gathered in her eyes. She hurried to Khalid's room and stuffed three changes of clothes, a toothbrush, hat, and sneakers into his backpack. Tomorrow, she told herself, she'd add water, sesame bars, dates, and flatbread, and then sew the $540 she'd stashed in the tea canister into the lining of his bag.

Huda turned a circle, eyes like lighthouse lamps. Khalid's Chewbacca doll lay beside his pillow. Should she pack it as well? She picked up the toy and hugged it to her chest. She pictured Khalid, six hundred miles away, all alone. *Can I really do this?* she asked. *Can I send my baby away?*

Huda wiped her eyes, then she grabbed the flashlight Khalid used for late-night sessions with Harry Potter and slid it into the backpack. The Corolla rattled into the street. Huda's heart pounded. She shoved the backpack into the closet and slammed the door shut.

Out in the kitchen, the eggplant's pale flesh was turning brown. Huda poured bread crumbs onto a plate and cracked two eggs into a bowl. She shot an anxious glance over her shoulder, and a string of egg white dribbled onto the counter. The front gate groaned.

Huda picked up a plank of eggplant and dipped it in egg wash. Abdul Amir's key jangled in the front door. Boots crunched over tile. Huda took a deep breath and pressed the dripping eggplant into the breadcrumbs.

"Sister, we've come at a bad time," muttered Abu Issa.

Huda wheeled around in shock, crumb-coated hands raised in the air.

"I didn't intend to interrupt your dinner preparations." Abu Issa stepped into the kitchen and sniffed. "Is that chicken with cardamom I smell?"

Huda's heart hammered so hard she feared it might tear a hole in her ribs.

"What are you doing here? How did—"

The front door slammed. More boots. Abdul Amir barreled into the kitchen.

"What's going on?" cried Huda.

Abdul Amir ignored her. Something in his eyes reminded her of Khalid by the lake at Martyr's Monument, when he said her brothers would be ashamed of her. Abdul Amir went straight to the fridge, pulled out a six-pack of beer, and then hurried out to the garden.

"Abu Issa, would you mind waiting in the living room?" Huda grabbed a paper towel and wiped bread crumbs from her trembling hands. "I need to speak with my husband for a moment."

"It's better if you leave him alone."

"Alone? Why?"

In the oven, chicken fat splattered and popped.

"Abdul Amir needs some space right now," said Abu Issa. "Let him be. There's no need for you to get involved in men's business."

Huda glanced through the window into the garden. Men's business. What did that mean? Abdul Amir hunched over the picnic table, one bottle of beer in his hand, the others waiting to be drained. When he'd looked at her in the kitchen, his face had been slack with shock. Was it possible he'd learned of her plan? Had he turned her in to the mukhabarat?

"I'm thirsty." Abu Issa frowned. "Can you do me the favor of pouring some juice, with ice, then join us in the living room?"

"Us?"

"My partner is here," he muttered darkly. "He's in the living room, waiting for you."

Goose bumps prickled Huda's skin. Was Abu Issa toying with her, with his request for cold juice? Did her husband intend to sit in the backyard and drink himself senseless, while the mukhabarat dragged his disloyal wife to Abu Ghraib? Her eyes swiveled to the knife on the chopping board. She thought of the gun that Abdul

Amir kept under the bed. But in the end, she set two glasses of mango juice on a tray and followed Abu Issa into the living room.

The Bolt Cutter paced the room with a rabid-dog gleam in his eyes. She laid the tray on the table, and he snatched up a glass in his fist. Huda stopped dead. The Bolt Cutter's knuckles were scraped raw. Flecks of blood stained his shirt. Was this men's business?

"Have you spoken with Ally Wilson recently?" Abu Issa didn't bother with his usual chitchat. "Is there anything you want to tell me?"

"No." Her answer came faster and louder than she intended.

"Are you sure?"

Huda battled the urge to run down the hall, out the door, and into the street. She prayed that Khalid would stay out late, that he wouldn't come home to find a man with bloodied hands in his living room—or his mother vanished to the dungeons of Abu Ghraib.

Abu Issa traded glances with the Bolt Cutter.

"Sit down, sister."

Huda's body refused to obey.

"The chicken is burning!" she cried, and bolted out the door.

She steeled herself for the thud of boots, for Abu Issa's hand on her shoulder, for the Bolt Cutter to grab her by the throat. She flung open the back door and hurried across the patio.

"What's going on, Abdul Amir? Why are the mukhabarat here?"

"Leave me alone." He turned his back to her. "I don't want to talk to you."

He knows.

"Why are they here?" She checked the kitchen window. "What's happened?"

"Leave me alone."

"Please, tell me."

Abdul Amir covered his eyes. His mouth contorted. A sob slipped out.

"Go away," he muttered. "I can't bear to look at you."

Huda's heart bucked like a train leaping the tracks. Had Abdul Amir turned her in? Why else would the Bolt Cutter be here, with bloodlust shining in his eyes?

"I'm so sorry," she whispered. "I truly am."

"You're not as sorry as I am," muttered Abdul Amir. "Please, I told you to leave me alone."

"Tell me you haven't—"

"Go, Huda." His voice split like wood under an axe. "The mukhabarat want to talk to you."

Abu Issa threw open the back door.

"What's going on here?"

Huda backed away, head swiveling left to right. She eyed the path at the side of the house and asked herself, *Can I outrun them?*

"I can't do this." Abdul Amir hung his head like a beaten dog. "How can I live with this on my conscience?"

"What's done is done." Abu Issa frowned.

"I should never have told you."

"We would have found out on our own, eventually."

The Bolt Cutter's bovine face loomed in the kitchen window. Huda wondered, had he come to drag her away? Or would he kill her in her own backyard? Someone whimpered. A moment, later, she realized it was her.

"I can't look my wife in the face." Abdul Amir clapped his hands to his eyes. "And God help me, what will I do if my son finds out? I can't do this. I'm going to the coffee shop."

He stumbled toward the back door.

"Don't go, please." Huda grabbed his elbow. "Please, don't leave me."

He shook her off and pushed past Abu Issa into the kitchen. Through the window, Huda saw the Bolt Cutter turn and stomp after him. Moments later, the front door slammed. Abu Issa advanced across the patio.

"What did Abdul Amir tell you?"

"Nothing." Huda sidled toward the side of the house. "Nothing at all."

"You're a bad liar," he said. "My partner will bring your husband back. We don't want Abdul Amir opening his mouth about any of this."

"Please, Abu Issa, I—"

"Your husband should have been more vigilant. This problem could have been nipped in the bud."

"It's not Abdul Amir's fault." Huda took another step toward the path of concrete slabs.

"I expected more from you, Huda."

"Please, don't let the Bolt Cutter hurt him."

"Bolt Cutter? That's what you call my partner?" Abu Issa laughed sourly. "I suppose it suits him."

Huda trembled. "I'm sorry."

"That damn fool is out of control." Abu Issa raked his hands across his scalp. "I hope he doesn't do anything stupid."

He stabbed his finger at her.

"Don't go anywhere. Don't talk to anyone. I'll be back."

Abu Issa spun on his heel, returned indoors, and disappeared past the kitchen window. Huda doubled over, breath coming in hard, hot gulps. She wanted to collapse on the soft green grass, but a voice inside her yelled, *Go, now, before the mukhabarat come back!*

Huda raced inside, snatched the tea canister from the pantry, and pried it open. Precious dollars and dinar spilled onto the counter. Huda ran to Khalid's bedroom and hauled his backpack from the closet. As she stuffed the cash in the bag, doubts rushed at her. Should she leave Khalid with his father? Should she take the money and flee to Basra? Deep inside, she knew it was pointless. Wherever she went, the mukhabarat would hunt her down.

"What the hell?" Abdul Amir's bulk filled the doorway. He stared at the rolls of cash in her hand and the backpack on the bed.

"What is this? Are you leaving me? Are you taking Khalid?"

"I'm not going anywhere." A spike of pain made Huda clutch her chest. "But it's not safe for Khalid here. The Bolt Cutter sat on our couch tonight, drinking our juice without washing the blood from his hands. Khalid can't be around this. It's too dangerous."

"I can barely look at you." Abdul Amir's face contorted as he stepped through the door.

"Please . . ." Every muscle in Huda's body tensed. "Don't—"

"An innocent man is dead, and it's my fault."

Huda couldn't breathe. She shook her head, but his words still didn't make sense.

"I told the mukhabarat about that driver, Hatim, ferrying Ally around." Abdul Amir slumped on the edge of the bed. "Abu Issa asked me to ride with them and point Hatim out. When they found him, they threw him in the back of their car. I thought they'd take him for questioning." He covered his face with his hands. "The Bolt Cutter got out of control."

Huda's mind replayed the Bolt Cutter's raw knuckles, the fresh blood on his shirt.

"Hatim's dead?"

"It was the Bolt Cutter's doing. Abu Issa wasn't happy about it. Extra paperwork, he said. He ordered me not to say anything, said it'd be bad for public morale." Abdul Amir tried to laugh, but it morphed into a sob. "I don't blame you for wanting to leave. And you're right, Khalid should go too. Take him with you to Basra, or back to your village, before the mukhabarat poison him too."

"So you didn't turn me in?"

Abdul Amir raised his red-veined eyes.

"Why would I do that?"

Huda battled to stay calm, while inside her everything whirled and spun.

"Why would I turn you in, Huda?"

"I thought the mukhabarat might be angry with me, about Ally traveling around unmonitored with Hatim. Abu Issa already said he was disappointed in me." The rolls of cash in her hand turned damp with sweat. "Where is Abu Issa, anyway? He left to find you and the Bolt Cutter. Did you see him?"

"They're waiting outside. I told them I needed to get my keys." Abdul Amir buried his face in his hands again. "They want me to go to the coffee shop and find out if people are talking about Hatim's death. They want to know if anyone is complaining."

"You better go," said Huda. "Don't let them get suspicious. Keep them away from here so I have time to pack . . . for Basra."

Another lie. Huda could hardly remember what honesty felt like.

Huda laid the phone back in its cradle. She wondered, had the mukhabarat been listening in? Rania was no fool. She used the code they'd agreed on to set their departure time. She sounded cool and collected—at least she would have to a stranger monitoring the line. But Huda had recognized the treble of sorrow in her voice.

"Who were you talking to?" Khalid dumped his school bag by the kitchen counter. "You sounded sort of upset."

"Upset? Not at all. I was organizing a trip to Lake Habbaniyah." Huda knew that some lies were best hidden in plain view. And if anything went wrong, if they had to abandon their plan, they could swim in the lake's warm waters, wash the falsehood away, and turn it into truth. "If I sounded stressed on the phone, it's because this trip is last-minute. We need to plan a few things."

"Who's *we*?"

"Mrs. Wilson, my old friend Rania Mansour, and her daughter, Hanan. And you too, my dear. Would you like a day off school?"

"A day off school?" Khalid punched the air. "Lake Habbaniyah, here I come."

He dug his lunch box from his bag.

"I thought Lake Habbaniyah had shut down? Bakr's cousin went there a couple of years ago. He said it was like a ghost town."

"It's true, the tourist resort is closed. But that means there'll be plenty of quiet beaches for us to enjoy. Now go wash your hands."

Huda struggled to keep her voice even. "There's roast chicken and eggplant fritters for dinner."

"We're not waiting for Dad?"

"He went to the coffee shop. I expect he'll be home late."

Khalid peered into her face. His green eyes narrowed.

"Your mascara is all smudged. You look like a raccoon. Have you two been arguing again?"

"No, not at all." Huda wiped her finger under her lids. "There's nothing for you to worry about."

"Is Dad coming to Lake Habbaniyah?"

"I wish he was, but he has other things to do here. Important things." Huda busied herself with the oven while Khalid washed his hands in the sink.

"Is that cardamom chicken, Mom? That's my favorite, you know."

"I know very well, my darling." Huda ladled a slice of eggplant onto his dinner plate. "I wanted to cook a special dinner for you."

"Where's your plate, Mom?"

"I'm not feeling hungry. But, please, sit down and get started before it gets cold."

Huda's lip quivered. She'd wanted so badly for them all to share a family meal together, to enjoy a few old jokes, and pretend that the moment would last forever. Instead, she hid her face from her son and bumbled about the kitchen, sick to her stomach.

She couldn't stop thinking of the taxi driver. Was Hatim's wife already washing his body and wrapping it in a shroud? Or was she in her kitchen, same as Huda, trying to keep her husband's dinner warm, telling herself he must have stopped to play a game of backgammon on the way home? She pictured the woman at the dinner table, listening to the tick of the clock on her wall.

Khalid sliced into his chicken.

"You're the best cook ever, Mom."

Huda smothered a sob and fled out the back door. In the garden, cicadas buzzed. Their cry cycled up and down, up and down, like a pulsing heart. Huda glanced through the kitchen window as Khalid bit into a slice of eggplant. What would he do when he learned the trip to Lake Habbaniyah was a ruse? Would he welcome a chance at freedom? Or, like his father, would he rather die than leave Iraq?

The waxy leaves of the orange tree scraped against the fence. On the horizon, the flames of al-Dora speared the gray evening. Huda tried to take a deep breath but her chest was tight as a drum. She knew she should go inside and finish packing but she couldn't leave the garden. She wiped her eyes and wondered, Would this be the last time she'd smell the apricot trees' perfume?

CHAPTER 27

Ally slumped over her desk. For the tenth time since she returned from the riverside, she pulled out her mother's postcards and thought about tearing them up. Ally knew it wasn't a good idea, but she removed Yusra's photo from her bag anyway.

The young nurse smiled at her. It was obvious from Yusra's straight-up stare, she would have struggled every day to still her tongue. Same as Ally's mother. With a shiver, she remembered Miriam Pachachi's warning, *Two can keep a secret only when one of them is dead.*

Ally wiped a tear away and wondered, could guilt have caused her mother's cancer? Did shame multiply inside her cells? Did she lie in that darkened bedroom and pop pills to kill the pain, or was it to keep the memories at bay, until the woman who wrote the postcards was thoroughly erased?

Like her mother, Ally had come to Baghdad dreaming of the possibilities under its enormous blue sky. Now, Huda was under the mukhabarat's boot. Khalid would end up in the fedayeen. Hanan could be raped and killed. Ally couldn't stop thinking about Rania's description of the wild dogs that Uday kept in a cage.

She put the postcards and photos away, crept to the bathroom, and splashed water on her face. She drank a glass of tepid water then lay down with sliced cucumbers on her eyes, while anger and guilt and fear galloped through her chest.

After the cucumber grew warm and floppy, Ally forced herself to get up and put a pot of water on the stove. She checked that she still had potatoes in the pantry, and cheese, butter, and green beans in the fridge for dinner, then lay down with a second round of sliced cucumber.

When the locks on the front door squealed, she didn't move.

"I'm home," Tom called.

"I've got a migraine coming on," she called from the darkened bedroom. "There's some dinner for you on the stove. I've taken a couple of ibuprofen. I'm going to try and get some sleep."

"Sorry, babe." He ambled to her bedside, bent down, and kissed her cheek. "I'll try not to wake you when I come to bed."

"Thanks," mumbled Ally. She wanted to scooch aside, pull him under the covers with her, and whisper everything she'd learned in his ear. But she knew he'd never agree to her smuggling Khalid and Hanan out of Iraq. Much less in an embassy vehicle. But what else could she do? Abandon Khalid? Leave Hanan to Uday? Look away while the regime destroyed more lives—just like it did with Yusra?

In forty-eight hours this will all be over, she told herself. She'll be safely in Jordan, where her secrets posed no threat to anyone, not her, not Rania and Huda, not Tom either. She rested her arm across her eyes to conceal her pink, mottled lids, and counted the seconds until he left for the kitchen.

In the morning, Ally pretended to sleep through Tom's alarm. She didn't want him looking in her eyes. If they were windows to the soul, surely he'd notice hers curled up in a ball, rocking back and forth, and gnawing its fingernails down to the quick. Once she was sure he was gone, she packed a small suitcase, then spent the rest of the day in front of the mirror, rehearsing lies, over and over again, until Tom returned from work once more.

"I'm in the bedroom," called Ally. She tucked the battered manila envelope into her suitcase and zipped it shut. "I'm doing some packing."

"You're packing?" Tom kissed her on the cheek and dumped his briefcase next to the bed.

Ally poked her head inside the wardrobe and rifled among her dresses. She'd already chosen her clothes, but suddenly she wasn't sure she could go through with her story. She repeated her lies so many times, the words had lost all meaning.

"I'm going to take up your suggestion, well, sort of . . ." Her laugh sounded so fake in her ears she was amazed that Tom didn't notice. She shoved her coats to one side. "I thought I'd take a little trip to Jordan. I'm overdue for some R and R. And maybe, to make you happy, I'll check out some apartments while I'm there."

"You will?" said Tom. "That's great. When do you want to go?"

"Tomorrow."

"So soon? I don't think that's possible."

"I talked to Huda already. She's got it all organized. The driver, the exit permit, and everything else. You don't need to worry about anything. You're busy enough."

He slipped his arm around her waist and turned her about.

"I'm never too busy for you."

"Yeah, right." Ally faked another laugh.

"I'm glad to see you feeling better." He smoothed a strand of hair away from her face. "I was sure that migraine was going to keep you in bed for at least another day or two. No offense, but you looked pretty horrendous last night."

"Thank you, love." She patted his cheek. "You have such a charming way with words."

Tom shifted Ally's suitcase off the bed and removed his shoes.

"Come here." He smiled slyly, and patted the mattress beside him. "You must be exhausted from all the packing." He reached for her hand and pulled her toward the bed. "Lie down, relax, with me."

"Relax?" Ally straddled his legs and pushed him backwards onto the mattress. "Is that what you're calling it now?"

"I'll call it anything you want."

He pulled her toward him, but she slipped out of his arms, rolled away, and clambered to her feet. She wished she could hide in bed with Tom, close her eyes, and forget about the world outside.

"Come back here," he said. "Lie down."

He looked at her, and her secrets lined up at the back of her throat, ready to leap out her mouth. She turned away and rummaged in the wardrobe again. Rania and Huda were right—she shouldn't tell Tom. Then if anything went wrong, he could truthfully tell the ambassador he hadn't known about their plan.

You can tell him all you want, as soon as everyone is safe, Huda had said. *Is it really lying, if you're honest in the end?*

As Ally pretended to search her dresser drawers, she wondered if Huda had always had such an elastic take on the truth, or was it the sort of motto that informants learned on the job? Did she repeat it in her head each time she invited Ally for a cup of coffee and a chat? When she said their friendship was real, was that another lie? Or was she just doing what was needed to survive?

"I admit, I'm glad you're getting out of Baghdad," said Tom. "But I didn't think it would be this sudden."

Ally gripped the edge of the dresser. He was too hard to resist, sprawled on the mattress, hand extended to her. Her body swayed toward him like the tide.

"Let's go for a walk." She retreated to the door. "I've been packing all day. I need to get out and clear my head."

Another lie. She didn't want to clear her head. She wanted to stuff it full of honking cars, and amber traffic signals flashing on and off. She wanted to replace all those clamoring secrets with carpet sellers offering tea, men playing backgammon outside the coffee shops, and boys riding donkey carts. She wanted sound, and light, and distractions. Anything but her and Tom, alone, with her lies on the tip of her tongue.

Out in the street, Tom took her hand and guided her past a pothole. It was still busy, and every minute or so a taxi driver slowed, tapped his horn, and called for them to get in. Ally scanned the sidewalk for Mohammad, but there was no sign of the little boy.

"You know the newspaper vendor and her son?" She clutched Tom's hand tight. "Will you drop some food off for them while I'm gone? Promise me you won't forget."

"Okay, I promise." Tom laughed. "I think you're going to miss your little friend more than me."

Ally smiled wanly. Up ahead, at the coffee shop, men were smoking nargilah. Ally recognized a taxi driver out front, leaning against his car.

"That guy is friends with Hatim, the driver I use every now and again. He might know if he's working tonight. I'd like to say goodbye before I leave."

"Hello!" She picked her way across the sidewalk. "Have you seen my friend, Mr. Hatim?"

Behind his glasses, the taxi driver's eyes bulged. He hurled his cigarette on the ground and raced around the far side of his car.

"He must think we want a ride," Ally whispered to Tom.

The driver clambered into the driver's seat and fumbled for his keys. Ally bent down and tapped on the window.

"I'm looking for Hatim," she called through the glass.

The driver stamped his foot on the accelerator. His taxi lurched into the traffic and disappeared around the next corner. Ally glanced at Tom in surprise.

"Do I smell bad?"

Abdul Amir strode across the sidewalk, appearing as if from nowhere. Ally's heart accelerated. Huda had said she wasn't going to tell him their plan, but secrets had a very short life in Baghdad.

"What are you doing here, Mr. Tom?" Behind Abdul Amir's shoulder, the men at the backgammon tables lay down their dice and eyed them sternly.

"You need to go somewhere?" Abdul Amir waved them back in the direction they'd come from. "I can take you. My car is parked around the corner."

"Thanks, but there's no need," said Tom. "We're just stretching our legs."

Ally tried to copy Tom's diplomat smile, but it wouldn't stick to her lips. She knew Huda might be an unwilling informant, but she doubted Abdul Amir was losing sleep over it. Or was she wrong? The shadows under his eyes were purple as a bruise. His gaze flicked left and right and back again.

"Are you okay, Abdul Amir?" said Tom.

His green eyes continued to flick back and forth between them and a man in the doorway of a juice bar. Even without his leather jacket, Ally recognized mukhabarat keeping watch.

"Maybe we should go home." She tugged at Tom's arm. "I've got a few things to do."

Tom had spotted the mukhabarat too and was eyeing him from under his lids.

"Okay, let's go," he said.

As Abdul Amir herded them toward the Corolla, Ally glanced over her shoulder. It seemed like every man in the street was watching them, all with that same dead-eyed stare. Goose bumps prickled her arms.

Ally realized that Baghdad would never reveal all its secrets to her. But she had the answer she'd come for—she knew why her mother lost her smile. Ally would have to carry that terrible knowledge with her, across the ancient rivers of the Tigris and the Euphrates, through the baking Mesopotamian plains, and on, always. Even if Ally wanted to exile truth from her mind, she couldn't purge it, no more than Baghdad could expel every tiny pearl of desert sand. But, if fortune was on her side, she could help to write her story a new ending.

CHAPTER 28

Huda lay in bed and stared at the ceiling. The blades of the fan whistled overhead. Next to her, Abdul Amir stirred.

"No," he muttered. "Don't, don't . . ."

He slurred something Huda couldn't make out. He'd barely slept all night. He'd wanted to talk to Khalid before he came to bed, to pass on some fatherly words of courage before his son supposedly set off for Basra. Huda convinced him it was too risky. Khalid might let it slip to Bakr, then Bakr might tell his parents or a friend, and who knew where it would end. *A secret is like a dove,* she'd whispered, *once it leaves your hand it flies where it wants.*

Now, as Abdul Amir moaned, guilt spread its wings in Huda's chest. Could she really deprive her husband of his son? Abdul Amir cried out again. The sound bruised her insides. She reached over and turned the alarm clock off before it had a chance to chime.

Abdul Amir jerked awake.

"Is it time already?"

"Stay in bed," she whispered. "I'll go make us coffee."

"I want to come to the bus station with you." He dragged his hands across his face. "Khalid will notice that he's getting on a bus to Basra, not Lake Habbaniyah. When he does, I want to talk to him, man to man, father to son."

"No, you need to stay here in case the mukhabarat come by," Huda whispered in his ear. "You can pick the car up tonight, but in the meanwhile tell anyone who asks that I've gone on a day trip. When they work out that . . ." She shuddered, and forced herself to continue. "Please, tell them you knew nothing. Tell them you're furious. Tell them you'll divorce me. Say anything, but, please, don't try to take the blame. I don't want you to get hurt."

Huda swung her legs off the bed and slipped out of her nightgown.

"Huda, wait." Abdul Amir's fingers brushed against the curve of her back. "Lie down with me for just a few minutes more."

Huda quivered. Sixteen years of marriage was not something she could steal away from, without even a kiss goodbye. She slipped back under the sheets.

"Don't cry." He tightened his arm around her. "We're doing the right thing for our son."

She nestled alongside his chest, so close she could hear the echo of his heart. Should she tell him the truth? she asked herself. Surely he'd understand that Basra wasn't safe, that there was nowhere to hide in Iraq. Abdul Amir rolled over and stared at her with a tenderness Huda had thought long dead. Abruptly, love plunged its dagger into doubt.

"I'm not going to Basra." She held her breath for a moment, then continued on, her words tiptoeing out as quiet as ghosts. "I'm not going to the village either. I'm taking Khalid to Jordan. It's the only way he'll be safe."

Abdul Amir's eyes went round with shock.

"We are Iraqi. We don't abandon our country." He spoke too loud. They both flinched.

"I love our country too," Huda murmured into his ear. "But we need to go someplace the mukhabarat can't find us. If we stay in Iraq, they'll hunt us down. You know that."

"Khalid is Iraqi," he whispered. "This is his home."

"An innocent man has been murdered." She levered herself onto her elbows and stared into Abdul Amir's sea-green eyes. "I can see the guilt in your face. I know it's like acid eating you inside. Do you want that for your son? Do you want him in the fedayeen? Do you want him to become a man like the Bolt Cutter?"

"Of course not." Abdul Amir shook his head, like he was still trapped in his bad dream.

"Then you either help me to get our son to safety." She bit her lip. "Or you can tell the mukhabarat everything and leave Khalid without a mother."

He shook his head.

"Khalid belongs in Iraq."

"Until now, I did what the mukhabarat asked. I did what you asked too." She leaned close, breath brushing against his ear. "I ignored what my heart was telling me, and it only led to tears. Listen to yours now. Listen to your heart, I beg you."

Huda sunk deep into the front seat of the embassy Land Cruiser. In the side mirror, she could see Ghassan waiting outside Ally's gate. He hadn't yet noticed it was her behind the wheel. She squinted into the early-morning haze, and searched for the mukhabarat stationed in the vacant house next door.

"Mom, why are you looking so weird?" said Khalid.

"Me?" Huda glanced in the rearview mirror. "Weird?"

Khalid ran his hands over the soft leather of the back seat.

"The way you're smiling reminds me of the Joker."

"The Joker?"

"One of Batman's enemies." He rested his hands behind his head. "We're really traveling in style to Lake Habbaniyah. You'd think you'd be happy, but you're looking all weird instead."

The gate rattled. Ally hurried onto the sidewalk. Ghassan reached for her small suitcase, but she waved him off and strode stiffly on, head down, arms pumping like an automaton. She threw open the door and shoved her suitcase into the Land Cruiser.

"Let's go." She scrambled into the passenger's seat. "Now."

"What is it? What's happened?"

"I'll tell you, but first, let's go."

Ally glanced past her, her mouth a frightened circle. Ghassan rapped his knuckles on the window by Huda's ear. She waved at him, but the way that she raised her hand looked less like a greeting than an attempt to ward off a blow. The Land Cruiser jerked away from the curb. A pickup honked and swerved out of the way.

In the periphery of her vision, Huda spotted the mukhabarat spy lumber out of the neighboring yard. He watched the Land Cruiser circle past. Ally saw him too. Her eyes sparkled with fear. Huda could tell every nerve in her body was popping, just like hers.

The girl tugged a portable CD player from her handbag.

"Hey, Khalid." Her hand trembled as she passed her headphones to him. "I've got the new album by Usher. Why don't you have a listen?"

"Usher? Thanks, Mrs. Wilson."

They waited till Khalid slid the headphones over his ears and began to nod his head in time with the music. Ally leaned across the cabin.

"Abdul Amir called the house. He wanted to speak to Tom. When I asked him what it was about, he refused to tell me."

Huda's breath jammed in her throat.

"What did you do?"

"What could I do?" She glanced over her shoulder. "I hung up on him and then I left the phone off the hook. We better hope Tom doesn't notice and put it back on."

"When did he call?"

"About five minutes before you arrived."

Huda had thought she'd convinced Abdul Amir that Khalid wouldn't be safe in Iraq. But as they loaded the backpacks into the car, she saw doubt multiply in his eyes. Was Tom the only one he'd called? Was he phoning the mukhabarat right now?

Ally glanced over her shoulder again.

"Ghassan is talking to that creepy guy next door. They don't look happy." Her fingers knotted and unknotted in her lap. "Please tell me I'm being paranoid."

Huda said nothing, and accelerated past the blinking traffic lights.

CHAPTER 29

In Rania's garden, the eucalypts quivered. She paced back and forth, unable to still herself as the wind tugged at her hair. At the picnic table, Hanan pushed a fried egg around her plate.

"Eat your breakfast," she said. "We have to go soon."

With a clang, Hanan dropped her fork and covered her swollen eyes. A bolt of pain ran through Rania with all the force of an ax splitting wood. She wanted to wrap her daughter in her arms, throw her head back, and wail at the sky. But all she allowed herself was a brief squeeze of Hanan's shoulder. Even that felt dangerous, like it might send them both over the edge.

"You must be strong," she muttered, to herself as much as Hanan. "Tears will only give us away."

There had been many tears last night, out in the garden, under the watchful eye of the bronze mother curled around her child. The moon had been bright, so bright she could almost see her daughter's childhood ending, word by word, whisper by whisper.

"Don't send me away," Hanan had cried. "I'll behave. I swear, I'll be good."

"None of this is your fault." Rania's voice cracked. "And no one could wish for a better daughter."

"I want to stay with you."

Rania hugged her tight, so tight she could feel Hanan's heart hammering in her chest. Her bones felt as easily crushed as a bird's.

"I promise," said Rania, "I'll join you as soon as I can."

"Why, Mom? Why is this happening to us?"

Rania didn't know what to say or how to explain. Hanan's enormous amber stare kept her silent, pinned like a butterfly under glass. As the stars looked on, Rania had cursed Malik, and Uday, and his father. How many families had they torn apart? How many had they forced into exile? How many tears would Iraq's daughters have to weep?

The bell rang at the gate, jolting Rania back to the present.

"Try to finish that egg, darling." The words caught in her raw throat, and she hurried across the dry lawn.

Huda was alone at the gate. As Rania hustled her in off the sidewalk, she caught a glimpse of Ally in the front of the Land Cruiser, eyes wide as a lake, and Khalid in the backseat, bobbing his head back and forth.

"I can't eat this." Hanan appeared on the path, holding her plate of eggs. "If I do, I'll throw up."

The girl glanced at Huda and tried to smile, but her lips wobbled and tears flooded her eyes. Rania felt that ax again, the blade cleaving her in two. She put an arm around Hanan's shoulders and guided her toward the front door.

"Darling, go inside and freshen up," she said. "Splash some water on your face, then we'll leave."

Hanan sniffed and stumbled indoors. Huda shot Rania an irritated glance.

"I thought we agreed not to say anything until we got to Lake Habbaniyah."

"I couldn't do it."

"Listen to me," said Huda. "It's not too late for you. We can go together. All of us."

lowered the window. A hot, grainy wind swept into the
and ruffled her hair.

s-salaam alaikum." She smiled at the soldier. "We're with
ustralian embassy. The deputy ambassador's wife is making
to Jordan."

he soldier stared at Ally, eyes wandering up and down.
ustralian, did you say? Where's her identification?"

uda flipped open the glove box, removed Ally's passport and
permit, and passed the documents through the window.
young man snatched them from her hand and sauntered back
e guard post.

uda raised the window and turned up the air-conditioning.
'd been pulled over at two other checkpoints, but both times
soldiers had been older men who remembered the value of
pline and common courtesy—or if not, they knew it wasn't
to mess with anyone in a big expensive vehicle, carrying pa-
stamped with the Foreign Ministry's seal. Huda peeked at
young men at the guard post. They were a different sort, un-
dictable. They jostled about, sniggering, passing papers and
mits back and forth like trading cards.

The young soldier exited the guard post, cocky, rolling his
ulders and hips. The others followed. They reminded Huda of
ppy desert dogs creeping toward a camel, hoping to get in a
e before they got kicked. The first soldier, the alpha dog, strode
ard the Land Cruiser.

"Boys, guns, and testosterone." Ally eyed their approach. "It's
angerous mix."

Huda lowered the window. The burning wind rushed in again.
e extended her palm for the papers.

"Get out." The alpha dog yanked on the door handle. It was
cked but he kept yanking. "Get out, I said."

"Why?" Huda recoiled. "What's wrong?"

"Unlock the door and get out. Now."

Alarm flashed in Ally's eyes.

"What did he say? Is he telling us to get out of the car?"

"I can't leave my mother." Rania knit her fingers together anxiously and rubbed her scarred thumb. An engine purred outside.
A few moments later, a car door slammed. Ally barged through
the gate.

"A man just drove past," she hissed. "He was staring at me."

"Plenty of men stare at you," said Huda.

"I don't like this," said Ally. "Maybe we should call it all off."

Rania glanced at Huda. The look in her eyes made her wonder,
does she feel the same as me, like a woman about to hurl herself
from a bridge? After so many years and so much bad blood, Rania
realized Huda was probably the only person who understood how
she felt right now. But could she trust her and Ally to keep Hanan
safe?

"Get Khalid into my car." She dug the keys to her old Volvo
from her pocket and handed them to Ally. "I'll get Hanan ready."

She hurried down the hallway to her studio. The president
watched from the easel, with his hunting rifle tucked under his
arm. She fought back tears as she dug Hanan's backpack from its
hiding place in her storeroom of art supplies.

A floorboard creaked. Huda slipped through the door. In her
peripheral vision, Rania saw her recoil at the sight of the painting.
Would the portrait pay enough for Hanan's new life? Or would
Malik laugh and declare the honor of painting the president reward enough? Rania hunched her shoulders and wondered, If
Huda touched her arm, would she feel the shame burning beneath
her skin?

"The man who commissioned this painting is one of his men."
She gestured at the oil-paint Uday lurking by his father's side.
"He's demanded a viewing this afternoon."

Her absence would surely raise Malik's suspicions. Rania had
to stay here, perform as demanded, tell him stories and flatter his
pride. God willing, that would earn her daughter enough time to
escape.

CHAPTER 30

The tang of turpentine and the muddy scent of oil paint made it hard for Huda to breathe. She tried not to look at the painting of the president and his sons as Rania carried the backpack out to the hall. Hanan was waiting for them. She spotted the bag, and her lip twitched. Rania kissed her daughter's forehead, then bent close and whispered in her ear.

"Huda's son doesn't know everything that you do. She's going to tell him at Lake Habbaniyah." She rested her hands on Hanan's shoulders and stared into her face. "Remember, if anyone asks, this is simply a day trip. Understand?"

Hanan closed her eyes and gave a small nod of assent.

"Khalid is waiting in our car." Rania grabbed a pashmina scarf from the hall closet and herded her out the front door. "Please go and introduce yourself while I finish locking up."

"We should split up." Huda's heart thumped with each step across the cobblestones. "I'll take the Abu Ghraib expressway. You take Urdun Street."

In the Land Cruiser, Huda and Ally waited in silence as the Volvo pulled away from the curb in front of them. A flash of yel-

low moved in the rearview mirror. Huda [...] a long, low sedan sail through the cross st[...] a Chevy, not an Oldsmobile—but some[...] profile made Huda's heart jerk in her c[...] Cruiser into gear and jammed her foot on [...]

"Careful!" Ally clutched the dash.

Huda turned right at the first corner, t[...] mind she saw the driver of the Chevy do[...] ever closer. Ally glanced over her shoulder.[...]

"Did you see something?"

"I'm not sure."

"This is insane." Ally kneaded her tem[...] have agreed to this."

High walls and locked gates flashed [...] wrenched the wheel. The Land Cruiser bou[...] strewn alley.

"What did the man you saw earlier look[...] teeth as they hit a pothole. "Did you see his f[...]

"He was about my age. He had dark hair, [...] tache."

"That could be anyone."

"He looked familiar." Ally twisted about. "[...] like one of the men who trailed me to the emb[...] was right before I hired Abdul Amir."

"Stay calm," said Huda. "We just need to sti[...]

She rolled to a stop at a broken traffic sign[...] ently, like a loyal citizen should—then she turn[...] accelerated toward the Abu Ghraib expressway[...] eyes and clutched her seat belt at her chest. Hu[...] praying for them.

The soldier swaggered toward the Land Cr[...] soldiers watched from the sandbagged checkpoi[...] boys like him, with Kalashnikovs dangling at thei[...]

"Stay calm," whispered Huda.

"Stay here," said Huda. "Let me handle this."

She unlocked the door and slid out onto the highway's dusty shoulder. The soldier was taller than she'd realized, and the sun pouring over his shoulder stung her eyes. A truck rumbled by, wheels churning up dust and exhaust fumes. The desert wind gathered it all up and sent it whistling back toward Baghdad along with a million grains of sand.

"How can I help you?" Huda wanted to sound calm and in control, but she had to shriek over the traffic and the wind. A line of vehicles snaked toward the checkpoint. Were Abu Issa and the Bolt Cutter out there, waiting to swoop in? What about Abdul Amir? Had he changed his mind? Was he hunting them too?

"The deputy ambassador's wife has all the correct travel permits," Huda told the soldier. "There shouldn't be a problem."

"What about you?"

"Me?"

"I want to see your travel permit."

"I don't need one. A driver from the embassy in Jordan is meeting us at the border crossing. He'll take her to Amman and I will return to Baghdad."

Alpha Dog's lip curled back in a sneer.

"Since when do women work as drivers? That's a man's job." He cast a sly glance at his two sidekicks. "Just like a soldier is a real man's job."

The soldiers smirked and slunk closer. Their guns clattered. Alpha Dog spat a blob of phlegm near Huda's feet. *Get back in the car!* a voice inside her screamed. *Go home and beg Abdul Amir's forgiveness before it's too late.*

Huda took a deep breath, straightened her spine, and tried to reproduce Rania's commanding presence.

"Our beloved president has been at the forefront of equality for the last twenty years." She glared at the soldiers like they were Khalid and Bakr skipping school. "You should know your own country's history better than that. The president has said that every woman has a role to play in the development of our glorious nation. This is the wish of the president himself, President Saddam Hussein." The words hit them like a slap to the face. The three young men shied away. Huda pressed on, wielding the president's name like a bludgeon.

"Our leader, Saddam Hussein, has granted women some of the highest positions in government. The minister of education is a woman. The chief scientific officer for National Security is too. So why should I, a loyal Iraqi woman just like them, not be fit to drive the car of a foreigner? Do you think an Iraqi woman is not good enough for that? Do you not believe the words of our great president, Saddam Hussein, when he says Iraqis are the equal of any nation?"

"Okay, okay," muttered the alpha soldier. "Don't get worked up."

"I want the documents now." Huda thrust out her palm. "They have been signed and stamped at the Ministry of Foreign Affairs. If you have a problem, I am sure the officials there would be interested to know of it. What is your name and rank, young man?"

Traffic at the checkpoint backed up. Men hung out car windows and cursed. Horns honked.

"You're lucky that I'm too busy to bother myself with the likes of you." Huda snatched the documents back. "Now get back to work, before I change my mind and report you."

She returned quickly to the car, knowing the presence of the shiny embassy Land Cruiser would be noted by the others in the queue. It would swiftly find the ears of the local mukhabarat, before traveling on to God knows where. Abu Ghraib was not far away. Perhaps whispers would surf the gritty wind, past the razor wire, and find their way to the darkest cell—the cell where they locked prisoners who once dreamed they could defy the regime. No, Huda told herself, as the sun bit the thin skin on her cheek. Traitors like them were already long dead.

Huda found Khalid on the shore of the lake, a mile or so from the derelict Hotel Habbaniyah. He had his back to her, his toes in the water, and his hands raised high above his head. He swayed slightly as the breeze washed over him. No one else was visible on the long stretch of beach. Far out on the enormous lake, the fishing fleet was reduced to a few squiggles. Huda slipped off her shoes and padded across the sand. Khalid spun about, grinning.

"Mom, finally, you're here. Did you pack a towel for me? Where's Mrs. Wilson and Mrs. Mansour?" He kicked at the water and sent spray flying back toward the lake. "What about Hanan? Is she going to swim?"

"Hanan's mother has to go back to Baghdad. And Mrs. Wilson and Hanan are waiting for us in the Land Cruiser."

"Why? We just got here. I'm not ready to go back to Baghdad."

Huda tried to take a calming breath, but the brackish air lodged in her throat.

"We're not going back to Baghdad," she said.

"Good, I was worried for a moment." He threw his arms wide and inhaled. "Because I could get used to the smell of freedom."

"Freedom?"

"Freedom from math class, anyway." He whooped and kicked the water again. "Bakr is going to die of envy."

He swung toward her, face shining.

"What is it, Mom?" The joy in Khalid's eyes flickered, then slowly disappeared. "What's happened? How come you look so sad?"

"This is going to be a shock." She reached for his hands. "We're not going back to Baghdad." A flock of water birds rose shrieking from the lake and flapped across the water. Huda took a deep breath. "We're going to Jordan."

Khalid blinked.

"Jordan?"

"Yes, and Hanan is coming too."

"What about our picnic? The swimming?"

"I don't want to scare you, but we have to leave Iraq." Huda squeezed his hands. "Today. Now."

Shock ballooned in Khalid's eyes.

"Is this a joke?"

"No, my son. We're going to stay in Jordan until it's safe for us to return."

Khalid pulled free of her grip.

"This is crazy. Does Dad know about this?"

"Your dad agrees that we can't stay. It's not safe."

"This makes no sense. We are Iraqis. We belong here." Khalid stamped his foot. Muddy water splashed against Huda's shins. "Is this because you're working for the mukhabarat? Are you having regrets? Are you running away to mend your conscience?"

"That's not it."

"I'm not leaving my country just because you sold out to the mukhabarat."

"Listen carefully, my son." Huda knew the beach was deserted, but she couldn't stop herself from scanning the long crescent of sand. "We're leaving because they want to put you in the fedayeen."

"The fedayeen? Me?" Khalid's voice cracked. He lurched away from the water's edge.

For a moment, Huda thought he was going to bolt into the scrub.

"I can't join the fedayeen. They make every cadet shoot a prisoner in the head. If you don't, they shoot you instead." He opened his mouth wide, like a small child about to wail.

"This is why we're going to Jordan." Huda tried to draw him into a hug. "You'll be safe there."

Khalid pushed her away.

"This is your fault. If not for you, the mukhabarat wouldn't even know my name." He clutched at his dark hair. "Is this some sort of sick reward for all your dirty work? Men like Abu Issa and his stupid partner probably have wet dreams about joining the fedayeen."

"Khalid! Watch your mouth."

"Why? If you had such high morals, you wouldn't be a mukhabarat spy."

The wind dragged a tear from Huda's eye.

"I had no choice."

"You could have refused, Mom." Khalid's face twisted in disgust. "And now it's me who has to pay the price."

He stumbled away from her. Huda wiped her eyes and followed him to the parking lot.

The Land Cruiser rumbled away from the lake, kicking up a trail of dust. Huda watched Rania dwindle in the rearview mirror. She stood tall and waved fiercely. Huda's throat ached. Rania had always been brave, rarely allowing anyone to see a chink in her elegant armor. But Huda knew that as soon as they rounded the corner, she'd slide onto the hard-packed earth and weep her heart out.

"Your mom will join you in Jordan soon." Huda prayed that was true. She reached behind her seat and patted Hanan's knee. The girl hiccupped wretchedly. "Trust me. It'll be okay."

"Trust you?" Khalid snorted. "We're running away from our own country."

"Please, let's all settle down." Huda gripped the wheel as the Land Cruiser bucked over the ruts in the dirt track. A flock of birds burst from a stand of salt cedar. Khalid glowered as they squawked toward the sky.

"This is all your fault, Mom."

Ally glanced over her shoulder. Huda didn't know how much she'd understood, but Khalid's anger needed no translation.

"Khalid, your mom only wants to keep you safe. Hanan's mom is doing the same."

"It's not the same," said Khalid, in schoolboy English. "Hanan's mom is not a dirty spy."

"Khalid!" gasped Huda.

"Come on." Ally shook her head. "That's not fair."

He slapped his palm against his forehead.

"Do you not understand?"

"Khalid, stop it." Huda tried to catch his eye in the rearview mirror. "No one wants to hear this."

"I think Mrs. Wilson would like to hear that the mukhabarat pay you to watch her." He hunched his shoulders like it was winter. "She should know you are not really her friend."

Ally sighed like the breeze on the lake.

"I know you're shocked." She swiveled toward him. "I was too, believe me. I felt like a fool. I was angry. Real angry." She paused and glanced at Huda. "But the truth is, if I was in your mom's position, I would have done the same thing."

Huda winced.

"Thank you."

She reached across and squeezed Ally's hand. She wondered, did the young woman realize that even now, if she had no other choice, she'd give her up to save her son? Her DNA was curled inside Khalid's cells. That trumped everything: fear of the mukhabarat, greed, even a true and loyal friend like the one seated beside her. As Huda steered the Land Cruiser past a hedge of salt cedar, shame tightened its fingers around her throat.

"Please," she said, "don't feel that you have to defend me to—"

She slammed her foot on the brake. An old yellow Chevy blocked the track. The Bolt Cutter was at the wheel. He caught Huda's eye and laughed, teeth flashing in the dark cabin.

Ally pressed her hand to her mouth. "That's the guy I saw this morning."

"Mom, do something." Khalid's voice squeaked. "Don't let him hurt us."

"Everyone, stay calm." Huda's fingernails dug into the wheel. "Remember, we're on a day trip to Lake Habbaniyah."

The Bolt Cutter slid out of the Chevy and lumbered toward the Land Cruiser, smirking like a glutton served a platter of steak. Huda slid her foot toward the accelerator. Should she run him down? The Bolt Cutter laughed and tugged a revolver from his pocket, as if he'd read her mind.

Huda shot a glance at Ally. She was pale as bone. In the back seat, Hanan huddled in a ball, clutching her mother's scarf. Khalid's eyes bulged, the whites too bright, pupils wide as the lake. The Bolt Cutter would see right through their day-tripper tale. Even if Hanan's weeping didn't give them away, the animal in him would sniff out their fear.

Where was Abu Issa? she wondered. She'd never dealt with the Bolt Cutter on his own. Panic pounded at her chest.

"Ally, I'm leaving the keys in the ignition." She reached for her door. "If anything happens to me, drive straight to the highway and keep going. Fifteen miles from the border, remember, make that detour. The compass is in the glove box."

"Wait." Ally twisted her wedding ring from her finger and pressed it into Huda's palm. "Take this. Maybe if you give it to him, he'll leave us alone."

"Are you sure?"

Ally nodded.

"Mom, don't go." Khalid lurched toward the front seat. "Don't do it."

"I love you, my darling." She touched his cheek. "Never doubt that."

Huda slid out of the Land Cruiser and hurried toward the Bolt Cutter.

"Well, well." The Bolt Cutter's gun swung lazily at his side. "It's my lucky day."

"What are you doing?" She frowned. "You've frightened the diplomat's wife. She thinks you're going to rob us."

"Rob you?" The Bolt Cutter laughed. "That's not exactly what I had in mind."

He tried to catch her eye, but she kept her gaze on his feet. She didn't want to get his blood up.

"Where's Abu Issa? Does he know you're here?"

"The old man's got no idea. This is, how do you say, off-the-books." The Bolt Cutter snorted. "All Abu Issa cares about is his precious paperwork and his goddamn regulations."

He flexed his fingers and swapped the gun from his right hand to his left. Huda followed its passage back and forth, dark snout gleaming in the sun.

"Abu Issa is nothing but a spineless bureaucrat." The Bolt Cutter stepped closer. "Don't you realize, Huda, I'm the real mukhabarat?"

Huda tried not to tremble.

"I'm supposed to be taking the diplomat's wife sightseeing. Now she thinks we're being robbed. How am I going to explain this? You should go before you make the situation worse."

The Bolt Cutter squinted at the Land Cruiser.

"I can see the foreign slut sitting up front, but who's that in the back seat? Is it your friend Rania Mansour?" He peered over her shoulder. "Or is that her sexy little daughter? And that's Khalid cuddled up next to her, right?"

Huda stiffened.

"I thought if I brought the kids along, Ally would be more relaxed and feel more comfortable opening up to me." Her heart thumped like a mallet against her ribs. "But she's not going to feel relaxed now that a man with a gun has blocked our way. I'm going to tell her you're a security guard from the old hotel and you got carried away. I'll tell her you're sorry for the mistake."

"Sorry?" The Bolt Cutter rocked on his heels. "Why would I be sorry? And why would I leave when I've just found you sneaking out of Baghdad in a diplomatic vehicle?" He took another step toward her. "If I search your car, what will I find?"

"Nothing, nothing at all."

"I tell you what I'd like to search." Once again, the Bolt Cutter swapped his gun from hand to hand. "I'd like to search that foreign slut. Oh, yeah, then I'll do the same to the Mansour girl. What's her name? Hanan, right? Yeah, I think I'm going to take her in for questioning." He bared his teeth. "If you know what I mean."

"You can't do that."

"Don't tell me what to do," the Bolt Cutter growled. "If I want to take the girl, I will. And then, Huda, I'll come over to your house tomorrow night and show you a video tape of what I did to her. Maybe when I leave, I'll take Khalid with me. Give him a little tour of Abu Ghraib." He snickered. "I'm not Abu Issa, remember. I'm not interested in drinking tea and making nice."

Huda searched for a way out. On her left, patchy scrub led to a tiny beach and a stretch of reed-clogged lake. On the right, head-high grass rippled in the breeze, so thick that four bodies could lie out there for days and no one would be the wiser. Only the birds would see them. Eventually, a circle of vultures in the sky would give their corpses away.

"Tell me what you want," said Huda.

The Bolt Cutter tilted his head, eyed her up and down.

"I'm going to search your vehicle and everything in it, especially that girl in the back seat. Abu Issa likes to complain that I'm not *thorough*. Well, I'm gonna be real thorough with her."

He laughed and slapped his hand against his tree-trunk thigh. A memory flashed through Huda's mind: her mother had taken her to see a gypsy caravan with a dancing bear. As the animal loomed over her, swaying clumsily, she realized it could kill her with one swipe of its hairy paw. The Bolt Cutter came toward her, and Huda felt that same bone-deep chill.

"Back to the Land Cruiser." He put his hand on the back of her neck and spun her about. "Get going. Now."

Huda knew if he looked hard enough, he'd find her passport hidden in the lining of her handbag. He'd probably find Khalid's birth certificate and Hanan's as well. How would she explain that? Even an oaf like the Bolt Cutter would realize they planned to flee. On the far side of the windshield, Khalid leaned forward and whispered urgently into Ally's ear. Huda prayed the girl wouldn't hesitate, and that she'd slide into the driver's seat, stomp her foot on the accelerator, and mow the Bolt Cutter down.

The Bolt Cutter shoved Huda between the shoulder blades. Khalid was right. She should have said no to the mukhabarat from the very beginning. Perhaps they would have sent her to Abu Ghraib, but at least it would have been her alone—not Khalid, not Hanan, and not Ally. Her diplomatic ID wouldn't save her now. Not with a man like this.

Huda whirled about and shoved the Bolt Cutter in the chest.

"Leave them alone!" she shouted. "They haven't done anything wrong."

The Bolt Cutter blinked in surprise.

"I guess my gut was right. You're hiding something." He smirked and brushed her imaginary hand print from his chest. "If you like, you can confess now. But I'd love an excuse to beat it out of you. In fact, it'll be my pleasure."

Huda eyed the rippling grass, the scrub, the lake.

"Listen, you need to come with me." She tipped her head toward the water. "The diplomat's wife can't see this or all our hard work will be ruined. And there's a nice piece of gold in it for you."

"What are you babbling about?"

Huda uncurled her hand. Ally's wedding ring glittered in her palm.

"Come on." She sidled toward the hedge of prickly salt cedar. "The longer we're out here, the more suspicious she'll get."

The Bolt Cutter lumbered after her. Huda hurried toward the beach.

"This better be good or—"

Huda spun on her heel, wound her arm back, and slapped his face.

The Bolt Cutter's mouth fell open. He touched his cheek. Huda prayed that she'd hear the Land Cruiser roar to life. If Ally kept her foot to the floor, she'd easily outrun the Bolt Cutter's old Chevy. Huda slapped the Bolt Cutter again, grunting with effort.

"Shame on you." She drew herself up tall. "What would your mother think? Does she know you spend your day harassing women and threatening young boys?"

"What the . . . ?"

"Do you have a sister?" Huda had succeeded in bluffing the soldiers at the checkpoint. She prayed she could do it again. "Would you like someone to treat her like that?"

The Bolt Cutter's fleshy lips twisted. His palm hit her mouth like an oar and she tumbled onto the dirt. She tasted the metallic tang of blood.

"You're going to regret that, you stupid bitch. And so will your son and the two whores with him." The Bolt Cutter glanced toward the tiny beach. "And if Abu Issa somehow finds out, I'll tell him you had an unfortunate accident while swimming. What's he going to do, anyway? File another report? Put another black mark in my personnel file?"

The Bolt Cutter leaned over her, blocking out the sun.

"Of course, I'll have to make sure that foreign slut doesn't open her mouth. And the poor little rich girl too, after I've had some fun with her."

Huda stared up at him. She'd often imagined how it might end. She'd never dreamed it would be washed in a lake's cool breeze, surrounded by grass, with water birds soaring overhead. The Bolt Cutter glanced toward the lake.

"How long can you hold your breath, Huda?" He reached down and grabbed her by the shirt. "Let's go find out."

Huda jerked and twisted like a fish pulled from a river but the Bolt Cutter barely noticed. He dragged her toward the shore.

"Don't do this!" she cried. "You're making a mistake."

"I'm sure I'll find enough proof in your vehicle to justify a few bodies, but if not, I'll plant something. I've done it before." He dragged her through a patch of spiky rushes. "I've got to tell you, I'm looking forward to feeling your body go limp. That moment is always so good."

"Don't!"

"Clean up shouldn't be a hassle. I know how to get rid of a body fast, even four of them." He laughed carelessly. "And I know a guy in Fallujah who'll pay real good money for that fancy Land Cruiser. He'll give it a new paint job and have it over the border into Syria before sundown."

"Listen to me." Huda grabbed at his ankle. "Uday Hussein won't like this. I swear, he's going to hang your head on your mother's gate."

The Bolt Cutter stopped. He stared down at her, face haloed by sunlight.

"What did you say?"

"The president's son has marked Hanan Mansour for himself. Uday's expecting her at his palace this weekend."

The Bolt Cutter blinked, brain creaking like a rusty cog.

"Uday has plans for the girl." Huda crawled to her knees. "You can drown me in this lake, but that'll be nothing compared to what he'll do if you touch her before he does."

He shook his head like an angry water buffalo.

"I saw you this morning outside Rania Mansour's house." Huda wiped blood from the corner of her mouth. "I told her exactly who you are. If her daughter doesn't show up, she'll know who's to blame. Don't you know Rania is the president's favorite artist? She's painting his portrait right now. These aren't ordinary people you're messing with. They're not like you and me."

The Bolt Cutter growled and kicked at the muddy beach. Blobs of silt splattered against the water.

"If you're smart, you'll get back in your car and leave." Huda staggered to her feet. "I'll tell the diplomat's wife she was right, you were a robber. I'll say a group of fishermen scared you off."

She rummaged in her pocket and pulled out Ally's wedding ring.

"Here," she said, "take this and go."

The Bolt Cutter snatched the ring from her hand.

"Maybe your friend in Fallujah buys jewelry too." Huda tugged a twig from her hair. "But I want twenty-five percent of whatever you make off that ring, understand? We can both work together and make some money. Or Rania Mansour can call the president's palace and mention your name."

The Bolt Cutter scowled.

"Fifteen percent," he grunted. "I'll give you fifteen percent of what I get for the ring. Not a dinar more."

Huda nodded curtly. The Bolt Cutter grumbled and stuck his gun in his pocket. Huda attempted to straighten her clothes. As soon as he left with the ring, she'd climb in the Land Cruiser and drive to the border. Tonight, she and Khalid would be in Jordan. So would Hanan. She could picture it now, clear as sunlight on the lake.

"Hurry up," she said. "We don't want the diplomat's wife raising the alarm."

"If you say so." The Bolt Cutter shrugged and turned away from the beach.

A loud crack split the air. The Bolt Cutter jerked backward. He clutched his chest and blood spurted between his fingers. Another crack. Huda shrieked and covered her head. The Bolt Cutter spun 180 degrees and smashed face-first into the dirt, like a tree felled by an ax. Khalid barreled out of the scrub. He sprinted past Huda and shoved an old revolver against the back of the Bolt Cutter's skull.

"No, Khalid," screamed Huda. "Don't!"

The boy's arm flexed. Another crack. Blood sprayed across the sand. Three more. Then all that remained was rustling wind and a faint *click, click, click*, as Khalid pulled the trigger again and again.

Afterward, Huda remembered only snatches: the heat of the gun as she removed it from Khalid's fingers; how he dropped to his knees and hid his face in his hands; how his heaving back reminded her of Abdul Amir weeping over the dead taxi driver. Huda wasn't sure exactly how much time passed before Ally and Hanan crept from the scrub, but she remembered that Ally took pains to keep her face averted from the pink fan of blood across the beach.

"Where did he get the gun?" Huda's anguish echoed across the lake.

"My mom gave it to me when we said goodbye." Hanan whimpered. "She had it in the closet, wrapped in a scarf."

Huda silently cursed Rania. Why didn't she tell her about the gun?

"Hanan, you need to get Khalid back to the Land Cruiser." Huda barely recognized her own voice. It was as if she'd been possessed by a jinni, as if some other force was moving her lips and operating her limbs. She hauled Khalid to his feet.

"My darling, it's not your fault." She gripped his shoulders. "You had no choice. He was going to kill me."

Khalid stared right through her, eyes as blank as a carp's. Did he realize she was lying? Or had he learned how to hide the truth, even from himself? Despite her shock, she saw bitter irony bleeding on the shore. She'd done everything she could: lied, stole, blackmailed. Still, she couldn't outwit fate.

Huda called Hanan over. The girl took Khalid's arm, and they stumbled away like sleepwalkers. Out on the lake, there was no sign of the fishing fleet. They'd sailed beyond the horizon. All Huda could see was the blurry line where sky met water. She glanced at the Bolt Cutter's corpse.

"Ally, help me drag him out of sight."

The girl grabbed the Bolt Cutter's left ankle. Huda took hold of the Bolt Cutter's other foot. It was as heavy as a concrete slab. The two women leaned their weight toward the sand and grunted. The body didn't budge.

"This isn't going to work." Huda released her grip. The Bolt Cutter's boot thudded onto the beach. She rifled through his jeans pocket, leaving his mukhabarat ID, but taking his keys. "I'll hide his car in the grass. Then we need to get out of here. Fast. No one will stop us once we're on the highway."

The two women staggered toward the track.

"Wait!" cried Huda.

She hurried back and ferreted through the Bolt Cutter's pockets again.

"We can't forget this." She passed Ally her wedding ring. Huda took her hand, and the two of them lurched through the salt cedar. As they neared the track, Ally stopped and stared up into space. The birds had fled at the sound of the gun. Not a single cloud stood witness in the sky. Huda told herself there was no time to search the heavens. No time for regret. No time to rage against fate. Yet her tears defied her, and a chasm opened in her chest, vast as the endless blue.

CHAPTER 31

Outside Amman's Abdali bus station, an old woman elbowed her way to the curb and broke into a joyful wail. Huda shuffled aside as the woman's ululations spiraled high into the air, above the honk of taxis, the beseechments of ragged boys selling water and dates, and the roar of double-deckers departing for Mecca. A bug-splattered minivan chugged up the hill and rolled to a stop alongside the curb. Passengers tumbled out, stiff-limbed, blinking at the sun. The old woman swooped on a young man in blue jeans, her arms wide like a blackbird's wings.

Huda called to a roaming ticket seller.

"Has the minivan from Ruwaished arrived?"

"Not yet." He glanced at his watch. "But soon, inshallah."

A people smuggler had transported Rania across the border shortly before dawn, but once on Jordanian soil he claimed engine trouble and dumped his passengers in the closest town. Rania had already been on the road for twelve hours when she called to say she'd finish the journey by minivan. She sounded numb, distant as the moon.

The scratchy call transported Huda two months back in time,

to when she crossed the Iraqi frontier in the Land Cruiser. She'd felt like an astronaut cut loose from her craft, watching her world grow ever more distant, while space unfurled around her, full of stars but deadly cold. The air too thin to breathe.

Unlike Rania's long trek, it took Huda less than half that time to flee from Lake Habbaniyah to the border, rocketing along the jet-black highway, overtaking filthy oil tankers and the occasional pickup truck. Not one of them—Huda, Ally, Khalid, or Hanan— spoke more than a couple of words the whole way. They stared at the flinty plains and tried to erase from their minds the red fan of blood on the beach. Perhaps they thought if they stayed silent, it would be as if it never really happened.

Fifteen miles from the border, Huda took the compass from the glove box. She switched the Land Cruiser to four-wheel drive, turned off the highway, and plowed through the gray sand. She wasn't sure of the exact moment they crossed into Jordan, there were no markers that deep in the desert, but eventually they found a dirt track and passed a pickup truck with Jordanian plates. It was almost too easy.

Huda remembered thinking that the highway should have been rougher, the desert should have bogged them down, they should have been made to get out and flail at the burning sands with their bare hands, they should have been made to suffer somehow, not simply roll across an invisible line and leave their country behind. Even now, as the old woman hugged her grandson and trilled her happiness to the sky, Huda expected someone to grab her by the back of her neck and call her to account.

On the far side of the road, two young women strolled out of a juice bar. One of them had long curly hair like Hanan, and Rania too, when she was young. Hanan had left for London a month ago, after one of Rania's friends found her a scholarship at a school popular with exiled Iraqis. Rania would soon follow Hanan to London. She had connections to smooth her passage. Much had changed, but she was still a Mansour. Despite Huda's best intentions, she tasted resentment in her mouth.

Rania should have told her about the gun hidden in the pashmina scarf. If she had, their escape would have gone differently. Huda often tried to talk to Khalid about the Bolt Cutter, and all that happened at the lake. But every time, the light went out behind his eyes.

"It wasn't your fault," Huda told him repeatedly.

"Do we have to talk about this?" Khalid would turn away and pull a dog-earned comic from his schoolbag.

"It must have been very frightening. You must feel upset or confused or . . . something?"

Khalid would shrug, then find some reason to slip away, often to the mosque. Huda knew she should be grateful he found solace in God, but sometimes he returned with a flat look in his eyes, like someone had pulled out a plug, or snipped a crucial wire. The local imam seemed generous and kind, but whenever Huda imagined prayer time, it was the white-bearded cleric from the Khan Murjan she saw railing from the pulpit, and Khalid bowed down before him.

She pushed the thought away, then stood on her tiptoes and searched for Ally's dark, shining hair bobbing above the crowd. The girl promised she'd meet her here. Huda shifted uneasily. Maybe she'd changed her mind. Perhaps Ally didn't want to stand on the sidewalk, checking her watch and making chitchat, while the past bore down on them like a runaway bus. As Huda scanned the roadside, she thought it fitting penance for a liar like her, that she could no longer keep faith in anyone else's word.

A young man pushed a cart with a vat of steaming chickpea stew along the sidewalk. Huda's stomach growled.

"Huda!" Ally darted through the traffic and hurried onto the curb. "Is she here? Has Rania's van arrived?"

"Not yet. But soon, inshallah."

"Is Khalid with you?" Ally waved off a hawker selling lukewarm Pepsi. "I was hoping I'd get a chance to see him."

"He's at school."

"How's he doing?"

"He's fine," she lied. "He's adjusting. It's a new place, a new country, after all."

The girl peeked at her from the corner of her eye, then looked away. Silence rose between them, filled the spaces between the honk, hiss, and hubbub of the bus station. Abdul Amir liked to say the past was dead. But their silence kept it alive, quivering inside them.

"So how's the new job working out?" Ally adjusted her handbag under her arm.

"Everyone is very nice, thank you." Huda bobbed her head. "Not as kind as Mr. Tom, of course, but very welcoming."

Instead of being fired for taking the Land Cruiser, as she expected, Huda managed to get a part-time job at the Australian embassy in Amman—largely thanks to Ally. She'd told Tom and the ambassador that when she learned the mukhabarat were harassing Huda and Khalid, she convinced them to escape with her. It was all her idea, she said.

Ally didn't tell them that Hanan was in the back seat when they crossed the border. And she didn't tell them about the Bolt Cutter. Huda wondered, when Ally saw Tom in person, would she be able to hold her secrets inside? Or would she turn to him late at night and whisper in his ear of the red fan of blood and how it was so very bright against the pale sand?

Huda had thought that once she left Iraq, she could leave all the lies and manipulation behind. But lies didn't take kindly to being forgotten, they clung to her pant leg, even as she ran for the door.

"I hope Khalid's doing okay." Ally smiled, but Huda thought she saw mistrust surface in her deep blue gaze. As Huda knew too well, to forgive was one thing, to forget another. Deception, betrayal, death, these could not simply be exiled from memory. Even forgiveness was not a one-off, or guaranteed to last forever.

Huda noticed two young men gawking at Ally. The women traded glances and rolled their eyes in unison.

"Shall I give them a lecture on respectability?" said Huda.

"Respectability?" Ally glanced behind her, and from side to side. She leaned against Huda's shoulder and muttered, "Hang on, I better find some first."

"I would lend you some," Huda deadpanned. "But I lost mine years ago. I think it was back when I was dealing blackjack at that casino on the river."

The two women bent their heads together and snickered.

Maybe forgiveness was a daily exercise, Huda thought, kept alive by unremarkable acts, like waiting with a friend for a late bus to come in, or sharing bad jokes. Perhaps Ally's broken trust could be repaired. And maybe in turn, Huda could forgive Rania for her costly secrets. But it would take work, and something even more difficult, truth.

Huda took a breath.

"I lied to you earlier." She glanced at Ally. "Khalid is not doing fine. He's depressed. He won't talk to me."

Ally looped her arm around Huda's shoulders.

"What about Abdul Amir? Maybe Khalid will talk to him?"

"You're right." Huda nodded. "He'd probably understand what Khalid is feeling better than anyone else."

"How is he doing? Is he still in Basra?"

"He's staying with his family, in his village." Huda stared at the sidewalk.

Abdul Amir had done what she asked, and denounced her to the mukhabarat. He said he knew nothing about her escape plan, and that he planned to divorce her. Luckily, Abu Issa was sympathetic, but Abdul Amir was locked up in Abu Ghraib for a week anyway. Abu Issa promised he'd be treated well, so Abdul Amir was beaten only three times, and had his fingernails ripped out on only one hand. Huda sighed and rubbed her eyes. Not many people got to walk out of Abu Ghraib, let alone with all four limbs pretty much intact.

As for the Bolt Cutter, Abu Issa almost seemed pleased that he'd vanished. He told Abdul Amir he'd recommended his partner be punished for killing Hatim—not for the murder, but that he'd done it without prior authorization—only the Bolt Cutter went AWOL first. Or so he believed. *Good riddance to that fool*, he said. *He's got no respect for his superiors.*

Huda still feared the regime would learn the truth about the Bolt Cutter. But as time passed, she figured the fishermen at Lake Habbaniyah had found his corpse and the mukhabarat ID in his pocket. The tribes in that area loathed the regime. They would have gladly fed his body to the carp out in the depths of the lake, sold his car to the cross-border smugglers, and erased all signs that he was ever there. Huda wished it was as easy to wipe him from Khalid's memory.

"Are you okay?" Ally touched Huda's arm. "You seem a million miles away."

A grimy minivan lurched to a stop at the curb. The crowd shuffled closer, waiting for the doors to slide open. Rania emerged first, tossing a silky scarf around her shoulders. Somehow, she made the act of clambering from the ripped bucket seats look as graceful as ballet, but when she straightened up she had the numb look of a soldier fresh from the front lines.

Huda wanted to rush forward and embrace her, but her feet wouldn't move. It was Ally who stepped forward, pulling Huda behind her.

"Rania, thank goodness you're here." The young woman paused. "I'm sorry about your mom. Please, accept my condolences."

"Allah has set a term for everyone," replied Rania. She bent down to retrieve her suitcase, but not before Huda saw the brief glint of tears in her eyes.

"May Allah make heaven her abode," said Huda quietly, hoping the ritual words of condolence provided a little comfort. Rania had never been a traditional woman, but she was clearly trying to honor the Muslim custom of limiting public displays of grief.

"We've been so worried about you," said Ally.

"I left just in time." Rania paused and glanced over her shoulder. Even now, far from Baghdad, she couldn't bring herself to speak freely. "His son is traveling to Basra this weekend. Malik told me he plans to send for Hanan." Rania shuddered. "He's going to be furious when he finds out she's not there."

"You'll feel much better when you and Hanan are together." Huda touched Rania's shoulder and pointed up the hill to a small café. "You must be thirsty. Let's order a cool drink and you can tell us all about your plans for London."

Rania met Huda's gaze for the first time.

"I can't thank you enough; truly, I wish I could." The shadows under Rania's eyes were the color of storm clouds. She glanced at Ally. "Or you, my dear. I will always be in your debt."

Behind them, a bus honked and took off, spewing gray exhaust from its tail pipe. The three woman started toward the café.

"How about we order coffee to go with that cool drink." Ally grinned slyly at Huda. "Maybe you can look at the grounds and predict what the future has in store?"

They reached the top of the hill and paused to survey the city. Limestone houses gleamed under a cloudless sky that seemed to stretch on forever. Baghdad was six hundred miles away, and Huda didn't know if they could ever return. But she took comfort that the three of them could stare into the same blue heaven, and hold on to hope for paradise.

AUTHOR'S NOTE

When the Apricots Bloom is a work of fiction, but it is inspired by my real-life experiences living in Iraq under the Saddam Hussein regime and later during the Iraq War. I was thirty-one when I arrived in Baghdad, and like the character Ally in this book, I suddenly went from being a journalist and professional in my own right to "a dependent spouse," the unflattering visa category for the partners of diplomats and UN workers. And as in this novel, I developed a close relationship with a woman like Huda—an informant secretly reporting back to the regime on where I went, what I saw, and who I spoke with.

Once the regime fell, the truth came out. I didn't blame the woman who so often called herself my *Iraqi sister.* I understood that *no* was not an option with the mukhabarat. And by then, I was no longer the same naive person who first journeyed to Baghdad. As I recounted in my 2007 memoir, my former workplace had been destroyed by a suicide bombing. I buried a dear friend, survived sexual assault, and learned that under extreme circumstances good people can make bad choices. As the tyranny of Saddam's regime was replaced by the chaos of war, it became clear that the best of intentions could go horribly wrong.

More than ten years later, I was still dwelling on all that happened in Iraq. PTSD was partly to blame, but I also couldn't stop wondering, Had it been just a job for my *sister*? Were we simply informant and target? Or had we been friends too? Sometimes real life is just as complex as fiction—motivations blurred, lines crossed and redrawn. And so I started work on this novel, exploring questions of truth, loyalty, and friendship that I had left unanswered in Baghdad.

While this experience inspired the starting point for *When the*

Apricots Bloom, and many small details came straight from reality, the plot is a work of fiction. I am not Ally. Huda does not exist. Neither does Rania. However, I did my best to paint an accurate portrait of life under Saddam Hussein at that moment in time. I'm indebted to Ban al-Dhayi, Samir al-Badri, and Ghada Kachachi for their encouragement, feedback, and advice in this endeavor. That said, any mistakes or alternations in fact are mine alone. I'd also like to thank my agent, Heather Jackson; my editor, John Scognamiglio at Kensington; as well as Natasha, Zaha, Jennifer, Sahar, Fatemeh, Wendra, Chelsea, Chris at Petworth Neighborhood Library, and the other members of my two writing groups. My wonderful husband, Geoff, went above and beyond. I truly could not have done this without him.

I also want to acknowledge the important discussion around *our own voices*. The publishing industry has marginalized authors outside of the white, Western mainstream for far too long. This needs to change. In this polarized era, we need more diverse books, written by diverse authors, in settings and situations that reflect the deep richness of our world. At the same time, like PEN America, I don't believe in setting "rigid rules" about who has the right to tell which stories, or that an author should be confined to creating only characters with a similar background or genetic code. I've spent more than twenty years living outside of my home country, in Iraq, Thailand, Sri Lanka, Brazil, and the United States and Canada. I've lived in tiny rural communities and heaving metropolises. Throughout, I've found that while we might pray in a certain way, cover our hair or not, bake our bread flat or leavened, at heart we want the same things—safety, peace, love. We share far more in common than that which divides us. I hope this book shows that.

WHEN THE APRICOTS BLOOM

ABOUT THIS GUIDE

The suggested questions are included to enhance your group's reading of Gina Wilkinson's *When the Apricots Bloom*.

Discussion Questions

1. *When the Apricots Bloom* takes place in Baghdad, during the rule of the dictator Saddam Hussein, at a time when Western sanctions kept Iraq virtually cut off from the rest of the world. What did you learn about life for ordinary Iraqis, like Huda, that surprised you?

2. If you were in Huda's situation, how would you have responded to the orders from the secret police? Should Huda have felt guilty about any of her actions? What about the money she pockets when Ally buys a lemon tree, or her threats later to the nurseryman?

3. Compared to Huda, how does Rania handle pressure from the regime? To what extent does her family's status protect her, or is that just an illusion? Rania is also an artist— a respected role in Iraqi society. How does this compare to prevailing attitudes toward artists in your own culture?

4. Ally is desperate to find a connection with her mother. Given the restrictions she's under, do you think her subterfuge is justified, or is her search for clues to her mother's past irresponsible? What would you have done differently? Were you surprised by her mother's history?

5. Huda's husband, Abdul Amir, plays a key role in the book. To what extent does he influence Huda's decisions? At the end of the novel, how do you feel about his character? How did your perception of him alter over time?

6. The starting point for *When the Apricots Bloom* was inspired by the author's own experiences, when she was befriended by a woman working as an informant for Saddam

Hussein's secret police. Did her portrayal of life in Baghdad seem realistic to you? How believable was the relationship between the three women?

7. The novel alternates between Huda's, Rania's, and Ally's points of view. How are their worldviews and attitudes reflected in their narrative styles? Do you prefer one to the other? How would the novel have differed if it had been told from only one perspective?

8. In the Author's Note, the author references the debate over "our own voices." To what extent do you agree or disagree with her statements? Do you think it was appropriate for her to write from the point of view of an Iraqi woman?

9. *When the Apricots Bloom* ends with Huda, Rania, and Ally reuniting in Jordan. What do you think the future holds for them? Did this epilogue strengthen the book, or would it have had more impact if it ended with the previous chapter?

Connect with
Us

Visit us online at
KensingtonBooks.com
to read more from your favorite authors, see books
by series, view reading group guides, and more.

Join us on social media

for sneak peeks, chances to win books and prize packs,
and to share your thoughts with other readers.

facebook.com/kensingtonpublishing
twitter.com/kensingtonbooks

Tell us what you think!

To share your thoughts, submit a review,
or sign up for our eNewsletters, please visit:
KensingtonBooks.com/TellUs.